I LOVE
LIKING YOU A LOT

GREG HATALA

Savant Books and Publications
Honolulu, HI, USA
2022

Published in the USA by Aignos Publishing LLC
An imprint of Savant Books and Publications LLC
2630 Kapiolani Blvd #1601
Honolulu, HI 96826
http://www.aignospublishing.com

Printed in the USA

Edited by Michael Davis
Original cover art by Vanessa Castillo
Cover by Daniel S. Janik
Excerpts from "Hello, Dolly!" used by permission of The Estate of
Michael Stewart, all rights reserved.

13 digit ISBN: 9781737643104

First Edition: July 2022
Library of Congress Control Number: 2022932844

Without you, there's nothing.

Chapter 1

"I didn't name you Douglas MacArthur Halecki for you to end up a sissy!"

Whack!

The leather belt cracked against the bare skin of Doug's butt. Once again, Doug had been marched out to the barn for a strapping. He was bent over a sawhorse beneath the harsh fluorescent light, trying to keep from slipping on the slick concrete floor. Doug's father had ordered him to drop his jeans and underwear, which he'd never done before.

Whack!

"Sissy? Why am I a sissy?" yelled Doug.

"'Cause if you're telling the truth, only a sissy runs away. Men handle things face to face. And if you're lying…"

Whack! Another swing of the belt.

"…then you ratted out your buddies and only a sissy tells on his buddies!"

Doug's father was the same height as him but the Army and years of warehouse work had made him heavier and solid. There was no 'give' in him, no flab, no hint of weakness. Save the fact he wasn't even 5'8", he looked like he could've walked out of one of those World War II recruitment posters.

Whack!

"And don't you dare ever use language like that in front of your mother again!"

Sissy. Doug hated that word and all the other ones. Fairy. Cupcake. Pussy. He grimaced and stared straight ahead, trying not to cry, deciding not to ask any more stupid questions. It'd be over sooner.

Doug's father walked around in front of Doug. Both were breathing heavily, bursts of steam coming from their mouths. "That's it. Now think about it!" He put his belt back on. Doug waited until his father went in the back door of the house before leaving the barn.

He walked slowly to his 'private spot' in the woods. A meandering path through the brush and trees led to a flat-topped stump, the only one without jagged edges. It was far enough from his house that no one could see him. His house, much like his spot in the woods, was far from everything, especially houses where any of his friends lived. His parents called it his new home, but to Doug, it felt like one of those prisons they build far away from everyone because no one wants to know the inmates exist.

The spot was a jumble of browns and grays, with a canopy of treetops blocking out much of the sunlight. It wasn't relaxing or inspiring, it was a place to get away, smoke without getting in trouble, and think.

Today, Doug had a lot to think about. There had been some bad days in his young life; this was one of the worst. Doug stuffed his hand into his pocket and found he'd left his cigarettes in his car, then realized that had been about the only thing that had gone right. "Would've been twice the strapping if they'd found them," he thought.

Doug rested his elbows on his knees, staring blankly at the ground.

"Douglas!"

Doug opened his eyes and found himself in room twelve at Blessed Sacrament High School the day before. He was leaning his chair back against the edge of the radiator, staring at the asbestos-paneled ceiling. Doug was in a math appointment, but the only numbers he was considering were how many girls might look his way now that he'd be driving a cool car. Three weeks earlier, he'd turned 17. Now, it was only one more day until his driver's road test.

"Douglas! Mr. Halecki!"

Sister Angelica barked out his name. Doug was startled; his head banged against the windowsill. He sat up straight and blushed.

"I said, what kind of function is this?" She was pointing to an equation on the blackboard that read 'f(x) = x^3.'

"Um, uh, it...it's a fox in a fix?"

"It's a cubic function," said Louise Grant from a few desks away.

"Thank you, Louise. As always, I can count on you to take things seriously."

The room became silent. Then, the sound of Barry Bennett's pencil grinding came from the sharpener attached to the wall in the back of the room. Barry was the star of the basketball team. Everyone glanced back at him and he paused; when they looked away, he went back to sharpening. It became a game, with him pausing every time someone looked. He finally stopped and sat down when Sister Angelica smiled at him. She turned back to Doug.

"As for you, Mr. Halecki, since you think equations are a joke, I have a special assignment for you. Solve all the problems in chapters three and four by Monday and make sure you show your work."

"...All the problems?" Doug stuttered.

"All of them," Sister Angelica responded.

"That doesn't mean us, does it?" asked Andy Swanson.

"No, only Mr. Halecki," she replied, looking directly at him. Her wimple, a nun's stiff, squared-off head covering, made her seem taller and more threatening. There was a paleness to her skin that, combined with her age of what was probably about 140, brought the Grim Reaper to mind. "Perhaps you should aspire to the level of Louise, not that you could ever match her. You have God-given ability, but waste too much time being childish. Perhaps we should send you back to third grade to feel more at home!"

Doug's face turned bright red again as kids around the classroom laughed.

"Halecki!" Barry hollered. "Halecki! Did they call you Becky in third grade? Becky Halecki?"

Basketball players were like gods at Blessed Sacrament. Kids always laughed at Barry's insults, as long as they weren't the target.

"Becky Halecki! Becky Halecki!" said Barry in a falsetto voice.

The classroom rocked with laughter. Doug could see Sister Angelica smiling.

"Or better yet—Pecky! Halecki the pecker! Peckerrrrr! Peckerrrrr!"

The laughter went on. Doug tried to compress himself into the desk.

Barry stood up and made a blessing motion with his hand. "I now hereby christen you Pecky Halecki!" Doug felt as if his desk had somehow become a pedestal and he was ten feet in the air. The bell rang for lunch; Doug waited until everyone left, including Andy, before gathering his things and leaving himself.

Doug spent the rest of the day trying to stay away from as many people as possible. At the day's final bell, Doug went to his locker. Christine Holloway's locker was right next to his. There were lockers on both sides of the narrow hall making things tight and crowded at the end of the day. He fiddled with loose papers and restacked the books on the shelf, waiting for her to arrive.

When she walked up and began dialing her combination, Doug went to say something, then stopped. He inhaled to start again.

"Hi Christine!" he said cheerily. His voice cracked and leapt an octave.

"Oh, hi Doug," she responded.

Christine didn't say anything else but seemed to be staring at Doug's face. More specifically, the large zit he'd picked at. Doug tried to turn slightly to make it less visible.

The hallway continued filling up with students. Someone walked by and said "Hey, Pecky Halecki!" Someone else jostled him and he bumped against Christine. A lot of him bumped against her. He could feel his upper arm come in contact with one of her boobs. Christine wore her uniform dress really short; his hand brushed against her thigh.

Doug couldn't help it; he felt a boner coming on. He turned so he almost had his back to her.

"Sorry!" he said. "Someone pushed me. It gets hard…"

Christine glanced down for a fraction of a second. Then she turned, closed her locker and walked away.

"to…keep…your…balance…" Doug trailed off. He remained facing his locker until his boner subsided.

Doug was seventeen and had never kissed a girl. Never held a girl's hand. Never hugged any female who wasn't his mother, sister or a seventy-year-old aunt. First base? Second base? Those were just baseball terms. At school, there were couples everywhere. He wanted to be half of a couple but didn't have a clue how they formed.

Doug spent all Friday night and Saturday morning working on the math problems. The new system at Blessed Sacrament supposedly didn't have homework—but here he was, doing what sure felt like homework.

Between Doug's freshman and sophomore years the school had switched to something radically different and more confusing than what school had always been. Supposedly, it was better preparation for college. Closer interaction between students and teachers through classes called "laps" with short "mods" and "resource rooms" instead of long class periods and traditional classrooms. Students amassed credits and all work was done in school. To Doug, all this new system accomplished was create more opportunities for him to be bullied, like on Friday in class.

"Douglas! Are you ready yet?" his mother yelled from the kitchen. "You have your driving test today!"

Doug rolled his eyes. Did she honestly think he'd forget it?

He hurried to finish the math problems at his small formica-topped desk across from his bed. His room, the smallest of three bedrooms, was at the end of a short hall that started at the kitchen; his parents' room was across the hall from his and his sister Linda's was next to theirs. It was hardly big enough to hold the bare necessities—bed, nightstand, dresser, desk.

It was like a prison cell. For the past two years, he felt confined to it with breaks only for school and jobs. He'd delivered papers for years to be able to buy a car. A car and a license meant freedom. Not having to beg a parent for a ride somewhere. Girls were impressed by guys with cars. It meant you were a man.

Doug had always been skinny. Having to get glasses in second grade made it worse; he thought he looked like Sherman on the Rocky and Bullwinkle Show. Bullies found him to be an ideal target. Girls didn't notice him at all.

Doug had stopped telling his parents about the bullies long ago. Once in grade school, after a particularly rough session of being knocked to the ground repeatedly, he'd told his mother, who called the school. The boys she reported retaliated by targeting Doug even worse.

There was one place Doug could escape—his neighborhood. All that mattered there was having fun. When chores were done on weekends it was time for things like throwing footballs and riding bikes—no one gave you grades on those.

So right after eighth grade, his parents suddenly decided to move.

He was enrolled in a high school where he knew almost no one. As freshman and sophomore years passed, girls' skirts got shorter and their boobs got larger but Doug's cluelessness about them, and most everything else, remained exactly the same.

He'd even started buying cigarettes junior year, lighting up whenever a girl was around, hoping it looked cool. Then he lit up when he felt nervous because girls didn't pay attention. Doug was now going through half a pack a day; it took a lot of breath mints to keep his parents from finding out.

"Don't forget to bring your permit!" yelled Doug's mother. She was near the back door with her coat on and her hand on the doorknob.

"It's already in the glovebox, Ma!" he yelled back. "Jesus," he muttered. He hurried to the back door, took the four steps leading down to it in one jump, put on his coat and left.

Doug had phoned his old buddy Dwight Tucker that morning to tell him he'd be coming to visit the old neighborhood. Now, he had to ask his mother. Driving back home, he waited for her to say something about having passed his test.

"Slow down!" she said sharply.

"Ma, uh…" he began.

"I heard you on the phone," she interrupted. "Don't think having a license means you don't have to ask permission for things anymore!"

Doug grimaced. There was no privacy in that house. Someone was always listening in.

"I know, Ma. I wasn't going to ask you unless I passed because then it wouldn't make any sense anyway,"

"Why not?" his mother responded. "I could've driven you there!"

Doug grimaced again. She'd missed the whole point. He pulled the car into the driveway at his house. "So, can I?"

"Be home for dinner."

When Doug drove down the street to Dwight's house, only a few things had changed in the middle-class neighborhood of similar-looking houses and similar-looking people. The Andersons house was green now instead of brown and the Baxters had a German shepherd, romping around the front yard. When he turned into the Tucker's driveway, he noticed the big pine tree in front of their house had been cut down.

His friends hanging out on the back steps were a little taller and their hair was longer, but they still looked pretty much the same. Doug got out and pointed to his 1972 Javelin. "Whaddya think? Nice, huh?"

"Hey, Halecki, long time no see!" Dwight said. "You're just in time!"

"For what? A football game? Where are we playin'?"

"You'll take us where we need to go."

"I don't get it. Where do we need…"

Before Doug could finish, the boys ran over and pinned him to the ground.

"What the fuck?" yelled Doug. "What the hell is going on?" He struggled but his legs and arms were trapped.

"Things have changed since you left." Dwight squatted down and spit next to Doug's face. "New people showed up. People that don't fit. People we don't like." Dwight leaned forward, pressing his knee into Doug's ribs. "Like the ones your parents sold your old place to."

Doug's old house, up the street from the Tuckers', had been bought by a young Hispanic couple. Holly Hill had a lot of Hispanic people—but Doug's old neighborhood didn't. "Relax, asshole, you're just taking us for a ride to Eat-Mor," sneered Dwight as they dragged Doug to his feet.

He motioned toward Doug's car. "Or we fuck you and that up."

Doug had just pulled into a parking space in front of the Eat-Mor and put the car in 'park' when Dwight reached over and snatched the keys from the ignition. He grinned, spinning them on his finger, then got out with the other boys. Doug lit a cigarette after they'd gone inside. He finished it and lit another one as he waited, wondering what was going on.

The boys came running out of the doors of the store, whooping and hollering, carrying what looked like every egg carton in the supermarket. "Drive!" yelled Dwight, tossing him the keys as they piled into the car. "To your old house. Follow your nose, you'll smell it." Laughter filled the car.

Doug stopped on the street as Dwight instructed. The house fronted a large stand of woods. "Your parents brought 'em in, it's only fair you help us show 'em they don't belong." The boys lined up along the street and started pelting the house with eggs.

"Dirty spics!" someone yelled. "Go back to beanerville!" someone else hollered. Doug hunched down behind the car; the others were intent on throwing eggs and weren't paying attention to him. He was scared; all he'd wanted to do was hang out like the old days. He'd never been involved in anything like this before. He could see a face peering out of a window when an egg shattered the glass.

Doug closed his eyes and prayed it would be over soon.

After they'd thrown all the eggs, the boys took off running for the woods, leaving the empty cartons scattered on the ground. "Hey! Hey!" A man came out of the house shouting after the running boys. Dwight stopped and turned back toward the house. "Halecki! You coulda hurt somebody, Halecki!" he yelled.

"Halecki?" said Mr. Rodriguez, turning and seeing Doug getting into his car. "Ernest Halecki's son? You did this? Why?"

Doug was trembling in fear. He started the car and sped away. In the mirror, he could see the man standing in the street, shaking his fist.

When he got home, Doug's parents were sitting at the kitchen table. They both had their arms crossed.

"Where were you?" his father demanded, angrily.

"I was over the old neighborhood," Doug said, nervously

"Doing what?" his mother asked, just as angrily.

"Hanging out, that's all," Doug looked away.

"Hanging out the window of your car throwing eggs!" his father yelled, standing up. "Mr. Rodriguez called!"

His mother also stood up. "You broke a window right in front of Mrs. Rodriguez!" she yelled. "She could've been hurt!"

"I didn't throw any eggs!" Doug yelled back. "They made me drive there!"

His parents had moved away from the table toward Doug, standing side-by-side.

"Who's THEY?" his father yelled. The second word echoed through the house.

Doug tensed. Violating the 'no-telling' rule all boys learned mattered little now.

"Dwight Tucker! His brother Dave! Robbie, Russell, they were all there!"

Doug's mother looked at his father, then at the phone mounted on the wall. "You'd better be telling the truth!" She snatched the phone off the hook. "What's their phone number?"

"Nine-one-nine, nine-five-three-six."

Mrs. Halecki punched the numbers into the phone, then glared at Doug as the she waited for an answer. Mr. Halecki was standing behind her with his hands on his hips. Doug tried to inch back imperceptibly

10

from the two of them.

"My son tells me your son made him throw eggs at our old house," she said. It was silent for a few moments as she listened, nodding her head a couple of times.

"Alright, Mrs. Tucker. I'm sorry for bothering you." She hung up, then looked at Doug's father first, shaking her head 'no.'

"She said Dwight said it was all your idea."

"WHAT?!!" yelled Doug. "He's a God damn liar!"

"No, *you* are," yelled his father. In one swift motion, he took off his belt, strode forward and strapped Doug across the butt.

"OUCH! DAMN IT! What the hell is going on?" Doug screamed, reaching back to cover his butt. "They jumped me!"

His mother had a disgusted look on her face. "She said you took everyone for a ride, then pulled up in front of the house. Dwight said you had eggs in your trunk. She said Dwight and his brother took off running when they saw what you were doing."

"Here's what you're doing NOW," yelled his father. He was standing over Doug who'd sunk to his knees, cowering with his arms over his head. "You're going to call the Rodriguezes and apologize. You're going there tomorrow and clean up the mess if it takes all day. You're going to find out how much that window cost and pay them. And then…"

He whipped Doug with the belt again, striking him on his raised arms.

"…you will use that car to go to school and work and nothing else. School and work. NOTHING else. Do you UNDERSTAND?!"

"I didn't do it!" Doug sobbed. "I didn't do a fucking thing!"

Doug felt the belt again. "Out to the barn. NOW!" his father barked.

It had been an absolutely rotten couple of days. Doug stared at the treetops. He lowered his head to his knees and started sobbing.

"Douglas!"

"Douglas! Telephone!" his mother was yelling at the top of her lungs.

Doug jumped up and ran toward the house, trying to clean his glasses with his shirt as he ran. His mother was standing in the kitchen as he came in.

"It's Ed Sherman." Doug looked hopefully at the phone his mother was holding—uncovered. "And no, you can't go anywhere. Your father said you're grounded. You can talk to him right here."

Doug's shoulders slumped as he took the phone.

"Hello, Ed?"

"Yeah, hi, Doug," said Ed, softly. "I heard. Sorry, man. Umm, say I was asking about an assignment."

The next day, Doug went to the Rodriguez house as instructed. The couple lectured him about responsibility as he scrubbed the driveway and steps on his hands and knees. They told him the window would cost 50 dollars to replace. He worked silently, moving from spot to spot they pointed out.

It was late afternoon when he finally finished and drove away. Within minutes, it was as if a hailstorm had erupted; his car was being pelted with eggs. They splattered against his side window and drummed off the door and fenders. The group of boys in the field he'd driven past were doubled over, laughing, shouting and giving him the finger. Doug felt completely humiliated, first from spending all day cleaning and being lectured and now this.

Doug drove to a self-serve car wash before returning home. He put a quarter in the box and pointed the soapy jet at his car. No matter how hard he tried, the egg goop and bits of shell wouldn't come out from where they'd wedged into the gaps in the car. He put in another quarter and tried to blast the bits free again with little success.

He stared at the mess in frustration. He saw the steam rising off the car's shiny metal skin. Then, something strange came over him. It was like the first time he'd masturbated—surprising, shocking and wonderful at the same time. It was the feeling of doing something kids couldn't. He felt it welling up in him and escaping out of every pore.

This car, this big, fast, deadly piece of metal, was *his*. He *was* a man.

"Those assholes aren't gonna fuck up MY car!" he snarled. He fed the machine two quarters for the high-pressure jet, working the nozzle up and down, left and right. Little by little, the eggshell pieces and gluey yolk washed off the car into the drain.

A million thoughts flooded his head at once. Last week, he was a little boy, at the mercy of his parents. Today, he was a man and could go wherever he wanted. Being home and getting yelled at could be solved…by not being home as much. He could make plans at school so there was no listening in and if the plans were school-related his parents had to allow them. Doug stared into the swirling suds on the floor trying to capture all the ideas flashing through his head.

A big, muscular man with a skin-tight sweatshirt stood near the entrance of the stall with his hands on his hips. "Hey, kid, are you about fucking done in there?" Doug jumped. "If you ain't gonna do more, stop wasting my fucking time!"

Doug hurried to put back the sprayer—and stopped. Without looking back, he dropped in another quarter and rinsed his car, slowly, one more time.

Chapter 2

"Palomma, right?"

Palomma looked up from her desk in homeroom on Monday. Paula Carino was standing in front of her.

"Some of us were going to that new shoe store downtown after school, think you'd be interested?"

Palomma froze.

"Uh, no, no thanks," she stuttered. "I have to, uh, be somewhere."

"*No problema*!" said Paula, cheerily. "Maybe next time!"

She walked out of the classroom. Palomma waited until she was gone to exhale.

The Holly Hill Public Library was three blocks from Blessed Sacrament, heading away from the center of town toward an area of stately homes and doctors' offices. Palomma walked to the library after school, headed for the fiction section and sat in 'her seat.'

The window next to it faced a large tree in the courtyard. In spring, birds perched on it singing; in winter, it often wore a sequined dress of ice crystals on its bare branches. Here, surrounded by all her book friends and the beauty of her tree companion, the rest of the world disappeared.

Palomma found the bustle of the resource rooms in the new system at school uncomfortable. The constant background buzz was distracting; at the library, the blessed silence let her study and read in peace.

The silence was suddenly interrupted by the vocal clatter of a group of girls in the center of the library's main circulation section. One of them was Palomma's younger sister, Gemma.

Gemma had on her Lourdes Academy uniform—a sharp, solid green compared to Blessed Sacrament's muted tartan skirts and white blouses. When Palomma won a scholarship to Blessed Sacrament, Gemma told their parents she wanted to go to the other local Catholic school. Gemma had a knack for being assertive that perfectly offset Palomma's complete lack of self-confidence.

"Where's Life Magazine?" one of the girls asked, quite loudly. The librarian shushed her, and the girls giggled. They spoke to each other in loud whispers and giggled some more. Palomma turned away and rested her head on her hand, covering one ear. She didn't hear Gemma walk up.

"Hey, big sis!"

"Hi, Gemma," Palomma whispered back.

"What time's Mom picking us up?"

"Five."

"Cool, I'll be back here by five!" Gemma called out "Wait up!" and rejoined her friends walking out of the library.

The sound of laughter forced Palomma to revisit something she'd been trying desperately to forget.

Earlier that day, Palomma had gone to the church basement for lunch, heading straight for the table where she and her best friend Christine Holloway always sat. At the far end of the table was a group of girls with cheerleaders Karen Jamison and Lauren Carrier holding sway.

Standing in a cluster in various stylish poses, they looked like mannequins in a store, one with a hand on her hip, another cupping a hand beside her mouth to whisper. All their skirts had the same length—or lack of it—high up the thigh, far higher than Palomma's uniforms. The tops were unbuttoned the same three buttons, showing the maximum amount of cleavage without revealing any of their bras. Each girl had one of the current 'hip' hairstyles, like Karen's Jane Fonda-esque shag and Lauren's wedge haircut *a la* Dorothy Hamill.

Palomma set her tray on the table. Lunch today was spaghetti, a tiny pile of wilted lettuce and a buttered roll. She picked at the lettuce, not wanting to finish before Christine came. But instead of Christine, Karen and Lauren were moving toward her.

"Hi Palomma!" said Lauren. "Where did you go to get your hair done to look like Farrah Fawcett?"

Palomma certainly knew *who* the two girls were but had never, ever interacted with them in any way. They were cheerleaders, pretty and popular, and intimidated Palomma. They were 'cool kids' and Palomma wasn't. Now, they were talking to her at lunch!

"I didn't go anywhere!" she replied, beaming. "It's natural! All I have to do is brush it!"

The two girls looked at each other and giggled.

Karen spoke up from Palomma's other side. "Verrrrry interesting. Your chest is naturally that way too, right?"

Palomma was stunned.

"Um, yeah, I mean, um, I don't..."

"Oh, we're SURE you don't!" said Lauren. They both started laughing. Palomma was the center of attention, spreading in waves across the room. Palomma heard kids repeat what the girls had said. She felt her face turning bright red.

"You've heard of Kleenex, right?" said Karen, in a voice loud enough to carry across the nine rows of tables in the room. "How about toilet paper? You might try using a whole roll!"

"Yeah, and if the boys got fresh you could tell them 'Please don't squeeze the Charmin!'" yelled Lauren.

17

Laughter erupted again.

Palomma was burning with embarrassment. She looked around and saw kids pointing. Not wanting to see or hear any more, Palomma stood up, emptied her uneaten lunch into a trash can and hurried out of the lunchroom. She dashed into the girls' bathroom at school, closed the stall door and cried until the bell rang.

Back at home, after Mrs. Rossi had picked them up at the library, Gemma rushed straight for the phone upstairs. Palomma walked to her room.

"Not too long," her mother said while setting the dining room table. "Dinner will be ready soon!"

When Palomma was in elementary school, her mother grew concerned with her self-isolation. Mr. and Mrs. Rossi met Christine's parents at St. Michael's Church when both girls were in fifth grade; when Palomma's mother heard Christine was an only child, she suggested playdates for the two of them.

Hesitant at first, over the course of a few get-togethers Palomma gradually began to find that Christine was similarly shy and self-conscious. Soon she had a best friend to share her tales of make-believe with.

Both girls had reasons to want to blend into the background. Having each other made up for their lack of social skills. They sat on their beds giggling over pictures of David Cassidy and Scott Baio in Teen Beat. They did homework together, watched TV together and consoled each other if kids at school were mean to either one of them.

Most of the time, they'd gotten together at Christine's house—Christine preferred that. But it suited Palomma's imagination; Christine's canopied bed could be a castle, her huge collection of stuffed animals the characters in their dramas.

Palomma's father was a corporate accountant, and his company sent him to Chicago for a full-year company audit after Palomma graduated eighth grade; the family had moved with him. It was a shock for Palomma, away from her only friend in a strange, scary city. When they returned, her parents bought a new, larger house and Palomma had a bedroom to herself instead of sharing with Gemma.

But she also found on her return that Christine was no longer interested in dolls and imagination. It had been replaced by a real world of dances, parties and flirting with boys. Christine had picked up on those things pretty fast, while Palomma knew nothing about any of them.

After dinner, Palomma had returned to her room to write in her diary when the doorbell rang.

"Hello Christine!" said Mrs. Rossi. "I didn't know you were coming over!"

Neither had Palomma.

"Hi, Mrs. Rossi! Can Palomma come with me to the mall?"

Christine never had to ask if Palomma was home at night. She was always home.

"Palomma!" her mother called upstairs. "Christine's here to take you to the mall!"

Palomma closed her diary and went downstairs.

"Don't stay out too late," said Mrs. Rossi as Palomma put on her coat. "And no boys' houses!" added Mr. Rossi from the living room.

After arriving at the mall, Palomma followed Christine from JC Penney's to Rovner's to Fayva, watching her look through racks of the latest jeans and sizzler dresses and trying on higher and higher platform shoes. She waited while Christine gossiped with other girls. Then she helped Christine carry her new shoes and jeans back to her car.

"You're quiet tonight," said Christine as she drove away from the mall. "Cat got your tongue?"

"No," Palomma said softly. She sniffled.

"Didja hear what Margie was saying about Barry Bennett?" Christine asked. "Looks like him and Karen Jamison are officially a couple!"

"I heard," whispered Palomma. She sniffled again.

"What are you crying about?"

"Nothing, it's not important," replied Palomma, turning her head away from Christine.

Christine drove in silence for a while longer before letting out a loud sigh. "I heard something happened today with you in the lunchroom. You know, I didn't want to say anything…"

She paused, knowing Palomma would want to know the rest.

"What…didn't you want to say?" asked Palomma.

They'd arrived at Palomma's house. Christine pulled into the driveway and turned off the car. She turned toward Palomma.

"Look, it's your life, like they say, you gotta do your own thing…"

Palomma waited. They looked at each other for a while. Christine shrugged.

"My own thing?" said Palomma.

Christine let out another exaggerated sigh. "Maybe you don't, um, maybe you haven't, you know…"

Palomma's wide-eyed confusion flustered Christine.

Christine looked straight ahead again. "Maybe people wouldn't say things like that if you didn't look like your mother."

Palomma inhaled sharply. "My mother?" she blurted out. "What's wrong with my mother?"

"Nothing's wrong with your mother," answered Christine. "It's just you look like an old…like someone's mother!"

Palomma looked down at her drab, unstylish slacks.

"You remember how I used to look!" exclaimed Christine. "They used to call me four-eyes, Porky Pig, God! But if you want to keep looking like those women at church, jeez!"

She trailed off. Palomma was trying to keep from crying again.

"All I'm trying to say is maybe people wouldn't pick on you if you stop giving 'em a reason to."

Palomma said goodbye, got out and went to her room. She buried her face in a pillow so no one would hear her crying.

A girl growing up in an Italian, Catholic home knew the rules. No boys' houses. No talking to boys on the phone. Even if Palomma had known any boys it would all be off-limits anyway.

But puberty made it hard not to think about kissing and making out. Sex was everywhere—on TV, in the movies, in songs and certainly in Palomma's imagination. And now it was constantly in Palomma's ear, thanks to Christine. She told Palomma a lot of stories about boys that sounded farfetched, but Palomma had no stories of her own and couldn't lie because Christine would know she was lying. And lying was a sin anyway. So she listened.

As long as the biggest things in life had been getting A's and playing make-believe, Palomma had been content. As long as her best friend was interested in the same things, she was happy. Now the only thing that mattered was kissing a boy. Making out with a boy. Something to brag about to other girls about at lunchtime. The 'other girls' being Palomma and pretty much no one else.

That night, Palomma lay in bed wide awake. The whole incident kept playing over and over in her head. It wasn't just the meanness of the girls that upset her; they were also probably right. Boys weren't ever going to look at a flat-chested, frumpy, unpopular girl.

She glanced at the romance novel on her nightstand. In books, they didn't tell you how big a girl's boobs were, they talked about how big her boyfriend's love was for her. Palomma closed her eyes and thought about the scenes she'd read. Without thinking, she started touching herself where no boy was supposed to until marriage.

After a few minutes, she sat straight up. A wave of guilt washed over her.

It was supposed to be wrong. She hadn't even thought about how to do it, it came naturally. It was supposed to be a sin—but it felt so good. Was she a sinner? Was having sex next? What if a boy tried to get her to? What if she didn't say no?

She was overwhelmed with fear but knew she couldn't mention it to the priest at Sunday confession. She knelt down and said nine Hail Mary's.

One morning, a few days after the incident at lunch and desperate to change things, Palomma cinched up her uniform dress, hiding the folds under her belt; it had risen above her knees. She took a deep breath and walked downstairs.

"Bye, Mom!" she said as she passed her mother in the kitchen. She tried not to sound nervous. "I'm going outside to wait for Christine!"

"Bye, dear," her Mom replied, walking out and drying her hands on a dishtowel. She looked her up and down.

Palomma felt herself turning white as a sheet.

"Have a good day!" she said, returning to the kitchen.

Oh my God. She hadn't died.

Chapter 3

A week after the egg incident, Doug's mother walked into his room. She always walked right in without knocking, as if Doug was still five years old.

"Your friend Ed called again—he asked if you could help him work on his car."

Doug didn't respond. He anticipated the next sentence.

"I told him you'd be right over."

Doug's eyes opened wide in surprise.

"I thought I was…"

"Your father said you could go," she continued. "He said it'll teach you some useful skills. He said Ed knows more than you about cars. He said it's time you started learning important things." She waved her finger forward on each 'he said.'

Doug didn't say a word. Out of the house was out of the house.

"Be back for dinner," his mother said as he left. "And nowhere else but Ed's house!"

"Grab a 9/16th box wrench," said Ed.

Ed and Doug were hunched over a 1964 Corvair in Ed's backyard.

"I'm surprised your folks let you come," said Ed, tightening a nut. "I thought you were grounded."

"I still am," Doug answered glumly. He stood up straight. "I'm here because I'm supposed to be learning"—he adopted a nasally, sarcastic voice—"'important things.' You're supposed to teach me about cars."

"You already know about cars."

"I know that, you know that, but *he* doesn't know that," replied Doug, motioning with his thumb. "Maybe while I'm here, you can teach me about raking leaves, or painting, or any other bullshit my father says is important."

"I got enough to do around here too," said Ed. "Don't take it out on me."

Ed met Doug when they attended St. John's Elementary School. At first, they steered clear of each other; Doug avoided guys like Ed who were bigger than him and Ed avoided smart kids like Doug. Ed had a few run-ins with bullies making fun of his second-hand clothes, but they left him alone after he'd slugged one of them. It wasn't until eighth grade that they ended up sitting next to each other in class.

One day, though, Doug came back from recess with a bloody nose. He was trying to hide it and wasn't succeeding.

"You, umm, got a little…blood there," Ed whispered.

Doug didn't respond.

"Need a Kleenex? I think I got one."

Doug looked at him. "Yeah, thanks," he whispered.

Ed couldn't think of anything else to say so he opened his history book. Doug watched out of the corner of his eye.

"Did you, uh, how do you think you did on the take-home quiz?" Doug finally asked.

Ed didn't look up. "I'm lucky if I got any right," he muttered.

Doug held a piece of paper behind his book. "Here, just don't copy 'em all," he said.

"Don't worry," replied Ed. "I'm dumb enough to be smart enough to miss enough to keep looking dumb."

Doug started to laugh out loud, then covered his mouth. He smiled, waiting until Ed was done copying answers.

They started hanging around together almost all the time. Ed knew Doug wouldn't call him stupid; Doug knew bullies wouldn't risk a beating from Ed.

"I'm not taking it out on you," said Doug. "I'm just sick of it."

The telephone rang in the house; Ed's mother stepped out the back door, looked around and went back in.

"Like that," grumbled Doug. "Guaran-damn-teed that was my mother calling to make sure I was here."

"The battery cable's good. Bring your car back here to jump it."

Doug drove his car around the house on the grass. It wasn't easy; there was something piled everywhere, tools, old car parts, scrap metal, bricks. It looked more like a junkyard than a backyard.

"You ever think about cleaning some of this crap up?" asked Doug as he got out.

Ed started to hook up the jumper cables. "And when do you suggest I do *that*?" he answered, straightening up. "Oh, I know, when the maid comes, right?"

He got behind the wheel and cranked over the Corvair; it started. Ed got out and unhooked the cables.

"We got two rules here." He closed Doug's hood. "If it works, keep it; if it breaks, fix it. Makin' things all spic and span ain't high on the list."

Ed watched the Corvair's engine run. "They got my Dad sunup to sundown at the country club, like he's the only one there who can do anything. My mom is nine hours at the canning plant. I hardly ever even talk with them anymore." He looked up at Doug. "Someone's got to help keep up with crap like laundry and dishes. It's not like there's anyone else to get the shit done. I never had a sister like you."

"Then what are you doing at Catholic school?" asked Doug. "All I ever hear from my parents is how much it costs!"

Ed slowly walked in front of Doug, wiping his hands on a rag. "My folks want me to go to college. My Dad gets a few bucks from the rich people to regrip their golf clubs. My Mom makes jam and pies, sells 'em at a farm stand. I strip junkers and sell the parts. *That's* how I'm at Catholic school. I don't really want to be but it's what they want. The golf team's about the only thing that makes it bearable." He tossed the rag onto Doug's car. "You got any other comments about my family?"

Years back, when his father had found work at the country club, Ed would tag along. He saw men playing golf; it looked like fun. Using a club his father fished out of a pond and golf balls he found in the woods, he'd started hitting balls in the fields near his house.

He had a knack for golf. His swing didn't look pretty, but he could hit the ball a long way. Ed would sneak onto the course to play a hole sometimes before his father went home; word of his ability spread to the club pro. Soon they let him use the driving range late in the day in return for picking up the balls.

At Blessed Sacrament, he'd made the golf team as a freshman; a wealthier supporter of the team saw his old clubs and gave him a new set. Ed even taught Doug how to play and gave him his old clubs; they spent some fun Saturday afternoons at Fox Hollow Golf Course, the small public course in town. Doug planned on trying out for the team.

Ed saw the golfers on TV and the thousands of dollars they won. He was getting closer to being able to play like them someday. Maybe golf was the little crack, the opening for him and his parents.

Ed and Doug stared at each other while the Corvair continued to run. Doug picked up the rag and handed it back to Ed.

"I'm sorry, man," Doug said. "I was talking shit."

"Seriously, it can't be that bad at your new home, right?" he asked.

"It's a *house*." Doug snarled the last word. "Where we *used* to live was my home."

Ed shut off the Corvair. "This shitbox has run long enough. Let's go get a Coke."

Doug looked back over his shoulder toward the house. "I'm not supposed to…"

Ed interrupted. "I'll tell my Mom we're still here. She'll catch on."

After stopping at a gas station and buying sodas, Doug pulled onto a dirt road and drove back into a farm field. This time of year, the fields were vast expanses of dry beige dirt; the only things visible in any direction were flat, featureless stretches of dull ground.

"That's the kind of shit I mean," said Doug as they sat on the hood of the car. "Your Mom sticks up for you."

"We gotta have each other's backs here in the sticks," answered Ed. "No one else will. Your folks giving you shit?"

"All I hear is how great this fucking new house is," said Doug, "shittons of work to do on it, out in the middle of nowhere, no friends close by." Doug stopped and lit a cigarette. "Yeah, friends. Like last week, when you called."

He told Ed the whole story about his old neighborhood. When he finished, Ed leaned back and took a long drink. "That sucks if you can't count on your folks to back you."

Ed turned quickly toward Doug. "That came out wrong."

Doug blew out a cloud of smoke. "Say what you want, there isn't much anyone could say that'd piss me off about now."

"This just start?" asked Ed.

"I *wish*," replied Doug. "It's been goin' on a long time. It's like it's a pain in the ass to have kids or something." Doug stopped and thought for a moment. "Your Dad taught you to shave, right?"

"Yeah, so what?"

"You know who taught *me*?" asked Doug.

"Who?"

"My *sister*!" said Doug, angrily. "Lin saw a big gash on my face one day and showed me."

"I remember," Ed smirked. "It looked like you had two mouths."

"Fuck you!" Doug laughed, throwing his soda can at Ed.

Ed ducked. "Man, I hope she wasn't the one that taught you, um, you know…"

"A book."

"A book what?"

"My mother gave me a fucking *book*," answered Doug. "Becoming a Young Christian Man—a Publication of the Diocese of Camden," he sing-songed while holding his hands like he was praying.

"Did it have pictures?" asked Ed. He moved his closed fist up and down.

"Gimme that fucking Coke can so I can throw it at you again!" laughed Doug.

Ed and Doug spent the rest of the afternoon trading stories about their childhoods before Doug brought Ed home and went home himself.

At around the same time, Christine was in her room, standing in front of a full-length mirror.

Breasts are the rite of passage from little girls to young women the world takes notice of most. Boys in particular. Which is why girls can't wait to get their first bra.

Christine was fortunate; she'd developed bigger breasts than other girls at a younger age. Boys immediately paid more attention to her when she walked into their seventh-grade classroom after summer vacation wearing a real bra—not a trainer, like the other girls.

Attention from boys was new and exciting. She started to look at the things women did to attract attention. Charlie's Angels were so popular, boys hung posters of them on their bedroom walls instead of Dr. J and Mike Schmidt. In high school, Christine talked her mother into taking her to a salon to have her hair done like Farrah Fawcett.

But it looked too much like Palomma's curly hair. She had it straightened and dyed to look like Kate Jackson's. It hung down past her shoulders and she practiced flipping it in front of the mirror. Christine decided Jackson was sexier than Farrah anyway. But none of Charlie's Angels wore glasses; what boy would be interested in her with them on?

One day during sophomore year, Christine walked up to her mother in the kitchen while she was making dinner.

"Mommy?" she said. "I, um, broke my glasses."

"Let me see," said Mrs. Holloway, taking the glasses from Christine.

"It wasn't my fault!" continued Christine. "I was cleaning them when some boy rushed by and knocked them out of my hand; before I could pick them up, someone stepped on them!" She acted out the motions of being bumped into and dropping them.

"That's the second time this month," said Mrs. Holloway, handing them back to Christine. "Maybe it's time for some thicker frames!"

"Or maybe…" Christine said in a kittenish voice, "I could get a pair of contact lenses?" She moved closer to her mother.

"Contact lenses? They're very expensive, dear. I don't know…"

"But they can't get stepped on! Or get knocked out of your hand!" Christine started talking faster. "Oh please, Mommy, please?" Christine looked at her mother with her hands folded and wide, pleading eyes.

Mrs. Holloway hesitated. "I'm going to have to ask your father."

"Of course, Mommy!" said Christine. She pirouetted, and happily walked out of the kitchen. Ask her father? Contact lenses were as good as hers.

It wasn't only Christine's appearance changing…she was learning how to get her way. And she liked it.

Christine had gotten very good at getting her parents to do almost anything she asked. When she got her driver's license junior year, she'd pointed out a Ford Mustang to her father when they drove past Crescent Motors and talked about how she'd give anything to have it in red. She talked about it pretty much nonstop. A week later, it was sitting in her driveway.

Christine also found boys were eager to do favors for her if they thought they'd get to kiss her someday or whatever they were hoping for. That was the whole point. Let them hope; nothing would happen.

Monday at school, Palomma sat in homeroom getting herself organized for the day ahead. It was one of the few places she was during the day Christine wasn't.

Elementary school used to be safe for Palomma—she'd been content to take her notes, do her homework and blend into the background. The system she'd come back to at Blessed Sacrament had changed everything. Students met with teachers at 'appointments' and made their own schedules. There was no background to blend into anymore. Participation was a major part of the grading.

Classrooms weren't what they used to be. Most of the 'resource rooms' had tables in the center seating four students each. Desks remained around the perimeter of the rooms with a few pulled up in a circle around the teacher's desk.

There was constant movement. Students could change rooms every twenty minutes if they wanted. They could talk in the classrooms instead of being silent. All these things were foreign and uncomfortable for Palomma.

All the groups Palomma ended up in were with Christine, at Christine's insistence. Christine was acting differently. She used to do her own work; now, Christine wanted help and convinced Palomma to provide it. Palomma struggled with her conscience. The 'help' she provided was cheating, and cheating was a sin. But she didn't want to think about possibly losing her best friend if she didn't.

And despite all Palomma did, Christine never returned the favor by helping Palomma with something she *was* good at—boys.

After the experiment with her hemline earlier in the year, she'd listened to the girls' stories at lunch more intently and heard a lot about makeup. Palomma started off borrowing her mother's, and now when she looked in the mirror she looked a little less plain.

Her breasts had grown a little too. When her mother took her to Soloff's to buy new uniforms, they were a little shorter and tighter than the ones Palomma used to wear. Her mother didn't seem to notice.

There were some new people at Blessed Sacrament that hadn't been in her eighth-grade class; with the new system, Palomma was beginning to notice some of them, like Ed Sherman, Andy Swanson and Doug Halecki.

Ed acted tough sometimes—but Palomma sensed it was just an act. She'd never heard him make fun of anyone except Doug and Andy, who gave it right back. He was clearly close to Doug; it was like they had what Palomma used to have with Christine—a friendship based in trust.

Andy was kind of immature. You could count on Andy to say or do something inappropriate in class—and him to think it was the funniest thing ever. Doug was a peculiar mix of smart, funny, nervous, boisterous, silly and serious.

Andy Swanson had moved to Holly Hill sophomore year and had been awarded a 'need' scholarship to Blessed Sacrament. Every year, the school enrolled a couple of students with their tuition covered by the church. When school started, Andy realized he stood out like a sore thumb in his uniform from the second-hand store downtown. But he had a plan.

After everyone else had left the locker room to go to gym class at the beginning of the year, Andy took a blazer, shirt and pants; he detoured to his locker, stashing them before heading into the gym himself.

Andy figured it was too bad Jeffrey Lattimore had to wear gym clothes the rest of the day. Everyone figured the basketball players had thrown his clothes in the dumpster as a prank, exactly what Andy had counted on.

Back then, Andy decided he and Doug should be friends. They were the same height, both wore glasses and both were socially inept. As time passed, though, Doug's social skills improved a little; Andy's didn't. Most kids would walk away when they saw him coming.

That night, Palomma was reading at home after school when her mother knocked on her bedroom door. "Dear, your sister needs a ride home from the mall, could you pick her up? She'll be behind the movie theater."

Palomma didn't mind going to get Gemma. It was a chance to drive, and she didn't get too many opportunities. She hadn't really been reading anyway, more thinking.

She'd been trying everything she could think of to get boys' attention but wasn't getting anywhere. It wasn't fair. All a girl like Christine had to do was wear a short skirt and wiggle her butt.

As she pulled up behind the movie theater, Palomma could see Gemma on the sidewalk, talking to a short, chubby boy. When she saw Palomma arrive, she gave him a kiss on the cheek. He waved to her as she walked away.

Palomma squinted her eyes as if to convince herself she'd seen what she'd seen. Gemma broke into a trot and approached the car. She opened the passenger door and jumped in.

"You won't believe who I saw!" Gemma said.

Palomma stared straight ahead. "I don't believe what I just saw!" she said, curtly. "I didn't know you were going out with anyone!" She began to drive toward the mall exit.

"I'm not. What makes you think I am?"

Palomma slowed and turned sharply into a section of the lot furthest from the mall, pulled up along the curb and put the car in park. She turned to face Gemma. "Then explain to me why you're kissing a boy out in the open and you're not going steady with him!"

Gemma turned to Palomma with a wry smile. "What part do you want me to explain?" she asked. She began counting on her fingers. "The part where your lips touch him? The part where you talk to him? Or maybe I should start at the part where, you know, you're somewhere a boy actually is."

Palomma felt her cheeks flush. She didn't say another word all the way home.

All through dinner, Gemma tried to get a rise out of Palomma without success. She even flicked a pea at her when her parents weren't looking. After dinner, Palomma walked into Gemma's room and closed the door.

"You're going to get us both in trouble if you keep it up!" she whispered, standing at the foot of Gemma's bed. "*You're* going to get in trouble out there!"

Gemma was leaning against the headboard thumbing through a Teen Beat magazine. Without setting it down, she looked at Palomma. "Why are you whispering?"

"Gemma! Stop it! Mom will hear!" Palomma said.

"And?" answered Gemma. "What if she does? I'm not a little baby!"

Palomma was about to respond when Gemma put the magazine down and slid over so she was sitting on the edge of the bed. Palomma sat down on the end.

"It was a little peck," she said. "That's Anthony, he's a nice guy and he likes it when I do that."

"And you don't see a problem with teasing him?" Palomma whispered back. "You don't worry what people will say about you?"

"I'm pretty sure he's..." Gemma started. "Um, wait, you know about...homos, right?"

Palomma blushed. "Yes, I know about homosexuals. They're men who...like other men instead of women."

"I'm pretty sure Anthony is," said Gemma, "I figured I'd help him out —people see a girl kiss him, maybe they won't think that about him. Even you could figure it out."

"Excuse me?" Palomma snarled.

Gemma leaned back. "Daddy says you're going to be a lawyer. Looks to me like you're working on being a nun."

Palomma was getting angry. "And what are YOU working on being, huh? Kissing boys right out in the open?"

"I'll bet you haven't kissed any anywhere ever," answered Gemma.

Palomma looked down at her lap and started rocking back and forth a tiny bit. Gemma realized she'd hurt her sister's feelings. She leaned closer.

"All I mean is you can be you, but I need to be me. I'm not gonna end up like Mom," she whispered, "spending the rest of my life cooking, cleaning and having babies. One thing I know is I won't get anywhere if I don't go anywhere. If I don't do things. If I act like..." She stopped.

"You don't have to finish it," said Palomma dejectedly. She got up and walked back to her room.

Palomma wanted to be angry with her sister but couldn't. She was right. All Palomma was worried about was attracting a boy, for what? To get married right out of high school? Spend the rest of her life as a housewife?

"Like when Mom was my age," Palomma whispered out loud.

Palomma always assumed her father had wanted a son and she was supposed to fill the role. He told everyone she was going to law school someday. It seemed like pressure she didn't want. But she thought about what Gemma said, and began to see it differently. Maybe it was a push. It would be a way out of the same life generations of women had little choice in.

Times were changing, but Palomma hadn't been.

I Love Liking You A Lot

Chapter 4

It was March of junior year. Some of the fun things associated with third-year students like getting class rings were offset by realities that couldn't be put off any longer. College applications were coming due; important senior-year activities were only months away.

Palomma was sitting in room six. It was a popular room because Mrs. DiBiase was the moderator, a teacher far more in tune with teenagers than the nuns. It was the resource room for English and many activities were based there, like the school newspaper.

Palomma was in a desk in the corner trying hard not to so much as glance in the direction of Karen and Lauren, who were sitting at a table in the center.

It had been a few months since they'd made fun of her at lunch, but she still didn't want to do anything to attract their attention. But she also wanted to see if they were talking about her. But why would they be talking about her? She wasn't cool like them.

Why couldn't anything in her life be a *good* kind of confusing?

At the mod change, Doug walked in, looking dejected. He plopped down in a desk on the other side of the room.

Palomma went back to worrying about the cheerleaders but kept glancing at Doug. There was something about his body language that made Palomma feel she could sense his emotions. It wasn't the usual joking, clowning Doug. And he wasn't with his friends as he almost always was. It occurred to Palomma this would be a great opportunity to practice talking to a boy.

She hesitated for a moment, stood up, added one quick skirt fold under her belt, shot a quick glance at the two cheerleaders, who weren't looking at her, and walked over to where he was sitting.

"Umm, Doug?" she asked, nervously, standing in front of him. "I was wondering if maybe you could take a look at this application I'm doing?"

"Huh?" Doug jumped. He'd been lost in thought.

"Unless you're busy. It's not important, I just think you're really good at writing."

"Oh, uh, okay, sure," stammered Doug. He barely knew Palomma; he had to think for a second of her name. "What do you want me to do?"

Palomma noticed Doug's eyes hadn't moved off the papers she was holding down to her legs at any point. Darn it.

She handed the pages to Doug. "It's for my application to Bryn Mawr. I'm supposed to tell them why I'd be a benefit to their college. Maybe you could tell me if it makes sense. I mean, you write so well, those fake horoscopes you wrote in the school paper had me laughing so hard…" She sat down in the desk next to him.

Doug was half-listening as he quickly flipped through the pages.

"It looks fine, I guess." He set it on the desk and looked away. Palomma feared she'd made a mistake in trying this when Doug started talking again. "I was going to start one of those today…"

Palomma waited for him to finish the sentence. He didn't.

"Why not?" she said. "You could probably write it with your eyes closed, way better than mine."

"Yeah," Doug answered. "'Course, now…"

Palomma waited for Doug to continue; he didn't. "So why…" she began to say.

"I'm gonna major in journalism." Doug began talking, more to himself than Palomma. He wasn't even looking at her. "The thing I wanted more than anything was the school article in the Daily Record. That's not writing for some stupid school paper, it's the real deal. I could make a big thing about in my essay. The article I submitted when they announced the tryouts was one of the best things I ever wrote." He trailed off, staring blankly at the door.

Doug turned back from the door and started reading her essay again.

"You didn't get it?" Palomma asked.

"Yeah. No. Sort of," he answered.

Palomma had a confused look on her face.

Doug turned toward her. "They called me down to the office and told me this time there'll be two people doing it."

"Who's the other person?"

"Christine Holloway."

Palomma didn't say anything, but remembered Christine asking for help with an article about school events. Palomma had thought it was for the school newspaper; she'd pretty much written the whole thing.

"It had always been one person before," said Doug, looking away again. "They said this was the first time they split it. God knows why. Colleges'll probably think I wasn't good enough to do it on my own." He looked down at the pages again. "This looks good. Looks like exactly what they'd want."

They sat silently for a few seconds. She looked at the papers Doug was still holding.

"That application has a ton of lines to put down your activities," she said. "I figured if they put that many lines it was probably good if you had stuff to fill it up. There are a lot of other things going on, maybe if you did some of them too it'd look better? A bunch of good things, all of them added up?"

Doug looked at her.

"Like the yearbook. Didn't you hear the announcement this morning? You could be on yearbook. I could never do anything like that."

"I don't know," Doug muttered.

"You're on the golf team, aren't you?" asked Palomma, recalling an article in the school paper.

"In this school, I'm amazed you even know there IS a golf team. All anyone cares about is basketball."

"There's Welcome Week, and from what I heard they do a bunch of skits. You could probably write some really good ones. Even act in them."

Doug smiled.

"Speaking of acting, how about the school play?" Palomma asked. "Last I heard there weren't many boys trying out, and Sue O'Brien said you sing really well. Who knows, maybe you'd get the lead role? That'd look really good!"

"What's the play?" Doug asked.

"Hello Dolly."

"The lead role is, um, a girl, isn't it? You know, Barbra Streisand?"

"Yeah, no, I meant the guy's role. I think it's her husband."

Doug leaned back, thinking. Palomma suggestions would give him reasons to get out of the house. Skits and plays would bring the attention he loved. His parents couldn't say no if they were school activities. His smile got a little bigger; he wanted to hear more.

"What do you have to do?" asked Doug.

Palomma felt a glow inside. She had to struggle to keep a huge grin from breaking out on her face. She was talking to a boy, just the two of them, and he was interested in what she was saying. And he was smiling at her!

"I've got the sheet they sent around," said Palomma. "I was going to sign up for chorus for the same reason—to fill up some space on the application."

She noticed some other pieces of paper she'd saved.

"You know what would look really good on a college application?" she said suddenly. "Class president!"

Lauren suddenly looked over at them from the center of the room.

Doug rolled his eyes. "Yeah, right. There's only 75 kids in our class."

"You don't have to put that on the applications," said Palomma.

"Doesn't matter if there were a thousand, 'cause no one would vote for me."

"I would," said Palomma. Immediately, she felt she'd said it too quickly.

"You barely know me," answered Doug.

Palomma was about to continue when she stopped and glanced at Lauren. She leaned in very close to Doug.

"I know the two who *are* running," she whispered. "Louise Grant and Karen Jamison." Doug made a sour face. "See?" Palomma leaned even closer. "No one likes either of them, but no one else runs. I'll bet kids would vote for *anyone…*"

Palomma stopped with her mouth still open. She leaned back and blushed.

Doug chuckled. "That's it, maybe I could run as Anyone Halecki. I could count on three votes, me, Andy and Ed. You said you would, that's four. Practically a landslide."

Palomma laughed; she was glad Doug thought it was a joke. "I'll bet Christine would vote for you, and most of the boys probably would anyway because you're a boy!"

"Thanks for noticing," said Doug. "And you're a girl!"

Palomma blushed again.

"I didn't mean anything bad!" Doug blurted out, seeing her reaction and suddenly feeling nervous. "I was just making a joke!"

An odd feeling came over Palomma. She and Doug were talking like boys and girls talk when they're flirting. She was trying to think of something else to say when Christine walked into the room.

Christine slowed down as she passed Karen and Lauren, giving them a little wave. They ignored her. She continued to where Palomma and Doug were, sitting down on the other side of Doug.

"Doug Halecki! Partner! Now we know who the best writers are in school!" she gushed. She hadn't even looked at Palomma.

Doug hadn't seen Christine walk in. He also didn't expect her to sit down next to him. He tried to think of something to say. "Congratulations, Christine, I'm sure it's important..." came out of his mouth. Christine talked right over him.

"You bet!" she answered. "With all the things I'm doing, I'll probably get a full scholarship! And as far as the article..."

She leaned closer and touched Doug's arm. "You'll do a great job!"

Doug felt himself start to shake a little; this was the closest his face had ever been to the face of a girl to whom he wasn't related. She smelled pretty, perfumy. He could feel her breath on his cheek and it felt warm and sexy. He shot a glance downward and could see a little bit of Christine's boobs through the opening in her blouse. He looked back up immediately and made sure his eyes didn't move again.

"Come on, we need to figure out how we'll work this!" She started to walk away; Doug got up and followed.

Palomma watched them walk out. When she saw Lauren was glaring at her, she hurriedly gathered her books and left too.

That night, Doug stood amid clouds of steam in the kitchen of the Amerihost Inn, second-guessing wanting to be a dishwasher.

"Get those damn monkey dishes done! This ain't a vacation!" yelled the chef.

When Doug got his license, he applied for a job at there. He was hired to clean the bathrooms on weekends, a disgusting job. He stuck with it hoping a dishwasher position would open up, imagining it would be like doing the dishes at home—washing plates in a sink, chatting with co-workers. After three months had passed, they reassigned him to the kitchen. When he arrived for this, his first night, he thought he'd stepped into Hell.

Clouds of steam spewed from the front of a massive, noisy metal machine. More steam rose from the dishes as they came out the end. The floor was slick from water and grease.

The chef handed Doug an apron. "It's simple. One—make sure the water temperature never goes below 160 degrees. You got that? Never below. Crank up the gas if the needle even gets close. Two—never stick your hand in the garbage disposal." He flicked on the disposal and it made a horrendous grinding sound. "Three—never drop silverware in the disposal. Four—if you do, stick your hand in there and get it out. Five—my pots are the priority. Got it?"

Doug paused trying to let it all sink in. "Wait! How do you tie this…"

The chef walked back to the ovens.

When he began the shift at 5 p.m., he managed to sort of keep up. Busboys would wheel a cart into the kitchen, piling the dirty dishes, cups, glasses and utensils at his station. Doug would rinse them, stack them in trays and slide the trays into the dishwashing unit. When they came out the other end, he'd take them to their places in the kitchen. He started to get a little rhythm going.

Then 7 p.m. came, and hell broke loose.

The number of carts coming in from the dining room tripled, quadrupled. Tons of dishes were wheeled in from somewhere to his right—it was the banquet room with an event going on. Busboys would shove things into any possible space, shooting dirty looks at Doug. He started jamming everything into the machine without rinsing.

"The monkey dishes, damn it!"

"Salad bowls! We're out of salad bowls!"

The head waitress, Loretta, tall and thin with her hair in a bun, dropped a stack of silverware next to Doug. "These are filthy! Rinse 'em off *right* before you send 'em through!"

"Where are my pots?" yelled the chef.

A fork slipped into the disposal; When Doug flicked it on the grinding echoed through the kitchen.

"What the hell are you DOING over there?" yelled Loretta.

Doug was burning with self-consciousness. It seemed everyone in the kitchen—waitresses, busboys, the chef—was focused on him. He was going as fast as he could but couldn't keep up.

"Salad bowls!"

"Monkey dishes!"

"Send cups through, for Christ's sake!"

Suddenly, another waitress, a short, round woman named Lily, dashed into the kitchen. "Cool it!" she said in an exaggerated whisper, holding her finger to her lips.

Doug didn't cool it. He was desperately trying to make a dent in the mountain of dirty dishes.

He glanced up to see a man in a three-piece brown polyester suit in the entrance to the kitchen. He was no taller than Doug, but a lot wider.

He looked around at everyone and bellowed "How y'all doin' tonight?"

Doug was startled. It was a southern accent straight out of the Beverly Hillbillies.

The man walked around looking things over. He asked the waitresses questions, saying "Fiiiiiine, fiiiine," as he walked away before they'd finished answering. Doug was still rinsing dishes when he heard the man say, "What's y'all's name?"

Doug turned; he was standing behind him. "Doug, sir. Doug Halecki."

"Well, Mr. Doug Halecki, if we had a hotel full of people stirrin' up as much dust as you, we'd make a million a night! Keep it up!" He slapped Doug hard on the back.

Everyone in the kitchen was staring at Doug.

"I'll leave y'all to your business!" he said as he walked out of the kitchen.

It remained silent for a few seconds. Then Lily adopted a mocking accent. "You just keep stirrrrrrrin' up dust, Mr. High-lecki!" Everyone burst out laughing. Doug blushed harder than he ever had before.

When the laughter died down, the regular kitchen bustle returned. Doug felt someone else come up behind him. He turned to see another waitress, a younger woman named Rena.

"Load up all the small stuff first," she said in a low voice. "Monkey dishes, cups, saucers, silverware. Plates after that. Oh, try this with the disposal."

She picked up a saucer and placed it over the opening.

"Keeps things from falling in. When the garbage starts to pile up, slide the saucer out and run it."

"Thanks," whispered Doug. "Thanks...um..."

"Rena," she replied. "Don't worry. You'll get it."

Dishes finally stopped coming in and Doug finished all of them and the chef's pots by 11:30. He sat at the break table in a corner, exhausted, smoking a cigarette. His shirt was soaked and he could smell the stink of spilled food coming off his jeans

"You did good," said Rena as she sat down. She reached for his cigarette pack. "May I?"

"Oh...sure!" said Doug. He sat up straighter. "Your name was Rena, right?"

Rena looked at her watch. "Still is!"

Doug laughed and relaxed a little.

"You coming back for another night of this torture?" she asked.

"Um, yeah, I mean sure! Why wouldn't I?"

"Some people don't even make it through one night," she replied. "I've had to pitch in more than once."

"I'll try to get the hang of it," said Doug. "I wish the guy with the southern accent hadn't singled me out, though. I don't want to make any enemies."

"That's the new owner," said Rena. "From Louisiana, I think. Says he's going to make the place all fancy and upscale. Wouldn't bother me —higher prices mean bigger tips. And as far as the other people in here,"

She leaned closer to Doug.

"For most of 'em it went in one ear and nothing blocked it on its way out the other side, know what I mean?"

Doug chuckled.

"Don't forget to clock out!" said Rena as she stubbed out her cigarette and walked out of the kitchen.

Doug took off his apron and left too.

A week later at school, Christine walked into room three and sat down next to Palomma, who was taking notes from science book.

Room three was a study hall room. It only had tables and chairs and was bare of books and audio-visual equipment. Palomma used it to study; most kids used it as a break room.

"Didja see? Didja see? I made everything!"

Palomma didn't respond. She had seen. Everyone had come into their homerooms that morning to find a mimeographed sheet of paper on each desk listing the results of decisions on activities. Palomma had picked it up as eagerly as many others but wasn't overjoyed with what she saw.

She hadn't been kidding with Doug about trying to get involved in as many things as she could—and pretty much everything she'd put in for, Christine was there. She signed up for the spirit club, only to see Christine's name on the sheet too. She'd signed up for the school play chorus. So had Christine. She signed up for the prom committee; Christine did too.

Christine had racked up even more. She was art editor of the yearbook and student representative to the PTA.

"I was looking at the Bryn Mawr application. Honestly, I can't see how I'm going to fit all of this!" Christine went on. "And that's even before they hold club officer elections! Let's sit down tomorrow and figure out how I'm, um, how we're going to fit it all!"

"Sure, we'll do that," said Palomma. She twirled her pencil in her fingers.

"Doug Halecki won senior class president too! I wonder what made him even run? I was sure Karen Jamison had that stitched up. But the other one made me fall out of my desk—didja see? He's co-starring in the play!"

"Yeah, I saw," said Palomma, putting down the pencil. "I heard he sings really good."

"Melody Jannsen is *soooooooo* pissed!" said Christine. "She was sure she was going to get Dolly and Kim Casey got it!"

"I guess things work out that way sometimes," said Palomma.

"Whew! What a morning! I've gotta run and talk to the people on the clubs, see who's voting for me!" said Christine, and she hurried out of the room.

After getting home from school, Doug walked back to his thinking spot in the woods before dinner.

It seemed a lot brighter back there this day. The sun filtering through the trees and the smells of spring made Doug feel happier. He *was* happy. As hard as it was to believe, good things had started.

"Class president. Fucking class *president*!" Doug said out loud to a squirrel running past. "And Horace Vandergelder in Hello Dolly! This is so fucking *cool*!"

Doug sat down, lit a cigarette, took the mimeo out to look at again and smiled. He folded up the paper and put it back in his pocket. All these things were great, but he'd also started to make some headway in the one that was of greater importance to him. Girls.

After Doug got his driver's license and car earlier in the year, he'd stay after school if there was anything going on. Afterward, he'd sit behind the gym in his car hoping someone would ask about it. He'd spent a lot of time sitting by himself.

Then, it happened. A girl walked up to him and asked him for a ride home.

Doug was almost giddy when he realized this was a way to be with girls without having to approach them. It wasn't like when they used to ask for homework answers in grade school; now, when they needed a ride, they'd be sitting next to him for a while with no one else around.

The first couple of times, Doug was ecstatic when they asked. For the first couple of times, though, he couldn't think of a single thing to say.

Margie McGovern had asked the first time, and Doug spent what seemed like forever trying to summon up the courage to start a conversation. By the time Doug had decided to say, "How were your appointments today?" they'd reached her house. Melody Janssen had asked him too; she talked nonstop from the moment she got in. He didn't get the opportunity to try out his "appointments" line.

Frustrated, Doug had put a tape into his 8-track player as he left her house—and it was as if a cartoon lightbulb came on over his head.

A few days passed.

"Hey, Doug! Are you leaving anytime soon?" asked Sue O'Brien as she walked up to Doug's car.

"Uh, no, wait, yes! Yeah, I was just about to get going!"

"Cool! Any chance I could catch a ride to my house?"

"Sure!" said Doug. "Hop in!"

Sue got in the passenger side and Doug drove to the parking lot exit.

"Where do you live?" he asked.

"On Arnold Street. You know, out near the bowling alley?"

"Oh sure, I know where," said Doug, pulling out of the lot.

"Passenger's choice!" he said, pointing to the box of 8-track tapes at her feet. He'd rehearsed these lines driving home the past few days.

Sue picked up the box. "Wow!" she said. "You've got a lot of good stuff in here!" She ran her finger atop the tapes. "Eagles, Orleans, Raspberries, Blue Oyster Cult, Boston, Jethro Tull…"

She stopped and took one out.

"Aerosmith!'" she exclaimed, holding up a tape.

"Got it when it came out," said Doug.

Sue pushed the tape into the 8-track player. Doug waited about half a minute and started singing along.

Sue's mouth dropped open.

"My God, you sound just like him!" she said during the instrumental break.

"You like it?" asked Doug, smiling.

"Do some more!"

They drove along with Doug singing until 'Dream On' ended.

"That was so good!" said Sue. "I didn't know you could sing!"

"Someone was singing?" said Doug, and they both laughed.

Sue pointed out which house was hers and Doug pulled up in front. "Thanks for the ride, Doug!" she said as she opened the door. "I wanna hear another one the next time I need a ride home!"

Doug made sure he was at the end of the street before letting it out. "Woo-hooooooo!"

Doug was pretty darn good at singing. Years before, to make his paper route less boring, he brought a radio. One day, he'd stopped at an intersection and had been so engrossed in singing "Without You" by Nillson he hadn't noticed the car next to him with its windows down. Doug heard a horn and was afraid to turn and look, assuming they'd be laughing at him.

To his amazement, they were clapping and giving him the 'thumbs-up' sign.

It was attention. Doug craved attention. Would've eaten it three meals a day if such a thing was possible. He started making an effort to sing loud when he rode past people.

This was something that got him more comfortable talking to girls. And it looked like there were a lot of girls in these activities. And he knew exactly which one he wanted things to start happening with.

He'd be around Christine Holloway a lot in the coming senior year;

Doug decided he and Christine were meant to be together. They had been picked to co-write the school article. They were both in the play. They'd were on the prom committee. Their last names both started with 'H.' Those had to be more than coincidences.

The next week at school, Doug felt emboldened enough by his singing successes to try to approach Christine.

"Hi ladies! Is this seat taken?" Doug walked up to Christine and Palomma who were sitting at a table in room three. Doug sat down next to Christine. Palomma looked away and rolled her eyes.

Ever since the results of elections and play auditions had been announced, it seemed Doug was constantly hovering around. Pretty much every day he ended up in the same resource rooms when Christine and Palomma were there.

"I was wondering if you'd thought about my suggestion as far as the article," said Doug. He didn't even look at Palomma. "You know, we take turns writing and researching?"

"Oh, yes, Doug, I thought about that—maybe we can do it another way," replied Christine, turning toward him. "Maybe I could be the one who found the stories, and you could be the writer! Like a research director, you know?"

Doug looked like he was about to say something when Christine 'accidentally' brushed her shoulder against his. Palomma was pretending to be absorbed in studying but saw Doug blush out of the corner of her eye.

"Um, yeah, that might work," Doug stuttered.

When the bell rang for the change of mod, Christine and Palomma got up to leave. "Palomma?" Doug said, softly as Christine walked away.

Palomma stopped and turned around. "Doug?" she answered.

"Could I ask you a favor?" Doug whispered.

"Sure, what is it?"

"I, um, forgot to ask Christine for her phone number." Doug was speaking very fast. "You know, so we can talk about things about the article if we have to. I figured you'd have it, best friends and all!" Palomma stood quietly and tried to keep a frown off her face.

"It's in the phone book, Doug," she said, dispassionately. "She lives on Carlton Avenue."

Chapter 5

Traditionally at Blessed Sacrament, the senior class would plan Welcome Week activities for the incoming freshmen starting the first day of classes, culminating in a Welcome Day show.

Doug had succeeded in getting on the Welcome Week committee along with the other activities he'd put in for. The group consisted of Karen Jamison, Lauren Carrier, Melody Janssen and him, but who was on it wasn't what mattered.

What mattered was Doug had an idea, and the show would help him pull it off.

The group had to meet in the summer before school started. In July, Karen called a meeting at her house. Her family had money, certainly more than the Haleckis. Their house was a large, two-story brick structure with pillars in the heart of the 'refined' section of Holly Hill. Doug felt uncomfortable when he entered, passing an antique clock and a grand piano. There was even a marble statue in the foyer. It was all too upscale.

Once all four members were there, they sat at a table in the spacious, modern kitchen and Karen said, "The first order of business is to elect officers."

"The Welcome Week committee has officers?" asked Melody. "There's only four people!"

"I nominate Karen to be president," interrupted Lauren.

"All in favor?" asked Karen. Karen and Lauren immediately raised their hands. Doug and Melody paused and did the same.

"And I nominate Lauren to be vice-president," said Karen. Doug raised his hand without waiting, followed by Karen and Lauren. Melody eventually did too.

"Great, that's taken care of. Now about this welcome thing..."

Melody jumped up. "Me! Me! I have the greatest idea! Broadway! Show tunes, dance numbers, the smell of the greasepaint, the roar of the crowd!" She looked at each person breathlessly with an exaggerated smile on her face.

Karen remained expressionless while Lauren covered her mouth to keep from snickering.

Melody went on. "It'll be the best ever! Take a look at these scenes I wrote, you'll see how super it'll be!" She handed each person a sheaf of typewritten pages.

Each sheet had an outline for a skit. Some were one-person monologues, others called for only two characters. Melody's name appeared on each of them.

Karen thumbed through the pages. "Wow, Melody, it looks like you're the star of each of these." Lauren spoke up. "Do you have anything for other people to do? You know, like," she pointed back and forth between herself and Karen.

Melody went to answer when Doug interrupted.

"If it please the court, I have an idea everyone can be a part of. It's a news program! Holy News! Blessed Sacrament's best and only news program!"

Lauren started to speak. "That doesn't sound..."

"There's an anchor desk with four people—two of 'em are you and Karen."

Karen and Lauren looked at each other.

"You play cheerleaders."

They both smiled.

Karen pushed herself up from her chair. "I call an officers meeting," she said. She and Lauren walked into the living room. Doug and Melody watched them leave.

"Too bad about Dolly," Doug said to Melody. "What will you be again?"

Melody glared at him.

"What do we do?" whispered Lauren when they were out of earshot.

"What *can* we do? One thing's for sure, we're not doing that crap Melody had," answered Karen, motioning with her thumb back toward the kitchen, rolling her eyes.

Lauren grinned.

"How about if…" she began to whisper.

"…we let Doug do all the work?" Karen finished, smiling. "Payback for the class president crap!"

The girls returned to the kitchen and sat down. Karen looked at Doug with a serious expression on her face.

"We're considering your suggestion, Doug, but you're going to have to get us scripts right away."

Doug picked up the envelope he'd carried in, opened it and handed Karen a pile of typewritten pages. "Sorry, my carbon paper broke. You guys'll have to share."

Karen and Lauren looked at Doug's outline. There were quite a few skits with various members of the class suggested for roles. There was a weather report skit, a scene for the basketball team and three or four classroom routines. Karen and Lauren had a lot of funny lines. "It certainly looks like a lot of people can be in this. What do you think, Melody?"

Melody didn't answer. She was pouting.

Karen looked at Lauren. Lauren shrugged.

"We'll vote," said Karen. "All in favor of the news show, raise their hand." Doug, Karen and Lauren raised their hands. "A majority. Doug, have final scripts to me by August. And make sure Lauren and I have more good lines. That's it, we're done."

Melody rushed out the front door muttering to herself. Doug strode out to his car happily. He didn't mind Karen giving him orders, because the whole news-show concept had grown out of an idea he had to get things rolling with Christine.

Doug worked on the show during the rest of the summer, dropping off pages for different skits in Karen's mailbox. He never heard a peep from her and didn't figure to.

Late in August, Doug mailed an invitation to Christine to come to his house one morning. He described in the card a special skit he'd written that she'd star in, the funniest one in the show. The skit involved a blackboard; Doug explained she needed to come over to his house because it wouldn't fit in his car.

Time couldn't pass fast enough to get to the appointed day. Doug waited nervously. She must have gotten the invitation—the mail always got delivered. Doug kept checking the clock and looking out the window.

Around 10 a.m., Christine turned into the driveway, got out of her Mustang and rang the front doorbell. Doug opened it, trying to act nonchalant, first leaning against the frame of the doorway, then reaching up and holding onto the molding above it. "Oh, hi Christine! Thanks for coming over!" he said. "I see you got my invitation!"

Christine was wearing a tee shirt and jeans; God, she looked good.

"Hi, Doug!" she said. "If this will be the best part of the Welcome

Day show like you say, I couldn't turn it down!"

"Oh, it will be!" enthused Doug. "Let's go look at how it works!"

Doug stepped back and let her in. He closed the door and rushed to get in front of her to lead her to the basement.

Doug had drawn an outline of the United States on the board. "Okay, Christine, you'll be introduced as the weather girl, Stella Storm. You'll give a forecast for the country. Let me demonstrate."

Doug picked up a piece of chalk and began to read from the script.

"A high-pressure system has moved in across the Rocky Mountains"—Doug drew a vertical line down the left side of the map— "which could cause problems when it bumps into a low-pressure system in the south." He drew a horizontal line across the bottom. "The jet stream is still in the north"—he drew a horizontal line across the top —"and will keep pushing hot weather to the east coast." He drew a vertical line down the right side.

He glanced over at Christine. She was watching but didn't have any expression on her face. Doug cleared his throat.

"High temperatures are expected in Arizona," Doug made a big 'x' in the lower-left corner of the map—"while temperatures in New England will be much lower." He made another 'x' in the upper-right corner. "But heavy rains are expected in Kansas"—he made a third 'x' right in the middle—"and these should end up cancelling each other out in the week ahead."

Doug looked at Christine again. Then, he turned back to the board and, with a flourish, drew a line through all three 'x's'.

"Oh, wait! It's a tic-tac-toe game! Now I get it! That's cute, Doug!"

Christine smiled and looked at Doug. Doug looked at her.

And…

Doug froze.

He'd planned to say, "I want you to be the star of *my* show, too," and give her a big hug. Hopefully, when they pulled back from the hug, he'd look into her eyes soulfully and kiss her.

Doug hadn't figured out whether to keep his eyes open or closed. People on TV always closed their eyes kissing; Doug wanted to keep them open to see how Christine reacted. And he wasn't sure whether he should wait for her to stop first or be the one to stop and see if she wanted to kiss some more.

It didn't matter, though, because Doug had chickened out.

They stood there awkwardly. Doug was frozen like a statue while Christine shifted her weight from one foot to the other. A few seconds passed before she spoke. "That's funny, Doug. But I ought to be going, I'm getting together with someone later."

Doug was only half-listening to her because he was also cursing at himself in his mind. In a split second, all the confidence he'd had drained out of him like air escaping from a balloon—he was thinking it might have even made the same sound. After all the work and planning, Doug had blown it.

"Um, yeah, okay," Doug responded. "Here's your copy of the script."

Christine took it from Doug, folded it and tucked it into her back pocket. She walked up the basement steps and toward the front door. Doug followed; a part of him wanted to spin her around and kiss her but it was a really tiny part and his chickenness overruled it.

As they neared the front door Doug rushed ahead to open it; she walked right through toward her car without slowing down. "See ya, Doug!" she called out over her shoulder. She started the car and pulled out of the driveway.

Doug stood watching long after she'd driven away.

Doug had managed to get summer work in maintenance on some

days while still washing dishes a couple of nights. Little, the innkeeper, seemed to have taken a liking to Doug; he'd stopped to chat with him a couple of times that summer and had lemonade sent out to Doug when he was mowing the grass.

After chickening out with Christine that morning, Doug was glad to have to mow the whole front lawn of the hotel; it would help keep his mind off of her. He had put away the lawnmower around four o'clock and was clocking out when Little approached him.

"Another *fiiiine* job on the grass." Doug smiled; he'd grown to like the sound of that accent. "Listen, I got a surprise I think y'all are gonna love!" Little motioned for Doug to follow him and headed for the kitchen.

They walked through the back entrance to the kitchen. "I want you to meet Pete Baker," he said, approaching a short, skinny, long-haired teen sitting at the break table. Pete sprang up immediately when Little said his name. "I hired him as a dishwasher. He's gonna start trainin' tonight."

Doug was confused. "I thought I had the shift…"

"You sure do! Startin' tonight, it's as a busboy!" He patted Doug on the back and rubbed his hand up and down on it.

Doug grinned ear to ear. "Wow, thanks Mr. Little!"

Pete nervously rocked from one foot to the other.

"Just tryin' to give you young men a start," he said.

As they walked back toward the time clock, Little stopped and sniffed the air. He fanned in front of his nose, grimacing. "Someone's a little *gamy* around here!" he said. "Why don't y'all get cleaned up?".

"Oh, sorry, Mr. Little," said Doug. "I've gotta go home to change. I'll shower at home."

"No need to apologize son. But at least you could get that sweat off before gettin' in your car," Little persisted.

"No, it's okay, really," Doug replied, moving further away from Little. "I have to, um, do something in the yard first when I get home anyway."

"Use the shower in my office," Little said. "It's down here." He started walking away from Doug toward his office, stopped, turned and motioned toward the door.

"It's okay, Mr. Little," Doug said. "Really."

"Relax, son! You ain't got nothin' I ain't seen before!" Little gestured toward the door again.

Doug turned and ran out the door behind him.

Driving home, Doug was worried. Was Little trying to get him alone? He'd read about homosexuals but didn't think he'd ever met one. Was Little? Doug couldn't shake the feeling he'd seriously messed up by running out. All Little had suggested was a shower. Doug laid down in his bedroom before the evening shift but trying to rest made him overthink more. Little sure seemed eager to have Doug shower in his office. But maybe he *was* just trying to be helpful. Would he go back and not have a job at all?"

Doug's palms were sweaty when he got to work that night. He almost dropped a tray of water glasses while he was being trained when he saw Little came into the restaurant. Doug tried not to make eye contact with Little as he walked over to the bussing station. "How's it goin' son?" Little asked, patting Doug on the back and doing that rubbing thing he'd done in the kitchen.

Doug answered "Just fine, sir," and waited until Little walked away to move again. He decided he'd misinterpreted the whole thing; maybe people from the south just did things differently.

That same afternoon, Ed was going to mow the grass at his house but the key to the shed wasn't on its hook in the kitchen. He rummaged around the house but couldn't find it. He got in his car and drove to the golf course to see if his father had it.

Ed parked and walked around the side of the main building toward the maintenance shed. He heard voices inside. "Where's my Dad?" Ed asked at the door.

The group of workers standing inside looked at each other, then at Ed. "Um, he ain't here," one said. "He don't work here no more."

Ed took a few steps forward.

"If that's a joke, it ain't funny." He clenched is fists and walked up to the group. "Where is he?"

"Hey, we don't know!" said another man. "He got let go last week. It wasn't our fault or nothing!" Ed didn't say a word and left. He drove home and laid on the couch. Ed's mother told him dinner was ready; he grunted in response. She ate by herself.

It was almost dark when he heard his father's truck in the driveway. His boots crunched the gravel as he walked down the driveway to the front door. Ed's father flipped on the light in the kitchen, then started to go into the dark living room.

"Where were you?" Ed asked, hesitantly.

Ed's father stood in the doorway with a sheepish look on his face, like a kid caught red handed taking a cookie. He walked in and sat on the beat-up recliner next to Ed. He leaned forward, hung his head and let out a loud sigh. "I got laid off at the course. Like they don't have the money. Ha. I went to see a guy who said they needed people at Garden State Park; I've been picking up some work in the stables."

Ed waited a couple of seconds before speaking. "I guess I'll be going to Rumley High now, huh?"

"Why?" said his father. "That school is a piece of shit. Why would you want to go there?"

"It wouldn't cost anything for me to go there, that's why," answered

Ed, turning to look at his father while still hunched forward.

"Hell no!" said Ed's father, fairly loud and startling Ed. "Your mother wants you where you are. I want you there." Ed's Dad got up, went into the kitchen, and came back with a can of beer. He cracked it open and took a long pull. "You're going to college and Catholic school'll get you ready. Rumley'll get you ready to be in jail."

Ed shook his head back and forth. He'd miss his friends, but all that money going to high school when it didn't have to, seeing his parents sacrifice even more, how was he *not* supposed to feel guilty?

"We've already been through this crap!" Ed yelled, standing up. He threw his arms out to the side. "I can work in construction! They probably have good shop classes at Rumley! They don't have any at Blessed Sacrament!"

"Fine, do construction," Ed's father set his beer can down on an end table. "But it'd be better to learn how to run a construction business. That's what college is for, learning that stuff, getting smart. You could be a builder who knows his shit and runs the show." Then he pointed a thumb at himself. "Or you could be me, the asshole who does all the shit and gets paid shit."

Ed stood quietly. His father made sense. He sat back down on the couch.

"Fine," Ed said, "but you got to at least let me pull my weight. Every day I go to school I'll be thinking about the money we don't have." He got up and stood in front of his father's chair. "I'm going down to the track too and if they'll take me, I'll work after school, weekends. Don't even try saying no."

His father stood up and they shook hands. "Deal. Until I find something better."

Ed went with his father to the track the next day and was hired as general labor. The people who ran it were always interested in strong guys who took cash and didn't ask questions about insurance or vacations.

The day after his first night as a busboy, Doug paced back and forth in his kitchen at home. School was starting soon. Doug desperately tried to think of something else he could do because time was running out for him and Christine to be a couple on the first day of school. He'd chickened out when she was right there in his house, just the two of them; he was sure he'd chicken out again once school started.

A phone call. He could tell Christine he wanted her to be his girlfriend and take care of the kissing later. It'd be easier to say without her standing right in front of him anyway. He went to his room to get the piece of paper he'd written her phone number on, then started to dial her number on the hall phone; his finger slipped off the dial on the last number. He hung up and started again, slowly and carefully dialing each number.

"Hello?"

"Hi, Christine, it's Doug."

"Hi, Doug, what a surprise! What's going on?" She looked at the clock in her room.

"Not much. Are you in the middle of something? Because I could call back later."

"I probably only have a few minutes," she said. "I'll have to eat dinner in a little bit." She sat down on her bed.

Doug hesitated, trying to figure out how long 'a little bit' might be. He nervously tangled his finger into the phone cord.

"Ummm, okay. Christine, I called because, you know, the other day when we were working on the skit, there was something I wanted to say and didn't…"

Doug paused again, hoping Christine knew what he was talking about and would say it herself. She didn't say anything.

"We sure have been doing a lot of things together and it'll be even more this year, spending a lot of time together."

Christine was growing impatient with the repeated pauses from Doug. She looked up at the canopy over her bed, drumming her fingers on the comforter.

Doug moved the phone away from his mouth for a second and stared straight ahead. He took a deep breath, exhaled heavily and cleared his throat.

"I guess all I wanted to say, Christine," Doug blurted out rapidly, "Is that I was wondering if it'd be okay if I was your boyfriend?"

There was a long pause on Christine's end; Doug began sweating and was about to say "Hello?" when Christine responded.

"Oh, Doug!"

In the split-second after Christine said "Oh, Doug!" he frantically tried to figure it out. Was it an "Oh, Doug!" because she was happy? If it was, Doug felt stupid; she could've thrown her arms around him in person and made being boyfriend-girlfriend official.

It hadn't sounded like a disgusted "Oh, Doug!" She hadn't started laughing either. What did she mean, God damn it?!

Christine made it clear.

"Oh, Doug! That's soooooo sweet! I mean, I like you, you're so funny and talented! It's just, you're a really good *friend* and it would mess it up if we, I mean, I value you as a *friend*, a good *friend* and I hope we'll always be *friends*."

The words were coming out fast—Doug wasn't sure he'd caught all of them, but he understood the meaning. He just didn't want to.

Christine went on to say a few more things, but he didn't hear any of it—after all the dreaming and planning, it was over. There wasn't any room for 'maybe she meant.' Doug was a friend. Not a boyfriend.

"Oh, there's my Mom calling me! Gotta go! See ya!"

Doug heard the click on the other end. He stared at the receiver for a few seconds, gently hung it back on the hook and walked into his room.

As soon as he sat on the bed it felt like the tense knot in his stomach unraveled and dissolved and gushed out of his eyes as tears. He couldn't keep himself from crying but knew he needed to either get it over with soon or move—it was five o'clock, his father would be home soon. He couldn't let him hear.

He took some deep breaths but the tears wouldn't stop flowing. Was this heartbreak? If it was, he knew now why people wanted no part of it. He marched himself out to the woods because he felt like the crying wouldn't subside any time soon.

Doug sat on his stump. He didn't notice the sunlight occasionally glinting through gaps in the branches. He didn't notice the small animals skittering about. He didn't even notice his cigarette had burned down to the filter.

Christine had turned him down. Without the slightest hesitation.

Then, he stopped crying. He didn't feel the sadness he'd been feeling inside only a few seconds before. It was a strange feeling, different from the ones he always had in the past when something went wrong. He felt a little shaky, dizzy. He stood up and paced back and forth in front of the stump.

"She thinks she's such hot shit?" he said out loud, punching the air with his finger. "I'm the class president! I'm the star of the fucking school play! She'll change her mind!" A deer ran toward Doug through the woods, stopped fairly close and stared at Doug. He pointed toward it. "She'll want me, and I'll make her wait! You'll see!" The deer remained motionless for a couple more seconds before running back in the direction it had come from. Doug nodded his head in satisfaction.

Doug walked back to the house with a spring in his step, thinking up ways he could get back at Christine. He'd ignore her. He'd stop joking with her. *He'd* decide if he wanted to even be around her. A huge grin spread over his face.

If this was what confidence felt like, he wanted more of it, lots more.

Chapter 6

"This year is going to be the best one ever," Doug said, taking a deep drag on his cigarette.

On a September morning in Holly Hill in 1976, Doug Halecki and Ed Sherman were leaning against their cars outside Morelli's Grocery, a couple of blocks from Blessed Sacrament High School, in the part of the lot furthest from the store. The grocery was a small flat brick building. Chains of convenience stores were springing up throughout the state but Morelli's thrived; it was old-fashioned and carried items other stores didn't.

"My last good year was Kindergarten," replied Ed. "All you had to do was memorize the Pledge of Allegiance and not piss your pants. Everything else was playing."

Doug burst out laughing. "Eddie, my boy, you are getting funnier every day. Glad to see some of the master is finally rubbing off on you."

"You'd know all about rubbing one off," Ed retorted. He glanced at his watch. "I swear I never thought I'd hear myself say this, but we better get going pretty damn soon." Doug raised an eyebrow at Ed. Ed shrugged. "I can't start this year off with a late slip after all the detentions I had last year."

Doug blew out a huge cloud of smoke. "Not me! Don't you see? When we walk in there, senior year starts. Then it's just nine months from being over. The before part is way better; it's like waiting for your birthday and Christmas morning put together! All the good stuff is coming!"

"What kind of horseshit is that?" answered Ed. "You don't want high school to be over with?" Ed shook his head and looked toward the store. "I always knew there was something fucked up about you, Halecki."

Andy Swanson came out of the store, walking fast and looking over his shoulder.

"What the hell have you been doing?" asked Ed. "It doesn't take that long to buy a pack of smokes!"

Andy leaned against his 1968 Camaro and held up the pack of Marlboros. "I took the five-finger discount on 'em," he said. "It took that long for that *ass*-sistant manager in there to look the other way. So stop dippin' in my Kool-Aid!"

Doug looked down and shook his head.

Andy had gotten a summer job at a flower farm because he had his eye on something he thought would make him cool—a used Firebird the farm owner's son was selling. People would be impressed with a Firebird. Except it was still socially inept Andy driving.

"Great. Excellent," said Ed. "I'm worrying about getting a late slip and you're in their ripping off boags!"

Andy lit a cigarette. "Sit on it, Eddie boy!" Doug rolled his eyes again. "We're with Halecki. Halecki never gets in trouble, not since he got made all those things last year." He flicked the match in Doug's direction. "He's important now—a double BS, a Blessed Sacrament Big Shot. That makes us, your bodyguards, important too, right Halecki?" Andy struck a pose like the Fonz and held his thumbs up.

"Andy, is there anything on TV you haven't memorized?" said Doug.

"Maybe someday I'll understand how any of this shit happened with you, Halecki," Ed said. They started to get ready to leave when Ed saw the assistant store manager, Daniel Parrillo, walking toward them. Ed and Doug knew him from grade school; he'd been a year ahead of them and thought he was a big shot.

"If you jagoffs ain't buying anything, get the hell off the property," he barked, with his hands on his hips. Andy let out a muffled laugh. "Something's funny?" asked Parrillo. "Up your nose with a rubber hose!" replied Andy. He grinned, pleased with his 'comeback.'

Parrillo wasn't laughing. "You think I don't know you've been ripping me off?"

"Prove it," said Ed.

Parrillo stared at Ed, who stared back. They didn't move for about ten seconds. Doug got into his car and started it.

"I'll be watchin' you," said Parrillo, continuing to stare at Ed.

"Why me?" Ed asked, testily.

"Because you're a dirty hillbilly," he answered. "That's why. Get lost, all of you faggots!"

"Fuck you," Ed said and climbed in his car. He squealed his tires as he pulled out of the lot.

Christine and Palomma had already arrived at school.

"You tracked a little dirt in over there—shake out the mat," said Christine as she switched off the ignition.

Palomma stiffened. "Oh, sure." She picked up the mat and tipped the dirt out the door. She glanced over at Christine.

Her uniform dress was short last year; now, as Christine got out of the car, it had hiked up to the point where it was almost a shirt. And she didn't seem to be in too big a hurry to shimmy it down. Christine stood next to her car, getting herself just so. She smoothed her dress and squatted down to check her hair in the side mirror. Scooping up her books, she started toward the gym entrance to the school.

"She treats me like crap," thought Palomma as she got out of Christine's car. Then she nervously looked at Christine as if she might have somehow heard her thoughts. Palomma jumped as three cars raced by; Ed, Doug and Andy parked on the far side of the lot, got out of their cars and ran toward the gym doors. Palomma watched them laughing and pushing each other as they dashed away.

The gym was buzzing with activity. Students stood in groups or sat on the bleachers. Others passed through quickly on their way to home-room, trying to avoid getting run into by the boys playing tennis ball soccer. Doug was standing to the side as the ball got kicked back and forth.

"Hey Pecky! Get your ass in the game!" Andy yelled.

"Hold your pants on!" Doug answered.

Doug was waiting for Christine to leave the gym. A couple of min-utes before the first bell, Christine got up from the bleachers and walked past. 'Walked' wasn't the right word; more like 'sashayed'—purse over her shoulder, hair and butt flipping back and forth.

"Hey Halecki! There goes your girlfriend!" Andy shouted.

Everyone knew about Doug's infatuation with Christine. What they didn't know was how she'd turned him down a week before. Or what he planned to do about it.

Doug waited until Christine was a few steps away from him before running back onto the court toward Ed.

"Did she look?" asked Doug.

"Say what?" answered Ed.

"Christine!" said Doug.

"At what?" replied Ed.

Andy ran up chasing the tennis ball. He took a big swipe at it, missed and kicked Ed in the ankle.

"OWWW!" yelled Ed. He picked up the ball and held it in front of

Andy. "Tennis ball," he said. "Ankle," he said, pointing to his leg. "Moron!" he yelled, playfully slapping Andy in the head. He turned back to Doug.

"What about Christine?" he asked.

"Never mind," answered Doug.

"Don't let her see that hard-on, Halecki!" shouted Andy. Doug watched her leave the gym.

Palomma walked quickly into the gym past the boys. They didn't pay her any attention; she'd gotten used to the fact they didn't but wished they would. But if they had, she wouldn't have known what to do anyway. Truth was, the only thing she was certain about was being confused.

She'd tried shorter skirts and makeup but they hadn't made a difference as far as getting noticed; she wanted things to start happening with boys, but had run out of ideas. Palomma glanced at the clock, saw the bell was about to ring, and hurried toward homeroom.

She walked into room eight and looked for a desk, set her purse down and took out a hairbrush. Just like junior year, she'd ended up in a homeroom with Paula and without Christine.

Palomma envied Paula, who was everything she wasn't—the good wasn't's. She was outgoing and self-confident. She had a natural ability to look sexy but not slutty. She was funny and talked to boys without a hint of nervousness. And she wasn't friends with Christine.

"Hey, senior girl, welcome back!" said Paula, sitting next to Palomma.

"Hi, Paula," she answered.

"Check this out!" Paula held up a five-subject notebook. "And these," she added, holding a case full of pens and pencils. "And last but not least, these!" She held her foot out in front of her to show off her new platform shoes.

"Wow, it looks like you're ready for everything this year," said Palomma.

"I was born ready. Eveready. They named that battery after me!" said Paula. She looked at Palomma's face and smiled. "I see you've been copying me!"

Palomma was confused. "I don't have..." she began to say.

"Your eyes!" Paula pointed to her own eye. Palomma had used blue eyeshadow with mascara on her top and bottom lashes. "Almost a perfect match!"

"I thought maybe it was time to try new things." Palomma relaxed. Paula's personality always put Palomma at ease.

"It looks way better on your eyes. I wish I had eyes like yours!" said Paula.

"I wish I had a lot of what you have," said Palomma. "Starting with..."

"A fat ass?"

Palomma laughed. "Confidence, actually."

Things got hectic for Doug the moment school started. Welcome Week activities kicked in. Articles for the Daily Record began right away. Play rehearsals would start soon.

Doug was psyched for the Welcome Day show that Friday. There were a couple of rehearsals during the week; it looked like everyone was enjoying the skits he'd written. When the day of the show came, Doug sat on stage at the anchor desk with Karen and Lauren; it was clear the show was a hit. Even the teachers were laughing.

Christine did her routine and was...alright. She'd flubbed a few of the lines and Doug had to try to whisper them across the stage. She almost forgot to connect the 'x's' on the board. Doug realized he should have given it to someone who would have tried harder, since his kissing plan had failed anyway.

Doug had asked Palomma, like most of the seniors, if she wanted to be in a skit but she'd declined. She'd opted instead for stage crew, opening the curtain. At the final bows, the gym rocked with applause; after Palomma pulled the curtain closed, Doug turned to Karen and said, "We knocked 'em dead!" Karen ignored him and walked away with Lauren.

Doug started to walk backstage; Palomma was surprised when he stopped as he passed her. "Whaddya think? Was that cool or what!?" It took a second for Palomma to respond. "That was cool. Those skits were really funny!"

"Well, thanks…" Doug had started to reply, but noticed he'd lost her attention. Palomma had looked away at Christine watching them from across the stage. She walked up and touched Doug's arm.

"Wasn't that great?" she said, looking at Doug and turning her back toward Palomma. "Stella Storm! They loved it!"

There was an awkward silence; Doug looked at Christine, at Palomma, then back at Christine. He rubbed the back of his head.

"You did a good job," he said. Palomma was surprised at how flat the words came out.

"The best part was when…" Christine began to act out her role.

"Listen, I gotta go," said Doug. He turned quickly and walked away.

Christine stared after him with a surprised look. Palomma fought to keep a straight face but had to cover her mouth to stifle a giggle. Christine turned to Palomma, who quickly squatted down to pick up scene directions she'd laid on the floor. Christine looked like she was about to say something, then turned and left the stage. Palomma waited until she was out of earshot to let out the giggle.

Welcome Week had barely passed when Doug's next attention-getting opportunity started—the school play.

He'd never been in a play before. But he, no one else, would be the guy starring opposite Dolly, played by Kim Casey, a junior. Palomma had been right; he was the only boy from the senior class to audition.

"Hey, Horace!" Kim said, walking over to Doug as everyone in the cast gathered in the gym. "I guess there's nothing more for me to do than to go back to New York and tell the other girl, the heiress…"

Doug could feel his face burning; he didn't have a clue what Horace's response was. "Oooo, I guess someone hasn't learned all his lines yet! What are you waiting for Horace, opening night?" Kim sat down next to Doug.

Two people walked out on stage and the gym quieted. "Hello, per-formers, my name is Hannah Stern, and this is Peter Augustine. As you know, I'll be directing the show and choreographing it; Mr. Augustine will be our musical director."

"There will be rehearsals every weeknight at seven; missing re-hearsals for any reason is a no-no," Stern continued. "There better have been a death in the family, the family member being you." Everyone in the gym laughed. "Rehearsals will also be on Saturday nights starting in October."

"All we're gonna do is run through songs today," said Augustine as he sat down at a piano.

Kim had the first song, and she was a natural. She didn't try to imitate Streisand and gestured and acted while singing. She finished to loud cheers.

The second song was Doug's.

"Next, there's some business in the feed store; then it's time for Ho-race," said Augustine. "Ready?"

Doug knew this wasn't the time for a joke. "Ready."

Doug stood up. The piano sounded a few notes, and Doug started singing. He walked around and directed the lines in the song to different students. When he finished "It Takes a Woman," everyone began clapping and whooping. Even Stern applauded.

Doug relaxed. This was going to be great.

Palomma and Christine sat with the chorus. They joined in with the chorus songs, though neither sang particularly loud. Palomma smirked; this was something Christine was going to have to do without help.

It was funny, though, when Doug sang. Palomma watched him, like she watched all the other people—but she noticed Christine had been looking down at her script or at the piano—everywhere but at Doug.

At the end of the run-through came the reprise of "Hello, Dolly!" The script called for Kim and Doug to dance; Doug got up and, without thinking, took Kim in his arms – adrenaline will do that—and she leaned backward and performed a dip. Stern laughed. "We'll work out the dance later. Right now, just sing." They performed the song as well as if they'd already rehearsed it, followed by more whoops and yells. "We've made a really good start," said Stern. "Rehearsal tomorrow night."

The next day, Karen and Lauren were sitting in homeroom. They had chosen desks near the window. No one had chosen either of the desks at their sides.

"I still can't get used to it. Class president Halecki," said Karen.

"I heard the voting was fixed, and it was all Palomma Rossi's idea!"

"Who told you that?" said Karen.

"You didn't hear her that day in room six?" asked Lauren.

"Why would I be listening to anything she had to say?"

Lauren rolled her eyes. "I wasn't listening either until I heard her mention class president. She told Halecki everyone hated you and she'd get a bunch of people to vote for him if he ran."

"The little bitch!" snarled Karen. "A little teasing and she resorts to that! You can't trust those quiet ones! Don't worry, I'll get her back, for sure. It's just a matter of picking the right time."

"Like lunchtime!" said Lauren. They both laughed.

"You know, cheer captain counts more anyway. They give scholarships for that, not stupid class president. What's he, on the"—she adopted a sneering tone—"golf team?" Karen rolled her eyes. "That's like being on the safety patrol!"

They laughed again.

As the day began, Palomma sat in room six with Christine. Doug walked in and sat down to work on the newspaper article.

Christine had suggested the previous year she do the research for the article; now there was a problem, and Palomma had seen it coming. Christine didn't even want to do that. She wanted her name in the byline each week; she just didn't want to be bothered with actual work.

"What's going on next week?" Doug asked.

Christine looked down at the table and smiled. Then she looked up at Doug with the biggest eyes she could make.

"Doug, I'm *really* busy this week," she said. "There's *sooo* much going on. Do you think, maybe, you could do the article by yourself for a while? Until things, you know, calm down a little?" Christine did that 'thing' where she tilted her head and raised her eyebrows. Palomma had seen her do it before and seen Doug fall for it. This time was weird; Doug continued to look at her without changing his expression.

"C'mon, Christine, we'll do it like we agreed, okay?" Doug opened a notebook and wrote the date of the article at the top of the page.

"C'mon Doug, for a few weeks? For me?" She leaned forward. She almost sounded like a little girl.

"Why don't we…" Doug started to say.

Mrs. DiBiase spoke up from her desk. "Why don't we reduce the volume?"

Christine smiled at Doug again. "Don't be such a grouch," she whispered. "I just want to skip a couple of weeks."

"Then I guess your name won't be on it for a couple of weeks," Doug whispered. He didn't change his expression.

"You're lucky they didn't give it to me alone!" she said, a tiny bit louder.

"But then you'd have to do all the work alone." Doug crossed his arms.

Palomma was trying to act as if she was studying but was loving how Doug was cutting down Christine.

Christine's eyes were fiery. "You think you're so good, I'm as good at writing as you are!" she hissed.

Doug folded his hands in front of him. "But you don't want to actually write the article. Your logic just crashed and burned." He remained expressionless.

Christine breathed in and out heavily staring at Doug. Then she took a few mimeographed sheets of paper with a photo clipped to them from between her books and dropped them on the table.

"I hope you're satisfied! I got all this by myself!"

Doug shot a quick glance at what she'd dropped on the table. "Sister Teresa handed that to you, right?"

"Wha…" Christine yelped very loud, clapping her hand across her mouth. She leaned as far forward as she could and whispered in a snippy voice. "You're mad because you didn't get what you wanted. Right, *friend*?"

Palomma couldn't figure out why she stressed the last word so much.

"All I want right now," whispered Doug with an over emphasized innocence, "is an article partner who isn't so fucking lazy."

Doug smiled at her. A tiny sound escaped from Christine, like a little squeak. Everyone in room six was watching now. She picked up her books and stormed out of the room.

Palomma watched her go, then looked at Doug.

"I think she's mad at you," Palomma whispered, almost inaudibly.

"Whoop-de-doo," replied Doug, continuing to look at the photo.

"No, I mean I think she's *really* mad at you."

Doug looked at Palomma, shrugged and went back to writing the article.

Chapter 7

After school that day, Palomma sat in the tiny booth at PhotoQuik. At times like these, when it was like an oven, she second-guessed herself about wanting a part-time job.

At seventeen, she felt she should go to the mall and buy clothes herself instead of bringing her mother along to pay, and maybe say 'no.' Or tagging along with Christine. Christine didn't have a job but always had money, and took every opportunity to flaunt it when they'd gone shopping together.

Palomma had approached her father—nervously – after dinner one night as he read the newspaper in the living room.

"Daddy?" she said, softly. Mr. Rossi set down the newspaper.

"I'd like to, um, I was wondering if you'd, uh, if I could get a part-time job?"

"Yes, you may," he replied.

"Only because I think it would be a good thing for me to learn more responsibility and to not always be asking Mommy for money and college would see it on my application and..." She stopped with an astonished look on her face.

"I said yes, Palomma. Just remember to get your work papers at City Hall first."

Palomma was flabbergasted he'd agreed so easily. "Thank you, Daddy!" she said, smothering him with a hug. She ran back to her room beaming.

The first ad Palomma answered was PhotoQuik, and they called within days. As she stood in the kitchen chatting with the manager on the phone, she felt grown-up. She must have looked impressive on the application. It was a good sign for how her college application would be received too.

Palomma arrived for training at the small booth on the corner of Oak and First a few nights later. She wasn't allowed to leave the tiny booth, which didn't even have a fan. She couldn't make calls on the phone; it didn't have a dial and she could only answer it. The door was to be locked at all times. She wasn't even supposed to open the sliding window unless a customer drove up.

She realized a lot of new-hires probably didn't return for a second shift.

Palomma was sorting the developed film envelopes when a car she recognized pulled up. It was Doug. She slid open the window.

"Good afternoon, welcome to PhotoQuik! What can I help you with today, sir?" Palomma said cheerily.

"Yes, hello, I was wondering if you have anything for me in there?"

"Of course, sir," Palomma replied. "Let me check. What is your last name, please?"

"It's Halecki. H-A-L..."

"Thank you, sir. Hmmmmm, there doesn't seem to be anything under that name; when did you drop your film off, Mr. Halecki?"

"Oh, is that how it works?""

"Very funny, Doug." Palomma propped her chin in her hands, resting her elbows on the counter. "What brings you here?"

"Nothing, really," answered Doug. "I was on my way to work and remembered hearing Christine say you worked here. I figured I'd stop to see if you were working. Which you are. And I saw you. Now get back to work. Bye!"

Doug waved and drove off. Palomma watched him leave shaking her head. Always making jokes. She kind of wished she'd thought of something to say to make him stay a while, though. It would have been practice talking to a boy, even if it was Doug. She went back to sorting, but she was confused about how she felt about Doug.

He was a nice guy, no question. And when he'd started to come out of his shell junior year, she saw a side of him she hadn't before. For starters, he was really funny. Smart funny, not silly funny. When Danny Donovan let out an echoing fart in religion class, everyone laughed, even the priest. But anyone could fart. Doug thought up things no one else did. And Palomma liked to laugh.

Doug used to wear glasses; now he had contact lenses. He'd bragged about paying for them himself, something about his job and steam. Without glasses, Palomma noticed he had piercing blue eyes. He also was taking better care of himself; his skin was clearer, and he was even styling his hair.

Doug had always been nice enough to Palomma, but he'd had his 'boy' attention focused on Christine. Now that senior year had started, things had changed; Doug wasn't following Christine constantly. Palomma realized she missed him being around but didn't understand the feeling. She didn't look at him and feel…what? She didn't even know what you felt when you felt something.

He was a boy friend of hers, certainly. A friend who was a boy, that is. But a possible 'boyfriend?' You were supposed to feel different for that. Palomma shrugged and went back to sorting.

The next day, Doug was sitting in his car in the parking lot after school, debating what to do.

There were still a few hours before the start of play rehearsal. He could drive home, but gas was getting expensive. There had been an oil embargo; gas went from 45 cents to 75 cents a gallon. And there would probably be a chore waiting for him.

Doug noticed Palomma walking toward the church across the street. She had a pile of books in her arms that were causing her to lean forward from the weight. The pick-up spot for cars after school was defined by a yellow curb running the length of the side of the church. Palomma reached the curb and stopped, staring up the block away from Doug. Doug got out of his car and hollered, "Hey! Palomma! Need a ride?"

"Oh! Doug! I didn't see you there!" she yelled back. She started to walk toward his car.

"I could give you a ride home if you want," Doug said as she got closer.

"Oh, no, thanks, Doug," replied Palomma. "My Mom is on her way to get me."

"Shame, you could've heard me sing."

"Is that what you call it?" Palomma shot back.

"Oh, a wise girl!" Doug imitated Curly of the Three Stooges. Doug was always saying things from the Three Stooges. Palomma rolled her eyes; she thought the Three Stooges were stupid.

They stood for a couple of seconds in silence. Palomma shifted from one foot to the other. "Here, gimme those," said Doug, taking Palomma's books and setting them on his hood.

"Have you sent out those college applications?" Doug asked, turning back to Palomma.

"Sure, I sent them out. Did you?"

"Yeah, I did. I sent to Rutgers, Rider and Notre Dame."

"Notre Dame? That's far away, isn't it?" said Palomma. She rested a hand on Doug's fender.

"Indiana," said Doug. "I probably couldn't go there unless I got a full ride." He took out a cigarette. "I really want to go to Rutgers. Where do you want to go?"

"Bryn Mawr in Philadelphia," Palomma replied. "Christine and I will probably go there."

"Oh, yeah, Bryn Mawr; that's an all-girls college, isn't it?" Doug took a drag on his cigarette and gestured toward Palomma. "Incidentally, how come you don't ride home with Christine?"

"It gets to be a problem," Palomma responded, in a long run-on sentence. "She doesn't want to wait sometimes for me to get out and sometimes she has to do something after school"—Palomma was moving her hands around trying to illustrate the confusion—"and sometimes I have to do something after school and it hardly ever works out because she doesn't like to wait, like I said, so my Mom picks me up when there's something I need to stay for or she stays for."

"Oh," said Doug.

They stood looking at each other, saying nothing. Palomma wasn't sure if she should say what she was thinking. "Speaking of Christine, maybe you could tell me," she began, "what happened...I mean what's going on...you know, since school started..."

Palomma froze with her hand in mid-gesture; she'd talked herself into a corner and wished she'd never started. Doug leaned forward ever so slightly, waiting for her to continue when she saw her mother's car coming up Main Street. "Look, there's my Mom!" Palomma blurted out, reaching for her books. "I better get back to where I usually stand or she'll think something's wrong. You know mothers!" Palomma said the last few words over her shoulder as she ran back to the church.

Doug watched her, shrugged, and got back in his car.

Palomma arrived at the curb as her mother stopped. She set her books on the front seat next to her mother and climbed in.

"Who were you talking to?" her mother asked as they pulled away.

"That's Doug. Doug Halecki. He's the class president—he's in the play, too. He was asking me about college."

Paula sat down next to Palomma in homeroom at the end of school the next day. "So what are you wearing to the Harvest Dance?"

Palomma had seen the notices for the dance in the hallway. "I, um, I'm not going."

Paula busied herself with straightening her notebooks. "I was trying to decide between going in jeans or maybe…what?" Paula stopped in mid-sentence. "Not going? Not likely!"

"Christine said she's not going and no one asked me," said Palomma, softly. "Besides, I can't dance."

"You don't go to many dances, do you?" Paula laughed.

"Nope," said Palomma, softly. She looked toward the window.

"Hey, I didn't mean anything," replied Paula, resting her hand on Palomma's arm. "Sometimes I get diarrhea of the mouth and constipation of the brain, you know?" Palomma turned back to face her. "Listen, *no one* knows how to dance at dances! Well, maybe Tommy Terranova; everyone else kind of flops around." She mimed people tossing their arms around awkwardly; Palomma smiled. "And no one *asks* anyone to dances, that's so our parents. They're either already a couple or they show up with friends. Like you're going to show up with me."

"I don't know…" Palomma looked down at her lap, then up at Paula. "What if I say no?"

"I'll only pester you every waking moment, and I can pester with the best. I'm like a sand chigger." She dug the knuckle of her index finger into Palomma's arm. "I'll get under your skin so bad you'll beg me to go to the dance!"

"All right, I get the message," laughed Palomma. "Now about what to wear..."

"I was just busting," said Paula. "It's jeans. It's not the prom!" She crossed her arms. "How about a trip downtown to look at clothes?"

Palomma remembered. "Sounds like fun!" she answered.

Palomma had only been to father-daughter dances at her church. On Saturday night, she got a ride with Paula and stuck by her like a shadow after they entered. Paula walked around greeting a number of girls and they all ended up in a group by the bleachers.

Palomma was content to take it all in. The loud music, the people milling around. She chuckled when she realized Paula had been right— no one on the gym floor was very good at dancing. Palomma watched, tapping her foot to the music.

An hour passed quickly. A couple of the girls had found boys to dance with; Paula kept busy telling Palomma and the other girls the latest gossip.

The chatter in the group suddenly stopped and all the girls turned in the same direction; a boy was walking toward them. Palomma went back to watching the dancers but was startled when he walked up to her and said, "And who is this foxy lady I haven't met?"

Palomma let out an audible gasp. She glanced at Paula, who opened her eyes wide and bobbed her head forward.

Palomma had a look of panic on her face. Paula rolled her eyes and bobbed her head again.

"I'm Palomma," she said in a voice barely audible over the music. "Who...what's your name?"

"Daniel. Daniel Parrillo."

Palomma didn't know what to say next. "You're Italian!" she blurted out.

"Yep, all my life," he replied. "*Sei quasi più figa di me!*"

Palomma smiled; she knew some Italian but didn't understand that he'd said, "You're almost as hot as I am!"

"I'll agree with that!" she responded and laughed nervously.

Palomma suddenly became aware the girls were subtly inching away. She'd seen this happen at school for other girls when a boy approached—now, it was for her! She remembered the time Doug had stopped by PhotoQuik and tried to think of something to keep the conversation going this time.

"I don't remember seeing you at Blessed Sacrament; do you go to Holly Hill High?" she asked.

"Did," Daniel answered. "Class of '76. I graduated last year."

"Are you in college?" Palomma didn't know what to do with her hands so she held them behind her back.

"Nope," he said. "I've already got a job—I'm assistant manager at Morelli's Grocery."

Palomma felt shaky. The boys at school were all the same—boys. All they ever did was act silly. Daniel was different. He was tall and handsome. He was confident, walking up to a group of girls like that. He wasn't like a boy at all; he was more like a man.

Palomma kept feeling a word trying to come into her head.

"That's a beautiful name, Palomma," said Daniel. "Almost as beautiful as you!"

Palomma felt her knees getting weak. Suave. He was suave.

A slow dance came on. "May I have this dance?" Daniel asked. Palomma began to say, "I don't…" when she saw Paula moving a little closer and start coughing. Palomma glanced at her and began to say, "I'm not very good…" when Paula coughed again much louder.

Palomma blushed and said, "Yes."

Daniel led Palomma onto the dance floor. While they danced his hands were proper, like a gentleman. Palomma alternately kept looking up at his chest and down at her feet to make sure she didn't step on his.

After the song was over, they sat on the bleachers and talked most of the night; Daniel told her about his job, his new truck and asked her about her family. He didn't try to hold her hand or put his arm around her, politely sitting with his hands in his lap, though Palomma was dying for him to do it so the other girls would see.

The DJ announced the 'last dance' and Daniel escorted Palomma onto the floor again. This time, he put his arm around her gently; she tried to put her arm around his shoulders but could barely reach high enough. They switched to having their hands on each other's waists.

When the dance was over, they walked out of the gym to the parking lot; Daniel led her to a spot away from other kids and asked if he could give her a ride home, but Palomma knew what would happen if she got out of a car her parents hadn't seen before with a boy driving.

"No, that's alright, I'm riding home with a friend," she told him.

"May I call you?"

Palomma glanced nervously to the side. This was difficult too. She didn't have her own phone like Christine; giving a boy her phone number meant Palomma couldn't be sure she'd be the one to answer.

"Um…" She couldn't bring herself to make eye contact with him.

"Palomma, I had a really nice time with you tonight. I'd like to see you again soon. Can I call you?" Daniel repeated.

Palomma thought of her talk with Gemma.

"Um, sure," she said, and told him her number. She was impressed he didn't get anything to write it down.

"Great!" Daniel smiled. "Palomma, thanks for a wonderful evening! I know we'll be talking soon." He took her hand and kissed it.

Wow. It was the only word in Palomma's head.

"What's his name?" asked Paula as soon as Palomma got in the car.

"Daniel. Daniel Parrillo," answered Palomma.

"Where's he live?"

"I don't know," replied Palomma. "We didn't really talk about that."

"Ohhhhh, more important things, huh?" Paula reached across and playfully pushed Palomma's shoulder. Palomma stared dreamily out the window. She felt like the heroines in her books. *This was how it was supposed to feel.*

Gemma came into her room after she'd come home. "Is he cute?"

"Wha... wait, how did you know?" Palomma stammered, sitting up straight on her bed.

"Know? You walked into the house without touching the ground. What's there to know? So, is he cute?" Gemma sat down next to her.

"He's very handsome. Nice. Handsome and nice. His name is Daniel."

"Who introduced you?" asked Gemma.

"He...wow!" Palomma shook her head as if to clear it out. "He introduced himself. To me."

"Were you by yourself?" persisted Gemma.

Palomma leaned back on the bed. "There was a whole group of girls. He picked me," she said. A dreamy look came over her face.

"Did he try to kiss you? Did you let him?"

"No, he was a perfect gentleman," Palomma replied. She found herself dwelling a little longer on the word 'perfect.'

The sisters agreed to try to answer the phone before their parents. They even tried to coordinate it so one was downstairs when the other was upstairs, but when? Palomma had no idea when Daniel would call.

That he would call she was a certainty; phone numbers were a big deal. Even if your number was in the phone book, it was considered almost criminal for a boy to call a girl unless she'd given him permission.

Palomma had the downstairs turn when the phone rang on Saturday afternoon—with her mother standing next to it. Palomma dashed toward the kitchen. "I got it! I got it!" she yelled. She ducked in front of her mother and snatched the phone off the hook. Covering the mouthpiece, she turned to her mother. "Christine said she might call about going to the mall!"

"Oh, all right," said her mother. "I never saw you so excited about going to the mall before."

Palomma smiled sweetly and walked around the corner. "Hello?" she said, expectantly.

"Hello, I'm calling from the electric company to see if you'll participate in a short survey," said the voice on the other end.

Palomma's shoulders slumped. "Thanks, Christine. Maybe next weekend!" she said loud enough for her mother to hear. She walked back into the kitchen and hung up.

Gemma came downstairs. "Whatsa matter, you didn't want to do the survey?" she asked, giggling.

"Gemma!" whispered Palomma sharply. "You have to swear you won't listen in!" They both broke out giggling.

The weekend was almost over; Palomma was thumbing through National Geographic in the living room when the phone rang on Sunday night. Gemma got to it first upstairs.

"Palomma!" she called out. "Phone!"

When Palomma came upstairs to get it, Gemma had a huge grin on her face.

"Hello?"

"Hi, Palomma, it's Daniel. Are you doing anything?"

"Oh, not much, just reading." She didn't want him to think she'd been waiting for him to call. Even though she had. Palomma slipped into her room and closed the door.

"I was wondering if you'd enjoy going out to get something to eat with me next Friday. I know I'd enjoy taking you. Maybe some Italian?"

Palomma realized she didn't know what to say when a boy actually asked her out.

"Ummm, uh…listen, Daniel, could it be Saturday? Friday's a school day and I'll have play practice at night."

There was a pause on the other end. Palomma held her breath.

"Saturday would be good. You know what? That's even better!" replied Daniel. "See you at six on Saturday!"

Palomma only exhaled after he hung up.

Chapter 8

The following Monday, Director Stern was late for rehearsal; the cast members and crew were scattered around waiting for her arrival. Doug walked into the gym and saw Palomma and Christine sitting on the edge of the stage. He swaggered up to them.

"Hey, chorus girls, do you want the star's autograph?"

Christine pointed toward Doug and opened her mouth to say something when Palomma retorted, "Oh! You've learned how to write your name! I'm so proud of you, Douggie!" Christine stayed quiet.

Doug said, "You bet!" and hoisted himself up onto the stage—next to Palomma.

He took her mimeographed script and wrote 'Doug Halecki as Horace Vandergelder' across the top. Palomma took the script back and added "+ Christine" next to his name.

"Jesus, I don't share autograph space with anyone!" Doug grabbed Palomma's pen and crossed out what she'd written. He hoped Christine saw him do it.

"If it was my name, it'd have a page all to itself!" said Palomma, giving him a playful bump with her shoulder and taking back her script.

"I'm a victim of soy-cumstance!" said Doug, and he reached as if he was going to shove Palomma back, snapped his hand to his head and ran it through his hair. "Psyche!"

Christine slid off the stage and stood in front of them.

"Now now, Doug, we all can't be the big star, this is true," she said, "but remember, the show is called Hello Dolly, not Hello Horace!" She waited for Doug to say something in response; he didn't.

"Oh, look!" Doug shouted, standing up on the stage. "Mrs. Stern is here! What time is it, Mrs. Stern? Funny, you don't look dead!" Doug crossed his arms and tapped his foot.

"That's quite enough, Horace," she said as everyone laughed.

Doug looked down at Palomma and Christine, making an exaggerated bow. "Alas, ladies," he said, "I must go be a star. *Au revoir*!"

"*Bocca al lupo*!" said Palomma, and she giggled. Christine's looked at her with a frown. Palomma swung her legs around, stood up and walked backstage.

Christine sat alone for a few seconds before going backstage.

"Mrs. Stern sure knows what she's doing!" said Palomma as she and Christine drove home after rehearsal. "I'd love to see what those dances look like from in front!"

"Uh-huh," Christine mumbled.

Palomma waited to see if Christine was going to say anything. She didn't. "Can I turn on the radio?" asked Palomma.

"Uh-huh," Christine mumbled again.

Palomma hummed along with the music. Ahead, she saw the light had turned red at the intersection they were approaching, but Christine hadn't begun to slow down at all.

"Um, Christine, the light's red," said Palomma.

Christine didn't say anything.

They were coming up on the intersection rapidly; cars were going through on the crossing street. Palomma looked over at Christine. They were within a hundred feet of the light.

"Christine!" Palomma yelled. "The light's red!"

Christine looked up and slammed on the brakes. The Mustang's rear wheels locked up, skidding to a stop just before the intersection. Palomma was thrown forward, almost hitting the dashboard.

"Wow! Sorry!" said Christine. The light turned green and she drove through the intersection. "I guess I was a million miles away!"

Palomma didn't say a word the rest of the way, muttering a terse "Bye, Christine" as she got out of the car at her house.

Doug walked toward the rear of the gym after rehearsal, proud of how he'd given Christine the cold shoulder earlier. He was about to leave when he saw Valerie Pisani, a junior, standing by herself in the gym foyer.

Doug had noticed Valerie when the rehearsals had started. She was in the chorus and was kind of cute. Maybe it was her slightly gravelly voice; when Doug heard it, he thought it was kind of sexy.

Valerie was peering out into the parking lot. "Hey, Valerie!" said Doug, and she jumped. "Waitin' for your Mom?"

"Oh, hi, Doug, I didn't know anyone was still here!" she said. She sounded nervous. "Actually, Christine Holloway said she'd give me a ride home, but I don't see her anywhere. I think she forgot."

"I could give you a ride home."

"Would you?!" replied Valerie, her eyes brightening. Then she cleared her throat. "You would? Gee, thanks!"

Valerie got into Doug's car and told him she lived near Fox Hollow Golf Course. He was about to ask her to pick a tape when she started talking. And talking. She talked almost nonstop from the moment he started driving, but Doug didn't mind—for a change, she was the nervous one, not him.

Valerie pointed out one house after another, naming kids from school who lived in them. "And that's where Palomma Rossi lives!" she said as they passed another one.

Doug dropped her off at her house. "If you ever need a ride again, don't be afraid to ask!" he said. "I will! I mean, I won't!" answered Valerie. She got out and ran to her door.

On his way home, Doug slowed down a little as he drove past the house Valerie had said was Palomma's. "Nice house," he thought.

A couple of mornings later, Christine was driving to school. She and Palomma usually didn't talk much in the morning. The radio played as they rode along in silence.

They came to the same intersection as a couple of nights before, this time in the opposite direction. Palomma waited until the light changed and they'd started moving again before suddenly blurting out, "I have a boyfriend!"

Christine snapped her head toward Palomma and the car swerved toward the curb. She had to jerk the steering wheel to get it back to pointed straight.

"What?" said Christine, in astonishment.

"I said, I have a boyfriend," answered Palomma, smugly. "His name's Daniel."

"Does *he* know it?" asked Christine. She slowed to almost a stop; the car behind her blew its horn.

Palomma chuckled. "Good one, Christine. Yes, he knows it. *He* called *me.*"

Christine was at a loss for words. Of all the news she might have imagined hearing this morning, *that* wasn't it.

"When…where…how did you meet him?" she stuttered.

"At the dance."

"You didn't tell me you were going to the dance!" said Christine.

"You said you weren't going, so Paula took me."

Christine's turned onto Main Street and turned off the radio. Her head was spinning. Palomma claimed she had a boyfriend. Maybe she was lying? Christine shook her head almost imperceptibly and erased that thought immediately. Palomma didn't lie. Palomma didn't know *how* to lie.

They pulled into the parking lot. Palomma jumped out practically as soon as the car had stopped.

"Gotta run!" Palomma chirped as she closed the door and ran toward the school.

Christine sat in the car for a while after she'd left, staring straight ahead.

Room five, the religion resource room was usually empty; students took as few religion laps as they could get away with. Doug saw Valerie walk into the room at the mod change; he waited a few seconds, then went in too. It was time to get back to working on kissing a girl. Valerie had seemed interested the other night; junior girls might be the way to go.

Doug sat down six desks away from her, trying to think of something to say when Andy walked in and sat next to Doug.

"Didja ever get any from Christine?" he said.

"Um, not *now*," Doug whispered.

"Ding! That's a no!" said Andy, loud enough to make Valerie look in their direction.

"Why, did you?" Doug whispered.

"I laid off because you were into her," Andy said, far too loud. "Laid? Into her? Get it? Otherwise, I'd bogart that today!"

"Well, Romeo," Doug whispered, dripping with sarcasm, "since you've got it figured out…"

"*Fingered* out," Andy interrupted.

Doug peeked at Valerie. She was shaking her head with a disgusted look on her face.

Doug grimaced. "Your timing is impeccable," he said.

"Dy-no-mite!" exclaimed Andy, and he got up and left. Valerie gathered her things and left too.

Doug covered his face in his hands. He leaned back, staring at the ceiling.

"Hey, earth to Doug!"

Startled, Doug's head banged the radiator. He sat up, rubbing his head, to see Palomma standing in front of him. "Are you all right?" she asked.

"C'mon, Palomma, can't you see I was practicing my Transcendental Meditation? You know,"—he alternately held his hands out – "I'm okay, you're okay, one for all, all for me, every man for himself?"

Palomma giggled.

"You must be an expert at it; it looked like you were asleep." She sat down next to him.

"What's up?" Doug asked.

"Ummmm, nothing much." Palomma glanced around the room. Doug shifted in his desk. The bell rang for the end of the mod.

"Oh, are you supposed to be somewhere else?" she asked, turning to him.

"Palomma, are any of us where we're supposed to be?" Doug leaned on the radiator. "I should be an announcer on Monday Night Football! You're supposed to be…" Doug put a finger to his lips. "Wait, what are you going to be?"

"A lawyer," Palomma answered.

"Prove it," said Doug. "Tell me a lie."

Palomma didn't break eye contact. "You're a hunk."

Doug chuckled, licked his finger and pretended to make a mark in the air. "Good one. What's up?"

"Didn't you say once you went to St. John's for grade school?"

"Yeah," Doug replied. "Eight years."

"Did you know Daniel Parrillo?"

Doug thought for a second. "Yeah, I knew him, sort of. He was on the basketball team when I kept the stats."

"What was he like?" asked Palomma. She propped her chin in her hand.

Doug tried to read Palomma's body language. "Boyfriend?" he asked.

"No, not at all!" Palomma responded quickly, sitting up straight. "I met him with some people, we got to talking and he said he went to St. John's, that's all!"

Doug squinted his eyes a teensy bit.

"He was...I mean, he was a grade ahead, at St. John's grades didn't mix. Like on the playground, each class had its own little area, as you moved up your spot got better..." Doug could see a look of impatience cross Palomma's face.

"Then you didn't know him." Palomma leaned back in the desk, sounding disappointed.

"Oh, yeah, he was on the basketball team when I was, you know, a manager. Managers helped..." Doug saw Palomma lean forward again with a look of anticipation. "Okay, he wasn't the best player on the team, but he played a lot. I do remember he went out with a girl in my class, Patty Pearce, we were in sixth grade and he was in seventh."

"Wow, that's going back a while," said Palomma, leaning on her elbow again. "Why do you remember that?"

"Because, I mean, no one really had a girlfriend...you know, except him..." Doug realized Palomma was staring at him now. "ANYWAY, Patty was, um, I remember Patty because..."

"Just say it," Palomma admonished.

Doug looked down at the desktop. "Patty had the biggest boobs of all the sixth-grade girls."

They both looked down at their desks simultaneously, then back up again.

Palomma brushed some hair away from her eyes. "What does that have to do with my…" Palomma caught herself. "With Daniel Parrillo?"

"Just that I remember him telling guys before games about feeling her up, she was a cheerleader…" This time, Palomma was the only one to look down.

"Oh," said Palomma, brushing at her forehead again. "That's all you remember?"

Doug held up two fingers. "On my honor, Palomma, I didn't know him much. It was that way there and, well…"

"Well what?"

"I wasn't…a popular kid." Doug looked down. "You saw me freshman year."

"Actually, I didn't," Palomma replied. "I wasn't here freshman year."

"Really?" Doug said, looking up. "I thought all of you went to grade school together and came to the high school together?"

Palomma told Doug how her family had moved away after eighth grade and hadn't come back for a year. Doug told her how his family moved right before freshman year. Neither of them noticed the bell or a bunch of kids coming into the room, their homeroom. Finally, they both became aware of all the movement in the room.

Each waited for the other to say something. Palomma did first. "I have to hurry to get back to my homeroom!" she said, gathering her books. "I have to ask about a couple of things!"

Doug got up. Then he looked down and put his hands in his pockets.

"Parrillo's probably a really nice guy," he said softly. "I'm probably thinking of someone else."

Palomma smiled.

As they walked toward the door, Doug let Palomma pass in front of him, bowed slightly and extended his arm.

"Thank you, sir!" said Palomma. "You are quite welcome, m'lady!" replied Doug. He watched her walk all the way down the hall before turning to go to his homeroom.

"Palomma," he said softly to himself. "That's a pretty name."

The next morning, Ed was getting a textbook out of his locker; he had a history quiz that afternoon and figured he'd try to memorize a few names and dates during the class meeting. It was a typical mod change in the hall, crowds of students hurrying in both directions or socializing.

As he was closing his locker, someone bumped him and his shoulder smacked into the locker door. He dropped his book and rubbed his shoulder. Someone else plowed into him from the side, causing him to slam his other shoulder against the locker.

"OW!" he yelled. "Who's the clumsy asshole who…" He turned angrily and didn't see anyone. Then he looked down. Beth Wheeler was at his feet, picking up notebooks while rubbing her side.

"I may be an asshole," she said, standing up, "but I'm not clumsy. You stick out too far." She barely came up to Ed's chest. "And Jesus, what's your ass made of, concrete?"

Ed had noticed Beth before, thought she was really cute, but also saw how outgoing she was. She'd say anything to anyone. Ed figured a girl like her wouldn't even notice him. But here she was, very close to him, noticing him, talking to him.

"Sorry," said Ed.

"Never apologize for being built," she replied, wagging her finger. "If you got it, flaunt it!" She winked at him, gave him a hip check—which hit him in the thigh—and walked down the hall into the gym.

Ed watched her walk away and started toward the gym himself when Doug rushed up to him.

"Let's go over it once more," Doug said. Ed held his hand up.

"I got it!" he said. "You say 'class gift' and I say my piece." He leaned to look down the hall at Beth going into the gym.

"Don't mess it up," said Doug, "or I'll have to mess *you* up!"

Doug grinned at Ed and they both laughed.

Chapter 9

The senior class sat together in the bleachers. Doug was standing near the stage with Beth Wheeler and Cindy Bascomb. "Do I have to say all that 'call this meeting to order' crap?" Doug asked.

"You wanted the job," Beth replied.

Beth was class treasurer, as she'd been for the three previous years, and Cindy was secretary. Doug walked to the front of the assembled seniors, and the chatter subsided.

"All right, let's get this thing going," Doug said. "About fucking time," said Manny Sanchez. "Shut up, Manny," said Doug.

An exchange Doug couldn't have possibly imagined a couple of years ago.

Manny Sanchez had always scared Doug. His sheer size reminded Doug of bullies from his past. Doug was in a resource room junior year when the principal came in and walked over to Manny. She spoke in hushed tones until Manny shouted, "Bullshit! I wasn't even there!"

Everyone in the room stopped what they were doing.

"I beg your pardon?" said Sister Teresa, angrily. "You most certainly *were* there, Mr. Sanchez, and that is unacceptable language. Gather your things and come to the office."

Everyone knew he'd be suspended. 'Gather your things' was principal-speak for it.

"What's that all about?" Doug whispered to Danny Donovan, who always knew everything going on that wasn't related to schoolwork.

"Someone told the principal Manny was getting high in the bathroom first mod," replied Danny.

Doug scrunched up his face. Manny couldn't have been in the bathroom first mod because he'd been in room three flicking little pieces of paper at Doug. Every time Doug looked over, Manny pretended to be studying a textbook he was holding upside-down.

"Um, Sister, that's wrong," Doug called across the room.

Somehow, the room got even *quieter*.

"Excuse me, Mr. Halecki?" she replied. "What business is this of yours?"

Doug stood up. "I think I heard what you were saying—Manny was in room three with me first mod."

"With you? You were together?"

"No, I mean, I was in there and Manny was in there at the same time. I mean, we're not, you know…" He feigned embarrassment.

The other kids in the room were trying to stifle laughter.

The principal looked at Manny, who shrugged.

"Mr. Halecki, are you sure?"

"Sure, sister," Doug answered. "I mean, he is pretty good-looking."

Some of the kids in the room giggled. A glance around the room from the principal stopped it.

"All right, Mr. Sanchez, I'll have to look into this. In the meantime, I suggest you clean up your language or you'll be suspended." She strode out of the room. A few seconds passed before everyone went back to what they'd been doing.

When the mod ended, Doug got up to leave, passing Manny as he walked out. Manny tapped him on the arm and Doug stopped.

"Nothing but a bunch of horseshit." said Manny. "Thanks."

"That's a big 10-4, good buddy," said Doug.

"We've got some things to discuss, so let's get going."

"You just said that," Manny said.

"It's all yours," Doug replied, making an exaggerated gesture with his arms.

Manny slowly got up and walked to the front of the group.

"Pecky's got shit to say, so shut up." Manny returned to his seat.

"All right, the class is supposed to raise money for a gift to the school but first is the spirit club Pumpkin Hop. Congratulations, Palomma, on being elected club president!" The seniors gave her a polite round of applause.

The Pumpkin Hop was an annual Halloween dance; the tradition was to line the gym with pumpkins. Each year, the senior class was supposed to attempt to break the 'record' set by the previous class by stealing pumpkins from houses and farmstands.

Palomma stood up in the bleachers. "The Pumpkin Hop will be on October 25th and admission will be $2.50. I will be contacting local farmers to donate pumpkins for decorations." She quickly sat down.

"Okay, Palomma, thanks for a highly detailed report." Some of the seniors laughed. "Next on the list, we're supposed to do something to raise money for a class gift to the school," continued Doug.

"The whole school can come to the Pumpkin Hop," yelled Danny Donovan.

"That's the spirit club's fundraiser. Any suggestions?"

"Another dance!" Andy called out. "A movie!" said a voice from the back. "X-rated!" Manny yelled, followed by more laughter.

"Wait," Ed interjected, "How about a ping-pong tournament?"

Doug breathed a sigh of relief.

"That's a great idea! All in favor of having a ping-pong tournament, say aye!" said Doug, answered by a chorus of 'ayes.' "And I nominate

Ed Sherman to be in charge. All in favor, say aye!"

Beth interrupted. "Someone has to second it."

"Second what?"

"The proposal, then the nomination."

"Fine, I second them," said Doug.

"You can't second your own stuff, someone else has to," Beth said.

"Jesus Christ," Doug muttered.

"Can I? Can I?" said Cindy, who'd been sitting silently on the stage, writing.

"Start all over, Doug," said Beth.

Doug scowled at Beth. "I hereby propose the senior class sponsor a ding-dong tournament."

"Ping-pong," said Beth.

"TABLE TENNIS!" yelled Doug.

"Cindy, go!" said Beth.

"…What? Oh!" Cindy stood ramrod straight. "I second the motion."

"All in favor, say aye," said Doug. The gym echoed with 'ayes.' "And I nominate Ed Sherman to be in charge of it," he continued.

"In charge of what?" said Beth.

"You wanted that job just to annoy me, didn't you?" said Doug. Beth stuck her tongue out at Doug, who did it back. The class broke out in laughter.

Doug cleared his throat. "Sherman. Nominate. Run. Tournament. All in favor?"

"Wait for the second," shouted Beth. Doug covered his face with his hands.

Cindy had a big grin on her face. "I second the motion!" she chirped.

"Now?" asked Doug, sarcastically.

Beth nodded.

"Show of hands!" yelled Doug. Everyone raised their hand.

"It's 'say aye'" said Beth.

"I just changed it," said Doug. "Assassinate me."

Ed stood up. "And I appoint Halecki as my servant to do everything I tell him; first, second, third, finished."

Doug pointed at Ed and looked at Beth. She shrugged.

"Okay, anything else?" asked Doug. "Nothing? Then we're done."

"Next time make a motion to adjourn the meeting," Beth said to Doug as she picked up her books. She stuck her tongue out at him again and walked away. The seniors left the gym amid a buzz of conversations.

After the meeting, Christine and Palomma were getting ready for an appointment in room eight.

"You said your boyfriend's name is Daniel, right?" asked Christine.

Palomma let the tiniest of smiles creep across her lips. "Yep," she answered.

"Does he go to Holly Hill High?" Christine continued.

"Nope," replied Palomma, still looking at her notebook. "He graduated."

"Oh, he's in college!"

Palomma looked at Christine. "Actually, he already has a full-time job. He's an assistant manager at a grocery store."

"Where..." Christine began to ask.

"Oh look, here's the rest of our group!" said Palomma, cheerily. "Time to move!" She gathered her books and walked over to the teacher's desk.

That night, Christine lay on her bed and stared up at the canopy. "What's Happening" was on her portable TV. Rod Stewart's "Tonight's the Night" had just ended on her record player. But the only thing happening tonight was Christine couldn't stop thinking about Palomma's boyfriend. How did she get one first?

"This guy she met, he's probably a nerd like her," muttered Christine. "She never said what he looked like." But—maybe not. So that night, Christine decided to go hunting.

Her first stop was at Marvin's Market downtown. Christine walked around the aisles for a while looking for anyone who worked there. Finally, she saw a woman talking to an older man in an apron.

"Marvin, are these tomatoes fresh?" the woman asked.

"For you, Mrs. Belmonti, I get you the freshest!"

He turned and called out "Jose! *Muy rapido!*"

A young Hispanic man hurried over. "My assistant will get you some; how many do you need?"

Christine turned away, frustrated. She walked out to her car and drove to her next stop, Morelli's Market.

Christine remembered seeing Doug hanging out there in the morning but didn't have high hopes; Morelli's was kind of small. As she walked in, she shot a quick glance at the employee at the counter—his name tag read "Dan." Christine kept walking as if she didn't see him and pretended to look around in an aisle until the other customers had checked out.

She slowly walked to the counter. "Can I help you?" asked Daniel.

"A pack of Parliaments, please!" said Christine, looking up, pointing at the cigarette rack. She saw he was a good head taller than her.

"Sure! Will there be anything else?" he said, leaning forward and resting both hands on the counter.

"Well, hello there"—she looked at his nametag --"Dan!" She stuck out her chest a little further. "Wait, you're so tall, you don't look like a Dan, that's too little—you look more like a Daniel…"

"Some people call me that," he said, leaning closer. "What do some people call you?"

Christine leaned forward too. "Some people call me beautiful, but my name is Christine."

"Hi, beautiful, I'm glad to meet you. *Sei quasi più figa di me*!"

"*Oui, oui monsieur*!" answered Christine, leaning forward and smiling.

He rang up her cigarettes. Christine waited for her change and debated whether to ask about Palomma or not. Clearly, he'd been flirting. Maybe this wasn't the guy. He certainly was good looking and not all nervous and scared like other boys. He could probably attract any girl he wanted to.

Daniel handed her the change, lingering an extra second while touching her palm. "Drop in again, beautiful!"

Christine smiled and left the store, then stood in front of the window. She opened the pack of cigarettes and lit one. She had a hunch their conversation wasn't finished yet.

Daniel came outside and walked toward her.

"I've got to keep an eye out for customers, I'm the only one here tonight," he said, wiping his hands on his apron.

"Hmmmm, all by yourself," Christine said as he lit a cigarette of his own. "You better watch it, you could get in a lot of trouble like that!"

"Like, how?" Daniel kidded back, tossing away the match.

"Oh, I don't know, we could think of something," Christine responded, and they both laughed.

Christine's mind raced. If this *was* Palomma's boyfriend she should say something.

They smoked for a moment. Christine looked up as if she was thinking. "Daniel...Daniel...hey, I think you know one of my friends, she said she met someone named Daniel who works at a grocery. Her name's Palomma?"

Daniel looked up too as if he was thinking. "Palomma...yeah, I know a girl named that. Met her at a dance, I think."

Christine's shoulders slumped in deflation. It was him. But he sure wasn't acting like he had a girlfriend.

"She's my absolute best friend!" Christine gushed. "We've known each other since we were little girls!" She sang, "*It's a small world after all!*"

Christine giggled and took a puff. "You know what would be cool? Maybe the three of us could do something together sometime! That'd be fun!"

Daniel tossed away his cigarette.

"I don't know, I'm pretty busy here at the store." He locked eyes with Christine, who was looking at him with a big smile. Daniel put his hand to his chin. "But that would be cool, getting together with you. And Palomma, too!" he quickly added.

Christine dropped her cigarette, took a piece of paper and pen out of her purse and wrote down her number. "Give me a call when you can get free and we'll set something up! How's that?" She folded it and tucked the paper into his shirt pocket, her hand lingering for a moment.

Daniel looked at her hand and then into her eyes. "You know, I'm pretty sure we could do that sometime."

"Cool!" Christine said. "I've got to go, see ya!" She walked quickly to her car and drove away. Daniel watched her leave and went back inside.

That Saturday night, Daniel opened the door for Palomma, then got in the driver's side of his truck and drove out of the parking lot.

"Sorry about the diner. I tried to get reservations at the Ramblewood but they were full up."

"The diner was wonderful," said Palomma. She leaned over and kissed Daniel on the cheek.

The past few weeks had been a delightful blur for Palomma. She filled up so many pages in her diary she had to buy another one.

It hadn't been as hard as she thought to tell her Mom about Daniel. Palomma told her about the dance, emphasizing what a gentleman he'd been. The first time they went out, Daniel waited in his truck in front of her house, saying he was shy about meeting her parents. After the date, he'd stopped a little way up the street, explaining he wanted to kiss her goodnight and didn't want her to get in trouble.

On the second date, he'd stopped up the street again before dropping her off and they had long, tender kisses. Just like Palomma had imagined.

Palomma didn't want to rush him. Her mother seemed displeased when he didn't come to the door but Palomma figured he was working up to it. Sure enough, this evening he'd come to the door.

Palomma had purposely waited upstairs when she saw him pull into the driveway. "Is Palomma ready?" she heard him say when her Mom opened the door.

"I'll call her," her Mom had replied, but she didn't move at first. Daniel stood silently with his hands in his pockets. Gemma was peeping from the kitchen. Mrs. Rossi eventually turned and called upstairs. "Dear! Your date is here!" As they left, she'd said, "Her curfew is 11 o'clock."

Moving in baby steps was fine with Palomma. She wanted everything to last forever. Her father would have to meet him eventually, but there was still plenty of time, maybe Thanksgiving.

After leaving the diner, Palomma did a double-take when Daniel drove past her house. "Daniel, I..." she began to say.

"Just a sec," he interrupted. "I forgot to make a call when we were eating. Gotta check in at work, you know? See if everything's copacetic." He turned to her and grinned. "There's a pay phone up here at the golf course."

Daniel pulled into the deserted Fox Hollow parking lot. It looked so different at night to Palomma, no cars, no people, only two streetlamps lighting up the property. Daniel parked behind the building and walked to a phone booth.

Christine was in her room watching TV when her phone rang.

"Hello?"

"Remember me?" A deep voice came through the phone.

Christine sat up and inhaled sharply. She hadn't expected him to call so soon.

"Oh, Daniel! Sure! You want to get together with Palomma and me, huh?"

"I had a different idea. Hear me out. I was wondering if you'd like to get something to eat tomorrow, maybe about 7, the two of us?"

Christine almost dropped the phone. "Wow, that sounds nice! I'm sorry, Daniel, you surprised me, that's all, I wasn't expecting you to call."

"Surprises can be good, right?"

"Definitely! Tomorrow night sounds great!" said Christine.

"Listen, I gotta go!" he said.

"See you!" Christine replied. She hung up, flopped back on her back, closed her eyes and smiled.

Palomma thought Daniel had been on the phone for an inordinately long time; she waited patiently and watched.

Finally, he got back into the car. "Sorry, it was busy—they put me on hold." Daniel reached behind his seat and picked up a bottle of Southern Comfort. "As a reward for your patience, a toast! To a hot fox!" He unscrewed the cap and took a big swig. He handed the bottle to Palomma.

She froze.

"No, I mean I've never…what is that?"

"SoCo!" he said. "It's sweet like soda!"

Palomma had only ever had a drink at New Year's with her family when she sipped some of the traditional sambuca. That tasted like licorice; maybe all liquor tasted like something good. She took the bottle, put it to her lips and tipped it back.

Immediately, her throat burned. She swallowed and began coughing, handing the bottle back to Daniel.

"Oh…my…God…!" she rasped.

Daniel chuckled. "Atta girl!" He took another swig and handed her the bottle. "Have another!"

Palomma took the bottle hesitantly and put it to her lips. Daniel reached over and grabbed the bottom of the bottle, tipping it up higher. A flood of whiskey filled Palomma's mouth. She pressed her eyes closed tightly and swallowed again.

Palomma pushed the bottle away and breathed in and out heavily. "No more," she sputtered.

"Rookie!" he said, taking back the bottle, capping it and putting it behind the seat. "We'll get you used to it."

He laced his arm around her waist and pulled her toward him. Palomma put her hands on his shoulders and they began kissing. Daniel swallowed her up in both arms. They kissed for a long time and the windows of the truck began to steam up. The air got stagnant and it was harder to breathe. Daniel started fidgeting around, trying to move her this way or that; Palomma wanted to keep still.

She felt chills up her arms and legs, but not from kissing. She felt dizzy even though she was sitting down. The chills moved into her neck and through her jaw; she was sure something was coming up from her stomach. She pulled away and leaned over the floorboards on the passenger side, gagged a couple of times—and let out a huge belch.

"Damn!" exclaimed Daniel. "Thank God you didn't puke!"

Palomma kept her head down. She was dizzy and starting to sweat. Daniel reached over and tried to pull her toward him; she hung onto the dashboard with both hands. "I...don't...feel...good," she managed to say.

Daniel let go of her and started the truck.

Palomma rolled down the window and leaned out; the rush of cold air was like a slap in the face, but she needed it. She didn't want to walk in the house looking like she imagined she looked.

Daniel stopped in her driveway. "How about next week?" he asked.

Palomma took a couple of deep breaths and cleared her throat. "Whew! Yes, I'd like that," she said, turning to him. "I'm sorry about tonight."

"No problem." He pulled her close to him.

Palomma leaned forward for a kiss.

Daniel belched and started laughing.

Ed knew what it felt like to be treated like crap, more so now that he was shoveling it. As one of the youngest workers at the racetrack, he got the worst days, like today, Sunday, and the worst tasks, like cleaning up horse manure from the stalls and grounds.

"I will never use the word 'horseshit' again in my life," he grumbled as he filled a wheelbarrow.

But it paid, and there'd be more work in the summer when the Puerto Rican migrant workers left to pick crops at local farms. Money was still tight; the Shermans had been eating a lot of boxed mac and cheese.

Ed was cleaning out one of the last stalls of the day when he heard voices from outside the stall door.

"It's done," a man with a squeaky voice said. "Taken care of."

"They understand anyone who don't do what he's told will be in deep shit, right?" said the other, gruffly.

"I told you it's done," the first man replied. "Do I ever screw up?"

"There's always a first time."

Ed knew exactly what was being discussed. A fixed race.

It happened all the time at smaller tracks. Usually, jockeys held back their mounts in an unimportant claimer race to let the predetermined horse win. Smaller bets made by a number of cronies didn't look suspicious.

The jockeys didn't even have to be paid off; cooperating meant better rides and better purses. Not going along wasn't an option. Ed had an idea forming in his head on how to get his hands on a little much-needed money.

"Made it easy for your guys to remember," the first man said. "November 5th, sixth race, number seven. 5-6-7. It'll look like one of those coincidences the papers love."

They'd made it easy for Ed to remember too.

That night, Christine sat in Daniel's truck as they pulled out of the parking lot of the Ramblewood Inn.

She'd tried to convince herself all day this was just a weird coincidence—two guys named Daniel who worked at markets, and she and Palomma were dating them. But clearly, there was only one, and this was him. Christine justified it to herself; this was 1976. The magazines said going out with someone doesn't mean you're married. And Christine had tried way harder for way longer than Palomma anyway.

Daniel was speeding down the highway; the cars in the oncoming lane zipped by much faster than when Christine drove. "Ever really crank it up?" he asked, turning toward her. "You know, in your car?"

Christine shook her head. "Nope, I don't have the guts."

"Check these guts!" exclaimed Daniel. He swerved into the left lane and passed a line of six cars before diving back into the right lane just in time as a tractor-trailer came toward them. "That's 90 miles an hour!"

"Whew!" said Christine, fanning herself with her hand. "That was a rush!"

They pulled into the parking lot at Holly Hill High School. The public school was on the edge of town, far away from Blessed Sacrament and much larger. Daniel drove onto a dirt road behind the baseball field. "A toast!" he said, reaching behind the seat. "To a gorgeous chick!" Christine watched him take a swig from the bottle of Southern Comfort. She reached over and took it from him.

"My turn!" she said, taking a mouthful and swallowing. It burned but she tried not to show much reaction. "Whew!" she exclaimed. "That's good!"

"Impressive!" said Daniel. "Another!" and he took another swig. He went to hand the bottle to Christine again.

"No thanks, one's enough for me!" said Christine. "Besides..." she nuzzled close to him. "I was thinking of something else we can do with our mouths..."

"Damn!" said Daniel. "You are major cool!" Christine kissed him while sitting beside him and even let him put his hand on her boob briefly. She gently pushed it away and climbed onto his lap; one of the girls at school said it was a way to keep a boy under control.

And it was. Daniel put his hands on her butt and nothing else. They made out for fifteen minutes before she said, softly, "I better be getting home."

"At your service," said Daniel. He started the truck and drove her home.

Palomma looked up dreamily from writing in her diary that night. It was becoming her own personal romance novel.

On their first date, Daniel opened doors for her and held her chair when she sat down. At the movies on their second date, Palomma almost melted when Daniel put his arm around her; it felt good to be the girl with the arm around her instead of the one watching. The experience with whiskey hadn't been pleasant but she'd have to learn to drink sooner or later.

Palomma had suggested Daniel come by the school one night to see rehearsals. She could make a show of pointing him out and maybe he'd kiss her in front of everyone. But he told her he was working a lot more hours and didn't have free time during the week. She focused on how wonderful it felt and the loving times to come.

Chapter 10

When Palomma told him she didn't have a record player, Doug had volunteered his basement for the first prom committee meeting the following Tuesday night.

Doug had asked everyone to come to the back door so they could go straight down to the basement without risking interaction with his parents; Doug wanted no part of that. He'd arranged some folding chairs around a table where his sister Linda's old portable stereo sat. When everyone was downstairs, Doug handed out sodas and talked nonstop.

Linda peered down the basement steps. "Hey, Doug," she called. "C'mere a minute?" Doug walked up the steps. "Not so loud," she whispered. "Or you'll get a visit from Mom and Dad too."

"Gotcha," said Doug, turning to go back down.

Aside from Palomma, Christine and Doug were vice-chairs. Doug had talked Ed and Andy into building the decorations. Angela Cicarone was in charge of money and correspondence and Katie O'Connor and Paula Carino, entertainment.

Palomma had never been in charge of a group before, and now she had the prom committee and spirit club; she'd written herself notes on things to say but was nervous. "Let's get the meeting started, guys," Palomma said. The talking stopped and they looked at her. "Before anything else, we need to pick a song for the theme. Any suggestions?"

Doug piped up immediately. "I think we should do 'Go All the Way' by the Raspberries! Let me play it." He put a record on the turntable and everyone listened to the lyrics.

Palomma figured Doug was joking. When the song was done, she said, "We have one suggestion. I have one myself, 'Come Sail Away.'" She handed the Styx record to Doug. "Oh, yeah, that's a good one!" said Angela. "I've got that record!" said Katie. When it was finished, she asked for more suggestions.

"I have one," Christine said. "'Still the One?' I bought the single at the mall. I know how much you love it, Doug!" She handed him the record.

Doug started to sing along; Christine even joined in.

Palomma fumed inside. Christine couldn't have made it more obvious, picking a song Doug loved. But Palomma wasn't going to change her expression or tone.

"We've got three suggestions, anyone else? No?" asked Palomma. Angela, Katie and Paula shrugged. "What we should do now is figure out how to decorate for them and see what works best. Doug?"

"Decorations? I have no idea. That would be the decorations department's job, right Ed? Right Andy?" said Doug.

"Fuck you," they replied in unison.

"Well, without any decorations, I guess we can't use your song, sorry Doug. Christine, how about your song?"

Christine fluttered her eyes toward Doug. "I'm sure Doug could come up with something perfect! He always has great ideas!" Christine was pouring it on thick.

"Didn't you have any ideas at all, Christine?" asked Palomma. "I mean, you suggested the song, not Doug…"

Everyone was completely silent waiting for Christine to answer. "I, um, guess we could, do something with numbers because it's 'Still the One'…" she began.

Doug interrupted.

"Wait, I got it! I got it! We could build a big moonshine still with a number one on it, you know 'still' the 'one?'" He stood up and acted out his idea. "And we'd fill it with lemonade and have it at every table, because it's yellow and looks like 'number one'?"

Katie, Paula and Angela burst out laughing.

Paula chimed in with a suggestion about everyone having to remain completely 'still.' Ed and Andy started tossing in their own 'Wait! Wait!' jokes. When Palomma looked at Christine, she was not smiling.

"Those are some interesting ideas," said Palomma, trying not to laugh. "For mine, I was thinking of a nautical theme."

Palomma described how they could hang ropes and nets, maybe build a lighthouse, even a bridge people crossed to enter.

"We could do that," said Ed. "They'd be pretty easy."

"All we'd need is a place big enough to build it," added Andy.

"Problem solved," said Doug. "We have a barn, and the whole second floor is empty."

"A barn?" said Christine. "Will we have to work with cows?" She laughed at her own joke, looking around at the others. No one else laughed.

"Udder-ly unnecessary," Doug shot back, emphasizing the pun. "I said second floor. Cows climb ladders at your house?"

Christine started to respond, then made a sour face. "Wait, what do you mean 'at my house?'"

"Nothing, Christine, I'm just milking it for all it's worth," Doug answered.

Palomma joined in laughing with everyone else. Everyone else except Christine.

The rest of the meeting went quickly, especially because Christine didn't say another word. Katie and Paula would get a list of places that hosted proms and names of DJs. Angela would get money from Beth to open a bank account. When everything on Palomma's list was covered, she said "I guess that's it. Come Sail Away!"

The group clapped—except Christine—and everyone got up to leave. Doug led them to the back door and held it open.

"Good meeting, guys!" said Doug as he walked out after them. He turned to Palomma. "'Come Sail Away' is a great idea. Mine blew."

"Thanks, Doug!" Palomma couldn't help noticing he didn't mention Christine's suggestion.

Christine started her car and pulled out of the driveway. For the few minutes it took to get to Landing Road, Palomma tried to make small talk. "That went well, don't you think?"

Christine didn't answer.

Palomma turned on the radio. If it was a movie, 'Come Sail Away' would've come on. It didn't—but it was 'Lady' by Styx. Palomma smiled.

October had arrived. School had started to settle into a routine of classes and activities. Doug and Ed were in room five for a religion appointment.

"I wish they'd tell us something new," said Ed as he thumbed through a textbook. "After eleven years, I've heard all this crap a hundred times."

"Maybe you could start your own religion," said Doug. "There's the Mormons, you could start the Shermans!"

"Helluva way to make money, that's for sure," said Ed. "Chant a few things and stick a basket in front of 'em." He drummed his pencil on the desk, waiting for the priest to arrive.

"Yeah, I could be the chant-it-clear, and you could be one of the three basketeers," said Doug. He waited, then held out his hand. "I said you could..."

"I heard you," said Ed. "It wasn't funny."

Ed watched Beth walk in and sit down at one of the appointment desks. He sat up straighter.

"That why you wanted to take this lap?" whispered Doug. Ed gave him a dirty look.

"Mornin' Beth," said Doug. "How're the senior class finances doin'?"

"I blew it all on a quarter pounder," she answered without looking up.

"Sure would be nice to have some money," Ed said softly, looking across the room.

Starting in October, play rehearsals were Monday through Saturday nights. Doug wouldn't be going to work for a while. Thankfully.

At school and at home, he'd been doing everything he could to keep acting normally. By the end of September, it had almost become impossible.

He'd had been promoted from busboy to weekday waiter in August; Doug felt it was another sign he'd impressed Mr. Little. It was nerve-wracking at first; customers for dinner at a fancy restaurant expected fancy service and Doug was new to everything.

"I didn't order a steak!"

"I'm sorry sir," said Doug, taking back the steak he'd placed in front of a well-dressed man and setting down lobster Newberg.

"I wanted this rare! This is burned!" snapped the man's wife.

"I'm sorry, ma'am. I'll get you another," Doug stammered.

"Maybe this month this time?" the man said sarcastically.

Doug hurried back into the kitchen. "I need another New York strip, rare!" he shouted to the chef.

"You wrote well," he yelled back.

"I didn't!" said Doug. "I…"

Rena pulled him aside.

"Trying to go faster makes you mess up, and that makes everything slower," she whispered. "I know you wrote it right. I'll check 'em before you take 'em out. We'll work as a team tonight."

Doug was too exhausted to do more than smile at her.

After a few nights, it got easier. And Rena had been right; upscale meant bigger tips. For this kind of money, he'd planned on trying to get more shifts when the play ended.

Doug lay in his room and thought back to a month before, when the bartender called Doug and said, "Mr. Little asked for you to bring his martini." Doug was excited; the boss asked for him! He practically ran to the bar, got the tray and headed to Little's office.

Doug knocked. Little called him in and said, "Y'all need a break. Sit down!"

Doug sat in the chair facing Little's desk.

"How's school?" he asked.

"It's good!" Doug answered happily. "I'm involved in lots of stuff this year!"

"Your folks?" Little asked. "They're good?"

"Very good!" replied Doug.

Little sipped at his martini. Doug tried to stay sitting up straight. Then Little looked at his watch. "Y'all better be getting back before they miss ya!" Doug took the empty carafe and glass and headed back to the kitchen.

The next week, Doug brought the drink, knocked and sat down when told to.

"How's school?" Little asked.

"Um, school's good," answered Doug.

"Family?"

"Them too," he replied.

This time, Little stood up and gulped down his drink. He walked around the desk and faced Doug. "Come here, son," he said, holding his arms out; Doug hesitantly got up.

Little wrapped his arms around Doug and hugged him.

"Ah'll bet the young ladies think you're a *priiiize* catch. Probably *liiinin'* up for ya." Little rubbed his hand up and down Doug's back again. "Yes sir, your gonna have to beat 'em off with a stick!"

Doug felt smothered. Doug's father never hugged him. He couldn't even remember the last time his mother hugged him. Doug squirmed, hoping Little would let go, but he wasn't budging. Little had pulled him so tight against him every part of the front of Doug was touching some part of the man. Doug tried wriggling away again.

"You're wrigglin' around like a catfish!" said Little. "What's botherin' ya?"

"N-nothing. I guess I'm…tired…"

"Y'all need to learn to relax!" Little lifted one arm around Doug's shoulder. "There's a lot goin' on at your age." Doug suddenly felt Little's other hand on his crotch. He froze and pressed his eyes closed.

"A young man like you needs to find ways to alleviate the stress." Little stretched out 'alleviate.' He slid his hand up Doug's crotch, then unzipped Doug's fly.

Doug let out a tiny gasp. He stiffened, feeling paralyzed.

"Relax, relax," Little whispered. "Shhhhhhhh…"

He had his fingers inside the zipper. Doug could feel Little worming them through his briefs. He didn't move until he felt Little touch his dick.

Doug pushed Little away. "Mr. Little, I, uh, I…I…"

Little stood still for a couple of seconds, then returned to his desk saying, "All right, son, you best be gettin' back."

Doug snatched the carafe and glass from the desk and hurried out of the office. In the hallway, Doug was shaking; he leaned against the wall in a corner. He was about to return to the kitchen when he realized his zipper was still down. He ducked back into the corner and straightened himself up.

The restaurant closed soon after, and Doug set up for breakfast in silence.

What should he do? Should he tell his parents? They wouldn't believe him, they'd think he was trying to get out of having to work. Doug could imagine it: "You think you're so important? Suppose we told Mr. Little what you were saying about him?!" If he quit, it'd be a trip to the barn for sure. They'd ground him from all his activities and probably even make him go beg for his job back.

It wasn't like he could tell any of the teachers. You didn't talk about things like that, especially with nuns and priests. Anything in the same hemisphere as sex seemed so disgusting to them he'd probably get in trouble for just saying it. Worse, what if Doug told someone and other kids heard about it? Jokes about homosexuals were all the rage. If one boy brushed up against another it would start. "What're you, a fag? Are you queer? Get away from me, you homo!"

"He's only touching me." Doug talked to himself on his drive home, trying to make sense of things. "That's not like..." He'd heard what guys like Little did with each other; would it hurt really bad? Doug shook his head to get the image out of his mind.

A couple of Saturdays later, Doug had a grim feeling about being at work. Little had called him to his office the previous week and had shoved his hand down the front of Doug's pants, rubbing him for quite a while until his phone had rung. Tonight, he kept looking to the bar, expecting to be called again. Toward closing time, Doug had planned to sneak to the time clock and leave when Florence, the hostess, pushed a cart toward him holding a tray with covered dinner plates.

"Mr. Little wants his meal delivered to his apartment."

Doug felt what a murderer must feel going to the electric chair. He considered asking her to give it to someone else, lie about having to get home, but he couldn't get any words out. He picked up the tray and walked down the hall until he reached Little's apartment.

Doug stood, trembling. The tray was heavy; he couldn't stand there forever. He took a deep breath and knocked.

The door opened. Little was wearing a bathrobe.

"Set that down over here." Little pointed to a table in the middle of the room. He closed the door and Doug inched sideways to the table, trying to stay facing Little. The apartment was crammed with furniture and antiques with barely any room to move around.

As soon as Doug set the tray down, Little grabbed the carafe and gulped the martini. He sat down in an easy chair positioned with its back to the door. As he did, his robe came untied and opened in the front.

He wasn't wearing anything else.

Little leaned on one elbow in the chair, crossed his legs and looked Doug up and down. Doug stood like a statue, staring over Little's head at the door behind him.

"All right, then," said Little. He got up from the chair and moved toward Doug. He stood facing Doug and unbuckled his belt, unsnapped his pants and crouched to slide them down to his ankles. He stayed in the position with his face inches from Doug's crotch, staring. Then he slid Doug's briefs down.

Doug was trembling.

Little went back and sat in the chair, staring at Doug. "Touch it," he demanded.

Doug didn't move a muscle.

"I told y'all to touch it!" Little repeated harshly, pointing at Doug's crotch and leaning forward. "Sure as hell you know how!"

Doug remained motionless. He hadn't imagined this happening. He felt like he was going to start crying but gritted his teeth to hold back tears.

"Maybe I need to get y'all started!" said Little, getting up and moving toward Doug.

Doug felt a jolt go through him. This wasn't standing in Little's office with his zipper open. He was naked from the waist down with his pants around his ankles; running away wasn't an option. Doug pressed his eyes tightly closed and began stroking himself.

He knew that if he didn't get a boner, Little might get angry. Angrier. He pressed his eyes closed. He tried to remember what Christine's perfume smelled like; he tried to picture the time she sat next to him and he got a look down her blouse. He could almost feel her leg pressing against his.

Doug could hear Little breathing very heavily. He opened his eyes the barest of cracks and saw Little standing in front of him, masturbating. Doug almost stopped but realized Little in front of him was better than Little behind him. He tried to forget where he was. He pressed his eyes tightly shut, imagining Christine naked.

He felt Little's hand push his away and jerk him up and down. His hand was oily and slick and Doug couldn't help it—he ejaculated.

When he opened his eyes, Mr. Little was kneeling in front of him, wiping his face with a towel.

Doug frantically pulled up his pants and dashed for the door. He yanked the door closed behind him and peered up and down the hallway; seeing it was deserted, he snapped his pants and buckled his belt. He felt dirty and disgusting. His briefs were still tangled around his thighs under his pants, but all Doug could think about was getting out of there as quickly as possible. He hurried back to the lobby, ducked into the alcove behind the front desk and clocked out.

Doug drove home fast. He didn't care if he got pulled over, he didn't care about much of anything. He pressed down on the gas pedal and felt the car surge forward.

That was it. It must be. Christine must've known when she turned him down. All the girls must know. He was a homo. As much as he'd tried to fight it, Little had done to him just like Doug did to himself. A man. Two men doing it made you queer. Little had even picked him out —it must be obvious. No wonder he couldn't talk to girls—he'd probably known all along deep inside. Now it made sense.

Everything was different now. He'd have to just pretend to like girls. He'd never get married, the only people he could socialize with would be ones like Little, the fags. It was hard to focus, thoughts were coming at him like the trees zipping past on the side of the road.

The large trees lined the road. He tried to keep his eyes on the road but they kept getting drawn back to the trees.

He wouldn't feel it; it would be over in a split second. He'd read somewhere people never knew what hit them when they crashed into something at high speed. He'd need to make sure he picked out a tree thick enough to stop the car and was going fast enough...but he couldn't see the trees as anything other than a blur going this fast. If he slowed down to see, it wouldn't be fast enough. Maybe if he picked one out, stopped and turned around and came back.

What if he fucked up? What if he didn't pick the right tree? What if he glanced off it? What if he didn't die? His parents would never let him do anything ever again! If he was crippled, if he ended up in a wheel-chair, they'd have to feel sorry for him! Or maybe they'd tell him he deserved it.

Doug slammed on the brakes and skidded to a stop on the side of the road. He cried uncontrollably, pounding his fist on the steering wheel.

When he finally got home, Doug got undressed, tiptoed to the bathroom so as not to wake his parents, got in the shower, stood under the water and closed his eyes.

He hadn't done anything wrong. Yet like with the bullies, he felt ashamed because he took it. He couldn't get the image of Little wiping off his face out of his mind. The water poured over his head. He tried to think which was worse—Little touching him, or someone finding out. His father thought he was a sissy—how bad would he beat him if it turned out he was?

Doug turned off the water and dried himself. It's like when a girl gets raped, right? It isn't her fault and this wasn't Doug's! His father had always called him a sissy, maybe he was right in one way. He should have kicked Little in the face, beat him with something. Like real men would have done. Like those karate guys.

Doug realized he wouldn't have to go to work for the next couple of months. Maybe he could call in sick after that and pretend to go to work; he could find some way to kill the time, drive around, whatever. He turned out the lights and lay on his back in in bed, thinking about his old friends turning on him. And how no one was ever on his side. He stared at the ceiling in the dark.

Doug decided no one could ever find out. Ever. This would be his secret. He'd never tell his parents. He'd never tell anyone. He felt himself starting to cry again. He turned over and pressed his face into his pillow so his father wouldn't hear.

Chapter 11

A week later, Doug was sprawled on the couch after dinner, watching the Three Stooges on TV. It was Columbus Day, a day off from school with no rehearsal. Not having to go to work for the past couple of weeks had helped cloud the memories of Little's apartment.

He heard the phone ring in the kitchen. "Doug!" his mother called, "It's Christine from school!"

Doug sat up, startled. He yelled "Got it," trotted down the hall and picked up the extension there. He waited for his mother to hang up.

"Hello?" If his mother was wrong, he'd be really embarrassed saying "Hi Christine!" to someone else.

"Hi Douggie! I hope it's not too much trouble! I really need a favor!" It was Christine.

Doug paused, then said, "What is it?"

"My car's getting fixed, and my Mom gave me a ride to the mall. I was wondering if you could give me a ride home?" Christine asked sweetly. "I'll be done shopping at 9:30."

"Okay, I'll wait in front of Spaceport." Doug hung up and beamed. His plan was working. Christine had called *him* and wanted to get to-gether with *him*.

"I'm going to the mall," Doug called out to his mother.

He got there early and played some video games. But his mind start-ed to wander; he walked out and sat on a bench in the mall.

Christine *had* called him—for a ride.

Doug watched couples walking through the mall, holding hands, laughing. Boys with arms around girls' shoulders. Doug thought ignoring Christine would move things along toward *them* being a couple, but all he was tonight was a free taxi.

"Hi Doug!" Doug hadn't noticed Christine walk up from behind.

"Oh, hi Christine," Doug answered, quietly. "I'm parked down by the movie theater." They started walking; Doug saw that Christine kept a pretty big gap between them as she talked about who she'd seen at the mall that night. He'd probably been right about her 'knowing' about him.

Eventually, they walked out of the mall into the parking lot. Christine got into his car saying, "I really appreciate this, Doug!" As soon as he started the engine, she turned to him. "You don't have to be home right away, do you?"

Doug was confused. "Umm…"

"Good! Neither do I! Let's ride around for a while."

Doug turned on the radio. It played for about thirty seconds before Christine said, "Do you remember Daniel Parrillo?"

Doug turned down the radio.

"Yeah, he went to St. John's. Played basketball. Year ahead of me."

"He said he remembered you kept statistics."

"How do you know Dan Parrillo?" Doug asked. He thought it was weird Palomma had asked about the same guy.

"From the mall," she answered.

Christine didn't say anything else so Doug turned up the radio again. He was heading in the general direction of her house and was about to pass Strawbridge Park when Christine spoke up. "Let's stop here for a minute."

Doug was confused but did as she asked. He pulled into the gravel parking lot, up to a wooden barrier with the car facing the lake. There were five or six cars parked in various spots around the lot, most of them in the places furthest from lights.

Christine reached into her purse for a cigarette. Doug took one out and lit hers before lighting his. He cracked the window to let out the smoke. His shoulders slumped; he was 'parking' with a girl—but not really. Except for the location, it was hardly different than talking to Christine at school.

Christine took a couple of drags and stubbed out her cigarette in the ashtray. She turned in the seat to face Doug, who flipped his cigarette out the window. She started talking, nonstop, about Daniel. Doug nodded at the right times while trying to figure out what was going on; he'd assumed Palomma was going out with Parrillo from her asking about him at school. Now here was Christine chattering away about him. Maybe he'd misinterpreted. Maybe Palomma had been asking as a favor to Christine. It's not like he knew anything about that stuff.

Christine was talking about the places he'd taken her on dates when she stopped abruptly.

"The other day when we were, you know, out, I asked Daniel what he wanted to do, and he said 'you,'" she blurted out.

Doug was startled but tried not to show it.

"Ummm, you said no, right? If you mean what I think?"

"I told him no, of course. I told him…" she stopped in mid-sentence.

Doug tried to think of something to say. "Did he try to, uh, no, I mean…"

Christine jumped in. "No, no, nothing like that! It's just he keeps talking about it, and. oh, Doug!"

Christine put her arms around Doug's neck, burying her face in his chest.

Doug was stunned, frozen with his arms stretched away from her.

What was he supposed to say? Or do? He put his hand on her back to hug her, flinched when he touched her bra and pulled it away. He lightly rested his arms against her.

"Gee, Christine," he said. "I guess, I guess only you can decide what you want to do, with your, with…" Doug put his hands on her back again but continued looking over her shoulder. "I guess if he's trying to make you, if you don't say something…" Doug looked down at the top of her head. "Maybe later on you'll wish you *had* and…"

Christine pulled her face away from his chest and looked Doug directly in the eyes. And then she kissed him. *Really* hard.

Christine was turning her face this way and that, and her tongue started to play against his teeth; Doug opened his mouth and put out his tongue. She pulled closer against him. Christine was making little sounds, and Doug didn't know if a guy was supposed to make sounds too. He seemed to be doing fine with the French kissing though; Christine was doing the same things he was. He gave in to the urge to open his eyes; Christine's eyes were closed.

Alarm bells were going off in Doug's head. This was not at all how he'd thought he'd end up kissing a girl for the first time. Part of his brain was trying to make sense of what was happening; the other part was concerned whether he was doing everything right.

For five minutes, things were a blur. Doug kept opening his eyes, then closing them because he was afraid to have them open if she opened hers. He started to slide his hands toward her butt, then abruptly moved them back up. He also realized it was kind of hard to breathe during all this but didn't want to pull away.

Christine did. Doug inhaled deeply.

They sat with their arms around each other and their heads on each other's shoulder. Then, Christine leaned back, sighed, and said, "That was nice. I guess I'd better be getting home."

"Yeah, I guess," said Doug. He was feeling a little like being drunk, but not. It was neat.

Doug started the car and backed out; Christine continued leaning her head against him. In a few miles he turned onto her street and into her driveway.

"Thanks so much for caring," she said. Christine held Doug's face in both hands, kissed him and got out of the car. She gave him a little wave before turning the corner of the back of the house.

Doug knew he'd driven home because he was in his driveway—he just didn't remember actually doing it.

He got out of his car and rushed to the back door; Doug wanted to call her. It sure wouldn't be like the last time he did. He closed the back door quietly and tiptoed up the steps to find his father sitting at the kitchen table, reading the newspaper. "Where've you been?" he asked, sternly.

Doug looked at the clock; it wasn't even 11. "Someone needed a ride home so I gave 'em a ride home. What's the big deal?"

"Are you getting smart with me?" his father said, angrily. "Because as long as you live under this roof, you'll show respect and follow the rules!"

Doug flashed back to the day of the egg-throwing incident. It was time to stop backing down.

"No one's ever told me when I had to be home," he said.

"What are you talking about?" his father snapped back. "You know it's…"

He stopped.

"You never told me a time, and neither did Mom," Doug continued, "and it's only 11 anyway. Lin used to stay out 'til midnight when she was eighteen, and I'll be 18 next month." Doug tried to sound repentant. "But I'm sorry. Next time I'll let someone know what time I'll be home when I do someone a favor."

Doug's father had an odd look on his face, as if he was going to say something but couldn't.

"Fine," he finally said. "Make sure you say something next time." He went back to reading the newspaper. "And nothing after midnight." Doug stood for a moment, and saw his father shoot the slightest of glances up from the paper before immediately looking back down.

Doug reached for the phone in the hallway, then stopped. It was probably too late to call now anyway. Instead, he walked into his room and locked the door. He didn't even need to take out his magazine. He could still smell a little of Christine's perfume on him. He closed his eyes and thought back to kissing Christine in his car.

Doug felt as contented as he'd ever been as he lay in bed. Making out with Christine a few more times would erase any memories of what Little had done. He'd done everything right without having done it before. She enjoyed it, for sure. If she hadn't stopped when she did, Doug thought he'd come really close to touching her butt. He tried to recover all the thoughts he'd had the previous summer about things they'd do together; Strawbridge Park seemed to be a good place to make out.

Then, it all drained out of his head in an instant. "She's going out with Parrillo! Why else would he have said that?" he whispered to himself.

They weren't going to be a couple. She and Parrillo were the couple. What had seemed wonderful a short time ago didn't feel wonderful at all.

Palomma impatiently paced back and forth in her room the next Saturday night. Would 7 o'clock ever get there?

After a few dates, Daniel had finally made reservations at a nice restaurant. He'd told her she needed to wear a dress, making it a special night. She'd gone to have her hair done and tried out Paula's new suggestions for lipstick and eye shadow.

"That was wonderful!" said Palomma as they stepped out of the restaurant into the crisp, cold night. "What's next on the dance card this evening?"

"Dance card?" asked Daniel. He scrunched up his face. "Oh, you mean what are we going to do next. Whaddya say we drive around for a while?"

"Sure!" replied Palomma.

Daniel squealed his tires as he pulled out onto the highway. He roared down Route 73, passing cars and weaving back and forth between the lanes. "There's no brake pedal over there," he snickered, seeing Palomma sitting stiffly and pressing her feet against the floorboards.

"Do you think maybe we could go a little slower?" asked Palomma, softly.

"Slower?" answered Daniel. "No point in slower. If you ain't drivin' fast, you ain't drivin', like they say in Nascar!"

"I don't think we're anywhere near the Daytona 500," replied Palomma.

Daniel's face brightened. "I'm impressed! You know about the Great American Race!" He slowed down to around the speed limit. "We're almost where we're going anyway." Daniel exited the highway in the direction of Blessed Sacrament, passed the school and turned into the lot at Morelli's. Instead of stopping in front, he drove around back. The only light behind the building was a single bulb over the back door near the dumpster.

"No one will bother us back here."

Daniel slid over on the front seat, said "C'mere, beautiful!" and put his arm around her. He put his hand behind her head and pulled her toward him, kissing her; she hugged him. They French kissed and Palomma thought how she'd never, ever done that before a month ago, how naturally it had come. It felt good. She wrapped her arms around him tighter.

She felt Daniel's hand slide up to her boobs and didn't stop him. She continued to kiss him as he moved his hand around. Then she started to feel his other hand on her thigh and tensed.

"Mmmmmm, Palomma, I love you," he said. "You're so beautiful."

He moved his hand high on her leg and rubbed her. He pulled her head forward so that her neck was pinned on his shoulder. Palomma moved her arms in front of her and pushed him back gently with her forearms. "Not here…"

"Here, there, anywhere…" Daniel started to sing a line from the Beatles song.

"Um, uh, it's not very private here, you know? I mean, maybe next time…"

"Then how about something else *this time*?" he replied, emphasizing the last two words and reaching down. Palomma glanced down and could see he'd unzipped his pants; he leaned back against the door facing her.

Palomma froze.

"You're moving pretty fast, Daniel! You just said you loved me a few seconds ago!"

"I do," replied Daniel, and moved closer to her again. "Now it's your turn to show how much you love me."

Palomma slid away and leaned back against the passenger door. "What, you go right from I love you to, a blowjob?" She startled herself; she'd never said that word before.

"Jesus, Palomma, it's not like you don't want to!"

Palomma stared at him in disbelief.

"Want to?" she said, her anger rising. "Want to what? Have, do that…
in back of Morelli's?"

Palomma felt the words coming out by themselves. "Maybe I think
saying 'I love you' is special. Maybe I'm not ready to say it." She turned,
crossed her arms and faced straight ahead. "And maybe I'm not cool or
whatever, but if that's what cool girls do, I'll stay…uncool, thank you
very much."

There was silence for almost a minute. Palomma swore she heard a
sniffle. Daniel leaned back and wiped his hand across his eyes.

"I messed up, Palomma. Can I have another chance?" He held his
hand out. "Please?"

Palomma couldn't help it; she turned and touched his hand.

"Daniel, you're a real handsome guy, and I enjoy being with you. I
just think—I think it's way too early for us. Do you know what I mean?"

Daniel looked down at their hands.

"You're right. I was being a jerk." Daniel looked out the windshield
for a couple of seconds and sighed. He looked back at Palomma. "If I
say I'm sorry, will you forgive me?"

Palomma hesitated; she'd never heard an apology phrased like that.

"Um, yeah, sure Daniel…" The thought crossed her mind that maybe
all couples went through stuff like this. "I forgive you."

He pulled her toward him and began kissing her again, more harshly.
He pushed her hand down onto his crotch.

Palomma struggled. Daniel tried to keep her hand between his legs
but she managed to pull it away. He reached toward her and started to
push her skirt up. Palomma shoved him backward with both hands.

Daniel stared at Palomma with a sly look. Palomma breathed in and out heavily a few times.

"Nothing wrong with using our hands, that's making out. You liked it a minute ago!"

Palomma turned away from him and pulled the hem of her dress down as far as she could.

"Take me home Daniel. Take me home *now*," she said firmly.

Daniel stared at her. Then he scowled and turned toward the steering wheel.

"Typical," he sneered. "Tease, say no. Buncha shit!"

He started the truck, revved the engine a couple of times and spun the tires as he pulled away. Palomma sank down in her seat.

They rode to her house in silence. Daniel stopped in front of her house, staring straight ahead. Palomma also stared straight ahead. Then he shut the truck off and turned to Palomma. "Can we start over?" he asked, softly.

Palomma looked down at her lap. "I don't know," she said softly.

"I'll call you," he said.

Palomma leaned over, gave him a quick peck on the cheek and got out of the truck. She didn't look back. When she opened her front door, she heard tires squealing.

Palomma made her way up the stairs in the dark. When she passed Gemma's room, the door was open. She was listening to the radio while cutting photos from a magazine. Gemma heard Palomma walking down the hall and leaned eagerly out her door to catch her. "How was your date?" she whispered, excitedly.

"Over," Palomma replied. She started sobbing. She went into Gemma's room and collapsed in her arms, crying.

Palomma had convinced farm stands to donate pumpkins for the Pumpkin Hop on Friday the 25th; Andy, Doug, Ed and Danny had been picking them up and storing them in Danny's garage, which was always empty because Danny's mother didn't own a car. Danny used it to lift weights instead, which was what he was doing when the other boys arrived the day of the dance.

They went to start loading up the truck Ed had borrowed from his father when Andy called out, "Hey, lots of 'em are rotted!" He fanned the air in front of his nose. "Jesus, how'd you stand the smell?! It stinks like shit in here!"

Danny sat up on the bench press and let out a loud fart. "So does that."

"All right, all right, we'll load up the ones that ain't squishy," said Ed.

They filled the truck to the edge of the cargo bed with a lot of pumpkins still in the garage. "Looks like two trips, Eddie. Got enough gas?" Danny yelled. He turned around, bent over and farted again. "I do!"

Doug followed Ed's truck in his car on the first trip to the school. When they arrived, they found Palomma and Christine in the gym setting up a refreshments table. "Pumpkins are here!" Ed called out, leaning in the gym door. "Half of them, anyway."

The girls walked outside and looked at the truck brimming with pumpkins. "Half? That's *half*?" Palomma asked, incredulously, walking around the truck. "I must've been awfully persuasive!"

Andy began to respond. "A couple of the places only donated a couple, so I persuaded a few more into my car…"

"Wait! Don't tell me!" Palomma turned her back to Andy, covering her ears with her hands. "That way I can't get in trouble!" She laughed and pointed to the gym, "Start bringing them in."

"Sounds like someone's giving orders around here," Doug interjected. "What's the matter, you two have broken arms?"

"Fair enough," answered Palomma. "C'mon, Christine." Christine gave her a dirty look.

Danny stood on the tailgate and started handing down the pumpkins, with Palomma taking the smaller ones. "Ewww!" Christine pinched her nose after making one trip with one small pumpkin. "Now my clothes are going to smell like pumpkins!" Palomma rolled her eyes.

"How about you make sure the DJ's table is set up," said Palomma. That had been her coup. Every dance, people used a DJ from the local radio station. Palomma had called WIFI-92 in Philadelphia and learned Joey Styles, a popular DJ throughout the Delaware Valley, did dances—and they could afford him.

The boys had emptied the truck and returned to Danny's house. It was almost time for the start of the dance when they returned to the school with the rest. "Pumpkins are all in," Doug said, walking up to Palomma. "Anything else?"

"How many?" She couldn't resist. Even though other classes had stolen them, she wondered if they'd set a record.

"455. Not counting the rotten ones. Or the ones we threw at Donovan."

"Wow!" Palomma hadn't been prepared for that number. "That's a new record!"

"Make sure it gets announced," Doug said. "I've gotta go get changed because I stink."

"So what's different?" said Palomma as he started walking away. Doug held up his index finger and made an imaginary mark in the air.

Chapter 12

Palomma's mother picked her up and took her home and she dashed around her house getting ready. She'd just finished drying her hair when she heard a car horn outside. Palomma looked out of her bedroom window and saw Daniel's truck in the street.

Gemma walked in and looked too. "Ignore him, he'll get tired of waiting."

"No," answered Palomma. "*I'm* tired of this."

She put on a coat, walked down the stairs and out the front door. As she approached the truck, Daniel got out and leaned against the fender.

"Hello, Daniel," she said. Daniel stood silently, smoking a cigarette. He took his time taking a last drag and dropping it to the street and crushing it before speaking.

"About the other night. Look, you're a really nice girl, and I guess I wasn't thinking, and I'd really like the chance to start over."

Palomma was about to respond but thought better of it. She stood quietly.

"I mean, I've gone out with other girls, but never with someone who was as smart and…" he paused and looked up, searching for a word, "… as classy as you, and, I screwed up." He took a step towards her.

Palomma took a step back.

"Daniel, you scared me big time! I mean, I think you're a nice guy…"
Daniel interrupted. "Here it comes!"

"Here comes what?"

141

"You're a nice guy, I don't think of you like that, yeah yeah," he said, shaking his head back and forth in a mocking fashion. "Why did you go out with me in the first place?"

Palomma started getting angry.

"Because I thought we could go out and do things and have fun?" she answered.

"Depends on what you think is fun." He lit another cigarette. "Doing things ain't cheap."

And suddenly Palomma felt any feelings she'd had for Daniel vanish.

"I see, dating is like going to your store!" she said, snidely. "You spend money, you get something!"

Daniel took a long drag on his cigarette and flicked the butt into the street.

"I guess we got our wires crossed." He opened the truck door. "You need some time to get your act together. When you change your mind, you can find me at the store."

Palomma went back inside. Just as she finished getting ready Paula pulled into the driveway. "Bye, Mom, I'll call when it's done!" she yelled as she dashed through the front door.

Palomma began telling Paula about what had happened the moment she pulled away from the house. "All I wanted, darn it, I just wanted him to respect me!" Palomma said.

"You wanna know how to tell if a boy respects you?"

"How?" asked Palomma.

"It's simple. You don't until he doesn't."

"What is this, Kung Fu?" said Palomma impatiently, "am I supposed to snatch a pebble out of your hand or something?"

"Palomma, come on. You know what I'm talking about."

Palomma did know, now. Things are always easier to believe when they come from somewhere other than your own head.

"Some boys are really good at saying things to make girls think they're all about love and stuff. They don't know any more about love than you and me—but they know what they want for themselves. They think it's all a game, like...like..." Paula was stuck for an analogy.

"Like handball?" said Palomma

"Oh, that was bad. Whew, that stunk. You've been hanging around Doug too long," said Paula. "Don't tell me, let me guess, he told you he loved you. Boys that want to climb on top of you will always say they love you, like it means anything to them."

"Paula, you make it sound like boys are all rapists!" Palomma sounded upset.

"No, that's not what I mean" said Paula, softly. "I'm talking about the boys who think because they spent some money you owe them something. Shit, there are probably boys who say they love you and believe they do!"

"When'll *that* happen?" asked Palomma, frustrated.

"Patience, grasshopper!" answered Paula, and they both laughed.

Palomma sighed. "So how do you know?"

"When you do," said Paula. "And yeah, I thought that sounded stupid when I heard it. Trouble is, it's probably true."

The Pumpkin Hop was hopping. Manny and Ed had agreed to stand by the two gym entrances to make sure no one snuck in; Beth and Rose Montesano were collecting money at the door. Christine had agreed to hand out refreshments and Doug was taking care of the lights and sound. Palomma hurried from place to place making sure everything was running smoothly. After a series of songs, the music stopped.

"I just want to say it's a blast to be at Blessed Sacrament in Holly Hill New Jersey!" DJ Joey Styles shouted into the microphone.

The dancegoers cheered. "We'll get back to the music in a minute—but first, I wanna thank Palomma Rossi for inviting me here tonight to party with you!" He pointed at Palomma standing near the stage.

"Puh-low-MUH! Puh-low-MUH!" the kids chanted, pumping their fists in the air. Thankfully for her, there was no spotlight, so they couldn't see her turn bright red.

The turnout had been great; the gym was packed. Palomma did some calculations in her head; after refreshments and the DJ fee, the spirit club might make two hundred dollars.

"Whaddya think?" shouted Doug, walking up to Palomma.

"You pointed me out to him, didn't you?" she yelled. Doug bowed.

"How about a dance?" yelled Doug.

Palomma was surprised by the request. "You know how to dance?" she yelled.

"Oh, hell no," yelled Doug. "I just wanted to hear how those words sounded coming out of my mouth!" He walked off toward the back of the gym.

"How about a dance?" yelled Paula, walking up to Palomma.

"You too?" she yelled back.

"You too what?" yelled Paula.

"Yeah, let's dance!" said Palomma, and she joined Paula and a group of girls on the floor.

The night went by quickly. Styles played 'Last Dance Take a Chance' by Sugarloaf at five minutes to 10; when it was done, Palomma turned on the lights to a chorus of boos. She started to walk away but felt a sudden urge to grab the microphone.

"Thanks for coming everyone! And the class of '77 set a new school record tonight with four hundred..." she paused with a panicked look on her face. She looked around the room—it felt like there were a thousand people staring back at her. Right as her hands began to get sweaty, Doug shouted from the back of the room "55!"

Palomma snapped out of it. "A new record of 455 pumpkins for decorations! Good night!" The gym erupted in shouts and cheers. She walked away from the DJ table and felt like she was floating.

Doug, Andy, Ed and Danny made their way to the back of the gym and began breaking down the refreshment tables, drinking all the cups of punch that had been poured but not taken as they worked. Andy let out a huge belch and even Palomma burst out laughing. Then she saw Christine near the entrance putting on her coat. "Leaving so soon?" Palomma called out.

"Oh!" Christine sounded startled. "Oh, um, yeah," she yelled back, turning around. "A couple of people need rides home, and I said I'd take them. See ya!" She walked toward the exit. Palomma didn't see anyone going with her.

Doug walked over to where Palomma was standing with Beth. "How much did we make?" he asked.

"Lots," said Palomma, holding up the stack of money. "Beth, you brought something to carry it in, right?"

"Yeppers," said Beth.

The boys stood motionless in a half-circle around Palomma and Beth. Palomma said, "Um, what did you guys plan to do with the pumpkins?"

"Pumpkins?" Doug asked, "what pumpkins?"

"I don't see any pumpkins," said Danny.

"Why would there be any pumpkins?" added Andy.

Palomma hated it when they ganged up and teased her...and also loved it.

"I know you guys aren't the brightest, so I'll help." She picked up a small pumpkin near the stage. "This, gentlemen, is a pumpkin." She adopted a pose like the presenters on game shows. "Notice the orange hue, notice the stalk at the top. Notice..."

"Okay, okay, we got the notice," said Doug. "We'll get rid of them."

Rose leaned in the door to the gym and shouted, "They're smashing pumpkins! All over the lot! It's a mess!"

Palomma, Doug, Ed and the others took off running toward the doors.

Outside, a few cars roared away and the parking lot had smashed pumpkins everywhere.

"Assholes!" Andy yelled. "Who were they?"

"Hell if I know," said Doug. "I don't think they were ours."

Everyone knew what he meant—some girls had come with boys from other schools.

"God DAMN it!" Palomma yelled. "DAMN it!" She stomped her feet on the asphalt.

"Settle down, Palomma," said Danny. "You'll have a rupture."

"Girls don't rupture," said Doug.

"Could you guys be serious for one second?!" Palomma demanded, waving her arms around. "Can you imagine what's going to happen when the principal sees this? No, you *can't*, because she'll come for *me*, not you!"

Doug walked over to Palomma. "Seriously, Palomma, we'll take care of it. We don't want you getting in trouble, right guys?" He turned toward Danny, Ed and Andy, who all nodded.

Ed walked over to where a few kids who had yet to leave were hanging out. He drafted them to help while Doug and Andy went inside to find something to help move the pumpkins. They found a cart that had basketballs on it, emptied it, and started moving pumpkins into the foyer. Palomma gathered a few smaller pumpkins into her arms and carried them out.

After a couple of trips, she went back outside. Ed had found snow shovels in a janitorial closet; he and the helpers were scooping up pumpkin slop and putting it in the dumpster.

Palomma figured if Sister Teresa said anything about the dumpster, she'd explain some of the pumpkins rolled off the truck when they were taking them away. She knew if she blamed kids from another school, she'd get a lecture about responsibility. Christine would say she wasn't even there.

When she went back into the gym, Andy and Doug had finished moving the pumpkins to the foyer. Ed backed up the truck to the door to the gym and everyone started loading it. "Don't worry about gentle," said Danny. "They're garbage now." The group finished loading and Danny got in the passenger side of the truck. Doug and Andy got into his car. Danny rolled down his window. "Where's Ed?" Danny yelled to Doug. "Hell if I know," Doug yelled back, shrugging.

Inside the gym, Beth was muttering as she tried to stuff the moneybag into her small purse. Ed walked up and stood in front of her. "That's a lot of money for a girl to be carrying around."

"Sure is," she said, "and I hear there was some bullshit outside. I don't need this aggravation!"

"I could hold it for you until Monday," Ed volunteered. "No one's gonna mess with me."

"Could you? That'd be great! In fact," she took out a piece of paper from her bag and spent a few seconds writing on it. "If you were a real sweetheart, you'd take it to the Savings and Loan for me tomorrow." She leafed through the bills, mouthing numbers as she went. "Two hundred eighteen…there!" She bent down and wrote on the slip. "All you have to do is hand the money and this slip to the teller."

Ed reached for the moneybag.

"Unless that's putting you out…" Beth continued.

"No, yeah, I can, no problem." Ed waved to Beth and headed for the door as Palomma was coming back inside.

She had to make sure the building was empty. Palomma looked around and didn't see anything out of place, waited until Beth left and went to the phone booth in the hall to call home. She walked toward the back of the gym, stopped, took one last look around, and saw two pumpkins they'd missed sitting in the corner.

"Screw it," she said, turning and waving her hand. "They can wait until the janitors come in."

She flicked off the lights, pulled the gym doors behind her closed and jiggled them to make sure they were locked. Then she looked up to the sky.

"Thank you," she whispered.

As if on cue, her mother pulled up to the gym. Gemma was in the car too.

"Thought you might need some help," Gemma said.

"Nope, everything's fine." They couldn't see her grinning ear-to-ear in the dim light.

On the way to his car after school on Monday afternoon, Ed heard Beth calling after him. "Ed! Ed! Wait up!" she yelled, jogging toward him.

"Hey, thanks again for taking care of the money for me," she said. "You didn't have any problems, right?"

"Nope, none at all," he answered. He looked at his watch. "Hey, I gotta run, I gotta get to work!"

"Even if it's only 10-to-1, that's still a couple grand," he thought that night as he lay on his bed, thumbing through the money. When he'd seen the wad of bills at the pumpkin hop, he saw a chance to place a bet for more than the few bucks he had.

It was only a few days until the 5-6-7 setup. Of course he'd win. The fix was in. He put the money back in the bag.

It was a sure thing. These guys had been doing this stuff for years. "Hell," he thought, "It would take a scratch to mess it…"

Ed stared at the money bag.

There were a lot of scratches at the track. Sometimes it was an owner not wanting to run for a small purse. But sometimes, a horse woke up lame or sick.

"They'd cancel the race. Bets on scratches are refunded. Yeah. I'd put it in the bank and no one would know."

Unless they'd switched the plan to another horse. Or another race.

Ed realized he'd have no way of knowing. And if he bet the money and lost it…

Ed slammed the cash bag onto his bed.

I Love Liking You A Lot

Chapter 13

That same Monday, after lunch, Kim and Doug were called to the office. They stood in the hall waiting for the principal.

"Are we in trouble or something?" whispered Kim.

"If it was just me, probably," answered Doug. "With you too, I don't know what the hell's going on."

"Language, Mr Halecki," said Sister Teresa, walking out of the office. "There's going to be a publicity photo taken for the Daily Record after school. Be on stage in costume at three."

"Which costume?" asked Kim.

"The finale will do," the principal answered.

"Sister, I have a dentist's…" Doug began to speak but Sister Teresa walked back into the office. "… appointment." He looked at Kim; she shrugged. Doug decided to skip the appointment.

When he got home at 4:30, his mother was in the kitchen. She looked up from making dinner. "Where were you?" she demanded, crossing her arms.

"At school. They were taking pictures for the play."

"Dr. Fisher's office called. You didn't show up for your appointment. He was very angry!" She wagged her finger at Doug with her other hand on her hip.

"I *couldn't*," Doug fired back. "They told us middle of the day the newspaper was coming and we had to stay after and get into costume." Doug stretched his arms out to the side. "What was I supposed to do, skip that?"

"You could have called the dentist's office." She crossed her arms again. "That would've been the responsible thing to do."

"I didn't know the number!" Doug yelled back. "And don't say 'use the phone book,' because there's no phone book in the booth at school!"

"You could have found one if you really tried."

"God, what the hell did I do wrong?" Doug yelled, turning away. "They told me I had to stay!"

"Doctors' appointments are important. You don't skip them without telling someone." Her tone sounded like when Doug was five years old.

Doug got angrier.

"Yeah, right," he yelled. "Doctors' appointments are a hell of a lot more important than me starring in the fucking school play!"

"Lower your voice and watch your language or you're not going to be in anything!"

Doug stopped for a moment, breathing heavily. "Fine," he snarled. "I'll tell the school they have to find someone else to play my part two weeks before opening night because I missed a *reeeeeaaaallly* important dentist appointment and I'm grounded and that'll go over *reeeaaallly* good and how the hell am I going to get into college if I'm not out there doing things…"

"Like smoking? How long have you been smoking?"

"JESUS CHRIST, MOM!!" Doug yelled. "I'm SICK of this shit! Get the hell off my BACK!" He stomped down the hallway, slammed his bedroom door and flopped on the bed.

Doug stared at the ceiling until he heard his father come home. He slammed both fists at his sides into the mattress. Dinner would be in a few minutes. He'd get yelled at again. Probably the belt for skipping the appointment, and the cussing, and the smoking. He slunk to the kitchen when his mother called for dinner.

"You didn't take much," said Doug's father. "What's the matter, are you sick?"

"Huh?" Doug had been playing with his food, nervously waiting for his mother to tell his father what had happened. "Uh, no, just tired, I guess."

He shot a quick glance at his mother. She was looking at her plate, eating silently.

Doug was antsy; until dinner was over, the table cleared and dishes done, there was still a chance. But as he put the last dish away, he saw his mother walk into the living room, his father to their bedroom. Doug went back to his room to change for rehearsals. He heard the phone ring; "Doug! Telephone!" his mother hollered.

"Rehearsal's probably been cancelled," Doug thought. Trouble was, he'd wanted to get out of the house, just in case his mother did say something; now he'd be stuck there.

He stepped out into the hall and picked up the wall phone. "I got it!" he yelled.

"Hello?"

"Hi Doug! It's Christine!"

Doug gulped.

"Oh, hey, Christine. What's up?"

"My Daddy took my car to the shop and I don't have a ride to practice tonight. Could you give me one?" she asked, her voice hitting a lot of high notes.

Doug was taken by surprise. "Yeah, I guess. I was just getting ready to leave. Will you be ready when I get there?"

"Sure will! See you in a few!"

"I'm a yo-yo," Doug said to himself, as he pulled out of his driveway.

"A fucking yo-yo." Doug talked to himself a lot. As much as he wanted to feel like he'd made Christine 'come to him,' he hadn't done anything after they'd made out. He gripped the wheel with both hands, and then slammed the palm of his hand on the steering wheel.

Doug arrived at Christine's house and knocked on her front door; her father answered. "Oh, hello! Doug, right?" Mr. Holloway was a lean, angular man with a shock of gray hair. He extended his hand.

"Yes, hello Mr. Holloway," Doug replied, shaking his hand.

"Christine!" he called into the house, "Doug's here!" Mr. Holloway gestured into the living room. "Come on in, she'll be right out." Doug sat on a stuffed chair in the corner of the room.

She didn't come right out so Doug tried to make small talk. "That's a really nice car Christine has, Mr. Holloway. What's wrong with it?"

"Nothing, it was in for regular maintenance and they didn't finish."

Christine's mother came in, wearing an apron over her dress. "Hello, Doug! Christine's told us about you!"

Doug stood up and shook her hand. "Hi, Mrs. Holloway. Was any of it good?"

"You are funny, like she said!" laughed Christine's mother. "I'm sure she'll be ready in a minute. Christine!"

Doug sat down again and looked at his watch.

After he'd waited five more minutes, Christine walked casually into the room. "Hi Doug! I was on the phone."

"Don't be too late," her father said, and they walked out to Doug's car.

"Thanks *soooo* much for the ride," Christine said as she got in. "No big deal," Doug said, backing out of the driveway. He hesitated, then asked, "Do you need a ride home after too?" It was worth a try.

"No, I've got that covered." Doug's shoulders slumped.

As they drove to school, Doug thought back to Strawbridge Park. He wished he could think of something to say that might have them end up there again.

Christine broke the silence. "It's only nine days until opening night, Horace! Excited?"

Doug put parking out of his mind. "Yeah, a little scared too." He kept looking straight ahead.

"Never fear," Christine said, sliding over and touching Doug on the arm. "You'll be a smash hit! Broadway here you come!"

Doug took a deep breath—and put his arm over her shoulder. She didn't move away.

Now as Doug drove down Holly Avenue, he was drawing a blank. Should he talk? Keep quiet? Christine was leaning against him now, and she smelled really nice. Her hair tickled his face. The only thing he could think to do was to sing from the play. "*It takes a woman, all powdered and pink, to joyously clean out the drain in the sink…*"

Christine burst out laughing. "Oh Doug! You crack me up!" She put her hand on his knee.

As they turned toward the school, Doug was certain he heard Christine let out a tiny sigh; he wished he'd taken his time driving. As they walked into the gym together a few cast members in the gym hooted.

Doug approached the stage; Palomma was perched on its edge. "And what were you two doing, hmmm?" she said.

"I can't speak for Christine, but I was driving a car." Doug tried to sound mundane.

"How many hands on the wheel? Ten-and-two positions?" Palomma held her hands out in front of her as if on a steering wheel. She opened her palms. "Wait, maybe I shouldn't say anything about positions!" she exclaimed loudly.

Doug blushed again. *Damn* that.

He turned and noticed Christine was ignoring the kidding. She'd taken off her coat a little distance away, set it on the bleachers and gotten out her script.

Doug looked back to Palomma. "You have a dirty mind. I'm telling the nuns on you."

"You've been giving rides to the nuns *too*?" she shot back, hands on her hips. "Douggie, you need to slow down, save something for the show!"

Director Stern walked out from backstage. "Performers in the bleachers! Stage crew! First half-hour is scene change practice!" Doug, Palomma and Christine started to move to the bleachers when Christine spoke up. "Oh, shit! I have to go make a phone call!" She walked toward the pay phone in the hall.

"That's weird," said Palomma, watching her walk away.

"Weird?" said Doug

"Weird she has to call someone right after she gets here," Palomma responded, turning toward Doug. "Were her parents home when you picked her up? And wait—why did you pick her up? She has a car."

"Not tonight," said Doug. "Her car was being fixed or something. Yeah, her parents were home, I met them." He leaned forward, resting his elbows on his knees. "Spent a lot of time with them, she was taking so long to get ready."

"What's there to get ready?" replied Palomma, looking back toward the phone booth again.

"Something about a phone call. I figured it was you."

Palomma turned back. "If it was me, I would've known about it; since I didn't know, you should have known it wasn't me."

"Okay! Sue me!" said Doug, holding up his hands defensively. Sue O'Brien looked over at them from further down the bleachers. "Not you, another Sue," Doug said, waving at her.

"I think Sue likes you," said Palomma, and she poked Doug with her elbow. "You know what they say about younger women."

"What do they say?" asked Doug.

"Or maybe you're into older women! Christine is older than you by, like, a week, right? How many places did you stop with Christine on the way here?"

Doug blushed again. Palomma realized she might be going overboard with the teasing.

They watched the stage crew practice for a few minutes; Palomma looked back toward the hallway. "What the heck could she be doing for half an hour?"

It hadn't been a half-hour, but it was longer than you got for a dime. Doug also looked at the booth. They could see Christine was sitting on the floor of the booth twirling her hair with her free hand. Mrs. Stern walked to the front of the stage and called out, "Chorus! We're doing the restaurant scene! On stage now!"

"I'll go get her," said Palomma. She'd gotten about halfway when she saw Christine stand up. She looked around quickly, saw Palomma coming, hung up and came out of the booth.

"That's all for tonight! Good rehearsal! Tomorrow night, same time!" called out Mrs. Stern from the front of the stage at the end of the night. Cast members began putting on their coats to leave.

"Sure you don't need a ride?" Doug said, hopefully, walking toward Christine in back of the gym.

Christine shook her head 'no' and walked out the door.

Doug turned around. "Kim? You?" he asked, as she approached. "No, Horace, my Mom's here," said Kim.

"Valerie? Sue? Anyone? Does anyone need a ride?" Doug called out, turning one way and the other.

Palomma walked up behind him.

"You didn't ask me!" she said, crossing her arms and making a pouty face.

"By God, you are 100% correct!" Doug said, turning around. "Palomma, would you like a ride home?"

"Why would I possibly want a ride home with *you*?" Palomma fired back, laughing. It also got a laugh from those who were standing around.

Doug chuckled. "Seriously, though, do you need a ride?"

"As a matter of fact, yeah," Palomma responded. "It'll save me calling my Mom."

"You live out near Fox Meadow Golf Course, right?" Doug said as they drove down Main Street. "I gave Valerie Pisani a ride home and she pointed out your house."

"Yep, that's the place," said Palomma. She turned toward Doug. "Giving rides to Valerie Pisani *too*?"

"Are you going to start again?" he replied, laughing.

Doug put a tape into the 8-track player. "Have you heard of Blue Oyster Cult?" he asked. "Andy turned me on to them. They do 'Don't Fear the Reaper.'"

"I've heard it on the radio," said Palomma. "It's good."

Doug sang along for a while. There was a stretch where the song quieted with a light guitar riff and light cymbal, followed by an explosive guitar solo; at the point the solo started, Doug turned the volume all the way up.

"AAAAAAUUUUGGGHHHHHHH!" Palomma screamed.

Doug laughed. "You scared the shit out of me!" said Palomma.

"I'm sorry, I really like that part," Doug answered. "And did you just say 'shit'?"

"No…" said Palomma, not convincingly.

"Don't lie, you said shit. Palomma, what's next, smoking?" chided Doug.

"I'm always smoking," Palomma shot back. "Smoking hot."

Doug laughed. "I'm getting killed tonight. I need Christine to give me straight lines."

Palomma didn't respond.

In a few minutes, they turned onto Palomma's street; her house was on the right with a driveway alongside. "Driveway or front?" Doug asked.

"What? Oh, the driveway's fine."

Palomma picked up her purse and script off the floor. "See you tomorrow, Doug!" she said, opening the door. She had one leg out of the car when she turned back toward him, lowering her head inside the car door.

"Speaking of Christine," she said, looking down at the seat, "I've been curious about…" She couldn't do it. She wanted to know why Doug had been acting differently around Christine but was too afraid to say it.

"…about whether you heard anything about Christine getting a job?"

"Not a peep." He thought it strange Palomma wouldn't know.

"It's just she's been missing Friday rehearsals. I thought she got a job and had to work," Palomma said rapidly.

"I don't know, I have a tough time picturing Christine in a McDonald's uniform," said Doug. "God knows why Mrs. Stern doesn't get stern with her about missing rehearsals."

"Who knows?" said Palomma, shrugging as she stepped out. She closed the door.

Doug waited until she got into the house, started the car, backed out, and left.

After rehearsal, Christine had walked down to Morelli's where Daniel was waiting and got into his truck, sitting on his hand, which he'd stretched out on the passenger seat.

"Daniel!" she cried out in the faux-surprised way girls save for their boyfriends. "Rehearsal ran late tonight; I can't stay out much longer." He took the next right turn very sharply and Christine slid across the seat, ending up right next to him. "That's called a C.O.D. turn—Come over, dear!" he said. "Now let's…"

Christine interrupted Daniel; she saw Doug's car ahead of them with Palomma in the passenger seat.

"Daniel, you see that car up there? Follow it."

"That piece of shit? I can blow it off the road!" He punched the gas pedal, closing the distance.

"Not so fast, Speedy Gonzalez!" said Christine. "You don't need any more tickets. Stay back."

They followed at a distance with Doug's car always in sight. After about ten minutes, Christine saw the car turn onto Rotary Way.

"Daniel, drive past Palomma's house. You DO know which one it is, right?"

"Yeah, I know. Knew. Whatever," he replied, waving a hand.

As they started up Rotary Way, Daniel slowed to a crawl. Christine could see Doug's car in Palomma's driveway. "Not so fast," Christine said, motioning with her palm. "Slower, but not too slow."

"Slower-but-not-too-slow-Jesus" he muttered, shaking his head.

Christine stared out the window and saw Palomma get out and walk toward her house.

"What was that all about?" said Daniel.

Christine jumped. "Nothing! I was thinking, that's all."

"I'm thinking too," he replied, "I'm thinking there's no one at the golf course…"

"Daniel, not tonight. I told you I have to get home, I'm late as it is."

"You had time for whatever that was," he said. "It's time you paid me some attention."

"All right, just a little while."

They pulled into the golf course and drove to the far end of the lot. Christine climbed onto his lap again and they began to kiss. Within seconds, Christine felt Daniel's hand between her thighs. He'd tried it the last time they'd made out, and when she'd squeezed her legs together, he'd taken it away. This time he didn't and kept trying to push it further up her leg. Christine pulled her head back.

"Daniel, I told you, not yet!"

"And I told you what I wanted," he whispered as he tried to slide his other hand under her waistband.

Christine tried to push both of his hands away. "Daniel, I said I don't…"

She heard the sound of stones crunching under a car's tires in the parking lot. Christine slid over to the passenger side. A car door slammed shut, and a light shown through the window.

There was a tap on the glass; Daniel rolled the window down to see a policeman pointing his flashlight around the front seat.

"Didn't you see the 'No Trespassing' sign?" he said. Christine tilted her head forward so her hair would hide her face.

"I'm sorry, officer, you know how it is," said Daniel.

The policeman bent down, shining the light in Daniel's face.

"No liquor in the truck, Parrillo?"

"None, officer. We stopped, you know, to, you know." Daniel motioned with his head toward Christine.

The policeman shut off the flashlight and stood up straight. "Next time you're going to 'you know,' go to the drive-in, you know?" He pointed toward the entrance to the lot. "Now get lost." He walked back to his car.

Daniel started the truck and drove away slowly. "Why does that policeman know your name?" asked Christine.

"He, um, comes into the store a lot. For coffee."

Daniel pulled out of the parking lot. He hadn't gotten a quarter mile down the road when the police car's lights came on behind him. He pulled over. Christine was staring at him with fear in her eyes.

The policeman came to the window again.

"Officer, I wasn't speeding…" Daniel started to say.

"Your headlights, dummy," the policeman responded, pointing to the dashboard. "You forgot to turn on your headlights."

"Oh…thank you, officer!" said Daniel, turning on the headlights. The policeman shook his head and returned to his car. Christine took a hairbrush from her purse and turned the rearview mirror toward herself.

"How about…" Daniel started to speak.

"Uh-uh," interrupted Christine. "Nope. See what happens when you don't do what you're told?" She stopped brushing and faced him. "And another thing, you slow down when I'm with you!" She jabbed the hairbrush at him for emphasis. "I don't want MY name in the paper after you hit something!"

Daniel stared straight ahead and slowed down to the speed limit. Christine went back to brushing her hair.

The next morning at school the gym was its usual beehive of activity, Beth yelled to Ed while he played tennis ball soccer.

"Hey, thief!"

Ed jumped. He turned to see Beth walking toward him. "Time out, guys!" he yelled, and he turned toward her. He fidgeted, trying to think of an explanation as she approached.

Beth stood in front of him with her hands on her hips.

"You never gave me back my money bag!" she said.

Ed let out a huge sigh. "Oh yeah, sorry. I left it in my locker."

"Let's go get it." She started walking out of the gym to the lockers. Ed hurried to move alongside her.

"So, did you go to the track and double our money?" she asked.

"What?" Ed stopped walking.

"The track. Horses. Bets. Win. Place. Show. All that shit," said Beth, gesturing alternately with each hand.

"Oh, hell no. Why would you think I'd do something like that?" Ed chuckled, hoping he sounded convincing.

Beth reached up and put her hand behind his neck and pulled his head down. For a split second, he thought she was going to kiss him. Instead, she whispered, "Because you told me in religion you work at a race-track, you dumbass."

Their faces remained within inches. Ed smiled.

"I took excellent care of it," he said. "I slept with it at night."

Beth paused and let go of his head. Ed straightened up.

"That's a new one," she said. "Someday we're gonna have to have a little talk about what people should and shouldn't be in bed with. In the meantime, cough it up."

Ed's opened his locker, took out the bag and held it high so she couldn't reach it.

"You know, if I kicked you in the nuts, that bag would come down really fast."

Ed laughed and handed her the bag.

I Love Liking You A Lot

Chapter 14

November fifth was a beautiful day at Garden State Park. Patrons were engaged in various activities, watching horses getting exercised and studying the Racing Form for tips before the day's card began.

Preparing to place the bet had been easy—Ed changed the singles and fives from the dance into twenties. He cut school because his mother wouldn't call him in sick if he wasn't actually sick.

But actually doing it, placing the bet, wasn't turning out to be as easy as Ed thought it would be.

Ed's father never gambled. He'd taken Ed aside at the track and pointed out the destitute men trying to scrape together two bucks to place another bet, the one that would change their luck. Except it was always the next one, and the next one.

He'd made Ed promise to never gamble; he was pretty persuasive. "You're gonna drink, so did I. You're gonna screw around and you'll probably get high; as long as someone else is buying, so what? But gambling is for stupid assholes, and I sure as hell didn't raise one."

Ed tried to convince himself this wasn't gambling—the race was fixed.

He'd repeated, "November fifth, sixth, number seven" to himself all week. He tried to act interested in the earlier races, but really only wanted the clock to move faster.

There wasn't going to be any problem. He'd win, he'd deposit the $218 Beth gave him in the bank and keep the rest. He'd plop a big stack of cash down on the kitchen table. His mother would be so happy; they could go out for something to eat for the first time in God-knows-how-long.

And in a couple of seconds, his father would ask him where it came from.

What was he going to say, he held up a store?

He'd tell them he borrowed it from the club at school for a little while, big deal, so what? He'd point to all the money. And his father would say it was stealing, the ends didn't justify the means. He'd remind Ed of his promise to never gamble.

Ed realized he could tap dance around it, but he wasn't good with words like Doug. Whatever he said would be bullshit and would sound like it.

Ed and his father trusted each other without hesitation—Ed knew no matter what, there would always be one person that had his back. Except now he'd have betrayed that trust.

It was getting close to the start of the sixth race, and Ed saw some commotion in the paddock. Nothing had changed on the tote board, no scratches; what was going on down there? The grooms led the horses to the starting gate. It looked like there was a delay in stall number seven; a track worker had his arms outstretched as if confused. Ed knew he had to get over to the window and place his bet fast or they'd shut down wagers for the race—but something might be going on, if he could only see.

The next day, Ed took the $218 and deposited it in the bank.

After the bank, Ed drove to the library and checked a newspaper. The number seven had indeed started the race and had won, like it was supposed to. Ed put it back and walked out of the library. He told school his car broke and he didn't have a ride; they bought it and simply marked him absent.

"Doug, I need a favor!" Palomma said in the hallway after that day's lunchtime dress rehearsal.

Doug stopped near his locker. "Sure, what's up?"

"My Mom's been letting me use the car a lot more…"

"It needs a tune-up? Geez, I don't know Palomma, I'm a little busy the next few days."

Palomma crossed her arms and tapped her foot. "I'll wait until you're finished."

"I'm done," said Doug.

"I can't use it tonight, Mom has a meeting at church. I know it's short notice, but could you give me a ride both ways?"

"Sure, no problem. I'll pick you up about 6:30."

"I'm sorry to put you out; I could give you gas money."

"Palomma, I gave Kim a ride home to Palmyra the other night," said Doug. "What are you, a couple-few miles from school? I'll see you at 6:30."

"Great, here's my number in case you need to call."

She reached into her purse and was about to hand him a slip of paper but hesitated for a second. The whole scene of Daniel asking for her number came flashing back. Doug took it and shot a quick glance at her. Palomma looked down and pretended to rearrange things in her purse.

While they'd been talking, Christine walked by; Doug saw her drift a little closer to them as she passed as if trying to hear what they were saying. Doug tapped Palomma on the arm, winked, and said, "Where do you want to go after rehearsal tonight?"

Doug motioned with his shoulder toward Christine, winking again; Palomma caught on.

"Let me see, let me see…how about the Homestead?" she said,

putting a finger to her chin.

"They'll card us there. The Carousel doesn't card, you'll get in."

"Carousel it is! See you later, my darling!" said Palomma, over-emphasizing the words.

"*Au revoir, mon cherie!*" replied Doug, walking away.

They both shot a glance at Christine, who'd never turned around but had come to a complete stop. Doug and Palomma looked at each other and covered their mouths to keep from laughing.

"You're not her type, you know."

Doug had walked down the hall to room six and had barely reached a table when Christine came up behind him and spoke. He sat down; she sat down next to him; usually, she sat across from him.

"Type?" asked Doug, turning to her. "Her type?"

"Look, I consider you a friend," she said, "and I don't want you get hurt." Her tone was oddly serious.

Doug thought for a second. "You're talking about Palomma, right? In the hall? Hell, we were just kidding around."

Christine blushed and looked away.

"Oh…yeah, I knew, I was funning with you!" she said, turning back to him with an exaggerated smile. "Gotcha!" Christine tried to act as if she knew it had all been a joke. "I can tell you someone who's got a major crush on you!"

"Sister Teresa?"

"No, really!!" said Christine, touching Doug on the arm. "Jackie Jardine is always talking about you!"

"You had the first half right," Doug replied, pulling a notebook out of his book pile. "Jackie Jardine is always talking."

"You love it, you know you do!" Christine said. She wrote "Jackie & Doug" on the notebook and drew a heart around it.

Doug sighed. "Let's get to work on the article."

Christine got up, walked around to the other side of the table and sat down.

Doug went to room seven when they'd finished working. He often ended the day there; he and Ed could play table golf. The game involved knocking a balled-up scrap of paper with the eraser end of a pencil toward 'holes,' little circles drawn on the table.

Doug sat down; Ed was staring out the window with his arms crossed over his chest. "Golf?"

"Huh?" Ed turned his head. "Oh. What'ya want?"

Doug sat at the table next to the desk Ed was sitting in. "Something eating you?" he replied.

Ed looked back out the window. "Naaah, nothing. Nothing major. I thought there was a chance of making more money at work, it didn't happen." He turned toward Doug. "Same old shit, different day. What else is fucking new, you try to get somewhere, you get nowhere." He moved over to the table across from Doug. "Christ, if I could just catch one break, it doesn't have to be..."

Ed looked up and saw Doug was staring at him.

"Yeah, right. Golf. Cool. I tee off first because you suck."

Ed rolled up a ball and tapped it with a pencil. Over time they'd come up with a variety of rules: the first shot had to be from the edge of the table; knocking the ball off the table was a one-stroke penalty.

While Doug was writing down Ed's score from the first hole, Ed folded his hands in front of him and rested his chin on them. "You're going out with Palomma now?"

"WHAT is going ON today?" Doug yelled.

"If you young men can't quiet down, you're going to have to leave," Miss Loman said from her desk. The students in an appointment with her also looked over.

"What is going on today?" Doug said in a loud, exaggerated whisper.

Loman shook her head.

"Nothing's going on. I saw you talking to her, and you said sweet-heart. What else would it mean?"

Doug batted the ball toward the hole in front of Ed and tapped it onto the circle.

"It was darling, and she said it," Doug replied. "Besides, mind your own business, we were kidding around."

Ed leaned back. "Don't get touchy! I was trying to act interested. Fuck you, instead."

"That's better," Doug said. They went back to playing.

After a few more holes, Ed said, "You gave up on Holloway?"

"I don't know," Doug said, leaning back and staring at the table. "I can't figure her out." Ed tapped the ball onto the hole. "Like, the other night she needed a ride, and she slid over next to me. She didn't even mind when I put my arm around her. Hell, she put her hand on my leg!"

Ed pushed the ball toward Doug. "Then what did you do next?"

"Nothing. Then we got there and she ignored me."

"It's a game, don't you get it?" Ed sounded exasperated. "She teases, you respond, she stops. You asshole, ever hear of playing hard to get?"

Doug thought for a second. "Maybe you're right."

"I'm always right," corrected Ed. The bell rang for homeroom. "Quick! We have to finish this game!" They furiously batted the ball of paper back and forth to complete nine holes.

That night, Palomma was already stepping out of the front door as Doug pulled into her driveway. She cut across the lawn and hopped into the passenger side.

"Thanks again," she said as she got in. "Sure you don't need gas money?"

"Nope, like I said, I'm good." Doug played music but didn't talk or sing all the way to school. Palomma figured he was nervous about opening night being only a day away.

The rehearsal was shorter because of the day's practice performance. Mrs. Stern called cast members onstage to work on specific scenes. There wasn't much for the chorus, so Palomma went backstage to watch from there. Christine was absent again, too. When it was over, Palomma sat in the bleachers until Doug came off the stage. "Ready?" he asked.

"Ready," she answered.

They walked out to his car in silence. This time Doug didn't even put music on. He pulled out of the parking lot and turned down Coles Avenue as if he was going to his own house.

"Damn!" he said, realizing his mistake. He turned to Palomma at the stop street. "Sorry, I'm…"

"I know. I am too and I'm just a chorus girl."

Doug smiled. He turned back to watch the road. At the next stop sign, he looked over at her again and smiled again.

To break the silence, Palomma told him about how her sister had asked if the guy who'd dropped her off the other night was the star of the play. "I told her, no, it's just Doug."

Doug laughed. "I guess I'm thinking about how cool this all is, I never did anything like this before. I remember…"

He stopped. Palomma noticed a sad look had come over his face. "Never mind, it's boring." he said.

"One thing you never are is boring," said Palomma. "Silly, but never boring."

"Thanks, I think I resemble that," said Doug,

Palomma grimaced. The Three Stooges again. "You were saying?"

she asked.

"I never got picked to be in the plays at St. John's," he began. "I never really got picked for anything. I wanted to, raised my hand, signed up..."

He turned toward Palomma at a red light. "Picked *on*, yeah. Picked *for*, nyet."

"That's mean," said Palomma.

Doug talked about grade school for a while until he noticed he'd driven past the turn for Palomma's house a couple of miles.

"Damn!" he said. He pulled to the side of the road. "I'm sorry, Palomma. I'll apologize to your parents for you being late."

"Doug, it is not a problem. I told you I needed a ride tonight because my Mom had a meeting; she's probably not even home yet!"

"What about your Dad?"

"He's working late."

"Ohhhh, okay." Doug made a u-turn and started back toward her house.

Doug stopped in her driveway but Palomma didn't get out right away. She turned to Doug and said, "You'll be great. Like Welcome Day. You're a natural!"

"I guess I'm scared and..." Doug hesitated, "then it's over. Then work starts again. And some things haven't been going good. You know..." He trailed off and stopped talking.

Palomma wasn't sure what other things Doug was talking about but thought it might have been about Christine. She was about to say something when Doug spoke up. "Like I said, sorry about running my mouth."

"You tell really good stories," said Palomma, gently touching his arm. "I enjoy them!" She started to get out of the car, and then stopped.

"You know, my Mom told me things happen for a reason. We're just not supposed to know the reason before they happen. See you tomorrow!" She closed the car door and walked toward her house.

Doug drove home feeling strange. He hadn't necessarily enjoyed thinking back to his grade school days, but this had been the first time he'd been able to tell anyone about them. He thought back to Palomma listening and realized something he'd never thought of before. Palomma was attractive—but it wasn't so much how she looked. It was her personality.

When Doug got home, he was surprised to see lights on, well past when his parents went to bed. Doug couldn't think of what he'd done wrong. He walked in the back door. took a deep breath and went into the living room. His parents were sitting in two chairs with the TV off.

"Okay, I messed up," he said. "I didn't say what time I'd be getting home…"

"Tomorrow's the big night, huh?" his father interrupted, leaning forward.

"What?" said Doug, confused. "Oh, yeah, the play. Yeah. Tomorrow's opening night." He was relieved he wasn't going to get yelled at and started walking down the hall to his room.

"Your picture was in today's paper!" his mother called after him. "The front page!"

"Who's the girl?" asked his father.

Doug stopped. His parents never asked him about activities he was involved in before. Now, all of a sudden they were interested, and Doug wasn't prepared for it. He walked back into the living room and stood in front of them.

"Kim Casey. She's a junior. She's Dolly," he answered.

"She's pretty," said his mother. "And so is her gown. I can see why you stayed for the photos now."

His mother winked at him. Doug couldn't believe it.

"You know the last time I saw our name in the paper?" asked his father, sitting back. "Back when you were born! And tonight, there it was, on the front page! A Halecki on the front page!" He reached for the paper next to Mrs. Halecki. "I can't wait to show the guys at work!"

Doug didn't say anything. This was all new and strange.

Doug's father examined the front page again. Then his mother spoke with a kind of hesitation in her voice Doug couldn't recall ever hearing. "I know it's the last minute," she said, "but are there any tickets left?"

Doug thought about the two free tickets everyone in the cast got, still in the desk drawer in his room.

"Um, yeah, I can get a couple," he answered.

"Good!" she responded. Doug was surprised by how relieved she sounded.

Doug started to turn again to go to his room.

"Tell him what else was in the paper, Ernest," said his mother in an admonishing tone. Doug stopped and turned around again.

"What? Oh," replied Doug's father. "It was in the police report. Your old friend Dwight Tucker got arrested."

"Tell him what for," said his mother. Doug sat down on the couch.

"The cops picked him up for vandalizing our old house. Spray painting cuss words on it."

When Doug's father didn't continue, his mother picked up the story.

"Mrs. Rodriguez took Polaroids of him doing it! How smart was that! She gave them to the police and they went to Dwight's house. Tell him what he said when they asked him if he'd done it!"

Doug's father looked at Doug. "Tucker told them someone who used to live in the Rodriguez house did it. They didn't print your name, though."

"Because they knew he was lying," his mother finished.

Doug's father stood up. "Speaking of taking pictures, can people take pictures at your show? I still got that Instamatic somewhere."

"Yeah, I never heard you couldn't," answered Doug.

"Could we come on Friday night?" asked his mother.

"Sure," said Doug. He stood up. "I'm pretty tired. Good night!"

The second Doug closed his bedroom door he was angry with himself. This was the kind of attention he wanted from his parents, but instead of talking to them some more, he left. He remembered what Palomma had said and was about to go back out to tell them more about the play when he heard their bedroom door close.

Doug went to bed and stared at the ceiling.

I Love Liking You A Lot

Chapter 15

It was Friday night, closing night, the final performance and the final scene.

"The front room, idiot! Well, go on! What are you waiting for?" said Doug.

"Horace Vandergelder, what is going on here?" responded Kim.

"Oh nothing, I just thought I'd have that front room done over in blue wallpaper."

Doug delivered a long speech referring to scenes from earlier in the show. When he finished, Kim looked up at the ceiling and said, "Thank you, Ephraim!" to her deceased husband.

The finale music began.

Doug sang, "Hello, Dolly, well hello, Dolly, it's so nice to have you here where you belong!" He took Kim's hand and led her to the front of the stage.

"I never knew, Dolly, without you, Dolly, life was awfully flat, and more than that, was awfully wrong." Doug put his arm around Fran's waist; they joined hands at face level, and began dancing.

The gym was silent except for the piano and the sound of their feet on the stage. They danced their eight bars, moved over to the prop store counter and stopped. Kim sang "So here's my hat, Horace, I'm stayin' where I'm at, Horace, Dolly'll never go awaaaayy…"

Doug interjected, "Wonderful Woman!"

And they both sang, "Agaaaaaaaaaaaiiin!"

After the last two notes, the gym erupted in applause.

Kim hugged Doug and planted a kiss flush on his lips, something she hadn't done the previous two nights. Doug wrapped her up in a hug as the audience cheered and whistled—and he realized he hadn't blushed.

After their final bows, cast members went to the classrooms that served as dressing rooms.

Doug got changed and walked down the hall toward the gym. He'd always hated the feeling when something enjoyable ended and the play had been more fun than he'd imagined. Turning the corner from the hall into the gym, he was surprised to see his parents still there, waiting near the bleachers.

"That was wonderful!" his mother said.

"Thanks, Mom."

His father studied him for a second with his hand to his chin.

"You know what would've looked even better?" he said. "If you had a mustache!"

Mr. Halecki smiled. Doug started laughing.

"They wouldn't let me try to grow one!" he answered, smiling. "They said it would be unfair to the other guys in school."

"How many other guys in the school were the star of the play?" his mother said, giving him a hug. Doug felt a warmth inside he honestly couldn't recall.

"Co-star," Doug corrected.

"I took pictures," his father said. "I don't know if they came out, but I got some of you and…what did you say her name was?"

"Kim," answered Doug. "Kim Casey. She's a junior"

They gym was almost empty by now; a custodian was folding and stacking chairs. "We better get going! It's past our bedtime!" said Doug's mother. They turned to leave.

"Hey, Dad," Doug called after them. "I could take your film to get developed if you want!"

"Deal," his father answered. "I'll leave it on the table. Don't stay out too late!"

They walked out of the gym. Doug watched them leave, then walked back to the stage and stared at it for a while.

After changing from their costumes and taking off their stage make-up, Christine and Palomma were on their way to the cast party. Christine lit a cigarette and held the pack toward Palomma; she didn't like smoking but took one and lit it.

"That was SO cool!" gushed Christine. "It sure was!" answered Palomma. They excitedly talked about how the final performance had gone. When they stopped at a traffic light, Christine suddenly changed the subject.

"How are things with Daniel?"

Palomma was startled. "Um, things, with Daniel..." She alternately looked down, out the side window and ahead.

"Ooooooo, lovers' secrets, huh?" Christine teased.

Palomma turned to look at Christine. "Things with Daniel...aren't."

"Whaaaa? What happened? Did you break up with him?" Christine sounded shocked.

"Yeah, sort of, I mean, I didn't say those words," said Palomma, turning back toward the window. "Could we change the subject?"

They drove for a few seconds in silence. Palomma's cigarette had gone out. She dropped the butt into the ashtray.

"Did he break up with you?" Christine asked.

"Urrrrgggghhhh!"

"Fine, fine, but you're my best friend," said Christine. "I want to know! What happened?"

Palomma figured this would go on until she answered.

"It really wasn't working out." She turned and sat with one knee bent toward Christine. "In the beginning, everything was fine, we went to a movie, to dinner, but he wanted to, uh, park and I thought we were just going to, um," Palomma felt herself blush. She began speaking very fast. "He tried to go way too far, and I got mad and he got mad when I wouldn't let him, then he apologized but he tried again and I got mad again and he stopped by my house and we got our wires crossed. That's it." She turned and sat facing straight ahead again.

"Oh," said Christine. "That sucks. Boys can really mess things up."

"They sure can." Palomma was surprised at how much better she felt telling Christine. She turned to face her as she'd been before. "You're my best friend and I should have told you. I guess I felt a little, you know, embarrassed, and…"

"Hey, you're probably better off!" Christine interrupted.

"It wasn't so much…" Palomma began to speak again.

"Did you see Melody after the show?" said Christine. "She wouldn't go anywhere near Kim! If you ask me, I didn't think she…"

Christine went on gossiping and Palomma tried to listen but was confused. Now it seemed Christine didn't want to hear anything else about Daniel even though Palomma wanted to tell her.

"Like I was saying," Palomma interrupted and tried to continue.

"Here's Mrs. Stern's studio!" said Christine cheerily.

Mrs. Stern hosted the party for all cast and crewmembers. A buffet table sat under the ballet rails on one side of the room and streamers hung from the ceiling. The soundtrack from 'Hello, Dolly!' was playing in the background. When Doug arrived, most everyone was already there.

Kim walked up to him holding a cup of punch.

"Oh my God, I made it through without cracking up!" she said.

"At what?" asked Doug. "My dancing?"

"No! In the restaurant scene! Every time you did that line 'I've lost my purse,' I thought I was gonna lose it! All I could picture was you swishing around, carrying a purse!"

Doug tried not to change expression. "Yeah, it was a dumb line, wasn't it? I guess that's what they called wallets back then." Doug saw Christine and Palomma sitting at one of the tables across the room and walked over to them.

Palomma stood up when she saw him coming. "See?" she said. "I told you! You were great, and that last performance was the *piece de resistance*!"

"Whew," he said. "I thought you were going to say it was a piece of something else!" Doug didn't know whether he should sit down or ignore Christine some more. He decided to sit at the next table.

"By the way, you forgot this in the dressing room," Palomma said to Christine, holding a necklace. "Keep it," she answered, "I have a new one." She pointed to a thin silver chain around her neck.

Kids came and went from Doug's table, telling stories and making jokes. Andy sat down next to Doug and poked him with his elbow, pointing down; when Doug looked, he saw Andy had a pint bottle of tequila. "Drop something," he said, and Doug caught on. He said "Oops!" and ducked down on his knees; Andy handed him the bottle and he took a swig.

Mrs. Stern was taking photos and Doug posed with various cast members. He also dropped something a couple more times. By the time the photos were done, he was feeling dizzily content. Then Doug felt something touch him. He turned his head to see Palomma holding a gray chain, trying to put it around his neck.

It was one he'd seen Christine wearing all the time.

Doug sat still while Palomma succeeded in securing the clasp. "Kim got flowers, you should've gotten something too!" Palomma said cheerily. Then she walked toward the refreshments table.

Doug thought for a second, then got out of his chair, turned and squatted in front of Christine. "Wanna get a smoke?" he asked.

Christine looked around. "Okay, I guess" she said. "Go ahead, I'll be out in a sec."

Doug walked outside, lit a cigarette and waited. Ed had talked about girls playing hard to get and Christine had barely said a word to Doug after the show; maybe this was all part of it. He had practically finished his cigarette when Christine finally came out.

"Christine, I…" Doug began. Christine interrupted.

"I know what you're going to say, and the answer is no."

Doug tried to speak again. "Christine, wait!" She cut him off again.

"Doug, Daniel is my boyfriend. You're just a friend." She looked away. "I needed someone that one night, and you helped."

Doug ran a hand through his hair. "Christine, I'm just mixed up. If you'd let me talk a little…"

Christine interrupted again. "There's nothing to talk about, Doug. We can be friends at school. Friends." Then she started walking away. "I've got to get going."

Doug watched her get in her car and leave before going back inside.

Ed was hanging out in a corner of the studio with other stage crewmembers when he saw Beth come out of the bathroom. "I'll be right back!" he said to Andy, and he walked quickly across the room.

"Looks like someone's got a boner for the loner!" yelled Andy.

Ed walked up to her. "Hey, Beth."

"Whoa!" she said, fanning in front of her face. "What have you been drinking, Vitalis?"

Ed had been having his share of Andy's tequila and felt emboldened.

"I don't want there to be any, um, bad stuff, you know, between us, and there's something I've been wanting to say, and uh, now that the play's over and everything, um…"

Beth interrupted. "Ed, I know you were doing something with the dance money. Did something. Whatever."

Ed's looked up, startled. "But the bank said the statements…"

"Go out monthly," finished Beth. "And they show the date a deposit was made, you bozo!" She reached up and playfully slapped him on the side of the head.

Ed turned away.

"Ed, I'm *busting* you," she said more gently. "You don't have to apologize for thinking about taking the money. *I've* thought about it plenty of times. What did you end up doing? I mean, I gotta believe you had some kind of plan."

They sat at a table and Ed told her the whole story of the fixed race and his fear of losing the money.

"Did the horse win?" she asked.

"Paid 11-to-1," Ed replied.

"Damn! That would've paid for some good times!"

Doug didn't drink anything else the rest of the night. Christine's words had sobered him up pretty quickly. It was approaching midnight when Palomma walked up to him.

"Doug, is there any chance you could give me another ride home? I couldn't find Christine and when I looked outside her car was gone."

Doug didn't want to let on they'd been talking outside…and she'd turned him down again. "You know, you're right. I haven't seen her either. Sure, I can give you a ride."

They walked out to his car. Doug didn't say anything as they started toward her house. Palomma glanced over at him from time to time but he didn't look back. She'd seen Christine go outside after Doug had; maybe they'd had an argument.

Palomma sighed. "That was a nice party." It was all she could think of.

"It was," said Doug. "And," he reached up and touched his neck, "I got a prize."

Palomma had intended her necklace 'move' to help Doug with Christine. Now she wondered if she should have left it alone.

A few weeks later, Palomma was laying on her bed, frustrated. Doug seemed to still be somewhat interested in Christine, but probably didn't know what to do. Palomma thought giving him her necklace at the cast party might be something he could start a conversation about, or even the play…

Then she suddenly had an idea; "That's it!" she said out loud. "Hello Dolly! Dolly was a matchmaker!" Doug and Christine were both turning eighteen soon—why not surprise them with a night out? Palomma checked her calendar and called the Ramblewood Inn to make a reservation.

The next day at school, she sought out Ed, Andy, Rose and Melody, telling them about her idea of a surprise dinner. Everyone seemed to like it and said they'd go. Late in the morning, she was in room six with Christine and Doug when Ed and Andy walked in and stood next to the table.

"Hey, Palomma," he said. "What time is the birthday party for these two supposed to be?"

Doug and Christine both looked at Palomma.

"Ed," Palomma said angrily, "do I need to buy you a dictionary so you can look up 'surprise'?"

"Shit, I forgot," he said. He turned to Doug and Christine. "I was playing with you, there's no party."

Palomma sighed. "Since the surprisees know, I was suggesting we all go out to dinner. You two are free on the 27th, aren't you? Doug, do you work Saturday nights?"

"Not yet," he said. "I'm good."

"Christine, are you free?" she asked. "I'll check my schedule, I could be," Christine replied. Palomma looked away and rolled her eyes.

"You two are the guests of honor; these two big mouths, Melody, Rose and I are going too," replied Palomma.

"Uh, hang on," said Andy. "I can't make it. I mean, I'd like to, for sure, but I'm working."

Doug looked down the table at Andy. "Since when do they grow flowers in the winter at night?" Andy gave him a dirty look.

"Who's paying?" Ed interjected as he sat down. "If we're going to McDonald's, I'll kick in a quarter." He'd gotten over his *faux pas* quickly.

"No, someplace nice. I made reservations at the Ramblewood Inn."

"You don't have to pay for me," said Christine. "I'm a big girl."

"Me, too," said Doug. "I'm a big girl too." He fluttered his eyelids.

"At least you finally admit it," said Ed.

Palomma smiled. Maybe it wasn't a surprise anymore, but it sounded like it was working out.

Later in the day, Palomma stopped at Doug's locker and asked if he would drive the night of the dinner. She hadn't wanted to ask—drive yourself to your own party? But Palomma trusted the way Doug drove, Ed's car was too small, and she certainly wasn't going to ask Christine.

The following day at school was uneventful, one of the rare days

Palomma and Christine had different things going on. It was only after she'd gotten home that Palomma realized it had been Christine's birthday.

That night, she phoned Christine. The line was busy. Palomma shrugged and went to her desk to write in her diary.

A little later, the phone rang. "Palomma!" her mother called, "It's Christine!"

Palomma answered. "Hello, Christine?"

"Hi, Palomma!"

"I tried to call, but your line was busy. How's it feel to be eighteen? Did you have wine with dinner?"

Christine laughed. "No, I did not! I was *soooo* disappointed!"

There was a pause, and then Christine spoke up.

"Palomma, since we're talking, there was something I wanted to ask about."

"Sure, um, what's up?" said Palomma.

"I was wondering if, I mean, would it be alright, oh shit, I'll just say it; would it bother you if I went on a date with Daniel Parrillo?"

Palomma's eyes opened very wide.

"Ummmmm, yeah, sure, I guess, I mean, no, it wouldn't bother me. Why would you ask?"

"I just thought since you'd gone out with him you might get mad if you heard he took me out," replied Christine.

"Uh, yeah, no, I mean, I told you we aren't going out anymore. How'd you meet Daniel?"

"It was so weird!" chattered Christine. "I was at the mall with someone at Orange Julius and she said my name and this guy said 'Christine? Christine Holloway?' and I looked, and Daniel was standing there."

Palomma stared at the floor and listened.

186

"I said how did you know my name and he said he knew you and you'd talked about your friend Christine Holloway and he didn't know any other Christines. We started talking, he hung out a little and boom!"

Palomma didn't respond. A few seconds went by.

"Whew! I'm glad we talked!" said Christine. "I was worried we wouldn't get the chance and, you know…" Christine trailed off.

"Completely understand," replied Palomma, flatly.

"Thanks! I'd better enjoy the rest of my birthday! Maybe I can find some of that wine!" Christine hung up.

Palomma realized she hadn't actually wished Christine a happy birthday, but that wasn't what was bothering her.

She also realized she'd never said anything to Daniel about Christine.

The next day, Palomma was in room three studying for a history appointment; the conversation from the previous night was making it difficult to focus on the Civil War. Doug walked in, plopped his books down on the desk next to her and sat down.

"Did you buy my birthday present yet?" he asked. "Time's running out!"

"Umm, no," said Palomma, not looking up from her notes.

"Good, you're going to. Okay, some ideas. I could use…" Doug started to count on his fingers.

"Doug, not now?" said Palomma curtly, turning toward him. "I've got to get ready for an appointment!"

"Okay! Okay! Calm down, Orville Moody!"

Palomma stared at him. "What does *that* mean?"

"Orville Moody. Pro golfer. Moody," Doug answered. His tone was flat now.

"Oh," said Palomma, looking back down at her work.

Doug sat for a couple of seconds. "Message received. Casting off!"

He stood up, saluted, picked up his books and walked out of the room.

Palomma looked at the door after he'd left. "Can't you ever be serious?" she mumbled.

She couldn't get the conversation with Christine out of her head. Since when did Christine ask her 'permission' for anything? Palomma wracked her brain but couldn't think of a single time she'd even mentioned Christine's name to Daniel. She shook her head back and forth a few times as if trying to shake the confusion out, then looked around to see if anyone had seen her do it.

It also occurred to her Christine wouldn't be asking about dating Daniel if she had any interest in Doug. But cancelling the dinner would look stupid now.

After her appointment, Palomma walked past room five and saw Doug sitting in the back. She paused, but realized she wasn't scheduled there. "Jesus, Palomma," she muttered, "break a rule for once!" She walked into the room, sitting down a couple of desks from Doug. She took out her appointment book, scratched out the '12' written for the mod, and wrote '5.'

Doug didn't appear to notice her; he was reading a paperback book. Palomma fiddled with taking things in and out of her purse for a couple of minutes, glancing at Doug. He shifted in his desk still looking at the book. Palomma got up, walked to a shelf and took a book, then sat down where she'd been.

"Whatcha reading?" she said.

Doug held up the book, 'Of Mice and Men.'

"I was going to take that lap," said Palomma. "Is it good?"

"It's okay," answered Doug. "Too many men, not enough mice."

Doug got up and sat in the desk next to Palomma. He stared intently at her. Palomma didn't know what was going on and stared back at him.

He rested his chin on his palm and furrowed his brow. "Can I help you with something?" she asked.

"I heard Palomma has a sister," answered Doug, looking at her from different angles, "I didn't know it was a twin sister." He held up both hands and framed her face with his fingers. "I'm trying to figure out if you're her or the other one."

"The other one what?"

"The other twin. The evil one, you know?" said Doug. "How come a hen can't lay a loaf of bread?"

Palomma had heard Doug repeat that Three Stooges line a dozen times. "It doesn't have the crust."

"It's 'because she ain't got the crust,'" he fired back, "close enough. Hi, Palomma, welcome back! Oh, I owe you an apology."

"For what?"

Doug rested his forearms on the desk. "Before, something was eating you and I acted like an ass. I should have asked you what was wrong."

"You don't have to apologize, Doug, and besides, I wouldn't have told you then."

They sat quietly for a few seconds, looking at each other.

"Now?" Doug said.

"Now what?"

"Are you going to tell me now? It's not then anymore, it's now. It's today. What is today, anyway?" Doug held his hands out at his sides.

"Wednesday," said Palomma. "We're all going out in three days." She rested her chin in her hand. "Or did you forget?"

"I have not forgotten," said Doug. "And you never told me where to pick you guys up, either."

"Oh, be at Rose's house at six o'clock. She's right down the street on Spruce, her house number is, is," Palomma rummaged through her purse. "I've got it here, wait a minute, here it is, 649."

Doug jotted the address into his appointment book.

She saw he still had the necklace on. "Um, Doug?" she asked. "Are you…"

Doug leaned forward and waited for her to finish the sentence.

"… going to take any more English lit laps? If you are, tell me if there's any room in the group, could you? Christine never wants to take them."

"Sure," answered Doug, sitting back. "No sweat. Tell you the truth, I'd rather have…"

Doug stopped and looked away. It was Palomma's turn to wait for the rest.

"Sure," he continued. "I'll look to see what they're offering. Maybe there's something new."

Neither of them spoke for a few seconds.

"All right," said Doug. "Now?"

"Now, what?"

"Are you going to tell me now what you were so upset about before?"

"Oh yeah!" said Palomma excitedly. Her facial expression changed to serious. "No."

Chapter 16

Saturday night, Doug parked on the street right behind Ed.

"I told you I'd give you a ride," Doug said to Ed. "You're practically on the way home from the Ramblewood!"

"I wanted to drive myself," said Ed. "Your piece of shit's too slow."

"Hardy har har," said Doug, as they walked toward Rose's house and rang the bell. "The birthday boy!" said Rose after opening the door. "Come on in! You too, Ed! The girls should be here any minute!" Doug and Ed stood in the living room, chatting with Rose. In about a minute, the doorbell rang again.

"Beth! I didn't know you were coming!" said Rose. "Come on in!"

"I didn't know I was coming either," she answered, "until last-minute-Jones over there asked me on Friday." She pointed toward Ed and looked at him. "My Mom dropped me off; I'm expecting a limo ride home!"

The doorbell rang again. Christine and Palomma walked in.

"I brought the birthday girl!" said Palomma. She noticed Beth standing near Ed. "Beth! Glad you could make it!"

"I'll second that!" said Ed to a chorus of laughter.

Palomma walked over to Doug. "Melody saw me Friday and said she couldn't make it. Ed was in the room and heard her beg off and asked if Beth could come instead."

Ed was behind Palomma and winked at Doug.

Doug liked Palomma's idea—a chance to go out and no one in the group was 'romantically involved.' Well, Ed was acting like it with Beth. Palomma, Ed and Rose got in the back of the car, Beth slid into the middle of the front seat with Christine on the outside. Doug held up a tape. "Palomma, looky what I bought! Styx!"

"Play it!" Palomma shouted. "Play it!"

The first track on the tape was "Lady," and everyone sang along. Next, "Come Sail Away" started. Doug stopped the tape.

"Hey!" Palomma yelled.

"I'm sorry, I don't want any hanky-panky going on back there." Ed started making smooching sounds.

"Rose, stop kissing Palomma!" Doug said to laughter.

Doug restarted the tape, turning down the volume. "I've never been to this restaurant, is it good?"

"I think I went to a reception there," said Rose. "But I'm not sure, it was in sixth grade."

"Yeah, that was like, ten years ago, right?" said Ed. "Twelve," replied Rose.

Doug laughed. He hadn't known Rose was a cut-up too.

"My boyfriend took me there already!" said Christine. No one responded.

The group entered and was seated. When the waitress came, Palomma pointed at Doug and Christine. "These two turned eighteen and want to order drinks!"

"Oh! Congratulations! Of course I'll have to see ID," said the waitress. Doug and Christine pulled out their licenses. She pretended to study them carefully.

"Everything's legal, what would you like?"

"I'd like a glass of red wine," answered Christine.

"I'll have a Schmidt's," said Doug.

The evening went well. The conversation was fun but not silly. Everyone seemed to enjoy acting like adults. Palomma was glad she thought of it.

Toward the end, Ed raised his soda. "A toast to being legal, which I'll be in a month!"

"Look out, world!" said Beth.

They clinked glasses and Doug added, "And I'd like to propose a toast to Palomma, for organizing this!"

"You're proposing to Palomma?" said Rose. "Here? Aren't you supposed to get down on one knee?"

Even though the lighting was dim, Doug still felt everyone saw him blush.

The check came; Beth and Rose figured out what everyone owed. "How about we pay for their appetizers as our gift?" asked Beth.

"Wait, no one had appetizers," said Ed.

"Nothing gets by you, does it, big boy?" replied Beth. Ed smiled. Everyone took out cash and Beth paid; they got their coats and went out to Doug's car.

On the way home, there wasn't much traffic. "Come on, Halecki, doesn't this piece of crap haul ass any faster?" chided Ed.

Doug sped up. "Sure it goes faster. You gonna pay my speeding ticket?"

Christine chimed in. "My boyfriend drove ninety miles an hour on Route 73!"

Doug glanced over at Christine.

"Ninety miles an hour!" he shouted. "Ninety miles an hour! You mean like this?" He accelerated. He lifted his foot off the gas after only a few seconds, slowed down and stopped at a light. "Hey everyone!" he said in a goofy voice, "that was 90 miles an hour!" Doug turned and sneered at Christine. "Make sure to tell your friends!"

Christine didn't say anything the rest of the way to Rose's house. She climbed out quickly and walked toward her car. Palomma started to follow; Doug got out and caught up to Palomma, reached out and touched her arm.

"Palomma?" he whispered. She stopped and turned toward him while Christine continued walking. "I just wanted to say thanks."

"Thanks?" Palomma asked. "For the dinner? It was no big deal."

"For helping. Or trying to help. No one ever did before."

Palomma stood quietly and crossed her hands in front of her.

"With Christine. With the necklace. With, whatever."

"Doug, I know you like her, and…"

"Liked," interrupted Doug.

"Oh," said Palomma. "Ummm,"

"Not your fault," said Doug. "As a matter of fact, without you giving me a little push, I wouldn't have, uh, I probably would have, Jesus, my mouth doesn't even work anymore."

Palomma was about to respond when Christine leaned on the horn for three full seconds. Palomma looked at Doug, then turned and walked toward the car.

Ed and Beth had gotten out of Doug's car and walked toward his. Ed bowed. "Your limo awaits."

"Great! You're gonna take me to it in this, right?" said Beth, pointing to his car. Ed laughed. "Hop in. You gotta tell me where you live."

"Just head down Landing," she said, and he started driving.

For all his 'advice' to Doug, Ed was nervous. He had never actually tried flirting with a girl before and couldn't think of anything to say. He turned on the radio instead. The neighborhoods they passed had houses getting progressively larger. After a couple more blocks, Beth said,

"Turn right at the next street. That's mine."

Ed turned. "The one at the end, there on the right," she pointed.

Ed stopped at the curb and ran around the car to open the passenger door. Beth got out, and Ed walked with her up the driveway to her front door. He was desperately trying to think of something.

When they reached her front door, he turned to her and said, "You got any more money you need me to guard?"

Beth also turned, smiled and was about to answer when Ed put his hands on her shoulders. "I'm good at taking care of a lot of things."

"I'll bet you are," answered Beth. Her arms remained at her sides.

Ed pulled her closer and leaned in to kiss her. Beth pulled her head back.

"How about a smoke?" she asked.

"I don't smoke," said Ed.

"Then you can watch me smoke," she replied. Ed let go of her.

"Man, it got chilly in a hurry," said Beth, shivering as she took out a cigarette.

"You want me to warm you up?" asked Ed.

"That's nice," Beth replied, tapping the cigarette on her palm. "Not too many people give a shit about other people anymore."

Ed took out his lighter and lit Beth's cigarette. She looked at the lighter.

"And people think I'm weird. You don't smoke, but you have a lighter."

"It's my Dad's," said Ed, snapping it shut. "I mean, it was my Dad's. He gave it to me."

"Your Dad smokes."

"Nope," said Ed.

Beth sighed. "I think I should be smoking something else for all that to make sense."

Ed took the cigarette from her fingers, tossed it away, looked down at her and quickly kissed her. She kept her lips pressed tightly together.

He leaned over and whispered in her ear. "We can go slower."

Beth moved backwards.

"How about a full stop?" she said.

Ed's shoulders slumped. He stuffed his hands in his pockets and turned away from her. Beth began to speak. "Ed…"

Ed cut her off.

"Not cool," he said harshly, still looking away. "Acting all into me when there's another guy!"

Beth spoke softly. "Who says it's a guy?"

Ed continued looking away. He turned back toward Beth, opened his mouth to say something, and stopped. He looked down, then back up. "Wow," he finally said. He backed away and stared at Beth. "You mean what I think you mean, right?"

"So you know, it isn't contagious." She moved forward. "I mean, I know most of you guys think with your dicks, but I thought you were different."

Ed opened his eyes wide.

"No, not *that*, Jesus Christ, that wouldn't even make sense," she continued, waving her hand. "I mean different like every girl wasn't a vagina with legs to you."

Ed looked away.

"See what I mean? That's so cool!" she said. "A big guy like you still blushes and stuff."

"You can't blame me, for tryin'," said Ed, looking at the ground. "I still think you're cute as hell. I didn't know. I just thought, like, you were into me."

Beth took Ed's hands in hers and this time he didn't back away. "Look, I get it," she said. "I'm sure as hell not gonna spread it around; 'Lizzy the Lezzy' would be way too easy for them." She brought his hands up to her chin level. "If I act totally bogus toward guys, it'll start, bet your ass. I'm sorry if you took it to mean something else, I was trying to, you know, act"—she made air quotes—"'normal.'"

She moved closer to Ed.

"You know what, though? If I *was* into guys, you'd be at the front of a really short line." She rested the side of her head against his chest.

"Yeah, well..." Ed's voice trailed off.

"Yeah, well really!" said Beth, reaching up and playfully tapping the side of Ed's head. "Quit selling yourself short." She motioned with a thumb toward herself. "Short? Get it?"

Ed chuckled.

"Big guy, you'll find her," said Beth, softly. "And 'til you do, I swear on your I-don't-smoke lighter I'll be the absolute best friend a guy could have who isn't his girlfriend. From what I've seen, girls are worse than guys at wanting what's already taken; the more they think I'm with you, the more they'll probably try to steal you away. I'd be pretty damn good at doing the act!"

Beth started making exaggerated gestures like a silent film actress. "Woe is me! Oh, woe is me! Ed left me for someone else!" She suddenly stopped.

"After all, I fooled you, didn't I?"

Ed put his hands on his hips and thought for a moment. "You are something else."

"God knows I've heard that a few times," Beth said sarcastically.

"No, no, that's not what I mean," Ed said, laughing. "I mean—you're different."

Beth stepped back, tapped her foot and crossed her arms. "Keep trying."

"How about this?" He put his hands on Beth's shoulders. "Hangin' around you'll teach me a shitload more than school does. How's that?"

"Very good," she replied. "A-plus."

"It'd be my very first one ever," said Ed. They hugged.

Ed waited until Beth closed her front door before driving home. He pulled into his driveway and was surprised to see lights still on. His parents never waited up for him when he stayed out late.

He walked into the kitchen and found his father at the table with papers scattered all over it. His was resting his forehead on his hand with his elbow on the table.

"What's this? You got homework?" Ed said, kiddingly.

His father looked up at him. Ed didn't want to believe it, but his cheeks were wet from crying.

"Don't worry about having to go to work tomorrow," his father said softly. "We don't have jobs anymore."

Ed stared for a second, then walked to the refrigerator. He took out two cans of beer and gestured toward his father, who nodded slightly. Ed sat at the table, pulled the tab and drank most of his in one draught.

"State came in and cracked down," said his father, idly toying with his can. "There was a fixed race a month ago, bunch of guys got busted. They said they had to get rid of the ones like us who weren't on the books. Casinos are comin' to AC, they're tryin' to make everything look squeaky clean."

Ed set down his can. "That seals it," he said softly. "I can hustle golf. Florida here I come."

Ed's mother burst out crying in the other room.

"Don't tell me the factory laid her off too!" said Ed.

Ed's Dad shook his head no and began to say something; Ed held up his hand.

"No," he said quietly but firmly. "No more bullshit. We don't have jobs and the three of us on Mom's pay won't keep the lights on."

"We'll figure something out," his father said, not all that convincingly.

"I have figured it out," said Ed. He stood up and paced in the kitchen. "I beat all the slobs around here; I can beat turkeys year-round down there, clean out those rich assholes, way more money than from the shit jobs we don't even have anymore!"

"Sometimes rich guys don't take kindly to people like us beatin' on 'em," his father said. "Who's gonna look out for you?"

Ed heard his mother sobbing in the other room. He was about to answer when his father stood up.

"Yeah, people like us. Hicks. Rubes. Whatever they can call it, I've heard it. I've *been* it, my whole damn life. Come with me." He took his coat from a hook on the back of the door and grabbed a flashlight from a drawer. Ed was puzzled by his father's tone but got his coat and followed.

They walked through the backyard into the woods. "This better not be another lecture about school," snarled Ed. "Get it through your head, that's not what's happening."

Ed's father didn't respond.

They walked deep into the woods. "Where are we going, anyway?" said Ed. "It's freezing out here!"

"We're almost there," his father said, softly.

After another minute, they stopped. Ed's father shone the flashlight around, settling on a pipe sticking up out of the ground with another one attached. There was a small piece of concrete in front of it. He handed the flashlight to Ed. "Read it."

Ed pointed the flashlight at the concrete. It had some letters scratched into it. "Mary Sherman…1961…an angel."

The pipe in front of the slab had been welded into a cross. It was hardly more than a foot tall, covered in rust. Ed stared at it, felt dizzy and leaned against a tree.

He'd never given it much thought before. A couple of times he swore he'd heard his parents talking about a girl as if she'd been part of the family. Ed had always been an only child. That had puzzled him. All the families in the area had more than one kid and it wasn't hard to see the purpose—more kids meant more ways to bring in a little money.

But his parents only had him. He wasn't stupid enough to think his parents didn't have sex; it was hard not to hear sometimes through the paper-thin walls.

And there was that candle.

Ed's mother had a picture of the Virgin Mary on a shelf in the kitchen; she lit the candle in front of it when she came home without fail. At bedtime, she'd say a prayer before blowing it out.

The Virgin Mary…Mary Sherman…

Ed slouched forward. It all made sense now.

"You had a sister, or you were supposed to," Ed's father said. "Folks like us called a midwife – couldn't afford hospitals. There was something wrong, I was going to get a doctor, she said not to bother…"

He started shaking. Then he began crying. Ed hugged him.

"I didn't make jackshit then either," he said between sobs. "No money for a funeral home, let alone a cemetery. I knew it was against the law so I had to go back here."

Now it was Ed's turn to break down crying.

"You're all Ma's got," his father whispered. "You're all I got. Don't you see? A Sherman's gotta climb out of this rut someday. We all do it if you do it."

They hugged again. Ed squeezed his father tightly.

"We'll figure something out," said Ed. He stared at the cross for a long time before turning with his father to go home. Walking back to his house, Ed counted his steps; he wanted to be sure he could find his way back.

Back in the house, he passed the candle, paused, and made the sign of the cross.

Chapter 17

It was Sunday, the day after the birthday dinner, Doug took a long walk in the woods. Things from the night before had him confused. He sat down on his stump and immediately got back up. He started toward the house but stopped.

He looked up at the treetops, sighed, and trotted back in the house.

Inside, Doug walked down the hall, dialed the phone and stretched the cord under his bedroom door. He sat on the floor with his back against his dresser.

Palomma was reading in her room when she heard her mother call out, "Palomma! Telephone!" Palomma picked up the phone and went into her bedroom.

"Hello?"

"Hi, Palomma, it's Doug. Is this a bad time to call?"

"No, not at all." She sat on the floor leaning against her bed. "What's up?"

"I was, I had been, I..." Doug stammered.

"Doug, you don't need to thank me again for the dinner!" interrupted Palomma.

Doug paused. "Yeah, the dinner last night; it was a lot of fun."

He took a deep breath.

"But you know, there was something a little uncomfortable last night, I mean it was for me, um, and I wanted to tell you, uh,...it was uncomfortable and I don't want you to think I had anything to do with it."

"Doug, what are you talking about?" Palomma pulled her knees up and rested her forearms on them. There was only a hum coming through the phone for a couple of seconds.

"Christine mentioned her boyfriend a couple of times," he said. "Do you know who she's talking about?"

"I suppose it's Daniel Parrillo," said Palomma. "She went on a date with him."

Doug took another deep breath. "Yeah, she was talking about Dan Parrillo, and I thought you were going out with him but maybe I was wrong but if I wasn't, I didn't know you'd broken up. All I know is I knew she was rubbing it in on me and it sounded like she was doing it to you too. I know how I felt, and I can imagine how you did too."

Palomma was quiet for a few seconds, taking in everything Doug said.

"Um, yeah, we did break up." She cocked her head to one side. "You said you knew she meant Daniel. How? Did you talk to her about me?"

"No, never," Doug answered quickly. "I've never talked about you with her."

"Then I'm even more confused. WHY would Christine tell you about him?"

Then it dawned on her.

"Oh, wait – I'm sorry, Doug. She told you before the dinner, right? She told me she met him a couple of weeks ago."

"Um, kind of, not really," Doug responded. "Wow, I'm sorry to hear you broke up. I guess it happened a while ago, huh?"

"A month ago. Right around the Pumpkin Hop."

There was a painfully long pause. The humming seemed to get louder.

"Doug? Are you still there?"

Doug felt himself getting shaky. He looked up at the ceiling; maybe the phone call had been a mistake.

"I honestly didn't know, Palomma," Doug finally said. "I mean, if I had…"

"You didn't know, so what?" Palomma interrupted. She was getting angry now. "We broke up. Christine told me she'd met Daniel. Now they're obviously going out."

Doug took a deep breath. "Okay, Palomma. There's something I want to tell you but promise you won't get mad at me."

Palomma stood up. "Not unless you keep beating around the bush! We broke up and they started going out, it's that simple!"

Doug sighed.

"Back on Columbus Day, Christine needed a ride home from the mall. I was taking her home and she said to drive around a little, so we did."

"And you asked her out and she said no, right?" interrupted Palomma.

"Palomma, this isn't easy, let me finish. I cut through Strawbridge Park, we stopped, and she started asking me about something I couldn't figure out at first. Then she said it was about Parrillo. She said his name."

Palomma sat down on the edge of her bed.

"Okay, it was like she wanted advice, and I said something, I don't remember what, and she said something and we, uh, we made out."

Doug blushed even though he was alone in his bedroom.

Palomma was taken by surprise with the 'made out,' but was also confused. "You said she was talking about Daniel? What about Daniel?"

"Palomma, this is why I wasn't sure I wanted to tell you. I figured you'd broken up and maybe introduced him to her. It was weird."

"When did you say it was?" asked Palomma, running her hand

through her hair.

"Early in October. Columbus Day."

Palomma stared at her window. She could hear Doug's voice coming from the earpiece. "Palomma? Hello?"

"I'm here," she said. "Look, I don't mean to…what was she asking about? Me?"

"No," answered Doug. "It wasn't about you. She never mentioned you. Like I told you, that's why I was confused."

"Then what was it?"

"She was talking about how he said he wanted, I knew she meant sex, and she didn't want to, umm…"

Palomma interrupted. "Doug, I'm glad you told me this. Really, I am." She exhaled heavily. "Like I said, we didn't break up until right before the dance. We both can do the math."

She sniffled. Doug heard it.

Doug tried to find something to say. "Palomma, I'm really sorry. Maybe she didn't know? I mean, about you and him? I was trying to tell you, I thought he was an asshole back in grade school."

Palomma tried to laugh. "You're saying he's an asshole and I dated him? Gee, thanks, Doug!" She looked up at the ceiling.

Doug realized she was trying to make a joke to keep from crying.

"No, no, all I'm saying is someone like him would probably go out with two girls at the same time."

"Doug, she knew," Palomma said, sliding back down to sit on the floor. "I told her back in September."

"Oh," said Doug.

Each could hear the sound of the other's breathing and nothing else.

"I'm, it's, how did she know him? Did you three go someplace together? This doesn't make sense," stumbled Doug.

"It makes sense in my life," said Palomma, laying back on the floor.

The floodgates opened. Palomma told Doug about Christine and the things that happened in the past couple of years. Doug listened without interrupting. After a while, she trailed off. "I guess you didn't need to hear all that stuff."

"Actually, I'm kind of, uh, I think it's cool you'd tell me."

"That's so nice," said Palomma. She sat up.

"Okay! Since we're baring our souls, you made out with Christine?"

"You just dive right in, huh?" said Doug. "Yeah, we were, um, you know."

"Was she good?"

"Uh…" Doug balked. "I don't know how much I was in a position to judge, seeing as how I, uh, hadn't, you know."

"That was your *first time*?" said Palomma in surprise. "You're probably the only boy who'd admit that!"

"Yeah, I'd say she was good. I mean, I enjoyed it!"

"Did you touch her boobs?"

"PALOMMA!" Doug realized he'd yelled it. "Palomma!" he faux-whispered, hunching over, "That's private! And no, I didn't. But I thought about touching her butt!"

They both started laughing.

"Then tell me," asked Palomma. "What happened between there and the play? Last year there were little hearts coming out of your head when you were around her, but this year you started paying more attention…" she caught herself. "You looked like you weren't interested anymore, then you're making out with her; you're tough to keep up with!"

It was Doug's turn to bare his soul. He told Palomma about the phone calls, the Welcome Week plan in his basement, the drive to rehearsal and the talk at the cast party.

"So we're both members of the club," Palomma said. "The screwed-by-Christine-Holloway club."

"But not in the Biblical sense," Doug quickly added. "You know, I figured something out you might find useful. Know how to tell when Christine's lying?"

"How?"

"Her lips move," said Doug. They both laughed.

"You'd know more about Christine's lips than I would, Douggie!"

"Palomma! Are you almost done?" her sister Gemma hollered from the hallway.

Palomma covered the mouthpiece. "I'm on the phone, Gemma! Jeez!"

"I KNOW!" Gemma looked in her bedroom. "And you've BEEN on for an hour. I'd like to use it!"

Palomma said to Doug, "I guess we've been tying up the phone!"

Doug answered, "Looks like we have."

"I guess I'll see you at school tomorrow," said Palomma.

"I guess I'll see you too," said Doug.

"Alright," said Palomma.

"Alright," said Doug.

"PALOMMA!" yelled Gemma.

"Bye, Doug."

"Bye, Palomma." They hung up at the exact same time.

Doug's mother, father and sister were seated at the kitchen table with Doug that night.

"Happy birthday to yooooooooou!!" they finished singing. Doug blew out the candles on the cake his mother had baked.

"You guys never could sing," Doug joked as his mother cut the cake.

"Listen to the big star," said Linda kiddingly, putting her hands on her hips and swiveling her shoulders.

"Who invited her?" Doug laughed, pointing with his thumb.

"You should be honored, I took off work tonight," she said.

"You know, I never told you about showing that paper to the guys at work," said Doug's father. "They were all impressed. Front page! One guy, he's a jackass anyway, said something about acting and whether you were a fag but I gave him what-for, believe you me!" Doug tensed.

"Dear, could we not use that language at the table?" said his mother.

"Anyway, they thought it was something. Really something."

"Linda was in the play her senior year, too!" said Mrs. Halecki.

"Oh Mom, Jeez! I carried something on stage, set it down and left!" said Linda.

"Did you trip and fall on your..." Doug caught himself. "Gluteous maximus?"

Linda laughed and gave Doug a playful shove on the shoulder.

"Everyone finished? Time for presents!" said Doug's mother, clearing the plates.

"Did you ask for four bagfulls of trucks like you used to every year?" asked Linda.

Mrs. Halecki put an envelope on the table.

"We honestly didn't know what to get, you didn't mention anything, so..."

Doug opened the card. There were five twenty-dollar bills inside.

"Wow! Thanks Mom and Dad!" Doug said.

"And your sister," his mother added.

"One of those twenties was mine," said Linda.

"We figured you didn't go to work for a while and were probably running low on money," his mother said.

"It's great!" said Doug, fanning out the bills in front of him.

Doug dried the dishes while his mother washed them. He was feeling strange, almost as if he was coming down with something. Shaky, jumpy, light-headed.

Lauren ran up to Karen excitedly on Dec. 3.

"Spaghetti day!" she chortled.

Karen had been plotting against Palomma from the day Lauren had told her about Doug Halecki deciding to run for class president. The day had arrived to carry out her plan.

"Make sure you get the spaghetti in her hair!" said Lauren as they went through the lunch line.

"Could I have a little more please?" Karen asked the server sweetly. "And extra sauce too?"

"Nice," said Lauren.

Palomma was sitting with Paula. After what Doug told her about Christine, she'd been trying to cut into their old habits. She didn't know where Christine was sitting, and frankly didn't care too much.

Karen and Lauren began to slowly walk down the aisle next to Palomma's table. As they'd planned, Lauren stumbled as they came up on Palomma, yelling "Ouch!" and falling forward into Karen's back. Karen yelled "Ouch!" and flipped the tray of food forward.

At that exact instant…Palomma bent down to her left to pick up her purse that had fallen off her chair. The tray full of spaghetti and salad landed on Paula.

Karen was frozen, horrified. Lauren slunk away as quickly as she could.

The lunchroom fell silent. Paula reached up and took handfuls of spaghetti and sauce from her hair and plopped it into her tray. "Excuse me," she said to Palomma, and pushed the food on her shoulders onto the floor. Palomma grabbed some unused napkins from the table and handed them to her; Paula daubed at her face.

"Paula, I'm so *sorry*!" Karen gushed. "Oh my God! I don't know what happened! Lauren pushed me and the next thing I knew…"

"A hundred," said Paula, turning to her.

"A hundred?" said Karen.

"Yeah, a hundred, as in bucks. Beans. Simoleans. Smackers. I'd say that'll cover a new uniform and a trip to the salon."

Kids at the tables around her laughed.

Karen's face turned crimson. She looked around, then dashed out of the lunchroom.

Paula held up a handful of spaghetti. "Split it with ya!" she yelled.

The room, including Palomma, dissolved in laughter.

The end of the semester kept everyone busy at school with tests and essays. A couple of weeks had passed since the dinner party; pretty much the only times Doug and Palomma interacted were when he and Christine were working on their article.

Doug sat in room six on Friday, shaking his head. Everything was last-minute with Christine. Finally, she came in and sat down. "What have we got next week?" asked Doug. He'd have to rush to get everything written by the end of the day.

"There's a blood drive, a guest speaker…lots going on," said Christine. Doug was frustrated she'd waited so long to gather everything but silently took the papers and began to write.

Palomma walked into the room the next mod and sat down at the table. As angry as she was Christine, Palomma was still scared of confrontations so she wasn't stopping everything they usually did.

"Is this assembly in the morning or afternoon?" asked Doug.

"Morning," answered Christine. "I mean afternoon. I don't know." Doug shook his head side to side ever so slightly.

Palomma noticed Christine jot something on a piece of paper she hid with her arm and slide it to Doug; she wondered what was suddenly so secret.

Doug looked at the page: "Douggie! Could you give me a ride home from school?"

He thought for a moment and wrote back, "Car's not working?"

Christine responded. "Sorta. Can you?"

Doug delayed before passing back his response. "Parrillo's working?"

Without looking up, she wrote in large block letters.

"None of your damn business."

Doug wrote back, "You made him my business at the park," and pushed the paper back.

When Christine read Doug's reply, her face flushed.

"You were supposed to forget that," she wrote, followed by all capital letters, "THANK YOU VERY MUCH."

Doug wrote back, "I can't give you a ride. Let Andy make out with you and ride with him."

Christine read the page; her jaw dropped. She looked at Doug, snatched the papers piled on the table, grabbed her books and rushed out of the room. Palomma had seen the notes being exchanged but was in the dark as to what had been written. She looked at Doug, curiosity in her eyes.

Doug opened his eyes wider and shrugged. He wrote on another sheet of paper:

"It wasn't about you."

"Whatever it was, I don't think she's going to talk to you for a while," was Palomma's written reply.

"I'm running out of paper," Doug whispered.

"Room five, next mod," Palomma whispered back.

"What was that all about?" asked Palomma as they sat down in room five.

"A rerun. She wanted a ride home again."

"I assume you said no. That's what made her so mad?"

"First I asked her why Parrillo couldn't."

"What's wrong with that?" Palomma answered. "A perfectly logical question, since she told you all about him."

"I also mentioned where she told me."

"Ohhhhh," said Palomma. She shrugged. "What, she's pretending that never happened?"

"My guess is she thought I'd think it might happen *again*," answered Doug. "I guess it didn't work."

They sat in silence for a minute.

"At least you got that out of the way. She won't be wanting rides anymore…wait, you know what I mean," stumbled Palomma, blushing.

"And I thought I was the only one with that problem!" said Doug.

"Sorry, bad choice of words," said Palomma. "Still, it's probably better now."

"One thing's not better," said Doug, looking toward the hallway.

"What?"

"She took all the article stuff," answered Doug. "I'll have to start over getting it all, and the deadline's today."

Palomma thought for a moment.

"I'll see if I can get it back for you. I'm not making any promises, but I'll try."

"You will?"

"I just said so."

"Marry me!"

"No," answered Palomma, and she got up to leave.

"That's okay, take your time, think about it," Doug said as she left.

Palomma regretted volunteering as soon as she left the room, but realized it was only fair. Doug had always been there when she needed something, the Pumpkin Hop, the prom meeting. The least she could do was try to help him now. She walked past room one, saw Christine at a table, walked in and sat down.

"Um, Christine," Palomma said quietly, "I don't want to get caught in the middle here, but Doug said you had the stuff for the article, and, um, I could give it to him if you want."

Christine didn't look up.

"Christine, I..." Palomma started again.

"What, Doug's your boyfriend now?" said Christine at a volume loud enough for those nearby to jump. "Oh, poor, poor Douggie, maybe he should have thought of that..." She didn't finish the sentence.

Palomma froze for a few moments, finally whispering, "I don't think that was necessary!"

Kids were shooting sidelong glances at them; a couple of girls were whispering to each other. "All right," Christine said, "it's all the rage these days." She tore a page from her notebook, wrote on it and slid it to Palomma.

"Tell your darling Doug to be a man and ask me!"

Palomma wrote back. "He's not my darling, he's my friend. At least we're friends that can trust each other."

Christine wrote back a huge question mark.

"You know what it means," wrote Palomma.

Christine scrunched up her face and furiously wrote back, "Friends get the whole story!"

Doug walked into the room and saw them. Christine grabbed the page back before Palomma had finished reading.

"Friends don't gang up, either!" she wrote.

Palomma wrote angrily. "Friends don't stab each other in the back!!!"

Christine leaned in close to Palomma; if people in the room didn't know better, it almost looked like they were about to kiss.

"What's that supposed to mean?" Christine hissed.

"It means they don't steal their friend's boyfriend," Palomma slowly whispered.

Christine grinned. "It's not my fault he dumped you. I was just being nice asking you!" she whispered.

Doug was trying to look like he wasn't watching. He wasn't being too successful.

"That would mean something," whispered Palomma, "If you hadn't already been going out with him!"

Christine put both hands palms down on the table. She shot a glance at Doug and leaned toward Palomma. Instinctively, Palomma tensed; she was afraid Christine was going to slap her.

"Believe what you want," she said. "I couldn't care less." She stood up, picked up a folder and dropped the article papers on the table. "I couldn't care less about that either." She turned and stormed out of the room.

Doug was looking at a book but felt Christine's eyes burning a hole in him.

Palomma knew everyone in the room was watching. Slowly, she straightened the loose papers, gathered up her books and purse and started to walk away, stopped at a desk, tore out a piece of notebook paper and wrote on it. She put it on top of the other papers and went to leave the room.

As she passed Doug, she dropped the papers in front of him. "Here's the article notes," she said, loud so people might assume what the whole scene had been about. She walked into the hall.

Doug looked down at the page on top.

"Lunch today. Pizza Hut. You're driving. I'm buying."

Chapter 18

Seniors were allowed to leave school property for lunch. Doug was waiting at his car in the church parking lot for Palomma.

"Grrrrrrrrrrrrrr!" she snarled as she got in.

"If it's worth anything, thanks," said Doug as they drove away. "For the article stuff."

"You owe me BIG time, buddy!" said Palomma. Doug noticed it was a kidding tone, not angry.

"I was looking for her, for you, for you and her because I figured I'd say some shit about the article being important and stuff," continued Doug as they drove, "because it wasn't fair you having to try to get it. I guess I was a little late, huh?"

"Just a touch!" Palomma held her hands really far apart.

They walked into Pizza Hut and sat at a table near the door. The restaurant was a hangout for Blessed Sacrament seniors nights and weekends and occasionally for lunch. Tiffany lamps hung over all the booths and tables, but they weren't what made it attractive; it was one of the only pizzerias that served beer.

"Order what you want," Palomma said. "This is on me."

"Why?" asked Doug.

"It'll keep your mouth busy while I do all the talking. And right now, I feel like talking."

"Wanna split something?" he asked, "like a small pie?"

Palomma looked around. No one else from Blessed Sacrament was there for lunch.

"Sure," she said.

The waitress came. "We'll have a small pepperoni pie," said Doug.

"Drinks?" asked the waitress.

"Coke," said Palomma.

"Beer," said Doug. The waitress waited while he took out his license. "I'll be right back with your drinks."

"Like I said, I'm sorry…" Doug began to say.

"Stop!" said Palomma, holding up her hand. "You apologize too much. In case you forgot, I volunteered to get that stuff back."

The waitress arrived with their drinks.

"That you did. Here's to you!" He held up his glass, and they clinked them together.

Doug set his glass down. "Can I have a sip?" said Palomma.

"Sure."

Palomma drank half the glass.

Doug took it back and examined it. "If that's a sip…"

"I'm paying, remember?"

The pizza arrived. "You got back everything you needed, right?" asked Palomma.

"For the article? Yeah, I'll finish it and drive it over after school."

"What was she going to do if you guys missed the deadline?"

"Does anyone ever know what she's going to do?" said Doug. They both laughed.

"She probably would've laped it to your tocker, I mean, taped it to your locker," said Palomma.

"Half a beer and she's drunk!" said Doug.

"I'm not so think as you drunk I am!" replied Palomma, putting her fists on her hips.

There was a pause.

"I'm *kidding*," she said, leaning forward.

"So why'd she get so pissed again?" asked Doug. "I thought she was gonna hit you!"

Palomma leaned closer and whispered, "We passed notes too. I told her I knew she was going out with Daniel before we broke up."

"Aha."

They munched on pizza for a little while.

"I mean, part of me didn't want that to happen," she said, "and part couldn't wait for it to happen so it would be over with. Does that make sense?"

"If it makes sense to anyone, it'd be me," said Doug. "I go through that constantly."

Palomma looked confused. "You've had arguments like that with her too?"

She gestured with the hand she was holding a slice of pizza with; a pepperoni slice flew off and landed in front of Doug on the table.

"No, no, no, that's not it," Doug replied, picking up the pepperoni and eating it. "Arguments with myself. You know, inside."

Palomma smiled.

"I guess it all dawned on me the other day, after we talked on the phone." Palomma looked out the window. "Maybe I shouldn't be telling you this."

"Why not?"

She turned back. "Because of how Christine treated you. It'd be like I was doing it now."

"Naahhh," said Doug. "You're about as much like Christine as… as…"

Palomma waited for Doug's comparison; she raised an eyebrow.

"… you were saying?" said Doug.

"It was all so…perfect in the beginning with him, and then it went right to…this is hard," stumbled Palomma.

"You don't have to go into detail."

"But then you, you know, I hear he's with Christine, and I thought I was, oh God…" Palomma put her hands over her face.

Doug leaned closer. "It's screwed up. Everything about it is. Screwed up for you, screwed up for me. If it means anything, you weren't the only one who felt, you know," Doug trailed off.

"Screwed?" Palomma finished.

"Yeah," Doug answered.

Palomma told Doug about Daniel's attempts at forcing himself on her, his false apologies and Christine's made-up story about meeting him. Doug didn't even seem to mind when she finished his beer. She glanced at her watch.

"Oh God, you still have your article to write! I'll get the check. And!" she interrupted Doug when he started to speak, "I'm paying for this!" She walked to the register. Then they walked out to Doug's car.

"Got any new tapes?" Palomma asked, picking up the tape box as Doug drove down Main Street.

"Only Styx from the party," said Doug. "Otherwise, same old same old."

"Someday I've got to dig through this and see what's in here," said Palomma.

It was only a short drive before they arrived back to the school. Doug noticed Palomma didn't immediately open the door.

She let out a sigh. "That was fun. Especially after this morning."

"It was," said Doug. "And you've got to let me return the favor some-day, let me pick up the check for something to eat. And drink."

There was a pause. Palomma smiled and turned toward Doug.

"Doug, are you asking me on a date?" Doug had never heard this co-quettish tone in Palomma's voice before

"Um, I," Doug started to stutter. "I was just saying it was really nice of you…"

"Because if you were," Palomma interrupted, "know what? I'll bet the answer would be yes."

Doug looked at Palomma. Her expression looked expectant. He straightened himself in the seat.

"Palomma," he said, "I was wondering if you'd maybe like to…I was thinking of going Christmas shopping tomorrow night, maybe you'd like to come with me. And I could buy you dinner."

Doug realized he was talking but wasn't consciously aware of forming the thoughts.

"That sounds like fun!" Palomma replied quickly. "Where do you want to go?"

"I was thinking the Deptford Mall."

"Nice! I haven't been there before!" said Palomma.

"How about I pick you up at six?" asked Doug. "And don't eat dinner!"

"Sounds great!" Palomma answered. She sat motionless for about a second; the look on her face had changed to satisfaction. She turned and got out.

"I actually asked a girl on a date!" Doug thought as he collapsed back on the seat and watched her walk back to school.

"Damn it!" Doug mouthed, looking out the window in room six, and he didn't have a steering wheel to hit.

All that time Doug had wasted chasing after, fantasizing about Christine.

"The whole school probably thinks I'm a wuss," Doug muttered. He looked down at the article he was frantically trying to finish with her name on it. "They're probably right."

He was shaken out of his funk by Palomma's voice. "Doug! I've gotta ask something!" She walked in with a folder full of papers.

"I thought you were going home?" asked Doug.

"I was," she answered. "Katie found me."

"Prom?"

"What else?"

"Okay, umm, let me finish typing this." Doug stared at the typewriter.

"Want me to type it?" asked Palomma. "I'm pretty good."

Doug held up his handwritten article. "If you can decipher this."

"I think I can, I've seen your chicken scratch," she answered, and sat down. "Double spaced?"

"Yeah. Hell, you can put your name instead of mine; at this point…" and his voice trailed off. He idly watched her type.

"*Finito*!" She pulled the page from the typewriter after a minute. "Wanna check it?

"Anyone who types that fast doesn't make mistakes," he said. "I guess there's going to be something in there now about Doug Halecki getting accepted to Trenton State Prison, right?"

Palomma laughed. "Did you apply?"

Doug licked his finger and made a mark in the air. He stuck the paper in his notebook. "Okay," he said, "Prom."

"Yeah, prom. Problem, prom."

"Christ, what now?"

"Katie and Paula waited too long to call around. Everyone's booked."

"Can we move it to another date?" Doug asked.

"Same thought I had; geniuses think alike!" Palomma gushed. Mrs.

DiBiase let out a sarcastic cough; Doug had completely forgotten the teacher was there.

"Yesssss?" Doug said, turning toward her.

"Hopefully, some of that typing is for the school newspaper," she said.

Doug walked over to her desk, took a folded sheet of paper out of his jacket pocket, and handed it to her with a flourish.

Mrs. DiBiase read some of it and chuckled. "What would we do without you?"

"Have a better newspaper?"

She laughed and made a mark in the air with her finger.

Doug walked back to Palomma.

"Turns out, the other dates are booked at those places too. We're either going to have it in the gym…"

Doug pretended to put his finger down his throat. "Gaaaaaaacccckk!"

"Or it occurred to me, didn't you say once you work at the AmeriHost Inn?"

"Uh, yeah, I guess I told you. I mean, yeah, I work there."

"Don't they have a ballroom?" she asked. "It'd be better than the gym, for sure."

"Palomma, I don't know how much it costs or anything, I've never had anything to do with that." Palomma was surprised at Doug's reaction; the look on his face was almost embarrassment.

"Maybe you could ask them about the date, that's all," she replied in a softer voice. "I mean, if it's booked, it doesn't matter anyway, right?"

Doug looked at the floor and thought about how Palomma had just bailed him out. "I'll ask," he said. "What's the date again?"

"May 19. It's a Thursday."

"Okay, I can't say I can ask right away, but as soon as I can."

"Thanks!" said Palomma, patting his hand. "See you tomorrow!"

Doug sat on his bed that night, making a list of things to do before his date. He crumpled it up. "Asshole!" he said to himself. "Making a stupid list!"

Unfortunately, Doug said it to himself out loud; he heard a knock on his door.

"Yeah?"

"You decent?" said his sister.

"Yeah, c'mon in."

"Couldn't help overhear," she said. "Something get messed up?"

"I've always been messed up," Doug answered.

Linda didn't reply as she sat on the end of the bed.

Doug let out a big sigh. "I have a date tomorrow night."

"Cool!" said Linda, perking up. "With who?"

"Palomma. Palomma Rossi," answered Doug.

"She's nice," said Linda. "I remember her from your meeting. I liked her."

Doug rocked back and forth without saying anything.

"Where are you taking her?" Linda asked.

"We're going to the Deptford Mall and then we'll get something to eat."

"That'll be fun."

"I'm scared," Doug blurted out, looking away.

Linda leaned over, resting on her elbow. "I guess that's a good thing," she said.

"How's being scared a good thing?"

"Because that means you don't think you know it all. Remember Billy Johnson?"

"The guy from your class? He took you out once, didn't he?"

"Just to Pizza Pete's, but he was an ass. He talked about all the girls he'd gone out with. I guess I was supposed to be impressed."

"Did anything happen?" Doug asked. "You know," he leaned forward slightly.

"He sure wanted it to. I told him I had a curfew."

"I didn't like him. Always showing off," said Doug.

"Back to your date," Linda said. "Don't go trying to show off."

"Lin, I…"

"Don't deny it," Linda interrupted. "I heard you after everyone got to that meeting in the basement, talking a mile a minute. I almost came down and slugged you."

"I acted pretty stupid, huh?" Doug asked. He was looking dejected.

"You were nervous. You were trying to impress people."

Doug didn't say anything.

"Palomma's nervous too," Linda continued. "Girls don't show it as much." She sat up again. "Look, answer me this. Do you like her?"

"Yeah, sure. She's fun to be around."

"Then be fun to be around too. She'll be more impressed by you being yourself."

Doug lowered his voice.

"Do I kiss her? I mean, this is the first, you know, 'official' date." asked Doug.

"Oh God, Doug! If you're having a good time, it'll happen. If it doesn't, that's not a biggie either."

Linda leaned forward and whispered.

"You *have* kissed a girl before, right?" Doug blushed.

"Good. That's a yes." Linda got up to leave.

"Hey Lin," said Doug. "Thanks. One more thing…"

Doug took a wildly patterned polyester shirt from his closet. "Should

I wear this?"

"Oh God no! You *must* have something else!" said Linda, laughing.

That same night, the phone rang after dinner at Palomma's house. For a split second, she thought it was Doug calling…to cancel?

"Palomma!" called her mother. "It's Christine!"

Palomma had a feeling of dread. She took the phone into her room. "Hello?"

"Hi, Palomma, it's me. Do you have a minute?"

"Um…sure. Yeah, I guess so."

"About today," Christine started. There was silence for a couple of seconds. "I wanted to say I'm sorry."

Palomma's eyes widened. She tried to think of something to say other than also apologizing. "I guess we just, needed, to…" She waited for Christine to pick up the train of thought. She didn't.

There was another ten-second pause. Christine broke the silence.

"Let's go out tomorrow night, me and you, like the old days. We could go to the Carousel!"

"Christine, I'm not 18 yet, you know that."

"But they never card at the Carousel! Come on, whaddya say?"

Palomma's mind was racing. She'd known Christine to stay mad for days about tiny things. Now, she wasn't just being friendly, she apologized.

"How about I pick you up at 8? That's not too late for you, is it?"

"Um, Christine, it sounds fun, but I'm going out tomorrow night."

Palomma swore she heard Christine inhale sharply.

"Going out? With someone?" Christine asked.

"Yeah," said Palomma.

"Who's the lucky fella?" Now Christine's voice sounded smarmy.

"Doug."

A long pause.

"Doug? Cool! Where are you two going?"

"We're going to the Deptford Mall to do some shopping," answered Palomma.

"What time?" asked Christine.

"Why are you asking?" answered Palomma, furrowing her brow.

"I just thought if you got back early enough, we could still go out."

"I don't think so; Doug's picking me up at six and said we'd eat dinner."

"Palomma and Douggie going on a date!" sing-songed Christine. "You better watch out! I hear he's an animal!" Palomma rolled her eyes.

"It'll be fun." Palomma couldn't think of anything more to say and didn't want the conversation to go on.

"I guess we'll do it another time then." Christine hung up.

Palomma hung up. "I'll have to thank Doug for getting me out of that!" she said to herself.

Christine immediately dialed Daniel's number.

"Hello, Daniel? Mmmmm, yeah, me too. Listen, scratch the Carousel tomorrow. Nope, new plan—pick me up tomorrow about six."

Doug's father needed help with chores Saturday morning, as usual. Today, Doug was glad there were chores. After he picked up sticks around the yard he got busy on straightening the basement. The last thing he wanted to do was stare at the clock. Which he checked every ten minutes anyway. When he was finished in the basement, he vacuumed his car. He tried to watch some TV but went back outside to clean his car's windows.

Palomma sat straight up in bed that morning, shaking. She'd had a bad dream.

She was in the middle of a crowd of kids in the lunchroom. Christine was making up stories about her having sex and Palomma tried to deny it, but her mouth was glued shut. People laughed, Christine named boy after boy. It was that damn phone call.

She didn't feel she could trust Christine anymore; even the call about the two of them going out felt like a trick. But when she and Doug were at Pizza Hut, she felt she could trust him. She didn't really know what she felt about him.

There had been times with Doug when she found herself wishing they'd lasted longer. Short rides home from school, him dropping by the photo booth—she didn't realize how much she'd enjoyed them until after they'd passed.

It was Christine, she thought. She'd had Doug wrapped around her finger so long Palomma hadn't gotten to know him. And now, she and Doug were going out on a date. It all seemed to be happening too fast.

"Guys do this all the time. It's like hanging out with Ed and Andy. No difference. Same thing." Doug was at his thinking spot talking to himself. Being with Palomma wasn't the issue. Doug felt very relaxed around her. The issue was Doug had no idea what to do on a date.

He thought about giving her a kiss when he first picked her up, then realized there was a high likelihood he'd bump heads with her and discarded that idea.

There was a Friendly's at the Deptford Mall, they could eat there, it wouldn't be too fancy or romantic.

He went back inside to his room and looked in his closet. Doug didn't have any 'date' clothes because he'd never been on one. Jeans; it was a mall and she'd probably wear jeans. Shirt; Linda made it clear the polyester shirt was out. He took out a blue button-down shirt. Naah, looked like school. Doug found a sweater in the back of the closet he hadn't worn in a while. Not too dressy, it would do. He looked at his watch again; it was 3 p.m. Plenty of time.

"Jeans?" Palomma asked as she stood in front of her mirror.

"Jeans," Gemma replied, sitting at her desk.

Palomma was a little nervous now. She laid out her underwear on the bed. She looked at the shoes she had on the floor of her closet.

"Wedgies?" she asked.

"Wear the sneakers. You won't trip and fall."

"Ha ha" said Palomma.

They were going to a mall to shop—but she'd used the word date. And Doug sounded like he was asking her on a date. But they were friends, and friends went to the mall and shopped, not on a date. For a date, you were supposed to feel something different, what it felt like when Daniel came up to her at the dance, when he asked her out.

"And look how that went," she said out loud.

"What?" said Gemma.

"Nothing," answered Palomma. She reached into her closet. "These jeans?"

"The other ones."

Doug showered and considered putting on some of his father's after shave, realized he'd smell like his father, and simply sprayed on Right Guard. He pulled on his sweater, tried it tucked in and loose, decided on tucked in, brushed his hair and put on his platform shoes.

He told his mother he'd be home before midnight and left at 5:30. Doug tried to drive to Palomma's house slowly but, hitting every green light on the way, he'd gotten to Palomma's street by 5:45. He continued to Fox Hollow Golf Course, sat in the parking lot for a few minutes and then started back toward her house.

Chapter 19

"Palomma! He's here!" Gemma called out.

Palomma ran out of the kitchen to the living room window. "Where?" she asked.

"Just kidding. Gotcha!"

"Mrrrggghhh."

Palomma went back into the kitchen, then walked slowly back out to the living room. She paused, thought for a second, the returned to the kitchen and walked out again, a little more quickly. Gemma, sitting on the couch, watched in amusement.

"I think you should run out, bend him back and kiss him in the doorway," she said, chuckling.

Palomma blushed and went upstairs to her room. She'd barely gotten there when the doorbell rang; her mother came out of the dining room and opened the front door.

"Hello, Mrs. Rossi?" said Doug. "I'm Doug Halecki, and I'm here to pick up Palomma."

"Hello, Doug, come in—I'll have Gemma get her."

Mrs. Rossi shut the door. Doug folded his hands in front of him, moved them behind his back, then let them hang at his sides. He remembered what he'd rehearsed. "This is a nice house, Mrs. Rossi!"

"Thank you, Doug. Do you live nearby?"

"Oh, no, we moved to a house on Woodpecker Lane a few years ago," he chattered. "It's all the way out near Cinnaminson. Not real way out..."

"Hi Doug!"

Palomma was coming down the stairs. Doug sighed quietly; he could stop running his mouth. "Mrs. Rossi," Doug asked, "what time should Palomma be home?"

He thought he detected a slight smile from Palomma's mother.

"She ought to be home by midnight," she replied. "Now, you two go have fun!"

Doug turned to Palomma. "You ready?"

Palomma replied, "No," turned toward the stairs, then spun around. "Of course I am, Doug!" She giggled. Doug made an imaginary mark in the air.

They walked out to his car. Doug opened the passenger door and held it for her. "My, what a gentleman!" Palomma said, getting in. Doug backed out of the driveway and started down the road.

"Pick some music," Doug said. Palomma picked up the tape box. "Hmmmm, I don't see the Hello Dolly soundtrack, how about Boston?"

The music began, and Doug kept the volume down. They talked. They talked about how the play had gone. They talked about the Pumpkin Hop. Doug realized how much fun it was talking with Palomma; she didn't steer everything back to herself.

There was a pause in the conversation just as Doug's favorite song, "More Than a Feeling," came on; he started singing along. He rocked his head back and forth and drummed on the wheel. Doug held the last note of the song as long as the singer did on the tape.

"Bravo!" said Palomma. "*Bravissimo!*"

"Wait, I know! That's Russian for 'don't sing anymore!'" Doug said. Palomma laughed so hard no sound was coming out.

Getting to the mall went by quickly. Doug found a parking space and they walked into the mall. "Let's go into Macy's first," Doug said. "I need to buy something for my sister, and I never know what to get her."

"Did she ask for anything?" said Palomma as they walked into Macy's.

"Yeah, clothes. She wanted tops, and, hell, Palomma. She's my sister."

"We'll work this out scientifically," Palomma said as they walked the aisles. "What kind of tops does she usually wear?"

"I don't know, tee shirts, long sleeves, usually things like you wear."

"Alright, it's a start." Palomma stopped at a rack. "Now, what size is she?"

Doug started to talk, then stopped. "I don't know, she's…" he scanned down Palomma's body and back up again. "She's about your size."

There was a split-second pause and he blushed a deep red.

"Wait, uh, you know what I mean," Doug stammered.

"Oh Doug!" Palomma laughed, "I know exactly what you mean!" She touched his arm.

Doug felt a chill go up his arm. He looked into Palomma's eyes and she looked back into his.

"Your eyes are so blue," she said softly. She cleared her throat. "Are your contact lenses tinted?"

"They're clear. What you see is what you get."

"Ohhhhh," she said, softly again.

Palomma was motionless for a couple of seconds, and then turned back to the clothing rack.

"Speaking of get, are you going to get something here or should we go somewhere else?"

"I totally trust your taste," Doug answered. "You choose, I buy."

Palomma selected a light blue pastel-plaid top and handed it to Doug.

"She'll like this. May I?" He held it in front of Palomma.

"Careful, Douggie, or that might end up going home with me!" They laughed and let out simultaneous sighs. "To the register!" said Doug.

"What other gifts are you looking for?" asked Palomma as they left Macy's and walked through the mall. They passed a Spencer Gifts store; the windows were jammed with black light posters, peace symbols, smiley face pillows and rock band medallions. Doug stopped and looked at the window.

"I ought to get something for Christine," he said.

They started laughing at the same time.

"Seriously, what would be something Christine needs?" Doug asked.

"Birth control?" answered Palomma, and this time he practically doubled over.

"Damn, you are good!" Doug said. Without thinking, he reached out to hold her hand. She didn't pull it away. Doug looked down at their clasped hands, then up at Palomma and smiled.

They walked hand-in-hand for a few minutes. "Let's go in here," Palomma said as they got to Berdan's clothing store.

"Now you help me pick something out," said Palomma. "Fair's fair."

"Who are you buying for?" Doug asked. "Your sister?"

"Myself, silly. You think you can take a girl to the mall and she isn't going to shop for herself?"

Palomma began looking at the designer jeans.

"What looks nice?" Palomma asked. "Not that boys know anything about clothes."

"Ha ha ha."

"How about this?" She held up a pair of Jordache jeans. "Jordache has the look that's right!" sang Doug, imitating the commercial.

"I'm gonna try them on!" said Palomma, heading for the dressing room.

Doug sat down. He figured this is what couples did and it felt weird and neat at the same time. He idly looked out the entrance of the store. He saw a girl near the entrance with long auburn hair…and a shirt like the one Christine had worn that night at Strawbridge Park…

Doug figured his mind was playing tricks on him; he could swear it was Christine peeking into the store.

Palomma came out of the dressing room, put a hand on her hip and struck a pose. "What do you think?"

Doug stood up and looked at her, more specifically, the bottom half of her.

"They're very nice," he said.

Palomma did a spin and put both hands on her hips.

"Douglas M. Halecki…it's 'M,' right? One of the reasons I like you is because you're honest. Don't start being not honest now! Now, again, what do you think?"

Doug took a deep breath. "You look really sexy!"

"Not too tight?" Palomma asked as she turned from side to side.

"Oh no. *Noooooo.* They're just right."

Palomma giggled. "Good thing, because I was buying them anyway!"

Palomma went back into the dressing room to change while Doug idly looked at the jeans on nearby racks. Palomma came out in about a minute.

"Ready?" she said. "Yep," Doug answered.

They went to the register. Doug looked at his watch. It dawned on him he hadn't looked at his watch since he'd arrived at Palomma's house.

"Oops!" Doug said. "I said we'd get something to eat!"

Palomma had forgotten about the time too but was getting hungry.

"How about Friendly's?" Doug asked. "Friendly's is good!" Palomma answered. She also noticed Doug didn't add "If that's okay..."

The stopped at a mall map and located Friendly's, walked to the restaurant and sat down across from each other in a booth.

"Okay, right back at you," said Doug after the waitress handed them menus. "Like yesterday; anything you want. As you can see,"—he gestured around the room—"I spare no expense!"

"Don't worry," said Palomma. "This is a date—boys pay on dates."

Doug smiled.

"Sorry I can't order a beer and let you guzzle most of it," he kidded.

"Guzzle? Guzzle? I'm insulted!" She put on a pouty face.

"It's okay," Doug said. "You're funny even when you're not drunk."

The waitress returned. "I'll have a chef's salad," said Palomma. "California burger for me," said Doug. "Medium rare." When she left, Doug told Palomma about having his first drink at the AmeriHost Inn. Palomma made a mental note to ask about the prom later.

After they finished eating, they sat over their sodas. "Dessert?" Doug asked.

"Oh God, no," answered Palomma. "I'm full."

She propped her chin in both hands.

"So, you started drinking at your job?" she asked. "Why couldn't I find a job like that?"

"You could have stashed a bottle at the PhotoQuik!"

"That place," she answered. "It's nice to have some money, but not that nice. Tell me about your job."

Doug looked down at his lap.

"Unless you don't want to," Palomma quickly added. "That's cool too."

Doug looked at the table, thinking of his decision to never tell anyone. He looked up. He was on a date with Palomma. This wasn't the time.

"The next time I'm there," said Doug, "I'll ask if that date's available."

Palomma thought his tone was unusually flat.

"Job stinks, huh?"

"I've been thinking about looking for another one," he said. "But if we do have the prom there, if it came down to them doing me a favor, I'd stay."

Palomma furrowed her brow at his answer. "I didn't mean you had to..." she began.

"I know you didn't," interrupted Doug. "It's just..."

He looked into Palomma's eyes. They seemed to get larger and softer. He couldn't do it.

"My boss can be an asshole sometimes, that's all," he said.

"Fair enough," answered Palomma. But she felt funny about the exchange. She smiled at Doug; he smiled back, and they both felt a blush coming on. Both turned toward their coats on the seats next to them.

"We ought to get going," said Palomma. "Let me leave the tip."

"El no-o," said Doug.

Doug put on his coat, left a tip and went to the register to pay the bill. Palomma put on her coat and moved toward the entrance. She was watching people walk by when she froze.

Doug came up and saw her looking intently into the mall. "What's up?" he asked.

Palomma jumped and turned to Doug. "Nothing! Let's go!" They walked out into the mall.

Palomma was almost certain she'd seen Daniel.

Doug didn't hesitate to reach over and hold Palomma's hand this time. It was a new experience for Doug; all the times he'd walked through stores before, he never had to avoid hitting people while holding someone's hand—it was a very pleasant dilemma.

"Shopped out yet?" Doug asked after they'd been the mall for almost an hour.

"Silly question," answered Palomma. "I'm a girl, remember?"

"That's something I'm not having any trouble remembering," said Doug. Palomma smiled. She'd been impressed with Daniel when she first met him because he seemed suave. Now she realized he probably said the same lines to every girl he met.

Doug was real. What he said was for her and only her. And it was honest. She'd had enough of fake lines and lies. For the first time, it was like honesty mattered as much to someone else as it did to her.

"Well, as much as I'd like to see you try on more jeans, the mall's closing," said Doug. "Let's be on our way!" They walked out to the parking lot.

Christine waved her arms to get Daniel's attention from the other side of the walkway and motioned for him to join her.

"They're leaving," Christine said as Daniel reached her. "And she didn't say anything about the rest of the night when I talked to her." They started walking behind at a distance.

"Maybe he's just taking her home," said Daniel. "From what you told me, I wouldn't be surprised."

"Yeah, maybe," answered Christine. "Let's stay with 'em."

Doug glanced at his watch as he drove down Route 73. It was 10 o'clock.

Now he felt stupid. Doug didn't know what to do next. "Where would you like to go now?" he asked Palomma, hoping she'd come up with something.

"Anywhere, as long as it's with you," she answered, sliding over on the bench seat next to Doug. She surprised herself; the words came out on their own and she hadn't thought about saying them.

Doug put his arm around Palomma. "How about we go someplace where it can be just the two of us?" Doug suggested.

He surprised himself; the words came out on their own and he hadn't thought about saying them. "That sounds really nice," said Palomma, snuggling closer.

Driving home so many times from the AmeriHost, Doug had found a shortcut through the Holly Hill Industrial Park; he'd never seen police back there on the nights he floored it and raced through the curves and straights. As they came up on it now, he turned into the entrance.

"Want some gum?" Palomma asked, reaching into her purse. "No… wait, yes," Doug answered. He drove into a cul-de-sac with no buildings or streetlights. He stopped next to the curb and turned to Palomma. "How's this?" he asked.

"It's dark!"

"I kind of thought that was the idea," Doug chuckled. "There's a used car lot on Route 38 lit up pretty bright, we could go there!"

"No, I mean it's *really* dark here! I can barely see you sitting there. How did you know about this place? Is this your 'secret spot?'" she teased.

"No, I," Doug stopped, realizing this wasn't the time for talking.

Palomma turned herself slightly to kiss Doug, but he'd moved his head away to take the gum out of his mouth and drop it in the ashtray.

"Oh…sorry!" he said. He sat back, put a hand on the steering wheel and pushed away from it slightly, turned and leaned over to kiss Palomma—to find she was leaning forward putting her gum in the ashtray. She sat back and they faced each other. Even in the dark, each could see the other trying not to giggle.

Doug put his arms around Palomma and kissed her. He was grateful now for the brief interlude he'd had with Christine. Palomma laced her arms around Doug's back and pulled him closer. Even after her experience with Daniel, there wasn't a hint of tension in Palomma when Doug had parked. As they hugged and kissed it felt nice. Not forced, not threatening, just really, really nice. And Doug was a pretty good kisser, too. She decided not to think about where he'd practiced.

Doug's hands weren't all over her. He seemed content with hugging and kissing and Palomma did too. They kissed with open mouths and relaxed into each other's embrace. They both wanted to forget everything from the past; all that mattered was this moment right now.

The car was suddenly filled with light.

"Jesus Christ!" Doug said, pulling away from Palomma.

There was a blinding light shining directly into the car from the side. "Is it the police?" asked Palomma, nervously.

"I don't know, I don't think so."

Doug was squinting and shading his eyes trying to see. It was a car, but he didn't see red and blue lights.

Doug slid behind the wheel and turned the key. "Whoever it is, I'm not waiting around to find out if I don't have to." Palomma was quiet; Doug glanced at her and could see she was scared. He threw the car into drive and screeched away without turning on his headlights.

Palomma imagined the worst. If it was the police, they'd chase Doug and pull him over. They might even arrest him for running away. She'd have to call her parents from the police station. Palomma started to feel sick like the night she drank whiskey with Daniel.

Doug kept glancing into his rearview mirror. Nothing seemed to be following him, so he turned on his headlights but kept going fast. He squinted and saw a car way back in the distance, just two tiny pinpoints of light; he couldn't be sure it had come from the same cul-de-sac.

He continued out of the industrial park onto Gardenia Road, still going fast. As he approached a traffic light, he took a look in the mirror and didn't see anything behind him. He slowed and stopped at the light.

"I'm sorry, I guess I messed up," Doug said.

"Doug, it's not your fault," Palomma answered. She turned on the seat. "You don't have to apologize. I told you before, you apologize too much!" She slid back over next to him. "You didn't do anything wrong tonight and, to tell you the truth, I can't think of anything you've ever done that needed an apology."

She touched his thigh. "Except for kissing. You really stink at it, you know?"

He looked at her; her lip trembled until she burst out laughing. Doug joined her.

The light turned green. "You're right," said Doug, continuing down the road. "Shit happens. This has been a wonderful night, and I'd like to spend more of it with you."

"Just not the used car lot," Palomma said. They both laughed again.

"No, I was thinking we could go for a walk. A walk on a beautiful night with a beautiful girl." He surprised himself again with his words.

Palomma nuzzled her head against Doug's neck. "Where are we going for this walk?"

"My house," Doug answered. "The cops only hang out there weeknights." Palomma couldn't stop another burst of laughter.

Doug pulled into the driveway on the side of his house, got out and walked into his backyard. "Shouldn't we go in first? Aren't your parents going to hear us?" Palomma whispered as she got out.

"My parents are sound asleep," said Doug. "By nine o'clock every night."

Doug's father had put up a huge floodlight near the side of the house.

Palomma stood under the light staring up with a quizzical look. "My Dad thinks it'll keep crooks away," explained Doug, coming up next to her. "I think it'll help 'em see what they're stealing." He extended his arm bent at the elbow toward Palomma. "And now, my dear." Palomma laced her arm into his.

They started to walk toward the woods. Palomma stopped. "No. Uh-uh. I'm not going in there." She pointed into the darkness. "That's creepy."

"Scaredy-cat!" Doug said. "It's not creepy! Okay, sometimes there's growling…"

"That's enough, Mr. Halecki, I said I'd go for a walk, not a safari."

"No worry," said Doug. "There's plenty of walking space over here."

They switched to holding hands.

"It's been quite a night," said Palomma.

"It's been quite a month," answered Doug.

They stopped and turned to each other. "It's been quite a year!" they said in unison and started laughing.

Palomma started swinging her arm back and forth as they held hands. Doug was quiet. "What're you thinking about?" she asked.

"Things are flying by so fast. All that anticipation for the play and then it's done. Know what I mean?" asked Doug.

"I do," said Palomma. "I guess that's life."

"Sometimes I wish it wasn't," answered Doug. "My life kind of sucked for so long, then things started happening and…"

"And what?"

"A lot of the good things were because of you. And I don't want them to end. Like tonight," Doug said softly.

Palomma stopped and turned to Doug. There was just enough moon-light to see each other's faces in a soft, innocent glow. She took his other hand in hers.

"Doug, there's something I want to tell you."

She hesitated.

"You make me smile. A lot. You make me laugh a lot too. I like smiling and laughing, I used to think there was more to everything than what was right there—I mean, I thought things were a lot more complicated."

"I think they are sometimes," said Doug.

"And sometimes not," said Palomma, "when you're with the right person."

It was still dark enough that Palomma couldn't see Doug blush.

"I wasted all that time on Christine," said Doug, staring into the darkness. "And now, I feel like an idiot."

"Why?" said Palomma. "If you hadn't been around her so much, you wouldn't have been around me and we wouldn't have gotten to know each other. I probably wouldn't be here with you right now."

"You are something," said Doug, and he hugged her. Palomma ran a hand up Doug's back to his neck.

"Are you still wearing that necklace?"

Doug hooked a finger under it. "Damn! You know I'd forgotten about it? You put it on; the least you could do is take it off!"

Palomma put her hands behind Doug's neck. "How am I supposed to unhook this thing in the dark?" she asked, fumbling with it.

"Like this." He took her hands in his and pulled them apart. The chain broke and Doug tossed it away into the brush.

Palomma still had her hands behind Doug's neck. "It's pretty chilly out here," she said.

Doug hugged her tight. He kissed her. And they kissed some more.

POW!

They both jumped; Palomma looked anxiously from side to side.

"Oh my God, what was that?"

Doug wondered the same thing. "I don't know," he answered. "A car, maybe?"

POW!

They jumped again. "That's too close!" said Palomma, looking around again. "A gun?"

"It sounds like—no, that's stupid," said Doug.

"Sounds like what?"

"Firecrackers. In December?"

Christine reached into her back pocket to get another firecracker, not realizing the match in her hand hadn't gone out.

Firecrackers went off again. They looked back toward Doug's house, but all they could see was the area lit by the streetlight.

Suddenly, the individual sounds turned into a chain of explosions.

"Those *are* firecrackers!" Doug said.

They heard a scream. Christine was running away through the light with smoke trailing behind. She dropped down to the ground and began sliding on her butt, got up, and ran around the front of the house.

Stones kicked up as a vehicle sped out of the driveway. Palomma and Doug stared into the distance.

"Are we drunk?" asked Doug

"If we are, let's get drunk more often," said Palomma. "I never saw anything like that!"

They started walking back toward Doug's car. There was still the scent of firecracker smoke in the air. "I was sure the lights would come on," said Palomma. "Your parents slept through that?"

"Very sound sleepers," Doug said. "And I think it's time I got you home. I'll bet your parents aren't asleep. Besides, too much excitement for one night isn't good for you."

"And if you know what's good for you..." responded Palomma.

Doug looked at her and waited.

"...Sorry, I couldn't think of anything."

"Air joke! Air joke!" said Doug.

Palomma punched him on the arm. "Quiet, you!"

Doug drove down Landing Road; he and Palomma were silent until they started talking at the same time.

"I swear that was," said Palomma, turning toward Doug.

"Damn, that's why!" said Doug, gesturing with his hand.

They looked at each other expectantly when Doug stopped at a stop sign.

"You first," they said at the same time. "No, you," they said simultaneously.

"Age before beauty," said Palomma.

Doug licked his finger and marked the air.

"Okay, I wasn't going to say anything because it would be about the dumbest thing I could do on a date with you," said Doug, "but I swear I saw Christine when you were trying on those jeans."

"And the last thing I was going to do was start talking about Daniel, but I saw him when we were at Friendly's."

"I never told Christine we were going out, or where!"

Palomma looked sheepishly at her lap. "I did."

"Okay," said Doug. "I mean, I like you weren't ashamed to say you were going out with me—wait, no, that's stupid."

"What's stupid?" asked Palomma.

"Who would follow someone while they were on a date?" Doug said, incredulously.

Palomma answered softly. "Someone with a smokin' hot ass?"

Doug almost drove off the road, he was laughing so hard.

They spent the rest of the trip joking about Christine setting her butt on fire. Soon they pulled into Palomma's driveway.

"This was…quite a night," said Palomma. "That will be a date that will live in infamy."

She turned to Doug.

"I had a wonderful time. I can't remember having a better night than this. Ever."

This time, their timing was impeccable. They kissed. They parted a few inches and sighed.

"*Danke schoen, mademoiselle*!" Doug whispered.

"*Danke schoen* is German," whispered Palomma. "*Mademoiselle* is French."

"Speaking of French," whispered Doug.

They kissed again. An outside light on Palomma's house came on.

Palomma gave him a last kiss before getting out and walking to her house.

"How was your date?" Gemma was still awake in her bedroom as Palomma passed.

"Over," she answered, walking into Gemma's room. "*Waaaaaay* too soon."

Gemma gave Palomma a hug. They sat on Gemma's bed and Palomma told her about everything that happened.

Chapter 20

Palomma drove herself to school Monday; her mother had let her have the car that day. In the church parking lot, Doug had just pulled in when Palomma got out of her car. They started walking toward the school, with Palomma slowing down a couple of times.

"You having clutch trouble?" asked Doug.

"I want to tell you something," said Palomma, moving closer. "Walk slower. Unless you can't wait to start school." Doug slowed practically to a stop.

"All right, all right, walk like a normal person. This is important." She took a deep breath.

"We went out on a date. You and me."

Doug nodded.

"I realized last night one of the reasons you and I, um, get along so well is, oh God, this is going to sound stupid."

Palomma took another deep breath.

"Okay," she said. "I think it's because we're weird."

Doug stopped. Palomma was afraid she'd offended him until he turned and she saw he was smiling.

"What's weird is I used to think that about myself and didn't want to," he said. "When your voice says it, it's not a bad thing anymore."

Ed jogged past them making smooching sounds.

"People can be so immature at times!" Palomma shouted after him.

They walked in the gym doors. Doug reached into his pocket and pulled out a tennis ball. "If you don't mind, though, I'm going to be weird *and* immature!"

Doug winked at Palomma, yelled "Hey Ed! Andy!" and kicked the tennis ball toward them. Palomma stood near the doorway until she saw Christine come in.

"Christine!" Palomma called. "I may have some good news about the prom!"

Christine didn't react but continued walking in Palomma's direction. Palomma sat down on the bleachers. Christine stood next to her.

"Sit down, let me show you this," said Palomma, sweetly.

"I'll stand."

Palomma stifled a giggle.

"Okay," she said. "Doug says he's going to check if we can have the prom at the AmeriHost ballroom and…"

Christine interrupted. "You decided this without asking me?"

She turned sharply and walked away.

Palomma watched her go.

"Yes, I did," she said, smiling.

"Talking to yourself?" said Manny as he came up behind Palomma.

"Yes, I am!" she said, looking at him and smiling wider.

A week went by, and Palomma hadn't seen much of Doug beyond quick 'hi's' in the hallway. Preparing for exams and writing essays kept everyone busy…and Doug was doing everything for the article by himself now. Palomma worried that Doug thought she was doing what Christine had done after they'd parked. She was nervous when Doug finally walked up to her in room eight while she studied for a French final.

"Hi, Palomma? Can I ask you something? Is this a good time?"

"Sure!" answered Palomma; she realized she'd sounded anxious. "I'm not busy," she said, more calmly. Doug sat down in the desk next to her and fought the urge to clear his throat.

"I really enjoyed going shopping with you—I mean, our date," he said.

"I did too," said Palomma, propping her chin on her hand.

Doug paused. "A little strange, though, you know?"

Palomma smiled. "That's one way to put it, yeah. It was a little strange."

Doug took a deep breath. "Um, Christmas is almost here, I know you'll be busy with your family and stuff,"—Doug slid his feet forward and back and folded his hands on the desk—"what I'm trying to say is I'd like to take you to a movie during the break. And maybe it would be best if we didn't tell anyone this time."

Palomma looked at him for a second and burst out laughing. Doug stiffened.

"Oh, I'm so sorry!" she said, touching his arm. "I'd love to go to a movie! I'm laughing because of what you said about not telling anyone!"

"Maybe we could tell, but the wrong movie," said Doug, and they both relaxed and laughed.

Christine walked in. Doug and Palomma stopped laughing abruptly.

"You were talking about me, weren't you?" said Christine.

"When?" Doug said. Palomma punched his arm.

"We've got that 'Grapes of Wrath' appointment to get ready for!" Palomma said. "Remember?" She and Doug stood up and started walking toward the door.

"I'll let you know when we talk about the prom," Palomma said softly to Christine as she passed. Christine stared at them as they walked out.

Doug had been dreading this night—the night he had to go back to work.

There wasn't much choice. He'd promised Palomma he'd ask about having the prom there. A couple of months of gasoline and cigarettes had eaten into his savings. Doug walked through the restaurant and into the kitchen, grateful Little wasn't there. This night, the restaurant was almost empty; a recent snowfall had kept people at home.

He saw someone new was washing dishes instead of Pete.

"Hey Doug, long time no see!" said Rena, sitting at the break table.

"I had the school play going on, all that," answered Doug, still looking at the dishwasher. "I didn't have any nights I could work. How've things been?"

"Pretty good," she replied. "Little said you took a leave of absence or whatever he called it." She nodded toward the dishwasher. "That's when he promoted Pete to waiter."

Doug sat down. "To waiter? No busboy in between?"

"He waits sometimes and buses other times," she said. "He only gets tables when Little's around, he says to keep an eye on him."

Doug tried not to change his expression.

He went into the restaurant; no one had been seated yet so he stood at his station. Then Doug tensed; he saw Little enter the dining room, look at the reservation sheet at the register, then look up at him. Little motioned with his index finger to come over.

"Glad y'all are back," he said in a muted voice. "Had to make some changes to handle things while you were gone." Little stretched out the word 'handle' and a chill went down Doug's spine. Doug needed to ask about the prom and didn't want to have to go to Little's office; this was his chance.

"Um, Mr. Little, I was wondering if you could do me, uh, us a favor?" he stuttered, trying not to make eye contact.

"Spit it out, son!" said Little, "ya know what I mean?" and he grinned lasciviously.

"I was wondering..." Doug started speaking rapidly. "I was wondering if the ballroom was available on May 19 it's a Thursday because I go to Blessed Sacrament High School and we need a place for our prom and I know it's late but maybe you could work it out for us because it would help us a lot." He stopped abruptly.

Little opened his mouth to answer when an elderly couple walked into the dining room, chattering about the weather. "How're y'all doin' this *fiiiiine* evenin'?" He asked their names, then looked at the reservation sheet. "Table seven, right this way."

Table seven was one of Doug's.

Little seated them and handed them menus. "Y'all will be waited on by this fine young man, Douglas," he said, gesturing at Doug. He began to walk away. Doug followed a couple of steps and whispered, "Mr. Little, our prom!"

Little stopped, turned and thought for a second. "See Erika about it," he whispered. "Now go wait your table."

The following week at school, on Tuesday, Palomma had stayed after in the library. Christmas vacation began after a half day on Wednesday; the school had a collection of catalogs with prom invitations and name cards she wanted to dig through before vacation. She was the only one there other than Sister Magdalene, the librarian.

She heard footsteps, looked up and saw Christine come in and sit two tables away.

Palomma tried to focus on her catalogs but couldn't fight the urge inside her. She got up and walked over to a shelf near Christine.

"I'm surprised you're not getting ready for a date," she whispered. She tried to make it sound sarcastic.

Christine pretended to ignore her.

"Or maybe school's not so easy if someone else isn't doing the work for you," she continued.

"Quiet please!" said Sister Magdalene.

"*Oooo*, Miss Goody Two Shoes getting in trouble!" whispered Christine. "And I heard you don't do *anything* that's a teensy bit bad!"

Palomma's face turned red in anger. She wished she could think of comebacks like Doug because she didn't want to say what she was thinking.

"What's the matter?" whispered Christine. "Cat got your tongue?" She leaned closer. "It sure wouldn't be Doug!"

"Stop it!" yelled Palomma.

"You started it!" yelled Christine.

"Enough!" snapped Sister Magdalene. "I expected more from you two young ladies. You both will have detention tomorrow! Christmas vacation starts later for you!"

Christine clapped her hand across her mouth, feigning shock.

"Palomma Rossi gets detention!" she hissed. "Who'd have thunk it!"

Palomma gathered her things and stormed out of the library.

The next day, the bell rang signaling the end of the half-day on Wednesday. Students rushed out of school to start their Christmas vacation. Except for two.

Christine walked into room three to find Palomma already there, sitting in a desk in the corner. Mrs. Loman had detention duty and was sitting behind her desk.

The room was silent as a church for the entire hour. Mrs. Loman graded papers while Palomma compared prom invitation prices she'd found the day before. Christine sat on the opposite side of the room from her, her chin resting in her hand, staring out the window. The hum of the fluorescent lights was the only noticeable sound.

At 1 p.m., Loman put her papers into a briefcase. "Detention's done," she said. "Have a good Christmas, both of you." Christine got up quickly. "And a very merry Christmas to you too!" she said to the teacher, hurrying out the door. Palomma put her papers away and got up to leave. She stopped at Loman's desk. "I'm sorry you had to stay extra," she said. "Not to worry," replied Loman. "It's my job."

Palomma smiled and left the classroom.

After stopping at her locker, she started toward the phone booth to call her mother and saw Doug standing near it.

"Thought you might need a ride," he said as she neared.

Palomma smiled and blushed. They walked through the gym and out the back doors.

The school was deserted by now as they walked toward the parking lot. Without saying anything, Doug stopped and took Palomma's pile of books and papers from her, tucked them under his left arm, and held out his right hand.

Palomma looked him in the eyes and took hold of his hand.

Pete Baker was a busboy on Doug's shift at the restaurant that night. When there was a lull, Doug walked over to the servers' station where Pete was stacking water glasses.

"Hi Pete, remember me?" he said, extending his hand.

"Doug, right?" answered Pete, shaking it.

"You're pretty good at remembering names," said Doug. "We only met for a minute, what, two months ago!"

"Wasn't too hard," said Pete. "Mr. Little talks about you a lot."

Doug paused for a second. "Anyway, how do you like working here? I heard you got started on waiting!"

"Surprised the heck out of me!" said Pete. He wiped his hands on a towel. "I was just getting the hang of busing, and Mr. Little called me into his office and asked me if I wanted to be a waiter. He said you were out for a while. He sure is a nice man, Mr. Little!"

Doug found himself unable to even respond with something inane.

Pete leaned back against the counter. "He calls down and I deliver him a drink a lot when I'm on, asks how things are goin' at school, offers advice, it's like havin' a father…"

Pete stopped and turned back to the stack of glasses.

"It's none of my business…" Doug began.

"Naah, it's cool," answered Pete. "I ain't never had one so it ain't like I know what to miss."

"Never?" said Doug.

"Mom says he split before I was born," Pete continued, idly wiping a glass with the towel. "She ain't never married again, some guys take her out, nothing serious. We get by." He looked back at Doug. "That's why I was glad to get promoted. Make a little more. Mr. Little says I might be able to go do other things too if I keep my nose clean."

Doug suddenly wanted to warn Pete, tell him what those 'other things' probably were. Florence the hostess walked up. "Doug, you've got people at table eight. Peter, Mr. Little called for a martini. And Peter, fix your bowtie!"

"Damn thing keeps fallin' off," Pete said as fiddled with it on his collar. "I need to get one with a better clip."

Doug didn't get a chance to talk with Pete the rest of the night; he was gone again when they'd finished the breakfast changeover.

The next morning, Christmas Eve, Palomma and Doug were on the phone setting up the prom committee schedule for the next semester. When they finished Doug asked, "What movie would you like to go to during break?"

"With who?"

"You're getting funnier every day. A regular Bob Hope. With me."

"Did you have anything else in mind?"

"Um, well," Doug wasn't sure what she meant.

"Because if it's not something really special, I wonder what that means you're thinking," Palomma interrupted.

"Oh! Ummm, I guess…" Doug tried to continue.

"I mean, it's one thing if a boy and a girl do something special, you know, like a fancy dinner or the prom, but if they're doing regular things, going to the mall or a movie, the boy needs to clarify exactly where he's coming from."

Palomma sounded very serious all of a sudden. "I, I, um…" Doug stuttered.

"In fact, it makes me a little worried,"

Doug began to sweat a little.

"…because all of this started kind of suddenly and we didn't have a lot of time to think and sometimes when things happen fast, I know I don't always make the right decision."

Doug had drawn in a breath but found he couldn't exhale.

"So, speaking for myself, I think I have to ask some hard questions about us and doing things together," Palomma said, followed by a long pause.

There was simply humming on the phone now for a few seconds.

"…we're officially going steady, right?" she asked.

Doug suddenly was able to exhale. He thought for a moment.

"Wait a minute, you rehearsed that, didn't you?"

Palomma giggled.

"This is a side of Palomma Rossi I don't think I've ever encountered before," Doug said.

"What side?"

"A devious one. What's next, Gemma's been listening the whole time?"

"Since you mentioned it," said Palomma, "of course not! I'm kidding!"

"I hope you weren't kidding about going steady," said Doug.

"As you go through life, Douglas Halecki, you will learn there are topics about which women *never* kid, and they all have to do with her heart."

"Okay," said Doug, "as far as next week, would you like to see a movie?"

"Which one?"

"Does it matter?"

"Nope."

Doug was in a bit of a daze after hanging up with Palomma. They were a couple; she said it herself. He took a walk in the woods to let everything sink in. He'd reached his thinking spot and was about to sit down.

BANG!

There were always hunters in the area. It never really fazed Doug or his family—but this one was really close. Doug hid behind a tree until he heard a whimper.

A light brown dog with fluffy hair was laying on its side about twenty feet away, blood running from its back leg.

"Damn it!" shouted Doug, looking around. "They can't tell the difference between a deer and a dog?"

The dog looked at him with wide eyes, part pain and part fear. Doug crawled over and tried to comfort him; the dog tried to get up, hurting himself and yelping in pain. "Don't move!" Doug said. "I'll be right back!"

Doug sprinted back to his house and climbed into his car. He sped out of the driveway and headed up the street to where a dirt road ran alongside the woods, getting as close as he could to where the dog lay.

"There, there, buddy," said Doug, after he'd returned, stroking the dog's head for a few seconds. Doug scooped him up; he was more awkward than heavy, but Doug didn't want to hurt the already-wounded leg. He started to carry the dog back to his car as fast as possible.

Maybe it was the movement. BANG! Another shot.

"Jesus mother fucking Christ!" Doug hollered at the top of his lungs. "Shove that fucking gun up your fucking ass!"

Doug finally got to his car, set the dog in the backseat and sped out of the woods. The only vet's office he could think of was the Petcare Animal Hospital, a few miles away.

There was a car in the parking lot when Doug got there. He started to lift the dog out of his car when the veterinarian came out to help.

"What happened to your dog?" he asked.

"It's not my dog," Doug said. "I found him in the woods. Shot in the leg."

"Let's get him inside."

Doug followed as the vet opened the doors and led Doug to an examination room with a metal table. "Set him there."

"I can't stay," said Doug. "My parents don't know where I am. Here." He took out his wallet and handed the vet a twenty-dollar bill. "It's all I have."

"It's still all you have." The vet pushed his hand away.

"Thanks," said Doug. He stopped in the doorway and turned around.

"He'll be fine," said the vet, and he began tending to the dog.

When Doug got home, his father was sitting on the bench by the back door. As Doug walked up, his mother came out of the house.

"Where did you go?" she asked. Doug was surprised; it sounded like concern instead of accusation. He sat down on the bench.

"I found a dog in the woods. He'd been shot and I took him down to Petcare."

"We heard shots," his father said. "That's what it was?"

Doug sat down and told them the story. When he finished, his father said, "You took quite a risk there, but he'd have bled to death for sure. You saved his life."

"Thanks," Doug said.

"Where'd that hole in your coat come from?" his father asked, pointing as he sat down. Doug looked down at the end of his coat to see a neat round hole.

He looked up at his father. Doug's eyes got very wide. He looked down at the hole and gingerly touched it. He was shivering—and he wasn't cold.

"Is that…" Doug stood up and stared into the woods.

Doug's father put his arm around his shoulder. "Yeah, it is," he said softly. "I guess you were being looked out for today."

Chapter 21

Two weeks after school started again, Doug had left a note on Christine's locker to meet him in room six. He didn't plan on doing the article by himself the rest of senior year, no matter how much trouble she caused. He wasn't going to stand for it.

"Although," he said out loud, "she might have to stand for it!" He started laughing.

"Did you say something?" said Palomma.

"Just an inside joke."

"Then keep it inside. Some of us are trying to study."

Doug was surprised when Christine walked in and sat down at the table.

"Or not," Doug said.

"I'm sorry, what?" said Christine.

"Nothing, I was just thinking out loud. Hi, Christine, wanna get started?"

"Sure!" said Christine. "I got your note and I know it's been a while, so I hope you don't mind but I went and got stuff and wrote a draft. You can make any changes you want, and I'll type it and deliver it. Will that work?"

"Christine, that's great!" said Doug. "You didn't have to do it all yourself!"

"Why not?" said Christine. "How many times did you? Tape it to my locker. Gotta run, I have an appointment. Bye!"

She shot a dirty look at Palomma before getting up and heading out the door.

Doug sat back in disbelief. Palomma was humming.

"I can't be awake," said Doug. "Pinch me."

Palomma socked him on the arm.

Doug winced. "Pinch is not spelled with a 'u'."

"Sorry, my error" she answered. "What's so important to interrupt my studying?"

"You didn't see that?" he asked.

"I saw it."

"And you heard it too?"

"Ears working fine."

There was a pause.

"Mouth working?" Doug asked.

"Yeah, okay, we had a little talk," she whispered. "Let's not do that note thing, it wastes paper."

"Wait a minute, wait a minute," said Doug. "If this is as good as I think ... Pizza Hut?"

"*Concordato*," said Palomma.

"Would you please stop that?" Doug said. Palomma giggled.

After they found a table at Pizza Hut and ordered drinks, Doug said, "Okay, before anyone interrupts, about this talk."

"Well," Palomma started. "You know it's been pretty...tense."

"Pretty."

"Okay, you had a golf meeting a couple of days after we got back from break, remember? I asked Christine for a ride home and she didn't even look up so I asked again and she snapped 'Ask your boyfriend.' I said, 'Maybe I'll ask yours.' She said, 'Go right ahead, you know what the answer will be.' Then I said, 'Don't be so sure, he seems to like driving all over the place, like the Deptford Mall,' and she said, 'What's that supposed to mean?'"

"Christine says that a lot," said Doug.

"Anyway," continued Palomma," she said, 'Big deal, you go to a mall, at least Daniel takes me good places,' and I said 'you mean like Doug's house? Or the fireworks store?' and she stared at me, said I was making up stories…"

Palomma took a breath. "Suck in some air," said Doug, "sounds like you're near the finish line."

"So I told her if she *was* concerned about people telling stories, it would be *reeeaaaalllly* unfortunate if a story about a certain person and firecrackers were to get around the school. She said 'Who's gonna do that, you? You wouldn't dare.' And I said 'Maybe, but who knows, the next issue of Doug's fake school paper, the one he passes around, maybe he'll write about it. I'll bet it would be really funny if he told it…'"

"And then?" asked Doug.

"Then, heck if I know, all of a sudden her face kind of went white and she mumbled I could have a ride home and you saw her yourself today."

Doug chuckled and looked down at the table.

Palomma looked at him. "Spill it."

"I was talking to Andy about the next issue of my fake paper and I made a sound "BANG!" and Christine was close enough to hear me."

They clinked their soda glasses together.

"Brilliant minds think alike!" said Palomma. "The firecrackers story?"

"Nope!" said Doug. "It was about when some guy shot at Andy when he was stealing pumpkins!"

Palomma crossed her arms and raised an eyebrow.

"Pumpkins for his own house."

"Hey guys, mind if we join you?" said Katie. She, Ed, Andy and Paula had walked in.

"Why, have we come apart?" said Doug. Palomma shook her head back and forth.

"Isn't he funny?" she said. "He should be on a stage—the first one leaving town."

"No fair, you're stealing my jokes!" said Doug.

"It wasn't supposed to be a joke."

"I ordered a pitcher of beer!" Ed announced. "I'm legal now!"

"Sit right down!" Doug said. "If there's not enough room, Palomma can find another table!"

"As long as I can still reach the pitcher of beer," she retorted.

"Did you get the wood donated, Doug?" Katie asked.

Doug glanced at Palomma. "I don't want to violate protocol here," he said.

Andy interrupted. "I'm going to violate the alcohol." He poured himself a glass.

"Ahem," Doug said. "I was saying. Shouldn't you ask the chairperson?"

"Why?" said Katie. "Didn't you do it?"

"Because Beth makes me do all that who-what-where bullshit at class meetings," Doug answered. Beth was sitting at a nearby table and gave Doug the finger without looking at him.

"There's no beer at class meetings," said Ed.

"Oughta be," said Andy as he drained his glass and refilled it.

"All right," said Katie. "Palomma, Miss Chairperson, has anyone obtained the stuff we need for prom decorations?"

"I'm glad you asked!" said Palomma. "I believe our, what are you again, Doug?"

"Douchebag!" coughed Andy.

"Asshole!" coughed Ed.

Doug ignored them. "Vice-chairman," he answered. "One of them."

"That's it,' said Palomma. "I believe our vice-chairperson…"

"Chair-MAN" interrupted Doug.

"Chair-*thing*," said Palomma, "has some good news."

"Yes, thank you, your majesty, Holly Hill Lumber donated all the wood."

Doug waited; no one said anything.

"All the wood. Free. *Gratis*," continued Doug.

"No nails?" said Ed.

"Paint?" said Andy

Palomma patted Doug on the head. "Cut him some slack, he's new at this. Besides, he's also working on where we can actually have the prom. He's going to see if we can have it at the AmeriHost Inn."

"What other options are there?" asked Paula

"Here?" said Andy.

"AmeriHost Inn! All in favor, say aye!" said Palomma.

"Wait, is this vote legal?" asked Ed. "One of the officers is missing."

"You have a quorum," Beth shouted from the other table.

"Seriously, Beth, how do you know all this useless shit?" yelled Doug. She gave him the finger again.

"Okay, let's talk about getting nails and paint when we get back to school. Room three, 16th mod," said Doug.

"Excuse me?" said Palomma.

"Oh, yeah," said Doug. "Ms. Chairperson Ma'am, may I ask the prom committee to meet in room three?"

"Yes, you may," she answered. "In fact, you did. Don't repeat it."

"Tyrant," whispered Doug.

"*Suddito*," whispered Palomma.

Christine walked up to Palomma at her locker after the final bell.

"Wow, it's so nice of you to let me know when there's a prom committee meeting!" she said, loud enough to be heard by almost everyone in the hallway.

"It was spur-of-the-moment," answered Palomma, quietly, still facing her locker. "I had no idea where you were."

"That's the best you can do?" Christine folded her arms across her chest.

"Okay," said Palomma in a low voice, turning toward her. "I hereby call a prom committee meeting consisting of the chairperson and one of the co-chairpeople. Let's go."

She walked down the hall until she saw an empty classroom. Christine followed right behind. Palomma closed the door.

Christine was about to say something when Palomma spoke first.

"So what now? Your feelings are all hurt because I didn't run around the school trying to find you?"

"*Excuuuuuuuse* me, Miss Important!" said Christine. "Look how big your head's gotten because you got put in charge of something!"

Palomma was about to respond; instead, she held up her index finger and turned to the blackboard. She wrote a few words quickly and pointed at them.

"Okay, let's see. Yearbook. Hmmmmm, no Palomma there! PTA Committee; nope, can't see Palomma there either. But look, here's the Spirit Club—and right there with Palomma is Christine Holloway. Prom Committee? Another Christine sighting. Looks like I can't be"—she made air quotes with her fingers—"'in charge' of anything without you trying to horn in on it!"

"Horn in on it?" Christine blurted. "You had everyone get together without me! You're freezing me out!"

Palomma stepped closer to Christine.

"It was pure coincidence," she said in a lower voice. "Doug and I went to Pizza Hut and the others walked in. Sorry it doesn't fit your poor-poor-me speech."

Christine went to talk; Palomma interrupted.

"You know, like your story about meeting Daniel—oooo, what a co-incidence!"

A sly smile spread across Christine's face.

"I *knew* that's what this was all about!" she said smugly. Christine moved toward Palomma, who backed away. "I didn't make Daniel break up with you; *you* broke up with *him*. He made the choice, not *me*!"

"After you did everything you could to…" Palomma began to say.

"Just like *you* said, Columbo!" she said sarcastically. "'Pure coinci-dence.' Besides, you made out fine, you ended up with a boyfriend. Oops, maybe I shouldn't say 'made out!' From what I hear…"

"Don't you DARE go there!" snarled Palomma.

"I'll go anywhere I want!"

"Oh, yeah, like spying on us. GOD!" Palomma stomped her foot. "Damn it, WHAT did I ever do to you? Huh? What?"

Christine fluttered her fingers in a wave and walked out of the room.

"I thought you were my best friend!" Palomma called after her.

Beth approached Ed as he was getting into his car after school. "Hey, limousine driver! I need a ride home!"

"I suppose," he answered, "if they let bums like me in your neigh-borhood."

"Don't worry, I'll talk you past the guards."

After the short drive, they pulled onto Beth's street. "Wait, stop here," she said. Ed stopped.

"That's my fucking father's car in the driveway. I don't need to deal with his shit."

"Say what?" asked Ed. Beth stared straight ahead.

"My father...Hah! Father!" she said. "He's a lawyer. Ever wonder how I know that shit about meetings and rules? It's all I ever heard him talking about—if he was even around. Anyway, when he ditched my Mom, his judge buddies helped him set it up so his child support was pretty much nothing. Mom 'got' the house; yeah, she got to live in the house is what it was. If she can't keep up the mortgage, it goes to him."

"Sounds like shit from the get-go. Sorry you've had to go through it," said Ed.

"I got used to it," she said. "We get legal things in the mail, about all we ever hear from him now. Except when he comes here to ask if I'm still..."

Ed had a puzzled look on his face.

"Just another thing he lied about to leave my Mom," said Beth. "Said she made me this way. Probably because she'd stopped fucking him. Oh yeah, he makes sure to pay for school, 'cause they're gonna fix me there."

Ed stared out the window for a few seconds. "I got an idea," he said. "How about I do for you what you were talking about with me? Wanna be my girlfriend for a few minutes?"

Beth thought for a moment and smiled. "Sounds like fun!"

He started the car and pulled up just as her father came out of the house.

"Now slide over here, put your arms around me and pretend."

Ed could see her father staring at them past Beth's head.

Beth leaned back. "I got an idea, too."

She got out of the car. "Daddy!" she cried out. "I want you to meet Ed!" Her mother came out and stood on the steps.

Ed slowly sauntered over.

"He's from school!"

Her father eyed him up and down. "Hmmmmm…"

Ed put his arm around Beth. "We've been going out for a month now," she said. "Ed, this is my Daddy!"

"Hi Mr. Wheeler," Ed said, shaking his hand. He made sure to squeeze hard.

"So you're…"

"Oh Daddy!" Beth said with a squeaky voice. "That's my business!"

He started to slowly walk toward his car. "It was nice meeting you, it was Ed, right?" he said as he passed.

"Bye Daddy!" said Beth. They waved as he drove away.

"You think he bought it?" said Ed.

"I would have!" she said. They high-fived.

"Thanks for the ride and thanks for the idea," she said. She walked up to her mother and hugged her.

Sunday had been picked as the day each week to work on prom decorations in Doug's barn. The following Sunday was the first gathering.

"How am I supposed to get up there?" Palomma stared at the folding ladder Doug had pulled down from the second floor.

"By climbing the ladder, Madame Chairperson," said Doug.

"Do I look like I go around climbing ladders?" said Palomma. "Especially wobbly ones?"

"It's either that, or we'll do all this without you seeing it."

"Up the ladder," said Palomma, and she gingerly began climbing.

Ed and Andy were already upstairs. Christine arrived last and didn't say a word as Doug pointed to the ladder.

"All right," said Ed. "Here's how I see it. Plywood will be good for the lighthouse; two-by-fours for the bridge, and the scraps will be name boards for the tables."

"Paint?" Palomma asked. "I mean, what colors should we get?"

"We figured white and red for the lighthouse, red for the bridge," said Andy.

"Sounds good," said Palomma. "I made a drawing of where I thought things could go." She sat on the floor and unrolled a large sheet of paper in front of her; Doug moved next to her and Andy and Ed sat across from them.

Christine didn't move closer.

Andy nudged Ed, motioning with his head toward Christine. Ed scowled at Andy. "Christine, you can't see from there," said Andy. He patted the floor next to him. Christine didn't respond.

"Any questions?" said Palomma.

"Yeah," said Andy. He turned to Doug. "How come there's no fucking heat up here?"

"Any questions that aren't stupid?" said Doug. Andy gave him the finger.

"Okay," said Palomma, rolling up the paper and standing up. "We can start next week after Ed picks up the wood." One by one, they began climbing down the ladder.

"Did you catch Holloway?" asked Ed as he and Andy walked toward his car.

"Back off, bugaloo!" said Andy. "Halecki's off and I'm on like stink on shit!"

"What happened with you and Melody Jannsen?" asked Ed as they got in his car. "I thought you were making a move on her?"

"Hell with that," answered Andy as they drove away. "And what do you know anyway, wastin' time with Wheeler! I heard she's a lesbo!"

Andy regaled Ed with stories of what he would do with Christine all the way back to his house.

Doug was down to one night waiting and one night's shift as dishwasher at work. He went back to washing dishes figuring Little wouldn't be as interested if he stunk.

This Wednesday night's waiter shift was slow. He was sitting at the break table during a lull when Florence walked into the kitchen.

"Doug, Mr. Little's martini needs delivery."

"Where?" Doug asked hesitantly.

"Office," she answered.

Doug tensed; but the office was better than the apartment. Doug walked to the bar with trepidation, picked up the drink tray and carried it to Little's office. He knocked and the door opened.

"Where've y'all been? I haven't seen you in a coon's age!" said Little, standing in the doorway. Doug walked in slowly.

Little gulped down the drink and walked toward Doug. The same routine, some stroking, the hand moving up his thigh, the opening of his zipper. Doug focused on a painting on the wall as he'd done before, trying to think about anything but what was going on.

There was a knock at the door.

Little said nothing.

Another knock.

"Mr. Little?" It was Erika from banquet sales. Doug silently begged her not to stop.

Little looked at Doug, shook his head ever so slightly from side to side and pointed down. Doug zipped up his pants.

Little opened the door.

"Hello, Mr. Little. Oh, hi Doug! I didn't know you were here!"

"He brought me a drink," said Little.

"What a coincidence! I was bringing contracts for you to approve—one's for Doug's prom!" She handed a manila folder to Little.

"Fine, fine, honey," said Little. "Thanks."

Erika and Doug stood motionless.

"Y'all need somethin' else?" asked Little. He sounded perturbed.

Erika began to back away toward the door. "I'm sorry, Mr. Little. I thought you'd sign them right now."

Little pushed the folder aside. "I need to give 'em a good lookin' and seein'."

"I better get back!" said Doug. He quickly grabbed the tray and empty carafe and moved toward the door, almost bumping into Erika. They left the office and Doug pulled the door closed.

"I'll let you know when I get it," Erika told Doug as they walked down the hall.

Christine and Daniel had gone out to dinner at a fancy restaurant Saturday night; he'd asked her to wear a dress. He'd picked her up in a car, explaining his truck was in the shop and he'd borrowed the car from a co-worker. After dinner, he drove to their usual parking spot behind the ball field.

Daniel turned off the ignition and got out the driver's side. "Come on," he said to Christine. She had a confused look on her face as she got out and walked around the car.

Daniel pushed the seat forward. "Get in the back."

Christine didn't move.

"Relax, I'm not gonna jump your bones tonight!" said Daniel, laughing. "But since we got a car, we could use a little more room for...exploration, you know?"

Christine vacillated. "Um, Daniel," she said softly. "I can't tonight.

It's that time of the month."

"Jesus fucking Christ!" Daniel yelled. Christine jumped. "I don't suppose you could have clued me in on that little fact before, huh?"

"Before?" Christine asked.

"Before I spent all that money!" Daniel snapped.

Christine didn't know what to say. She leaned toward him and said, "Maybe we could just, you know, cuddle tonight?"

"Fuck off!" he yelled and slapped her across the face.

Christine fell back against the car door with her eyes open wide, rubbing her face. Daniel pushed her into the front seat and got in himself, started the car and drove extremely fast to her house. He stopped a little way up the street from it.

"Sorry," he said.

Christine remained silent.

"I'm sorry, really," he repeated.

"You hit me," Christine whispered, sobbing.

Daniel suddenly covered his face. "Oh God, I'm sorry!" he said. "It's wrong, I know it's wrong!" He lowered his hands and looked at Christine. "I got hit so much growin' up, um, it's a defensive thing, you know? It's my stepfather's fault, he hit me so many times…"

His voice trailed off and he covered his face again.

Christine watched his shoulders shaking.

"Sometimes I get tense from work and, and I do the wrong thing." He wiped his eyes with the palm of his hand, then turned to Christine with a sad look on his face.

"All right," Christine said softly. "But never again."

"Never again," Daniel repeated.

Chapter 22

Doug picked up Palomma the next day to work on prom decorations. When they got back to his house, no one else had arrived yet. They climbed the ladder in the barn.

"Christine's not coming today," said Doug. "My Mom answered the phone. Something about getting hurt, I don't know…"

Palomma turned and faced Doug.

"About the prom…"

Doug looked around.

"That's what we're here to do, right?" asked Doug.

"I mean about it…and us."

Doug puzzled for a second. "Oh, *that* about-the-prom!" He slapped his own forehead. "I'm an asshole, okay? Here we are working on this crap and I never…"

He got down on one knee.

"Palomma, would you go to the prom with me?"

He saw a tear well up in Palomma's eye and roll down her cheek. Her lower lip trembled. "Why did you have to ask like *that*?" she said, looking away.

Doug stood up. "I never did it before. Did I do it wrong?"

"No, no, that's not what I'm talking about." Palomma turned back and took Doug's hand. "I'm worried about after it."

"Going down the shore?"

"No, I mean after, after." She turned away from Doug again.

"People go to the prom together," she said. "In a gown and a tux, just like, you know, other things with gowns and tuxes. Senior year ends, and some people…"

"I'm going to college," Doug interrupted. "So are you."

"And that's what happens, right?" Doug could hear Palomma's voice break a little. "Some people get married and they're together, and the others…"

She turned away and whispered, "Aren't."

"Why?" asked Doug.

"Because…*because that's what'll happen to me*!" Palomma blurted out and started crying.

Doug touched her arm. "Shhhhhh, don't cry."

Palomma kept sobbing. "It's not you, it's me! I'm a jinx!"

"What are you talking about?" asked Doug.

"Just when I start getting my hopes up about something, boom! It's gone!" she cried. "Starting high school—oops! Gotta move away! Have a best friend? Not anymore! Get a boyfriend—uh-oh! He's a jerk!"

She stopped and looked at Doug. "You know what, I mean who I'm talking about!"

Palomma sobbed a few more times. Doug thought for a moment.

"You see those woods back there?" said Doug, pointing. "Okay, I mean if there wasn't a wall the woods you'd see. I've walked a lot of circles around those woods."

"Please don't say anything about 'going around in circles' because I've heard all the clichés in my life I want to…" Palomma started to say, wiping her eyes.

"I wasn't going to," said Doug. "Actually, if I was going to use a cliche, I'd say sometimes I feel like I jumped into a lake without a clue how to swim."

274

"That's an analogy," said Palomma. She sniffled. Then giggled.

They looked at each other and laughed.

Doug sighed. "If we're weird like you said, what makes you think we won't do things different than other people? I mean, before, you were the only weirdo in it. I'm in it now too—we put the double weirdo whammy on whatever could happen!"

Palomma sighed. Doug sat down on the floor. Palomma sat facing him.

"Let's take a walk down memory lane, shall we?" said Doug. "You know, around the woods? *That's* a cliché, right? That's the right word?"

"As long as stuff doesn't start blowing up like on that other walk," said Palomma.

They both sighed.

"I never told you, but at the cast party, I was all set to ask Christine out again. *She* told *me* how it was gonna be. Friends. Period."

"I wondered what had gone on."

"Then you and me are friends, and somehow we go out, now were going steady, and damn it, I can't figure out anything anymore. So I'm not going to try."

Doug moved over to sit next to Palomma. "I'm only sure about one thing." His voice cracked. "I like you as much as a guy who doesn't know anything about love can."

Palomma stared into his eyes.

"I have a feeling," she whispered, "you'll know what it means when I say…"

She gave Doug a kiss.

"I love liking you a lot."

Doug kissed her back.

"I love liking you a lot too," said Doug. "And you never answered me about the prom."

"How's this?" said Palomma.

Palomma wrapped Doug in her arms and began to kiss him. She whispered, "It sure is cold up here!" Doug felt her hand moving up his thigh...and he tensed and backed up.

Palomma looked at him in confusion.

"Anybody home?" Ed shouted from downstairs.

Both of them stood up quickly and moved apart. "Yeah, Ed, up here!" Doug shouted.

Ed climbed the ladder and saw them across the room. "Do I smell hanky-panky?" he asked, kiddingly.

He saw Doug blush a deep red.

Palomma didn't. She stared at Doug for a few seconds.

Palomma ran up to Doug in the parking lot before school the following Wednesday. "Good! I'm glad I caught you! You didn't say your newspaper seminar yesterday was going to take all day!"

"I didn't know myself," said Doug.

"Any luck on the contract? For the prom?"

"They haven't told me yet," he said, shrugging. "I mean, I asked, right after I started working again, they just haven't told me."

"Maybe you have to be a little pushy," said Palomma, giving him a playful shove. "I mean, the prom's less than four months!"

Before Doug could answer, Palomma walked away.

"Florence, I need a minute; I gotta ask Erika something," said Doug to the hostess that night at the restaurant.

"Make it quick," said Florence.

Doug walked toward Erika's office and knocked on the door. "Come in!" said Erika.

"Um, I was wondering if that reservation, I mean, if the contract was ready for our prom in May. They're bugging me about it at school."

"You saw, I gave it to Mr. Little for approval two weeks ago!" said Erika. "He hasn't signed it yet?"

"No, I mean, I don't know," said Doug.

Erika picked up the phone and punched a button. "Hello? Mr. Little? I've got Doug Halecki in my office asking about his prom. Have you approved it yet? I see. I'll tell him. Thanks, Mr. Little."

She hung up. "He says to stop at his apartment and get it after changeover."

Doug could feel himself turning pale. "Uh, yeah, okay. Thanks, Erika." He hurried back to the restaurant.

When the final table had been reset for breakfast, Doug started down the hall to Little's apartment. He could feel his legs shaking.

He knocked. "Who is it?" Little called out.

"Doug Halecki," he replied, softly.

Little opened the door. He was wearing the same robe.

Doug didn't move. "Erika said I could get the contract for our prom."

"C'mon in, I'll get it," said Little, turning and walking to the table. He picked up a piece of paper and handed it to Doug. "This is it. All set for y'all."

Doug looked. The date was filled in and the meal cost, but there was no signature.

"Erika said it had to be signed," Doug said, hesitantly.

Little took the paper back. "How forgetful of me! Lemme get a pen."

As Little walked into the next room, Doug realized he was standing in the same spot as the last time he'd been in the apartment. Seconds seemed like hours as he waited to be able to leave.

He froze in horror. A bowtie, the kind the waiters wore, was on the floor next to the easy chair.

"Here you go!" said Little, walking back. "All John Handcocked, ready to go!" He set the contract on the table and put his hand out to shake. Doug began to shake his hand and Little squeezed it tightly. He locked eyes with Doug and continued to grip Doug's right hand, using his free left hand to unbuckle Doug's pants.

In a second, he had his pants and underwear down and was on his knees in front of Doug, gripping his hips. Doug closed his eyes as tightly as he could and felt Little's mouth on his dick.

Little would alternately suck it and masturbate it, pushing Doug's butt with the other hand. Doug couldn't help it; he got a boner. He felt as if he was going to collapse and tried not to look down.

Before long, he ejaculated.

He didn't even want to open his eyes but had to grab the contract. Doug hooked his thumbs under his belt and yanked his pants up, reached for the contract—and saw Little was completely naked. He dashed out the door and didn't even bother to go clock out.

Doug wasn't thinking about killing himself while driving home this time. He was trying not to throw up. He couldn't shake the feeling of a man's mouth on him; he rolled the window down to try to shock it out. It was below freezing outside, but Doug was numb from more than the cold.

His parents were sound asleep when he got home. He stripped off his pants, shirt and briefs and balled them up; then he put on a sweatshirt and jeans and crept out of the house and back into the woods and set the clothes on fire.

Doug watched the fire to make sure it didn't spread. It was time to stop kidding himself about it; he was queer. After all, he'd just had sex with a man.

Palomma had been pretty obvious about making out in the barn, and he'd frozen. He watched the flames dance in the darkness until nothing was left but charred cloth. He stepped on the embers and crept back into the house.

Doug curled up into a ball in bed and held off crying as long as he could.

"Thanks *so* much for getting the prom contract worked out!" said Palomma as she got into Doug's car after school the next day.

"Yeah, okay..." said Doug, staring out the driver's side window.

"'Course, if you'd waited a little bit longer, we'd have had to talk Pizza Hut into letting us use all the tables!" Palomma laughed.

"I said I was sorry for not getting to it," answered Doug. Palomma was surprised by his testiness.

"I was kidding!" she said. "Don't be such a grump!"

Doug didn't answer.

Palomma was quiet for a while as they drove to her house. "Valentine's Day is Wednesday, you know..." she finally began saying.

"Yeah, it sure is," said Doug.

"Did you have anything in mind?"

Doug took a second to answer. "I don't know, I guess we could do something," he said, dully.

"Precisely what I was thinking!" bubbled Palomma. "I thought maybe tomorrow night instead of next week! And I had this really great idea!"

Doug didn't say anything.

"Try not to get too excited," she said, sarcastically.

Doug sighed. "Okay, what is this great idea?"

"I'm glad you asked!" said Palomma, bubbling again. "How about you take me to the restaurant where you work? I heard it's *reeeeeeallly* fancy! I could get dressed up and you could get dressed up and we could..."

Doug interrupted. "Why the *hell* would I want to go back *there*?"

Palomma was taken aback by his response. "Uh, because you'd be taking me?" she said, softly. "Your sweetheart?"

"It's bad enough I have to put up with shit there, stay so late, my boss is an asshole, now you want me to go back when I'm not working? Christ, you can't think of anything else? *That* was your great idea?" Doug waved his hand angrily.

"Like you even had one?" she said sarcastically.

"It wouldn't have been as fucked up as *that*," he snarled.

He slammed his hand on the steering wheel. Palomma flinched.

Doug stared at the road until he heard a tiny sob. He tried to think of something to say but his mind was blank. He slammed the wheel again.

"Please stop that. You're scaring me," whispered Palomma.

Doug remained silent.

"I was just trying to think of something…" she reached over and touched his arm, "different."

Doug jerked his arm away.

"Different? Oh, that's a *great* choice of words! Different! Maybe I don't *want* to be different! Maybe I don't even want to go to a prom!" He was yelling now. "And don't expect me to apologize because you said I apologize too much and I'll be *damned* if I'm going to apologize when it isn't my fault!"

Doug stopped at a stop sign. He looked at Palomma and saw she was hiding her face in her hands, trembling.

He pulled into her driveway and turned to her.

"Look, I'm…"

Palomma spun away and opened the door. "You don't have to say *anything*." She got out and faced him through the open door. "In fact, I'd prefer you DIDN'T say anything. I'd prefer you keep your mouth SHUT if you can't even acknowledge me making an effort! Whatever that was all about, I'm not taking crap like that anymore! The feeling is mutual— I certainly don't want to go to the prom if it's with YOU! I'll be leaving now, so feel FREE to punch anything in the car you want to!"

She slammed the door shut and stormed toward her house.

Doug started to get out to follow her but stopped, started the car, and slowly backed out into the street.

Doug had his coat on and walked through the kitchen that night when his mother asked, "Where are you going? I thought you didn't work tonight?"

Doug thought for a second. "Uh, no, I mean yeah, they changed the schedule. I have to go in."

"In jeans?"

Doug looked down. "Yeah, I'm washing dishes tonight."

Doug didn't know where he was going but couldn't bear the thought of sitting at home. He knew he should apologize to Palomma—but he didn't think she'd even talk to him now. Maybe never again.

He stopped at Sheehan's liquor store and bought a bottle of Tequila Tango. He drove around Holly Hill aimlessly, hitting from the bottle from time to time. He didn't feel like he cared if got pulled over. A half-hour later, he drove to the industrial park and parked in the same cul-de-sac.

Doug lay back against the car door, lit a cigarette and swigged from the bottle. He lit another one as soon as he finished the first one. "So that's it, huh?" he shouted, drunkenly. "I'm a fag, right? I'm a fucking fag!"

He sat up, rolled down his window and tossed the bottle out; it smashed on the asphalt.

Doug didn't remember driving from the industrial park to St. John's church, but he was standing in front of its side door, which had always been unlocked in grade school; he tugged it and it opened.

Doug went inside. It was dark except for the flickering light of the votive candles in racks lining the walls. He walked to the back of the church and sat in a pew, staring at the floor with his chin propped in his hands. "Everything I think is wrong isn't. Or it is," he said out loud. "So why am I even fucking here?"

"If you figure out the answer, let me know," he heard a voice say. Father Paul Kiniski was standing next to the pew. Doug recognized his voice but didn't look up.

Father Paul's hair hung down past his collar. While other priests repeated the same religious cliches in their sermons, Father Paul talked about what was going on in the world. A lot of people badmouthed him, thought he was a hippie, a radical. Doug had always liked him and trusted him in grade school.

"It's fucked up. If I do it, it's fucking wrong, but it's not for other people. And I'm not apologizing for cussing in church. Add it to the fucking list!"

"Standing on this marble floor isn't doing my back any good," said Father Paul.

Doug slid over and Father Paul sat down. They sat in silence a full minute.

"It's wrong...I mean, it's not right...um, like, God says it's a sin, right?"

Father Paul looked at Doug but didn't respond.

Doug sat up straight, putting his hands on his knees. "Okay, I, um, have this friend, and someone did something to him."

Father Paul stood up. "If I hear 'I have a friend' one more time, I swear, I'm telling people to say Hail Marys every waking moment for the rest of their lives."

Doug looked up at him. "I'm not lying! His name's—you won't tell anyone, right?"

Father Paul raised an eyebrow, running a finger under his clerical collar. He sat down again.

"Yeah, okay. His name's Pete. I think someone did something wrong to him."

"You think?"

"Okay, I know."

"How do you know?"

"I was there, okay? I mean, I was where it happened, uh, after it happened, I mean in the same place…Jesus!" Doug lowered his head and started again.

"Okay, there's this girl I know."

Father Paul sighed very loud.

Doug looked up. "Palomma. Her name is Palomma."

"That's a really beautiful name."

"Yeah, anyway, some guy did something to her, you know, tried to make her do something."

"You were there too? They let you watch?" said Father Paul incredulously.

"No. She told me."

"Palomma's your girlfriend."

"Why would you say that?"

"Girls only tell those things to their best friend and their boyfriend," answered Father Paul. "Somewhere in all this is something to do with someone making someone do something, am I on the scent?"

"Yeah. Kind of. I mean, it's wrong, right? If someone, you know, makes you do something you don't want to, it's wrong, right?"

"Right. It's wrong."

"Except," Doug turned away. "Except, what if he—it was like he liked it?"

"He?"

"SHE!" Doug corrected himself. "She. I mean, she said as much."

"She told you that?" said Father Paul. "You've got a special woman there, hardly anyone's that open."

"Did I say she? I meant he. Pete."

Father Paul crossed his arms. "Pete's a guy, right?"

"Yeah, of course. What did you think I meant?"

"It's getting a little hard to follow you."

Doug took a deep breath. "Okay, fine. You want to hear it? Some guy made Pete do something he didn't want to, and Pete, you know, it happened. Now he thinks he's a queer." Doug sat back and stared straight ahead.

"Really?"

Doug looked at Father Paul. "You do know what a queer is, right?"

"I think the question here is whether you do."

"What do you mean, whether I do?" snapped Doug.

"Oh, sorry. Pete. Whether PETE knows." He turned in the pew to face Doug. "How well do you know Pete?"

"Good enough," said Doug.

"I suppose if he told you *that*," said Father Paul. "Ask him if he masturbates."

Doug flinched.

"Masturbates. Jerks off. Chokes the chicken. You've figured that out by now, right?"

Doug slammed the pew with his hand. "This is all bogus. One day it's don't play with yourself or you go to hell and now you're tellin' me I'm supposed to know how to play with myself. And what about the guy…"

Doug stopped in mid-sentence and looked away.

Father Paul leaned forward with his hands folded in his lap and spoke softly. "I'm not making light of any of this. I'm just trying to explain something. It's a safe bet your friend Pete masturbates. All guys do. I did. I liked girls, dated my share. I was a boob man, myself."

"And you became a priest," said Doug, sarcastically. "That makes zero sense."

"Yeah, it does." Father Paul said. "I liked girls, but I felt I needed to do something different, something that mattered, something to challenge myself, something difficult. There's no challenge in doing something easy."

"Yeah, so what? I deal with a lot of shit that isn't easy," said Doug.

"Maybe you're being challenged."

"Maybe I don't want to be."

"Maybe you don't have a choice."

Doug pointed at Father Paul. "I call bullshit. Why would God challenge you and make you do something wrong?"

"Like what?"

"Like…" Doug started vibrating, trying not to burst out crying. Father Paul put his arm around him.

"Your friend Pete touches himself, and if some man touched him and the same thing happened it means he took advantage of the way the human body's made. How much did you have to drink tonight?"

Doug tensed.

"You're eighteen, right? You're legal. I'm just saying—you caught a buzz, right?"

"Yeah."

"No matter how hard you might've tried NOT to, you still would have. It's how your body reacts to alcohol, not whether you want to get drunk or not. *Capish*?"

Doug smirked. "Palomma says that."

They sat in silence for a few seconds.

"Tell your friend Pete the thing he needs to worry about is not being anywhere near someone like that. I mean, the fact he's got a girlfriend—you know, like you do—and I'll bet he likes kissing her but dreads what that guy does to him, that's what he's counting on. Getting him confused. Getting him to give in."

He took his arm off Doug's shoulder.

"Pete's gonna be fine. Let me let you in on a something anyway. The guy who did stuff to…Pete, he's not a homosexual. He's a pedophile. It isn't because you're a guy he's doing that to you, it's because you're a teenage guy."

Doug suddenly sat straight up.

"To Pete, I mean. Pete's a teenager. Right?" said Father Paul.

"Right," answered Doug.

Father Paul stood up. Doug stood up and hugged him.

"Thanks, father," said Doug.

"You're welcome," Father Paul answered. "Two things. First, apologize to Palomma."

Doug went to say something; Father Paul cut him off.

"We males have a habit of taking out our problems on females because we know they won't kick us in the balls like we deserve. And second…"

Doug waited.

"Don't breathe out anywhere near the candles when you leave. This place'll go up in flames!"

Father Paul walked with Doug back to his car. "You're good to drive?" he asked.

"I'm good," answered Doug.

Chapter 23

Doug woke up the next day with a start; it was nearly noon on Saturday. He was still wearing the clothes he'd had on the night before. He never got to sleep late, his parents always woke him up for something he had to do. He sat up and tried to clear his head of the liquor and make sense of all the things that had happened.

He changed, brushed his teeth and headed out the door. "I gotta go somewhere, Ma, be back soon!" he called out to her in the laundry room before she could say anything.

Doug took a deep breath and rang Palomma's doorbell.

Almost a minute passed. Finally, Palomma opened the door.

"There's no other way for me to say I'm sorry except to say I'm sorry," Doug began softly, before she could say anything. "I couldn't have been a bigger asshole to you. If you never forgive me, I deserve it."

Palomma looked into Doug's eyes. The argument from the day before had locked an angry expression on her face.

"Come inside and close the door," she said, tersely.

As soon as he closed the door, Doug began to speak. "I know you were…"

"Not here," said Palomma, holding up her hand and looking around. "Let's go down in the basement. I've got things to say and you need to shut up and listen."

Doug followed Palomma down the basement stairs. Doug sat down on a sofa. Palomma sat on a stuffed chair five feet away.

"First of all, I was more than a little pissed when you didn't call yesterday! For all the times you apologized for every little thing when it was..."

Doug interrupted. "You're absolutely right. I could have. I *should* have, and I didn't."

Palomma paused, then began again. "I was trying to do something for you and I didn't appreciate your reaction at all." Her voice began to get a little louder with every sentence as she thought back to the day before. "*Most* girls would *expect* a boy to make the plans for Valentine's Day, surprise them, and there I was thinking things up and you treated me like dirt!" She stood up and pointed at Doug. "I get it, you don't like your job but I don't like that photo booth either, it was always like an oven in there, but I *deal* with it!" She kept stabbing the air at him with her finger. "Don't take it out on me because you don't like where you work!"

Palomma trailed off when she saw Doug hadn't taken his eyes off her the whole time she was speaking—but tears had rolled down his cheeks. She sat down where she'd been before.

"It isn't that I don't like my job," he began, softly. "It's just,"

Suddenly, it all came spilling out. In a hushed voice, Doug told her everything from months ago to the past week.

Palomma was frozen in shock. Doug didn't leave out any details and Palomma tried to picture things she couldn't possibly have imagined before. She couldn't even open her mouth to say anything, but slumped back into the chair stupefied, staring at Doug.

When Doug finished, he shrugged. "Like I said, I'm sorry. And I'm sorry for making you think, letting you think...wasting your time...with me." Doug covered his face.

Palomma whispered, "I, I, oh God..." She moved over and sat down next to him on the couch. "Doug that's horrible! For a grown man to—oh my God!" She stiffened; a clear picture of what Doug had described had suddenly appeared in her head. "How could you even have gone back there?" she whispered.

Then she gasped.

"Oh my God, *I made you go back there!*"

"No, you didn't," whispered Doug from behind his hands. "I didn't do a damn thing. I was afraid to quit. I let him play me like a drum. And I hid it from you."

"Have you told anyone? I mean, anyone else? Did you tell your parents?" she whispered.

Doug shook his head. "Palomma, my parents gave me a *book* about sex. And it sure didn't have that in it!"

Palomma leaned forward a little. "Maybe someone else?" she whispered. "You could tell the police or something! You can't let him get away with it!"

Doug sighed. "The chief of police was there every Friday for lunch in the summer. The mayor, all those big shots. Never paid. Him laughing with them. Who'd believe me?"

Doug looked away. "Thing is, I didn't want to tell anyone. I don't want anyone to know…what I am. Like that day in the barn…"

It took a second for Palomma to realize what Doug meant. She reached over and grasped his hand, pulling him toward her. She felt him shaking.

"The first time it happened," he said,—Palomma winced—"I told myself I wasn't going to let him do it again, but I did."

"You didn't have much choice," Palomma whispered.

"Don't you get it?" said Doug, pulling away from Palomma. "I could've quit! I told myself not to because of what my parents might say, but I guess the truth is," he dropped down to his knees and covered his face again, "maybe that's what I am. '

Palomma walked over and pulled Doug to his feet, took hold of his arm and turned him around.

"What you are is the most wonderful guy I know," she said softly. "I let people take advantage of me to get what they wanted too, screwing with my head, making me think things about myself I didn't want to. We can't let them do that anymore."

"We?" said Doug, hesitantly.

"Us. You and me. Remember what I told you—when it comes to the heart, women don't play games." She put his hand over her heart. "Mine tells me you were taken advantage of by a monster. Mine tells me what you are."

She squeezed Doug and gave him a long, wet kiss. Then she whispered, "You can touch my butt if you want!" Doug laughed, put both hands on it, picked her up and carried her to the couch. Doug held her in his lap and they kissed as passionately as either of them ever had.

"As far as that place goes, quit," said Palomma, firmly. "I'll help think up something to tell your parents if they get mad."

"What about the prom?" said Doug. "What if…"

"What if what?" said Palomma. "You got the contract, I checked, it's signed, it's totally legit. There's a benefit to having a girlfriend who's going to be a lawyer!"

Palomma slid off his lap and snuggled against him.

Doug sighed. "So, about Valentine's Day," he said. "If it's not too late, I'd like to take you up on your idea to go there for dinner. I'll call for a reservation for Monday. If that's okay."

Palomma hesitated. "But you don't have to…"

"You've done so much for me, and I think I need to do something for someone else. Someone there," he said.

"Okay," said Palomma. "Who else there…"

"Good," Doug said quickly. "Now I have to get home, I didn't tell my parents where I was going today!"

"How about fifteen more minutes?" said Palomma.

"How come?" asked Doug. Palomma gently touched his thigh.

"Oh."

When Doug got home, he walked to the barn and found his father tuning up the family car. He watched him work for a minute. "Need help with anything?" he finally asked.

His father looked up and pointed, "Yeah, get these spark plugs ready." Doug started to set the gap on the plugs as his father had shown him.

"You got in pretty late last night," his father said from under the hood.

Doug didn't respond. His father moved away from the engine, wiping his hands on a rag. "Busy night at the restaurant?"

"Um, I didn't go to work last night." Doug turned toward his father. "I, uh, okay, I lied to Mom because I needed to go somewhere and think about some things. I ended up at St. John's."

"You lied to your mother," his father said, almost matter-of-factly.

They stared at each other for a moment.

"If you need to think, that's a good place," said his father. "And"—he pretended to zip his lips shut—"mum's the word with Mom." He pointed at Doug. "But don't think you're sleeping 'til noon every Saturday!" It was the first time Doug had ever seen his father with a smirk on his face. "Okay, how about you swap out those plugs?"

Doug grinned. They went back under the hood and finished the tune-up together.

The phone rang after dinner. "Doug! It's Palomma from school!" said his mother.

Doug picked up the hall extension. "Got it, Ma!"

"Good news if you're not claustrophobic!" said Palomma. "I called my boss and asked about any hours at PhotoQuik. He's got another booth near your house and said he needs someone. I guess there aren't enough people stupid enough to lock themselves into those little things!"

"And we've got 6:30 reservations on Monday at the restaurant," said Doug.

After Palomma and Doug finished their dinner at the Amerihost on Monday night, Doug helped Palomma put her coat on and said, "Follow me." He led her to the time clock. Everyone's timecards were in their slots, with the week's pay envelope behind them. Doug pulled out Pete's timecard, took an envelope out of his pocket and slid it in the slot so Pete would see what he'd written on the front: 'To Pete, from Doug'. He replaced the card in front of it. Doug took his own paycheck from its slot.

"We've got one more delivery," he said, putting a finger to his lips. He crept quietly into the hall with Palomma following and leaned around a corner. "The coast is clear," he whispered. Doug tiptoed to an office door that had a sign reading "Innkeeper," took an envelope out of his other vest pocket and slipped it under the door. He took Palomma by the arm and hurried toward the door.

"I gave Pete my phone number," said Doug. "Told him to call me, I'd help him find another job. He needs to get out of there too." Palomma smiled.

"And I think you know what the second one was," said Doug as they drove away.

"What did you write on that one?" she asked.

"Two words," answered Doug.

"Clean ones?" said Palomma. They both laughed.

"Wait a sec," said Beth…and she started slapping herself in the face.

"What the fuck are you doing?" asked Ed.

"I don't blush good," she answered. Then she mussed up Ed's hair and stepped out of her bedroom.

"Daddy! I didn't know you were coming over today!" Her father was talking to her mother in the foyer.

"Hello, Elizabeth," he said. "I was just checking…on…"

He trailed off when he saw Ed step out of Beth's room behind her.

"Hi, Mr. Wheeler!" Ed said cheerily. He ran his hand through his hair.

"We were…studying!" said Beth. "Right Ed?"

"Oh yeah, studying!" he said.

"Where are your books?" her father asked.

"I was using Beth's," Ed replied.

Beth's father rested a finger on the side of his cheek. Her mother was trying desperately not to laugh.

"We better get going!" Beth said in a high-pitched voice. She took hold of Ed's hand and they turned sideways to pass her parents. As they started to go out the door, they heard her father ask her mother, "Do they usually go in her room?"

"You should have acted in Dolly instead of doing stage crew!" said Ed as they walked outside. "That pause before you said 'studying'…for a minute, *I* thought we'd been fooling around!"

"You're not bad yourself," she said. She imitated his voice. "Using her books. You should have had your shirt untucked though!"

"Next time," said Ed as they got into his car.

"We're gonna need more wood," Ed said in Doug's barn the following Sunday.

"Looks like we have enough," said Doug.

"Nope," said Ed, "unless you want a bridge you go up but can't come down."

"Wait," Andy said. "I think I'd have to be stoned for that to make sense."

"Since when do you need an excuse to get stoned?" said Doug. He pointed to the ladder. "To the lumberyard."

Ed and Andy climbed down. Doug paused before following them.

"Thanks again for showing up today, Christine!" he said, not trying to disguise the sarcasm. "Palomma'll show you what needs to be done."

Christine stared after him, turned to Palomma and said, "Yowsah, boss, what am I supposed to do?" also dripping with sarcasm.

"Those name boards need to be painted white," she said matter-of-factly.

"Painting?" said Christine. "You want me to get paint all over my nails? Don't you have gloves or something?"

Palomma smiled at her. "I guess you're just going to have to tough it out."

Christine walked to the corner where the boards were stacked. "Yes ma'am!"

The girls worked silently for a few minutes until Christine said, "These things should be white letters on red, not this way."

Palomma turned. "*What*?!" she said, sharply.

"I said they ought to be the other way around," Christine began, "if you want them to look *good*..."

"ENOUGH!" shouted Palomma, standing up. Christine jumped and stared at her.

"You know what we *ought* to be doing? We *ought* to be doing what everyone agreed on, *not* what Christine Holloway thinks is best!

Capish?!" Palomma pointed angrily at Christine. "I'll tell you one thing, here's what we're not gonna do! We're not going back to you taking charge of everything and we sure aren't going back to me backing down! I'm through letting you take advantage of me to get what you want! Those days are gone! *Finito*!"

Palomma breathed in and out heavily.

"All I was doing was making a suggestion," Christine snarled. "You didn't have to get so uppity about it. God!"

"I hate this shit," Palomma muttered, turning away. "I hate it."

"What?!" barked Christine. "You hate me? Say it to my face!"

"Oh, grow the fuck up!" snarled Palomma.

Christine turned her back.

"I know you hate me, you think you're faking me out?" she said flippantly. "You can stop pretending. That's all you ever did before anyway."

Palomma was about to respond when Christine stood up.

"Enough of all this crap! It's me. Not the nuns. You can ditch the goody two-shoes stuff. Show some guts and say it. You hate me. You're the one who always preaching about"—she put on a sneering voice – "honesty."

Palomma turned and stared at Christine. "Hate you? Pissed off at you about a lot of things, yeah, I'd say *that* was honest. Disappointed so many times? Honesty and a *half*. Hate you? I hate the stupid mind games, that's what! And why bring this out now, all of a sudden?"

"It's coming here," said Christine. "That's what it's all about anyway."

"Yeah, you would think that," Palomma muttered, looking away. She turned back. "Let's get this over with. We were friends way too long."

"Wow, you're in charge of deciding if we're still friends or not too?"

Christine sneered. They were facing each other, inches apart.

"Christine, you know I'm not lying because I stink at lying," said Palomma. "I thought we were friends, now I don't know what to think. God knows how *you* think."

"What's that supposed to mean?" said Christine, testily. "You know what I think? I think you're starting to think you're a big shot, you get to decide everything, that's what!"

"You can dish it out but you can't take it!" barked Palomma.

"Waaaaah waaaaah waaaaah," sing-songed Christine.

Palomma stared for a moment. "Okay, yeah, fine. I'm a big shot. Queen Palomma Rossi. You want me to say I hate you? Fine. I hate you. I hated it when I came back sophomore year and you treated me like crap, I hated it when you talked about boys and left me out…"

"It's not my fault I tried harder!" Christine fired back.

"Tried harder? TRIED harder? Oh yeah, I could've had my boobs hanging out at school, 'Hey, everyone, want a peek at my ass?' THAT would have got me attention from boys!" yelled Palomma.

"What's that supposed to mean?" said Christine, angrily.

"Doug's right, you do say that all the time!" yelled Palomma.

"See? You even talk about me behind my back!" yelled Christine.

"I don't date your boyfriend behind your back!" yelled Palomma.

"Are you gonna start that shit again?! Christ, I'm sick of this!" yelled Christine.

"You started it!" screamed Palomma.

They stomped away and separated as far apart as they could in the room. Christine sat muttering to herself.

A full five minutes passed before she heard Palomma walk over to her.

"I'm sorry," Palomma said softly. "I guess we should have talked about this stuff a long time ago, huh?"

Christine looked away. "What's to talk about?" she said, distantly.

"Is it Doug...and me?" Palomma whispered. "Is that why coming here is hard?"

"I...I don't know what you mean!" stuttered Christine. She went back to painting. Palomma sat down across from her.

"Okay, I admit it," said Palomma. "You knew about boys because at least you tried, I didn't. You want honest? Everyone knew more than me. My sister knew more than me. Doug worshipped you. I wished a boy would just *look* at me and you had him following you around like a puppy. This year starts and I don't know, he wasn't and I didn't know anything about flirting or stuff and he talks to me and you probably thought I was trying to steal him away from you and like I said I didn't have a clue how but then I met Daniel and all of a sudden I didn't care what boys at school thought about me and I don't know why but Doug was kidding with me and I kidded back..."

A tear rolled down Palomma's cheek. She looked down.

"Damn it, why?" she whispered.

Christine looked down at the floor too.

"Because...I was always jealous of you," she said softly.

Palomma was startled. "What did you say?" she asked, looking up suddenly.

Christine looked up. "I said because I was jealous of you."

Palomma suddenly felt as if her brain had shut down. Of all the things she might have expected to hear, that was definitely not one of them.

"Wow," said Palomma. "Christine, I..."

Christine interrupted. "All I ever did was try to be as good as you, and I sucked at it." Palomma could see she was trying hard not to cry.

"From day one, you did everything better. You thought up stuff I never could when we were kids. You aced all the tests. You never messed up, ever. You were pretty, I was ugly. I looked goofy and stupid. I hated myself. You went away and suddenly it was like I was free! You weren't one-upping me in everything! It was, God, it felt good!"

Christine looked away. "Then you came back, and I was right back where I was before."

Palomma struggled to find something to say. "Is that why you treated me like you did when I came back? You thought I was doing—whatever it was you thought I was doing, on purpose?"

Christine turned back to Palomma. "I don't know what I thought. No. Or, maybe yes." She stood up and stared at the wall. "All I know is you came back and you were as perfect as ever. I knew I couldn't beat you at school, I had to find something. And I did. I could get boys to pay attention to me and you couldn't. And when I saw you were jealous of it, I figured I'd finally beaten you at something. It felt great!"

Palomma started to say something, but Christine interrupted.

"Then you said you had a boyfriend. And you beat me *again*."

Christine stared at Palomma. She sobbed, sniffled, then burst out crying. Palomma stood up and they hugged.

"Everything was working," Christine stammered. "Everything. Doug was fawning over me and I got greedy. I figured I could do better. But it was like I woke up one day and nothing worked. You had a boyfriend and I didn't. Doug wasn't paying attention to me anymore, no one was, and I did everything wrong. Now I realize all the things I did wrong, not just…you know. I should've treated you nicer way back. I should've gone out with Doug like he wanted. And I lost the only…"

Christine stopped.

"No, you didn't," Palomma whispered. She looked Christine in the eyes.

"You're right, I preach about honesty. My best friend HAS to be honest. She can mess up, piss me off, hurt my feelings, but as long as she's honest, I can work out all those other things with her." Palomma motioned for them to sit down.

"We could repeat this stuff forever," she said softly. "It's done. It's not worth losing my best friend over."

Palomma put her hand on Christine's knee, and Christine rested hers on Palomma's

"Maybe it all happened for a reason anyway," said Palomma, "because now you're with Daniel and I'm with Doug."

They both laughed. They started sharing stories they never had before.

There was the sound of a truck pulling up to the barn. In a couple of minutes, Doug was climbing the ladder.

"How's painting coming?" he said. Christine and Palomma were still sitting on the floor together, talking.

"Got a lot done, I see," Doug said, sarcastically.

"Sure did," they said at the same time.

Chapter 24

"So you really have a boyfriend," said Melody, walking up to Doug and Palomma Monday in room five. "I guess hell froze over or something."

Melody waited, but neither responded. "Did she ask you or did you ask her?"

Doug looked up. "Who?"

"Palomma!"

Palomma looked up. "Hi, Melody! What's up?"

"I was just asking your boyfriend if he knows anything about going steady."

"Oh, you were talking to him?" said Palomma. "When?"

Palomma shot a quick glance at Doug, who nodded almost imperceptibly.

Melody waited. Doug and Palomma continued looking at their notebooks.

Melody tried to get a rise out of them again. "Are you going to the prom?"

"Prom?" Doug looked up. "Melody, this is kind of sudden, I wasn't really prepared; are you saying you want to go to the prom with me?"

"Me? What? Huh? No, I wasn't…" Melody sputtered.

Doug interrupted, "Because, you know, we come from different worlds, I mean, I was star of the school play while you…" Palomma stifled a laugh. "Anyway, I suppose it could work out."

Melody was flustered. "Doug Halecki, I am NOT asking you to the prom!"

Doug made a face. "Why not? What's wrong with me?"

"I don't have enough paper for the list," Palomma said.

"Don't you know you're supposed to ask her to the prom to prove you're going out?" demanded Melody.

Doug paused. "You know, I hadn't really given it much thought. Hey, Palomma—wanna go to the prom?"

"With who?" Palomma answered.

"Well, it sounds like Melody doesn't have a date—I mean, she asked me..."

"Yeah, I could go with Melody and you could ask Lauren Carrier!"

"Would I have to Carrier across the bridge?"

"That was really bad," said Palomma. "Even by your subterranean standards."

"Jesus!" shouted Melody as she got up and left the room.

"It took way too long to get rid of her," said Palomma.

"I couldn't help it, she was giving me straight lines," Doug answered.

A minute later, Lauren came into the room. She walked over to Palomma and Doug. Palomma looked up.

"Hi Lauren!" What a coincidence—we were just talking to Melody and now you come in!"

"What's that supposed to mean?" said Lauren.

"Don't say it!" Palomma said to Doug. Doug pretended to zip his lip.

Lauren looked at them. Palomma and Doug looked down at their notebooks.

Lauren sat down waiting for either of them to say something. When they didn't she blurted out, "Who did you ask to the prom, Doug?"

Doug rolled his eyes. "Don't tell me, let me guess—you bumped into

Melody."

"She was in the hall and ..."

"Problem is," Doug interrupted, "you didn't bump into her hard enough—knocking her right out the front door of the school would've been better."

"That would be violence," said Palomma. "I don't condone violence."

"What if it was an accident?" asked Doug. "You know, like firecrackers?"

"Okay, maybe," said Palomma. She saw Lauren staring with her mouth open, looking back and forth at them as they talked.

"Answer me!" shouted Lauren. Other people in the room looked.

"Answer me!" she whispered.

"I'm sorry, Lauren," Doug whispered. "If I'd have known you wanted me to ask you, I wouldn't have not asked Melody."

"That's a double-negative," said Palomma.

"In more ways than one!" Doug shot back.

"I knew that was your comeback before you even got the words out," said Palomma.

Doug looked at Lauren. "Oh, you're still here! Okay, we've gotta clear this up. What's the date of the prom anyway?"

"May 19," said Palomma.

Doug cleared his throat.

"You doing anything on May 19?" Doug asked. "Not you, Lauren, sorry, I meant Palomma."

"I don't think so."

"Would you like to go to the prom?"

"Sure," answered Palomma. "With who?"

"I'm free," said Doug. "What do you say, let's check it out."

"Sounds okay," said Palomma.

"Check it out? OKAY?" Lauren said. "What's wrong with you two?"

"I don't have enough paper," Palomma started to say.

"You used that already," interrupted Doug.

"She didn't hear it."

"This isn't a joke!" said Lauren. "Don't you know anything?"

Doug slid out of the desk onto one knee. Lauren smiled.

"Oh, sorry, I was tying my shoe," said Doug. "Was there something you wanted me to say?"

Lauren threw her hands up. "You two were made for each other!" she seethed and walked out of the room.

They watched her leave.

"You seemed particularly into that," said Doug. "Much funnier than usual."

Palomma punched Doug on the arm.

"I never told you about me and her," she said. "Remind me."

Later that week, Palomma was in her room. She realized it had been a long time since she and Christine had talked on the phone. After patching things up in Doug's barn, it could be like the old days again. She dialed the hall phone.

The phone rang a few times. "She's probably out with Daniel," thought Palomma.

"…Hello?" said Christine, hesitantly.

"Christine? It's Palomma. Is this a bad time?"

"Um, uh, no!" Christine cleared her throat. "No. What's up?"

Palomma closed her bedroom door. "Not much, I hadn't called in a while."

They both didn't say anything for a few seconds, then started at the same time.

"I guess I'm surprised, I thought you'd be doing something with

Doug…"

"I was surprised you answered, I thought you and Daniel would be doing…"

They laughed.

"You first," said Palomma.

"No, you," said Christine.

"Shoot fingers!" said Palomma. "One, two, three…shoot! What do you have?"

"Two," said Christine.

"Wait, we never called odds or evens!"

"We suck at this," said Christine

They laughed again.

"I'm older," said Christine, "I say you go first."

"Beauty before age?"

"Ha ha."

"Doug has a lot of golf matches," said Palomma, sitting down on the floor. "Today was all the way down in Ocean City."

"We were supposed to go out," said Christine, "but Daniel had to fill in for someone."

"That sucks."

"Yeah," Christine said.

"We usually try to do things on Saturdays anyway," said Palomma.

"So do we," said Christine. "Although, if Daniel had his way, it'd be tonight too."

"You said he was working?"

"He wants me to go there and hang out."

Palomma thought back to when the two of them parked behind the store.

"We're talking, so I guess you decided against a night at the grocery store," said Palomma.

"As a matter of fact, I'd just gotten off the phone with him when you called. I thought…" Christine's voice trailed off.

"It was him?"

"Yeah."

"You had a fight?"

"Kind of. I was hoping he was calling back to apologize, and you called," said Christine.

"I can hang up, maybe he's getting a busy signal."

"Maybe he deserves it," said Christine, distantly.

Palomma waited.

"I don't know, Palomma, I'm all messed up," Christine said. "Maybe it's payback for what I did to you."

"Christine, stop," said Palomma. "We've been through that."

Christine sighed. "It's, he doesn't…listen like he used to. Like driving a hundred miles an hour, he promised to stop, now he just ignores me. He says driving fast is better than…"

Christine took a moment before continuing.

"Did he, I mean, was he…God, I don't know how to say this."

"Just say it," said Palomma.

"Did he try to make you do…things?"

"Yeah, I guess," said Palomma. "Some boys want to call the shots all the time, don't they?"

"*Doug* did that?" Christine asked.

"Did what? No!" Palomma said quickly. "I mean, we *do*, um."

There was silence. Palomma cleared her throat.

"No," said Palomma. "If you're talking about trying to force me to have sex, no."

"I didn't think so," said Christine. "But can I ask you something, promise you won't get mad?"

"I guess," said Palomma.

"Did Daniel—get his way? I mean, you didn't have sex with him, did you?"

"I'm still a virgin, Christine, that's what you're asking, right?"

"You know, there's a lot of different things." Christine's voice trailed off as she finished the sentence.

"He wanted me to, and I didn't. Did Daniel make you do something you didn't want to?"

"Oh no!" Christine answered quickly. "No, I mean, if you're talking about, I mean, I thought he'd be satisfied with, uh, but he keeps bringing up the same thing, I say no and we fight. I'm pissed off at him, and then he apologizes, and I forgive him, and I go a little further. You see what I mean?"

"Christine, look, we're different people, I can't tell you…"

"Like you say, just say it," said Christine.

"Okay," Palomma replied. "I guess we—me and Daniel—had some nice dates, but I broke up with him because I, um, wasn't ready to go where he wanted to go."

There was a lengthy silence on Christine's end.

"Christine, I didn't mean…"

"It's like there's only one thing on his mind," Christine said. "We've gone to some nice places, sure, but he always, you know."

Palomma stayed quiet.

"I think about stuff I'd miss out on," she went on. "You know, not having a date for the prom, just sitting around the house."

"Christine, um, it's not like, I mean, you probably know a lot of other boys."

Palomma could barely hear Christine's response. "Maybe I used to exaggerate."

"What are you going to do?"

Christine sighed. "I'm not going to be all Miss Priss about it. I like making out and stuff. And Daniel, as long as he's asking instead of, you know,"

"I wonder if he tried to call?" asked Palomma.

Christine laughed. "That's his problem. I'm glad it was you instead. I better be going, I can't keep my eyes open!"

"Me too," said Palomma. "Good night!"

"Good night!"

Palomma tried to fall asleep but a jumble of voices filled her head. She went downstairs and watched TV instead.

Golf was a spring sport starting in March; the early matches could be dreadfully cold. Today was one of them; Doug was glad to get back to his warm home.

He walked in and couldn't believe his nose. "I smell steak!" he shouted.

The Haleckis had steak occasionally, but 'steak' like 'Salisbury Steak' is really hamburger. They couldn't afford much better. This was different. It smelled like the restaurant. It was incredible. His mother was setting out plates...with a slab of prime rib on each one.

"I guess you heard we won, huh?" Doug joked.

"Better than that," said Linda, "Dad won!"

Doug looked at his father, confused.

"They're opening a new frozen food division at Campbell's. I got put in charge of shipping and inventory!" said his father. "We're celebrating!"

"Oh, and it's nice you won, too," his mother added.

All through dinner, Doug's father talked about his new job. "It's really something," he said between mouthfuls. "You ought to see these new freezers they have! Big as this house! And a new fleet of trucks with refrigerators built right onto them!" It was the happiest Doug had ever seen his father.

When they finished, Linda left for a night class. Doug cleared the table and got ready to dry dishes when his father said, "Ma, why don't you take a break from washing tonight? I'll handle them."

Doug dried as his father washed in silence for a few minutes.

"I got that promotion because of you," his father said.

Doug almost dropped the dish he was drying. "What'd I do?" he said in confusion.

"You almost done? Let's go outside," replied his father.

"I never did anything during the war," his father said as they walked around the woods. "I was in Quartermaster Corps; I filled orders. I weighed about as much as you do now. I guess they thought I was too small or something. All my friends got sent over."

He stopped.

"Some of 'em didn't come back."

Doug was silent; his father had never talked about the war and he wasn't going to interrupt.

"I came home, your mother and I got married and, hell, warehouses were better than farming. You kids never went without." He suddenly stopped walking.

"But I still never fought." He put his hands into his pockets and gazed into the distance.

"I ran into one of my buddies last year, he'd been at Normandy. Got shot in the hip, still limps. He was telling me what he did after the war —went to college on the G.I. Bill, got a good job, kept moving up. I asked him, how'd you do it? Know what he said?"

Doug's father sat down on Doug's thinking stump.

"You gotta tell them what you want, they sure as hell ain't gonna ask."

Doug sat down on a log next to the stump.

"He told me *what* to do, yeah, years ago. You showed me *how* to do it." He turned to face Doug.

"Umm, how'd I do that?" Doug asked.

"You took risks," his father answered. "You tried things. All my life, I waited until someone told me what to do. Meanwhile, here you were in all kinds of different things. I didn't know all the stuff you were doing, your mother filled me in."

"I still don't get it, it's high school. It's not a job, it's not a war!"

"Risks," said his father, resting his elbows on his knees. "You took risks. I was too…" His voice wavered. "Scared. Yeah, I was scared. I just wouldn't admit it to myself."

Hearing his father admit he'd been scared jumbled up everything Doug had been thinking for years.

"That day with the dog around Christmas," his father continued. "I was telling your mother. I heard gunshots, you went and saved it. You came back and there was a bullet hole in your coat, and you didn't go all to pieces. I got to thinking about the war and the guys who did what they had to do and risked everything, and I got to thinking about you."

"I was scared shitless, Dad."

His father turned to him. "But you still did it!"

"I guess I didn't have time to think."

"Well, I did," replied his father. "Have time to think, I mean. When they sent around a paper about the new division, I thought, what's the risk compared to those guys who went up the beach? They turn me down? I'm no worse off. I put in for one of the management spots. Turns out I was the only one who applied before they posted it; they said I showed initiative."

They sat quietly for a minute. Absentmindedly, Doug pulled his cigarettes from his pocket…and quickly tried to stuff them back in.

"Smoked a ton in the service," his father chuckled. "Quit when they weren't free anymore. I'm not calling the kettle black, but you might want to think about quitting."

"I'll quit these if we eat more steak like that!" said Doug.

"Deal," said his father.

Spring had arrived. Doug was busy with the golf team and planning the ping-pong tournament along with the article and regular schoolwork. Palomma's activities were nearing the end as well as her classes.

"Hey guys, you goin' to that thing after school?" asked Ed, leaning into room three on Friday morning.

Doug and Palomma turned to each other with blank expressions.

"You forgot, didn't you?" said Palomma.

"Don't give me grief; I'll bet you forgot too," answered Doug. "Go ahead—what is 'that thing'?"

"It's, you know, one of those, after-school things. Okay, yeah, I forgot."

"It's the April Fool's barbecue at Bennett's house," Rose said, turning from the table. "You know, seniors only."

Palomma and Doug walked toward the backyard where people were gathering. Barry and his older brother Brian were pointing out the soda and food—and Barry's All-County trophy.

"I think we're supposed to bow to it," Doug whispered to Palomma, motioning with his thumb.

It was crowded in the small, fenced-in backyard. Someone knocked over a trash bucket of empty cans; bees swarmed out. Palomma had been standing with her back to it, and some of the bees flew up her dress.

"Oh! Ah! Ah!" she yelled. She jumped around swatting at them.

"OUCH!" she suddenly yelped. "I got stung! OUCH! Oh God, they're stinging me!"

Doug frantically tried to shoo the bees away. As he did, he saw Barry and Brian laughing uproariously.

"Where did they get you?!" Doug asked.

"On the leg! Oh God, it HURTS!" said Palomma.

"Come with me!" Doug took her hand and ran her to his car; he could hear laughter and voices behind them.

"Did you see her? She looked like a fucking go-go dancer!"

"Nah, it was like the Three Stooges—hey! hey! hey! hey!"

"She screamed like a little girl! Eeeeeeeeeek!!"

Doug opened the car door and helped Palomma lay across the seat. "Which leg?"

"This one." Palomma pointed to her right thigh.

Doug pushed her skirt up and saw she'd been stung more than once. Her thigh was starting to swell.

"I hate bees. *Hate* bees," said Doug. "Scared to death of the stupid things. I read what to do if you get stung, because I don't want to die from a stupid bee sting."

He looked at Palomma who'd opened her eyes wider. "Sorry, bad choice of words. You're not going to die."

"I didn't think so," said Palomma, "but it hurts!"

Doug found his old pocketknife in the glove compartment. "You're supposed to scrape something across the stings to get the stingers out."

He motioned toward her skirt. "Could you move this?" he said. Palomma pulled her skirt higher and watched what Doug was doing.

Doug ran the edge of the knife blade over the stings. As he moved his hand to scrape again, he bumped Palomma between her legs.

He looked Palomma in the eyes. "Sorry," he said.

Palomma smiled. "Are they out?"

Doug saw specks on the blade. "I'm pretty sure we got 'em!"

He and Palomma could still hear whooping and laughing.

"Assholes," said Doug, shaking his head. "Stupid assholes. You're not allergic to bees, are you?"

"I don't know," said Palomma. "I never got stung before. Do you understand *now* why I'm not a fan of the great outdoors?"

"The swelling's going down." He put his hand gently over the sting area—and looked into her eyes again.

"That feels good," she said softly. "Really good."

They heard voices approaching. Palomma sat up, straightened her dress, and said, "I came here for something to eat, and I'm gonna eat!" She sat up and got out of the car.

They walked back to the party and sat at a table. Ed asked, "Is she alright?"

"Looks like it," Doug answered. "Doesn't seem to be swelling up anymore."

"I'll bet something else is!"

Doug turned to see Barry and Brian.

"You go through a lot to get into a girl's dress," Barry said. "Trust me, it ain't that hard. You probably are, but ..." and they laughed again.

Doug pretended to ignore them.

"Plus you're too retarded to pick out one that's worth the effort," sneered Barry, cupping his hands in front of his chest. Doug glared at him.

"Why you mother…" Ed started to move toward Barry; Doug jumped up and stepped in front of him.

"My problem, not yours," said Doug, not breaking his stare at Barry.

"You sure?" asked Ed.

"Yep," said Doug.

"Oh yeah, you most definitely have a problem," said Barry, stepping in front of Doug. The two of them moved toward the driveway.

Palomma saw them but couldn't hear what was being said. She got up and took a few steps when Paula stopped her.

"It's boy shit," Paula said. "Stay right here, for Doug's sake."

"Seriously? They're going to fight, right? How stupid!" Palomma started to try to walk again.

Paula pulled her aside hard. Palomma almost fell.

"Back off!" she said in a stern voice that scared Palomma. "Sometimes boys fight to show off. Sometimes, they have to, or else."

"Or else what?"

"They spend a long time wishing they had," Paula answered.

Doug put his face close to Barry's. "You're a fucking asshole," said Doug.

"Only asshole here is you," said Barry. "So you're tough, huh? Getting some pussy makes you think you're a man, huh?"

"All you do is play with balls," Doug said.

"Fuck you," snarled Barry.

"Fuck yourself," snarled Doug.

They were silent for a few moments.

"Make your move, prick!" said Barry, giving Doug a two-handed shove in the chest. Doug shoved back. Barry tried to kick Doug in the nuts. Doug avoided the kick, and pushed Barry, who was off-balance and fell on his back. Doug jumped on top of him, pinning his shoulders down with his knees; he took of his belt, looped it and held it over Barry's face.

Barry's eyes got very wide.

"Some guy at work told me there's no such thing as a fair fight," snarled Doug.

Barry stayed silent.

"He said there's no referee," Doug continued, "no rules. Nothing."

Barry struggled but couldn't move. Everyone had gotten very quiet.

"He said let the other guy take the first shot. If he doesn't knock you out, grab whatever you can. He said it's a fight…"

He was inches from Barry's face now.

"… not a sissy basketball game."

Barry was breathing heavily. "You won't do it," he said. "You don't have the balls." His voice was a lot higher-pitched than before.

"Then come on," answered Doug, standing up and motioning with his hands, "since you're so fucking sure. Try kicking me again."

Doug had a weird feeling he'd never had before. He'd been bullied for years, and the only feeling he ever remembered was fear, wishing he could run away, wishing it was all over. This wasn't fear. It wasn't guilt. This was different. It was tingly and exciting, like nothing could possibly hurt him.

Doug didn't want to hit Barry, but he wasn't going to back down. Not again. Not ever again. He didn't care if he got in trouble with his parents. He wasn't thinking about whether Palomma would be angry. Everything was in this moment right now, and Doug wasn't scared. And he wasn't backing down.

Barry stood staring at Doug, breathing heavily. Then he walked away, waving a hand back at Doug. "Buncha shit!" he yelled.

It took a few seconds for people to start moving again; no one spoke until the Bennett brothers went into the house.

Palomma walked over and stood in front of Doug. "Listen to me, Douglas Halecki!" she whispered. "Part of me is pissed you were going to get into a fight over something stupid!"

She continued, more softly, before Doug could say anything. "But standing up to bullies, standing up for yourself, takes real guts, and I'm proud of you. I'd hug you right now but I think there's been enough of a show today."

"Let 'em buy tickets," said Doug.

"Yeah," said Palomma, and they walked down the driveway. She stopped.

"Why your belt?" she asked.

"I'll explain someday," said Doug.

Chapter 25

Christine saw Palomma and Doug leave the barbecue; shortly after, she saw Daniel pull up to the curb. She walked out to the street.

"I said six," said Christine. "You're early."

"Get in," said Daniel.

Palomma got out of Doug's car, said "Hi Mom!" and ran to her room. No sense mentioning the bee stings; her mother would make a big deal out of it.

She laid back on her bed. Her leg tingled a little but wasn't swollen like before. Her mind drifted back to Doug's car.

He'd touched her. By accident—but he had. And when he said 'sorry,' he didn't blush. And what getting shocked with electricity must feel like went through her when it happened.

She closed her eyes. She was thinking about Doug, leaning over her taking care of her; it wasn't hard to imagine him laying with her in bed.

Doug walked into his house, said "Hi, Mom!" and went to his room. No sense mentioning anything about the run-in with Barry; nothing had really happened anyway.

Doug had an adrenaline rush he'd never felt before. Not only had he 'won'—Barry was the one to back down—he hadn't felt any fear. Maybe for the first time ever.

It felt cool to stand up for Palomma. And when he touched her, Doug had seen a look on Palomma's face that sent a peculiar feeling through him. Doug laid back on his bed and relaxed. This felt really good.

"That counted as dinner, right?" Daniel asked as they drove away.

"I told my Mom I'd be eating there," Christine replied, "so yeah, I guess."

"If you got home later it wouldn't be a big deal, right?"

""How much later?" asked Christine. "I didn't mention doing any-thing else."

"Shame, I had a little surprise. But if you have to go home…"

"I can be later! I like surprises!" She slid over next to Daniel.

He drove to a part of Holly Hill Christine had never been to. They were getting further from houses and businesses. "How long does it take to get to this surprise?" she asked.

"Hold your pants on!" Daniel answered, snickering.

Daniel turned down a farm road, stopped and backed into a small area his truck barely fit into. They were surrounded by dense woods.

"Welcome to our little spot!"

"Wha…our little spot?" Christine repeated. "Where exactly are we?"

"It's a place I scoped out," he answered. "Nobody'll bother us here!"

"Bother us?" said Christine, looking around.

Daniel grabbed Christine, pushed her on her back on the front seat and laid on top of her.

"Ow!" said Christine. "That hurt! What're you doing?"

She saw he was undoing his belt. "Daniel, I said I didn't…"

"You've been waiting for me to take charge," he said. "Chicks get off on that."

He had his pants down and had reached up Christine's dress, trying to pull down her panties.

"Daniel! Stop! This isn't right!" She grabbed the top of her panties.

"I'm a man, you're not," he grunted. "I say what's right!"

"Daniel, NO!" said Christine. They struggled but Daniel was too strong.

"Shut up," he said. "Chicks want a man to be a man."

Palomma was lost in her imagination. She pictured Doug's blue eyes; she tried to recapture the tingling she'd felt when he'd touched her.

Doug thought about Palomma. He pictured when he was looking down at her in his car and the complete trust in her eyes. It was better, thinking about Palomma.

Daniel used both hands to pull Christine's panties down. She tried hitting Daniel, but her arms were pinned between their bodies. When she tried to scream he clamped his hand over her mouth and pushed her head back. Christine tried to think of any way to escape but couldn't move.

Daniel muttered, "Oh baby! Oh baby!"

When he got off of her, Christine slid against the passenger door, sobbing as she tried to straighten her clothes. Daniel had rolled down his window and was smoking a cigarette. She could see a tree was right outside her door; it wouldn't open a foot. And even if she could get out, where would she go? She had no idea where they were.

Daniel flicked his butt out the window, pulled the truck out of the trees and roared down the road. Christine balled herself up against the door.

Daniel lit another cigarette and held the pack toward Christine.

"You raped me," she whispered.

Daniel didn't respond but drove faster.

"You raped me," Christine said, louder.

"Bullshit I did," sneered Daniel. "You said it yourself, remember, dick tease? Huh?" He used a high-pitched voice. "'Not today, someday.' I decided someday was today."

He reached over and put his hand on her thigh. "And you loved it.

Admit it."

He stopped at an intersection; Christine tried to open the passenger door. Daniel grabbed her wrist and sped off. She yanked her arm free.

"You can't drive around forever, you stupid shit!" she yelled. "You've gotta stop sooner or later!" Christine breathed heavily in and out.

Daniel continued in silence to Christine's house but stopped a few houses up the block from it. He put the truck in park and took a deep breath.

"I fucked up." he said in a flat, emotionless voice. "If I say I'm sorry, will you forgive me? It'll be our little secret." He turned to her with an expressionless face.

"A secret?" snarled Christine. "That's what you want it to be?" She was yelling now. "How about I tell the cops our little secret? Huh?!" She got out, slammed the door and ran up the street to her house.

She could hear Daniel yelling. "You don't have the guts!"

Thankfully, Christine's father wasn't home and her mother was in the bathroom. She didn't see Christine run to her room.

"Knock knock!"

Gemma walked into Palomma's room

Palomma shot up to a sitting position on her bed.

"God! Don't you ever..." she trailed off.

Gemma looked at Palomma and smirked. "Don't *you* ever give me any crap about *my* skirts!" she said.

Palomma realized her skirt was hiked way up. She cleared her throat and smoothed it down.

Gemma sat down on the end of the bed. "I thought you went to a barbecue."

"I did," replied Palomma. "Where do you think I went?"

"People don't usually...do that after a dumb barbecue," said Gemma.

She playfully patted Palomma's foot.

"I, um, got stung by a bee. More than one," said Palomma.

She pointed.

"My God that must've hurt!" said Gemma.

Palomma blushed. "No, not *there*, on the leg. Here." She slid her skirt up.

"I never heard that one," said Gemma. "Bee stings make you feel like that?"

Palomma crossed her legs and leaned forward.

"You came in here for something, right?" she said, smiling.

"I was gonna ask you how things were going with Doug, that's all. I think I got my answer."

Palomma smiled. "Yeah."

Mrs. Halecki knocked on Doug's bedroom door. "Dinner!" she called.

Doug walked into the kitchen. "Sorry, I just remembered," his Mom said. "You had a barbccuc, right? You already ate."

Doug sat down at the table.

"Yeah, no, I mean, I went, but I didn't have any food."

"Why not?" asked his father.

"Wasn't hungry," answered Doug. He began to fill his plate. "How are things at the plant, Dad?"

Palomma was in her room that night writing in her diary when her mother called out, "Palomma! Telephone!"

Palomma's mother covered the phone. "It's Christine; she sounds like she's not feeling well."

"I'll go upstairs," said Palomma.

"Okay, Mom, I've got it!" she yelled. "Hi Christine!"

Palomma could barely hear her response. "Could we go somewhere?"

"Uh, sure, where?" said Palomma, confused.

"Anywhere," she whispered. "Could you drive?"

Palomma was scared by the sound of Christine's voice. It seemed lifeless.

"Absolutely," said Palomma. "I'll be there as soon as I can." She hung up.

"Mom, can I borrow the car? Christine wants me to come over," she asked. "I won't be out late." Her mother nodded and Palomma left.

"Me and Palomma are going out for a little while," Christine said to her mother when Palomma pulled into her driveway. She tried to sound normal.

"Where do you want to go?" asked Palomma. She was vacillating between curiosity and fear; for as long as she'd known Christine, she'd never heard anything like this tone in her voice.

"I don't know," said Christine, softly.

"The mall?"

"No," Christine answered distantly.

"The diner, maybe?"

"Someplace alone."

Palomma was coming up on Strawbridge Park. "Here okay?" she asked, hesitantly.

"Uh-huh," said Christine, without looking.

Palomma parked and shut off the car. Christine hadn't moved and Palomma didn't know what to say. "Got any cigarettes?" she finally asked. It was all she could think of.

"Yeah," said Christine, and she pushed her purse toward Palomma.

Palomma took out the pack and lighter. She handed one to Christine, who took it but just held it in her hand resting on her thigh. Palomma sat still and watched Christine. In the distance, they heard sirens.

"Sounds like the cops are chasing someone," said Palomma.

"I hope it's him…" said Christine. She barely whispered it.

"Him?"

Christine suddenly erupted.

"DANIEL! That's who! HIM! And I don't know why I'm saying his name! ASSHOLE! That's what I should call him! SHITHEAD! That's what he is!"

Palomma started to speak. "I guess you had an…"

"HE RAPED ME!!!!" Christine screamed. She collapsed face down on the front seat, sobbing uncontrollably.

Palomma felt as if she couldn't move a single muscle in her body.

"I hope they're going to get him!" she stammered between sobs. "I hope they throw him in jail! I hope he's DEAD! I hope he crashed and burned to death! I wish he was *dead*! I wish *I* was dead!" She collapsed again.

Palomma pulled at Christine to get her to sit up and hugged her as tight as she could. And they both cried.

Chapter 26

The next afternoon, the doorbell rang at Doug's house while he was watching a baseball game. "Doug! Palomma's here!" his mother called out.

Doug was surprised; Palomma had never come over his house when something wasn't planned; his parents hadn't even met her yet. He hurried to the living room and found Palomma and his mother talking at the door.

"Um, Mom, this is Palomma. Palomma Rossi," said Doug.

"You're just a little late, dear," she answered. "We already introduced ourselves. It's nice to meet you, Palomma!" she said. "That's such a beautiful name! I'll leave you two alone now." She walked away toward the kitchen.

"This is a surprise!" said Doug. "Come on in!"

"Do you think maybe you could come outside?" Palomma said softly.

Doug was confused by the look on her face. He stepped out and closed the door.

"What's up?" he asked. "Something bothering you? You look upset."

"Do you think maybe we could, um, take a walk in the woods like you wanted to on our first date?" she asked.

"Uh, sure, sure, yeah," Doug answered. He was even more confused now. They started around the house. Palomma reached over and took Doug's hand.

As they got near the woods, Doug stopped. "Are you sure?" he asked.

"There's a lot of bees and stuff this time of year. We could walk some-where else."

Palomma was silent as she walked into the woods, pulling Doug along. They stopped at the corner of the path. Palomma sat on Doug's stump. Doug sat on the log next to it.

"Christine called me this morning," Palomma began, softly. "She wanted to go for a drive last night. We ended up at Strawbridge Park."

Palomma began sobbing.

"Daniel raped her yesterday," she whispered.

"WHAT??!!!" Doug jumped up and yelled, so loud it echoed. "HE RAPED HER?! SHE GOT RAPED?!"

Palomma stood up. "And no more yelling, understand? That's why I wanted to come back here, in case you reacted like that. I didn't tell Christine I was gonna tell you—it'd be nice if the rest of the world didn't hear it too!"

Doug stared at her. He stuffed his hands in his pockets, took out his cigarettes and absentmindedly held the pack toward Palomma.

"Right now, I think I need one of those," she said.

They sat down and smoked in silence. Doug stared at the ground.

"Did she call the cops?" he said, softly.

"No," Palomma answered, quietly.

"Did her parents?!" asked Doug, his volume rising.

"She didn't tell them."

"Why the hell *not*?" Doug said angrily, standing up.

"Did *you* tell anyone? Or call anyone?" Palomma asked, looking up at him.

Doug sat back down.

"Did he…" Doug stopped and hit himself in the forehead with the butt of his hand.

"What?" asked Palomma.

"It was stupid," said Doug.

Palomma realized what Doug meant. "I asked. Christine said she thinks it's the wrong time of the month for her to get pregnant."

Doug stared into the woods. "Rape..." he muttered. "Rape..." He jumped up.

"If she's not gonna call the cops, maybe I should!" he said, angrily. "I didn't, maybe it means I shouldn't chicken out again! Did you ever think of that?"

"You think it's that easy?" said Palomma, standing up and facing him. "What if she doesn't *want* the cops called?"

"Why *wouldn't* she? You said it yourself—she got raped," said Doug. "It's a crime. Call the cops."

"It's not so simple," said Palomma.

"It's rape!" said Doug. "How much simpler can it be?"

Palomma let out a loud sigh.

"Remember what you were telling me about what happened to you?" she asked. "How I asked if you'd called the cops or told anyone? Remember what you told me?"

"Yeah, but this is different." said Doug.

"Is it?" asked Palomma. "Your boss forced you into sex and you didn't want to. What else would you call it?"

"I don't know, assault? I mean, he didn't..." Doug trailed off. "It's different when it's a girl."

"Why?"

"Because—she can get pregnant, that's why." Doug sat down and looked at the ground.

"Doug, I'm not comparing exactly what happened to you with her," said Palomma, stepping on her cigarette. "It's not as simple as people make it sound!"

She sat down.

"Okay. Let's say rape is when some guy grabs you, kidnaps you or something, forces you to have sex, has a gun or knife or something, right? That's rape, right?"

"Yeah, that's rape," said Doug. "He gets arrested and goes to jail."

"When you look things up, like I said, it's not so simple." She stared at the ground.

"Look things up?" asked Doug. "Look what up?"

"I went to the library," said Palomma. "This afternoon. They had articles about sexual assault, and the system is screwed up. In fact, it sucks."

"How?"

"First off, Christine said she agreed to go with him, it isn't like he kidnapped her."

"Yeah, okay, but I don't think Christine went along with having sex!"

Palomma leaned closer to Doug and whispered.

"How can she prove that?"

"I, I mean, she…"

"Don't you see?" said Palomma, angrily. "The article said they've been doing this to women forever. It would be her word against his. They'd make her admit she went with him willingly. If she said he forced her, he'd lie and say she suggested it or something. Her word against his."

"Who's 'they?'"

"A lawyer, if he got one. From what Christine said, it probably wouldn't even get to that. She said he's friends with the cops. A cop who knew his name saw the two of them parking before."

Doug looked down. "So if she called the cops, he could say she said yes and he'd get away with it.'"

"And they'd tell her it was going in the paper," said Palomma. "That she said she got raped. They wouldn't put his name in the paper, just hers."

"Why the fuck not?"

"They'd only put the guy's name in the paper if she pressed charges. He'd lie and the cops would believe him, not her. They'd drop the charges but it would have already been in the paper."

"I didn't know any of that shit," said Doug softly.

"Remember what you said about how you were scared people would find out what your boss did? Do you think Christine wants it all over the place? People would assume she was lying because no one went to jail, that she got mad at him about something and now she's trying to make it sound…" Palomma didn't finish the sentence. They stood quietly.

"What's she gonna do?" asked Doug.

"She doesn't know what to do," said Palomma. "She said he actually told her it should stay a secret between them, and then, and *then*…"

"He threatened her?" said Doug.

"He apologized!" she said. "She told me what he said and it was the exact same thing he'd said to me! Right after he…"

Palomma stopped and her eyes suddenly got very wide. She started shaking.

"*It could have been me!*" said Palomma, her voice cracking. "I mean, he…oh my God!"

Palomma fell into Doug's arms, crying.

"What are you talking about?" said Doug, holding her.

Palomma stepped back and wiped her eyes. "He took me to Morelli's because he figured it was a safe spot for him. I made him stop and he did that apology. He tried again and I yelled at him. If I'd started screaming, he probably realized someone would've heard me. So he took me home and apologized again."

She started pacing.

"This time, he made sure it was someplace where it wouldn't matter if she screamed. He probably thought she'd start liking it. Those articles talked about men fantasizing about raping a girl and her wanting them to do it. Except she didn't do what he thought. So he apologized again."

"I'm lost," said Doug.

"He's *practicing*! Each time, he tries to fix what didn't work! For all we know, he's going out with someone else at the same time as Christine—I mean, he did it to me! Maybe he's trying things on someone else too!"

Doug plumped back down on the log. "And he figures no one will go to the cops. 'cause he's got that covered."

"Someone's gonna be next, and then someone else," whispered Palomma. "And there's not a damn thing we can do about it!"

Palomma sat down.

Doug spoke softly. "Like I said, what's she going to do? What can she do? I mean, didn't the articles say anything?"

"They said she's screwed, in as many words," Palomma said, softly.

They both stared into the distance.

"GOD DAMN IT!!!!" Palomma yelled, so loud it echoed.

They started walking back to the house. Palomma stopped as they were leaving the woods.

"Doug, you have to promise me you won't say anything to anyone!" Palomma said. "Promise! She told me but she doesn't want anyone else to know!"

Doug stopped and turned toward her.

"I promise," he said softly.

"She probably feels so alone," said Palomma. "She probably feels like no one knows what she's going through."

It was Doug's turn to stop.

"Um, listen," he said, slowly. "I was thinking about what you said back there—I mean about what happened to me. Before I told you, I felt all alone too, and dirty and ashamed. I don't know if it would ever be any help…but if she, you know, gets to thinking really bad about herself or something, you could always tell her about what happened with me… maybe she wouldn't be so hard on herself 'cause I didn't call the cops or anything either."

Palomma looked into Doug's eyes and kissed him.

Doug's parents were sitting in the living room when they came back in. Doug's mother looked at them with concern. "Is something wrong?"

"No, Mrs. Halecki," said Palomma. "Something happened to someone I know and I was upset about it, that's all. Had to get it out of my system."

"It wasn't this, was it? Did you know this guy?" asked his father. He held out the day's issue of the Daily Record.

The headline read, "Fiery Crash on Route 73 Kills One."

Doug took the paper and began to read the article aloud.

"An accident on Landing Road Friday night took the life of a 19-year-old Holly Hill resident. Police said the victim, Daniel Parrillo, was traveling at a high rate of speed when he left the road and crashed head-on into a tree. The truck began to burn but firemen arrived in time to extinguish the fire."

"The victim was identified and pronounced dead at the scene."

Doug stopped reading and stared at the article. Palomma looked away.

"Did you know him?" Doug's mother asked.

"Um, yeah, I mean kind of," he answered, looking up. "He was a grade ahead of me at St. John's. On the basketball team."

"What a shame," she said. "Someone with his whole life ahead of him and just like that, it's all over. I hope he didn't suffer!"

"There's a lesson to be learned, though," said Doug's father. "Nothing good ever comes out of going so fast. It said they figured he'd been going 90 miles an hour! On Route 73! At least no one else was with him."

"Ernest!" said Doug's mother. "That's a horrible thing to say!"

Doug looked at Palomma. "But it's true," he said. Palomma nodded and whispered, "Can I use your phone to call Christine? She probably needs someone to talk to."

"Right down the hall," said Doug.

Mrs. Holloway answered the door later that day. "Hi Palomma. Christine said you were coming. She's in her room." Palomma walked in the door. "Oh, could you tell Doug thanks for giving her a ride home last night?"

"Sure, I'll tell him," said Palomma.

Mrs. Holloway stopped in the living room.

"She saw the paper," she said quietly. Mrs. Holloway looked toward Christine's room. "I know this is a horrible thing to say but thank God she wasn't with him yesterday. She could've…" She stopped in mid-sentence. "You know the way, go ahead in."

Palomma found Christine in bed, the covers up to her chin. She looked pale. Palomma closed the door behind her. She reached under the covers to take her hand and found her holding something.

"What are these?" she asked, incredulously, holding up the bottle.

"Sleeping pills," mumbled Christine.

"Sleep…where did you get sleeping pills?"

"The medicine cabinet."

"How many did you take?" asked Palomma anxiously, looking at the bottle.

"I don't know," said Christine. "Not enough."

"Enough? It says take two…"

Palomma stopped. Christine stared at her with terror in her eyes.

"*I killed him*!" Christine whispered. "I killed him! I wished he'd crash and burn to death and he did!"

Palomma gripped her hand. "Christine, no! It doesn't work like that! You *know* that. It was a horrible, horrible coincidence!"

"I killed him. I killed him. I killed him." Christine kept repeating it softly as she looked away.

Palomma sat down and pulled Christine up to hug her. "No, you didn't and you know it. He killed himself. He always drove too fast, it was one too many times." She held Christine by the shoulders. "He can't hurt you anymore."

Christine went limp and started crying again.

Palomma walked into the kitchen. "Mrs. Holloway, Christine wants me to stay the night, can I?"

"Certainly," she answered. "She doesn't seem to be running a fever. She threw up in the bathroom before; you two didn't eat anything last night, did you? Or dr…" she stopped herself.

"We didn't go anywhere. We just drove around," said Palomma.

"I should have known better, Palomma. I know you'd never let anything bad happen to Christine! She probably ate something at the barbecue that disagreed with her."

"Probably," said Palomma, walking back to Christine's room. She grabbed the pill bottle, slipped into the bathroom and put it in the cabinet.

"I've gotta call my Mom too," she said, reaching for Christine's phone. As she was about to pick up the receiver, it rang.

They both jumped. Palomma picked it up. "Hello?"

"Palomma? Good, it was you I wanted anyway," said Doug. "You left your purse at my house! Your license is in it, right? Do you want me to bring it to you?"

Palomma smiled. "Thanks, Doug, it can wait until tomorrow. I'm staying at Christine's tonight. Okay, bye,"

"I came from Doug's house," she told Christine as she hung up. "Like an airhead, I left my purse there."

Christine sat up suddenly.

"How did Doug know you were here?" asked Christine. There was fear in her voice.

Palomma stroked her hair.

"Because you and Doug have a lot more in common than you could ever know," she said softly. Palomma laid down beside Christine and they talked into the early morning hours until they both feel asleep.

It was mid-April. Doug was at his new job when a car he recognized pulled up to the booth. "Good evening, welcome to PhotoQuik! What can I help you with, ma'am?"

"Oh God, do I sound like that?"

"No, your voice is deeper," said Doug.

"Stick your arm out that window so I can punch it."

"Not a chance," said Doug. "It's chilly tonight! And you made me open the window and let whatever heat there was in here out!"

"Really? My booth has a heater!" said Palomma.

"And this booth is out in the sticks," said Doug. "Smart people like me have to use our brains!"

Doug reached back into the booth and held up a candle.

"It gives off a little heat, at least until someone who doesn't even have any film to drop off comes up and bothers me and makes me open the window," said Doug.

"Let me get this straight," said Palomma. "You're in a booth the size of a closet, filled to the top with film which is highly flammable, and you've got a lit candle in there?"

Doug propped his chin on his elbows. "We could always trade booths!"

"Oops! Look at the time! Gotta go!" said Palomma, and she drove away.

"Darn it, I tracked some dirt in here," said Christine the next morning in the church parking lot. She went to open the door to tip the floormat out.

"Christine, please! Look at all the filth on my side!"

Palomma had been driving Christine to school a lot. She'd been spending a lot of time at her house too. It had been a couple of weeks since the accident; Palomma had gone to the viewing with Christine and had been impressed with how well she handled it—and also angered by all the nice things people said about him. If they only knew the truth.

Later that morning, Doug was writing in room six when Christine and Palomma walked in and sat down. "That's okay, don't stand up," said Palomma.

"Thanks for doing the article the last couple of weeks," said Christine. "I really wanted to help, but, you know," she stopped. "Thanks for *all* your help."

She winked at Doug. Doug looked at Palomma. Palomma winked.

Doug smiled. "You guys got something in your eyes?"

"Hey, guess what? They posted who'll be doing the article next year!" said Christine, looking down at her notebook. "I saw it on the office tackboard. Jackie Jardine!"

"Yeah, so?" asked Doug.

"So someone's going to have to spend a *lot of time* with her, show her everything we do," she went on, still looking down. "Maybe even drive her to the Record office, show her where it is."

Doug looked at Palomma. Palomma looked at Christine. Christine was still looking down. "I hope you don't mind, I told her I'd do it," she said.

Palomma punched Doug in the arm.

"Whaaaa…?" he exclaimed.

"For even thinking it," said Palomma, laughing.

Ed was in room seven toward the end of the day waiting for Doug when an envelope plopped on the table in front of him. He looked up to see Beth standing next to him.

"Damn, you can sneak up on people," he said. "What's this?"

"A thank you. For those little performances at my house."

Beth sat down across from Ed. "My Mom got a letter from the bank saying the mortgage was paid off. She said he'd been preaching at her the last couple of times he came about how he'd been right all along, how they fixed me here. She told him he was absolutely right, a genius, way smarter than her, a whole bunch of things…"

She stood up and turned around; she had her fingers crossed behind her back.

"Since money's not so tight anymore, go ahead, open it!"

Ed raised an eyebrow. "Why do I get the idea there's $218 in here?" he said.

"ENNNNNGGGHHH!" Beth made a buzzer sound. "Wrong!" Miss Loman looked across the room at her.

Ed took out two tickets and a coupon.

"Prom tickets," she said. "And a free tuxedo at the mall. Doug said the class officers got those."

She leaned across the table and whispered.

"He said he told them I was a guy."

Ed sprayed Beth trying to stifle a laugh.

"If you two can't quiet down over there, you're going to have to leave," Miss Loman said from her desk.

Beth put a finger to her lips and made a ridiculously loud shushing sound to Ed.

Loman shook her head.

"How much do I owe you for the tickets?" asked Ed.

Beth folded her arms across her chest. "Get with it, big boy. This is 1977. I'm asking, I'm paying. I don't know about you, but I sure as hell want to go and I don't have a car."

She leaned toward him again.

"Besides, when my father hears we're going, maybe he'll start paying the electric bill."

Ed burst out laughing, got up and turned to the teacher's desk.

"We're leaving! We're leaving!"

Chapter 27

"Mommy, Daddy, there's something I wanted to ask you," said Christine as her family finished dinner that night.

"Sure, honey, what's up?" replied her father.

They sat at the kitchen table silently looking at each other for a few seconds.

"Can I, um, get a job?" Christine said, almost inaudibly, looking down at the table.

"Sure," said Mr. Holloway. "Where'd you have in mind?"

"You've been paying for everything and...huh?" said Christine in surprise.

"I want to know too," said Mrs. Holloway. "Did you have a place picked out?"

"You're not, I mean, you...I can?" Christine said, still surprised.

"Why couldn't you?" said Mr. Holloway.

"Because," Christine began to say.

"Because we didn't think you could?" he said. "The only way it'd be wrong was if you didn't think you could do it and we forced you."

"We only want you to be happy," said her mother. "It's all we've ever wanted for you."

Christine looked back and forth at them as they spoke, her eyes open wide with surprise. "I hope yes was the answer you wanted," said her father. "'Cause it's the only one we have!"

"Oh, it's the answer I wanted!" said Christine, laughing and crying at the same time. "I love you Mommy! I love you Daddy!"

She gave each of them a hug and started telling them about the clothing store she was going to apply to at the mall.

Karen and Lauren were eating lunch when they became aware of someone standing behind them.

They turned to find Doug and Manny—holding trays heaped with spaghetti.

"They serve spaghetti a lot, don't they?" said Manny.

The two girls stared. Karen moved closer to Barry. "You wouldn't dare!" she said.

"Could you hold this?" Doug asked Manny. "Certainly," he replied, taking Doug's tray in his left hand.

Doug bent down between the girls.

"What I *wouldn't* do," he whispered, "his sink to your level." He looked toward Barry.

"Right, Mary?"

Barry started to say something when Manny handed Doug his tray back. "I like that," he said. "Mary. It fits."

Doug and Manny slowly walked away. "Did they call you Becky in third grade?" asked Manny.

Doug laughed.

"Hello, ma'am, how can I…oh! It's you!"

Christine had gotten a job at Berdan's at the Moorestown Mall two weeks before. She'd walked up to a customer, not realizing it was Palomma.

"Hi Christine! Listen, you gotta help me out here."

"Picking out a gown? Sure! That's my job!" Christine leaned closer and whispered. "And trying to get you to buy the most expensive one!" They both laughed.

"Actually, I want to make sure mine doesn't look anything like yours. It'd be stupid if we matched."

Christine remained silent.

"Your gown," said Palomma. "The one *you're* wearing to the prom."

"Yeah, well," Christine looked away.

Palomma took a gown off the display. "I want to try this on; give me a hand in the dressing room."

"It's too big…"

Palomma interrupted. "I said I need help in the dressing room!"

When they got inside, Palomma closed the door. "You're going to the prom."

"By myself?" said Christine. "What'll that look like?"

"It'll look like you going to the prom. And sitting at our table. Doug said he'd pick you up and drive you home with us." Palomma put her hand on Christine's. "Tommy Terranova is going stag too. It'll look like nothing was going to keep you from your senior prom, that's what it'll look like!"

"It doesn't make any difference if I'm there or not," whispered Christine.

Palomma sighed. "It makes a difference to me! How could I have nice memories of the prom if my best friend wasn't at it?"

"You better not let Doug here you say that!" said Christine.

"Besides," continued Palomma. "If he starts to get fresh, I need you there to tell him "please don't squeeze the Charmin!"

Christine blushed. "Honest to God, I did NOT know that was gonna happen! If I had,"—she punched at the air—"bang! Zoom! To the moon!" They laughed.

"*I'm* asking you to the prom, Christine. You deserve to have someone ask you to the prom."

"But...he never bought tickets," said Christine.

"Let me let you in on a little secret," said Palomma, and she leaned within inches of Christine. "*We're the prom committee*! We sell the tickets! You got the money?"

Christine blushed. "My Mom and Dad told me they wanted me to go too. They gave me money for a ticket and way too much for a gown, shoes, everything." she said. She poked Palomma with her elbow. "Probably enough for two!"

"So we're here until we find gowns!" said Palomma. She looked at the price tag on the one she'd brought into the dressing room and jumped. "Oh my God! It better be enough for two of *these*!"

"I get an employee discount!" said Christine. "Tell you what, I'll get the gowns...and you get the film!"

"You look...beautiful"

Palomma, wearing a white prom gown with crossed shoulder straps, stood on the steps in her home.

"Thank you, Douggie!" Palomma replied, walking down. "Now, what do you say we paint the prom red? And shh shh shh..." She placed her finger to his lips.

"No jokes about already doing that in your barn."

"You're amazing," said Doug.

"You're perceptive," said Palomma.

They picked up Christine and drove to the Amerihost. Doug took Palomma's arm and crossed the bridge into the ballroom; then he went back and escorted Christine in. Ed and Beth were already at the table. Manny was there with Rose. Andy was there with his new girlfriend from Rumley High.

"Great job setting up the decorations, guys!" said Palomma.

"Lugging that bridge was a bitch," said Ed. He pointed at Doug. "Especially with only two sets of hands!"

"Wasn't even at his own house to help," muttered Andy. "I'll tell you one thing, there's plenty of heat up there now!"

"I had very important things to attend to!" said Doug.

"Things?" said Palomma. She punched him in the arm. "I'm a thing?"

"And when do we have to get this crap out of here?" said Ed. "I've got things to attend to too!" He turned toward Beth.

"I'm a thing, too" she said, looking around the table. "And damn proud of it!"

Everyone burst out laughing.

"Don't worry," said Doug. "The decorations are taken care of." He and Palomma winked at each other.

"I've just been handed the results of voting for class awards," the DJ announced.

"This is all on the up-and-up, right?" said Ed. "You guys didn't change things, did you?"

"Would we do a thing like that?" said Palomma. Everyone at the table stared at Doug.

"Most likely to succeed, Doug Halecki and Louise Grant!"

"With each other?" shouted Tommy. Everyone laughed.

"Biggest gossip: Tommy Terranova and Palomma Rossi!"

"Right back at ya, Tommy!" Doug yelled.

Palomma was shaking her head. "I *should* have changed that one."

The DJ said, "I was also given another category and asked to announce it now. A special vote was taken for prom king and queen." There was a buzz in the room.

"Special vote?" said Andy. "Who was part of this special vote? We weren't doing that one!"

"It was a quorum," said Palomma, "of one."

"For prom king and queen," the DJ continued, "Doug Halecki…"

Doug had a confused look on his face.

"… and Christine Holloway!"

Palomma looked at Doug and winked.

"Let's have the royal couple out here for a coronation dance!" Doug escorted Christine onto the dance floor.

"Thanks, Doug," she whispered. "This means a lot."

"Don't thank me, you know who to thank." Christine looked over Doug's shoulder at Palomma, who was grinning ear to ear.

Eventually the DJ announced, "Ladies and gentlemen, this is the last dance. Gents, bring your ladies to the dance floor for the final song, 'Come Sail Away.'"

"God, it seems like years ago!" said Palomma as they danced.

"At my house, playing this record," said Doug.

Palomma snuggled up against Doug. "It's gone by way too fast."

"I don't know," Doug answered. "If you Go All the Way back to when I asked you to Come Sail Away to the Deptford Mall, I think it's worked out just right that You're Still the One!"

Palomma smiled. "Why do you have to be so good with words?" she said. "But right now, actions speak louder than words."

Palomma kissed Doug as the last lyrics of the song played.

There was an after-prom party at Tommy's house. Ed, Andy, Katie, Paula and Christine surrounded Doug and Palomma.

"What about those decorations?"

"The prom chairperson will clear that up," said Doug.

"If you say we have to do it tonight, I'll pound you into the ground," said Ed.

"And I'll help," said Paula. "Pound, I mean"

"You won't have to haul them away tonight, or anytime," said

Palomma.

"Wait," said Christine. "We signed a contract!"

"So did the owner, and our future lawyer here read it very carefully," said Doug. "The box about cleanup after the event wasn't checked. The banquet manager said they'll drag 'em outside and all we have to do is come back next week and break them up!"

"Demolition party on Wednesday!" said Palomma.

It was coming down in buckets when Doug pulled into the cul-de-sac. "Is this the same one?" Palomma asked.

Doug shut off the engine. "I wasn't taking notes, but yeah, I'm pretty sure." He turned to Palomma.

"I suppose you're wondering why I asked you here."

"The thought crossed my mind," Palomma giggled.

"The last time we were here, things got stupid," said Doug. "And we're not quitters."

Palomma shook her head. "Nope, not us. Now shut up and kiss."

They leaned toward each other when Doug stopped.

"Wait!" said Doug. "How about we get away from steering wheels and all this junk? I think it's time," he pointed a thumb backwards, "to actually go back there."

"You are nuts," said Palomma. "I am not getting out of the car in this!"

"No need," said Doug, and he rolled over the front seat into the back.

Palomma smirked. "You practiced that, didn't you?"

Doug grinned.

"If you expect me to do that, forget it. I'll break something. And it's not breaking your car I'm worried about."

"Prop yourself on your elbows and face me." Palomma did, and Doug took hold of her arms and slid her over the front seat; Palomma ended up painlessly in the back.

Doug started to say something.

"Nope! Do not!" Palomma placed a finger over Doug's lips.

They hugged. Then, they looked each other deeply in the eyes and kissed.

They stopped, and Palomma let out a loud sigh. "I'll tell you a secret."

Doug leaned back as she rested her head on his chest.

"I was scared," she said. "You and I started going out…"

"That scared you?" asked Doug.

"No," Palomma answered. "It wasn't the start, it was…"

Doug kissed the top of her head.

"I'd just broken up once because it felt like I was a…possession."

"Not, like, 'The Exorcist' possession, right?" said Doug.

"Right," answered Palomma. "My head isn't going to spin around."

"Phew!"

"So many things get messed up because someone thinks they can decide how everything should be."

Doug wrapped his arms around Palomma.

"I never really trusted anyone like I've been able to trust you!"

"You know why, don't you?" asked Palomma. "Honesty. I never had to wonder whether what you said was true."

"Same for you," replied Doug. "You make it so easy."

They hugged.

Doug looked at her for a minute, listening to the rain and her breathing; he swore he could hear her heartbeat.

"I never told you I loved you," he said.

"Douggie doesn't wuv me," said Palomma. She stuck out her bottom lip.

Doug placed a little kiss on the lip.

"You see," continued Doug, "I do, I'm confused, and everything in between."

Palomma hugged Doug tight.

"I know exactly what you mean," she said. "There's too much to it to think we know."

"I have a really good teacher," said Doug.

Palomma blushed. They began to kiss.

When they stopped, Palomma let out a sigh and smiled.

"We needed something this year, deep down inside" she said. "We just didn't know it was us."

They began to kiss again. Then Palomma rolled on top of Doug and looked into his eyes, blue and sparkling.

"Doug, do you want to make love with me?"

Doug looked back into Palomma's eyes, the windows to her soul.

"Yes, and no."

"Perfect answer," Palomma replied.

They lay in each other's arms with nothing but the sound of the rain and their breathing. Maybe some people would think it could be better, but for now and for them, this was all they needed…and it was perfect.

"What is that smell?" said Palomma as she walked in her front door.

"You never had a pet?" asked Doug.

"Nope. Why?"

"Because that's the unmistakable smell of wet dog!"

They followed their noses into Palomma's kitchen; Gemma was sitting on the floor with a dog, drying it off with towels. The dog's tail started thumping hard against the floor.

"Oh, look at you!" said Palomma. "You're all wet! Gemma, how did… "

"He," said Gemma.

"Thanks. How did he get all wet—and wait, where did he come from in the first place?"

"Daddy came home with him," said Gemma. "He said he was visiting his friend Dr. Schad and this guy was laying there in his office. He said somehow he knew this dog was supposed to be ours. Dr. Schad didn't even charge him anything; he said the dog was brought in as a stray."

"He was all wet at the vet's office?" asked Palomma.

"Oh, that..." said Gemma. "He wanted to run around when he got home, it started pouring..."

"You're so cute!" said Palomma, rubbing his face with both hands. "Doug, isn't he adorable?"

"He certainly is," said Doug, who scratched the dog on the back, then slid his hand down to his back leg. Old wounds heal well with love.

About the Author

Greg Hatala is an internet news content provider, bus driver and substitute teacher in New Jersey. His career has ranged from nightclub janitor to columnist for a major regional newspaper. I LOVE LIKING YOU A LOT is his first novel.

Consider these other fine books from Savant Books and Publications and it's imprint Aignos Publishing

Essay, Essay, Essay by Yasuo Kobachi
Aloha from Coffee Island by Walter Miyanari
Footprints, Smiles and Little White Lies by Daniel S. Janik
The Illustrated Middle Earth by Daniel S. Janik
Last and Final Harvest by Daniel S. Janik
A Whale's Tale by Daniel S. Janik
Tropic of California by R. Page Kaufman
Tropic of California (the companion music CD) by R. Page Kaufman
The Village Curtain by Tony Tame
Dare to Love in Oz by William Maltese
The Interzone by Tatsuyuki Kobayashi
Today I Am a Man by Larry Rodness
The Bahrain Conspiracy by Bentley Gates
Called Home by Gloria Schumann
First Breath edited by Z. M. Oliver
The Jumper Chronicles by W. C. Peever
William Maltese's Flicker - #1 Book of Answers by William Maltese
My Unborn Child by Orest Stocco
Last Song of the Whales by Four Arrows
Perilous Panacea by Ronald Klueh
Falling but Fulfilled by Zachary M. Oliver
Mythical Voyage by Robin Ymer
Hello, Norma Jean by Sue Dolleris
Charlie No Face by David B. Seaburn
Number One Bestseller by Brian Morley
My Two Wives and Three Husbands by S. Stanley Gordon
In Dire Straits by Jim Currie
Wretched Land by Mila Komarnisky
Who's Killing All the Lawyers? by A. G. Hayes
Ammon's Horn by G. Amati
Wavelengths edited by Zachary M. Oliver
Communion by Jean Blasiar and Jonathan Marcantoni
The Oil Man by Leon Puissegur
Random Views of Asia from the Mid-Pacific by William E. Sharp
The Isla Vista Crucible by Reilly Ridgell
Blood Money by Scott Mastro

In the Himalayan Nights by Anoop Chandola
On My Behalf by Helen Doan
Chimney Bluffs by David B. Seaburn
The Loons by Sue Dolleris
Light Surfer by David Allan Williams
The Judas List by A. G. Hayes
Path of the Templar—Book 2 of The Jumper Chronicles by W. C. Peever
The Desperate Cycle by Tony Tame
Shutterbug by Buz Sawyer
Blessed are the Peacekeepers by Tom Donnelly and Mike Munger
Bellwether Messages edited by D. S. Janik
The Turtle Dances by Daniel S. Janik
The Lazarus Conspiracies by Richard Rose
Purple Haze by George B. Hudson
Imminent Danger by A. G. Hayes
Lullaby Moon (CD) by Malia Elliott of Leon & Malia
Volutions edited by Suzanne Langford
In the Eyes of the Son by Hans Brinckmann
The Hanging of Dr. Hanson by Bentley Gates
Flight of Destiny by Francis Powell
Elaine of Corbenic by Tima Z. Newman
Ballerina Birdies by Marina Yamamoto
More More Time by David B. Seabird
Crazy Like Me by Erin Lee
Cleopatra Unconquered by Helen R. Davis
Valedictory by Daniel Scott
The Chemical Factor by A. G. Hayes
Quantum Death by A. G. Hayes and Raymond Gaynor
Big Heaven by Charlotte Hebert
Captain Riddle's Treasure by GV Rama Rao
All Things Await by Seth Clabough
Tsunami Libido by Cate Burns
Finding Kate by A. G. Hayes
The Adventures of Purple Head, Buddha Monkey... by Erik/Forest Bracht
In the Shadows of My Mind by Andrew Massie
The Gumshoe by Richard Rose
In Search of Somatic Therapy by Setsuko Tsuchiya
Cereus by Z. Roux
The Solar Triangle by A. G. Hayes
Shadow and Light edited by Helen R. Davis
A Real Daughter by Lynne McKelvey
StoryTeller by Nicholas Bylotas
Bo Henry at Three Forks by Daniel Bradford

Kindred edited by Gary "Doc" Krinberg
Cleopatra Victorious by Helen R. Davis
The Dark Side of Sunshine by Paul Guzzo
Cazadores de Libros Perdidos by German William Cabasssa Barber [Spanish]
The Desert and the City by Derek Bickerton
The Overnight Family Man by Paul Guzzo
There is No Cholera in Zimbabwe by Zachary M. Oliver
John Doe by Buz Sawyers
The Piano Tuner's Wife by Jean Yamasaki Toyama
An Aura of Greatness by Brendan P. Burns
Polonio Pass by Doc Krinberg
Iwana by Alvaro Leiva
University and King by Jeffrey Ryan Long
The Surreal Adventures of Dr. Mingus by Jesus Richard Felix Rodriguez
Letters by Buz Sawyers
In the Heart of the Country by Derek Bickerton
El Camino De Regreso by Maricruz Acuna [Spanish]
Prepositions by Jean Yamasaki Toyama
Deep Slumber of Dogs by Doc Krinberg
Navel of the Sea by Elizabeth McKague
Entwined edited by Gary "Doc" Krinberg
Critical Writing: Stories as Phenomena by Jamie Dela Cruz
Truth and Tell Travel the Solar System by Helen R. Davis
Saddam's Parrot by Jim Currie
Beneath Them by Natalie Roers
Chang the Magic Cat by A. G. Hayes
Illegal by E. M. Duesel
Island Wildlife: Exiles, Expats and Exotic Others by Robert Friedman
The Winter Spider by Doc Krinberg
The Princess in My Head by J. G. Matheny
Comic Crusaders by Richard Rose
I'll Remember by Clif McCrady
The City and the Desert by Derek Bickerton
The Edge of Madness by Raymond Gaynor
'Til Then Our Written Love Will Have to Do by Cheri Woods
Aloha La'a Kea edited by Robert "Uhene" Maikai
Hawaii Kids Music Vol 1 by Leon and Malia
William Maltese's Flicker - #2 Book of Ascendency by William Maltese
Honeymoon Forever by R. Page Kaufman
Shep's Adventures by George Hudson

354

Greg Hatala

Retribution by Richard Rose
Poutine and Gin by Steve Rhinelander
The Immigrant's Grandson by Vern Turner
Lion's Way by Rita Ariyoshi
The Power of Dance by Setsuko Tsuchiya

Coming Soon
Hot Night in Budapest by Keith Rees

http://www.savantbooksandpublications.com
Enduring literary works for the twenty-first century

www.ingramcontent.com/pod-product-compliance
Lightning Source LLC
Chambersburg PA
CBHW051228260626
47162CB00002B/326